He Vowed to Possess Her

"Antonio . . ." She meant it as an objection, but instead it came out sensuously. His name hung in the air, the most beautiful word she had ever heard. But her cry seemed to spur him on and the once tender look in his eyes now gleamed with naked lust.

She knew that what he wanted should be saved for her wedding night, and even with her heart beating wildly, her passion uncontrollable, she silently cursed him for rendering her so helpless.

But then his lips returned to hers and she was without choice . . . consumed with feverish desire . . . ready to have him take her on their journey to rapture. . . .

The Kiss Flower

...omances by Glenna Finley

The Kiss Flower

GIMONE HALL

Ready
Reading
Collection

Ⓢ
A SIGNET BOOK

NEW AMERICAN LIBRARY

NAL BOOKS ARE AVAILABLE AT QUANTITY DISCOUNTS
WHEN USED TO PROMOTE PRODUCTS OR SERVICES.
FOR INFORMATION PLEASE WRITE TO PREMIUM MARKETING DIVISION,
NEW AMERICAN LIBRARY, 1633 BROADWAY,
NEW YORK, NEW YORK 10019.

Copyright © 1985 by Gimone Hall

SIGNET TRADEMARK REG. U.S. PAT. OFF. AND FOREIGN COUNTRIES
REGISTERED TRADEMARK—MARCA REGISTRADA
HECHO EN CHICAGO, U.S.A.

SIGNET, SIGNET CLASSIC, MENTOR, PLUME, MERIDIAN AND NAL BOOKS
are published by New American Library,
1633 Broadway, New York, New York 10019

First Printing, August, 1985

1 2 3 4 5 6 7 8 9

PRINTED IN THE UNITED STATES OF AMERICA

I

Long past midnight an awareness of danger invaded Susannah Dunbar's sleep. In her dreams she had been at the Gayoso House in Memphis, dancing, first a waltz and then a mischievous schottische, in her white tulle ball gown crossed by bands of royal-blue velvet. Men stood in line to sign her dance card—Tom Langworth and Edward Newland. And of course, Cort St. John. She couldn't dream of a ball without dreaming of *him*.

Susannah pulled the covers more tightly about her, trying to dismiss reality, the threat her senses had perceived through her dream. She tried to hold on to the vision of Cort's springy wheat-colored hair, the teasing, ardent sparkle of his eyes, the audacious squeeze of his hand at her waist as they danced.

But the sound came again from beyond her dream. Susannah's eyes flew open. She remembered that long ago the white dress had been torn up for rags. Tom Langworth had been buried last March in his Confederate uniform. Edward Newland had a wooden leg and would never waltz again. Cort St. John and her father, Colonel Josiah Dunbar, were serving with General Forrest's marauders, but she had not had word of them in months.

Susannah lay still, trying to listen, but it was almost impossible to separate the distant noise from the soft breathing of the younger girl who lay curled beside her in the enormous pineapple-post bed. In the dimness she glanced at the innocent, slumbering form of her sister, Rachel.

Rachel slept like a child, with her knees pulled up toward her chin and her Dutch doll quilt clutched to her chest. But at fifteen, Rachel wasn't a child. Moonlight flowed over the mallow pink of her cheeks and tangled in the pale gold of her hair. Her rosy mouth was even now set in an attitude of adolescent defiance. She was so lovely, so fragile, so determined not to be impeded by the delicate health that had plagued her from birth, a difficult birth that had claimed their mother's life. Susannah judged Rachel was dreaming of one of their many arguments—perhaps of her fury at Susannah's not allowing her to pin up her hair in a grown-up way until Papa came home to approve.

"You did, when you were my age, and you're only four years older now!" Rachel would say.

"It was different then." Then there had been

no woman-hungry Yankees in Memphis to notice a girl's blossoming. Susannah had trouble enough of her own managing the lecherous enemy officers, without adding Rachel to the problem.

"I'll be an old maid," Rachel would wail.

"Well, I'm getting to be one myself."

"But *you* have someone to think of!"

Cort St. John. Had she played her cards right, she might have been his wife before he had ridden off with her father to join General Forrest. But she had been young and silly then, enjoying the company of her other beaus, who hadn't left so quickly. She had Cort to think of, yes. And every day she wondered if he were still alive or if he were dead at the hands of one of the huge saber-waving expeditions that left Memphis bent on destroying the Mobile and Ohio Railroad and defeating the fabled Rebel general. But Susannah had battles of her own to fight.

She had battles to make old clothes do, to find feed for the milk cow and the one horse left from a fine stable, to keep firewood for the cookstove; and she had even had to make candles to provide light. Susannah had been raised to do none of these things; and when Papa had left Robin Hill, there had still been a large contingent of loyal slaves to do everything for her. They were all gone now, drifted away to the Union Army or somewhere North. Just as well. She didn't want to grow cotton to be made into Yankee uniforms. Only Uncle Arthur and Aunt Caroline were left, and they didn't think of themselves as slaves, but as family.

The worst of her battles had been to keep the

Yankees from encroaching on her property and her person. And now Susannah sensed such a battle was imminent. Creeping out of bed, she leaned out the window, hearing the sighing of the warm August wind in the leaves of the ancient live oaks lining the half-mile lane to the white-columned house. Above that came the rhythm of hoofbeats racing toward her. The horseman was a faraway shadow against the white shell road.

"What's wrong, Susannah?" Rachel was sitting up in bed.

"There's a Yankee coming."

"Just one this time? Let *me* handle the gun, then."

"Not a chance. You'd be too likely to shoot him."

Susannah put on her satin wrapper. "Hide under the bed, Rachel. If he comes upstairs, he'll be too busy ransacking the chifforobes to look there."

"Susannah, you're probably more likely to kill a Yankee than I am. You know what Colonel Spangler said the last time."

Susannah paused with her hand on the porcelain doorknob. "I remember, Rachel. Now, do as I say and get under the bed!"

The sweeping walnut staircase lay before her, still magnificent, but lacking the sheen it had had when there had been many hands to polish it. Halfway down, she realized her feet were bare, but it was too late to turn back. As she passed a mirror in a massive frame of carved limewood, her reflection startled her. She recoiled, imagining for an instant that the intruder was already within the house. An intruder or a ghost, for family legend was that the mirror was haunted by the ghost of a stern Virginia grandmother who had sent it along with her daughter to the wicked Memphis boomtown of 1840.

Although the sisters had spent many childhood hours frightening each other over the spectral image, Susannah had never seen a ghost in the mirror, unless her own reflection tonight might qualify. The dim, myopic mirror saw only what it had always seen—a small girlish figure of the right height to reach just under a man's chin, allowing him to breathe the scent of flowers she used to pin among her heavy auburn tresses. The mirror failed to record that her ivory skin had tanned, nor did it see the appealing sprinkle of freckles across her dainty nose, the result of her bonnet having fallen askew while she chopped wood or hoed the garden. But more than anything, the mirror did not notice the steely core beneath her seemingly soft femininity. It did not see the steadfast determination that had profoundly altered her since the Union Army had occupied Memphis; the girl in the mirror no longer existed.

Downstairs in Papa's study, where cigar smoke still seemed to permeate the camelback sofas, she removed a pistol from a secret compartment in the desk and pulled back the hammer with shaking fingers. Fortunate for her that Colonel Spangler hadn't confiscated the pistol after the last time. No, not fortunate. She had seen to it that he did not.

Last time there had been at least a dozen interlopers, all drunk as skunks after a rowdy evening at Bell's Tavern. Susannah had chosen not to open the door when they'd banged on it. After all, it had been made of solid oak, secured with fine English locks, openable only with eight-inch brass keys. But the soldiers had smashed windows and slashed down the draperies with their swords as they burst through. They'd helped themselves to provisions, broken several Windsor chairs, and turned the place upside down searching for valuables, most of which had already been sold.

She'd stood frozen until one of them, finding no souvenir to his liking, had decided to take a lock of her hair. As he'd lifted the strand to cut it, she'd taken a pistol from her pocket and fired. The shot had gone over the soldier's head, shattering a bisque pitcher on the mantel. She would have shot again with better aim, but the gun had needed reloading, and they had all ridden off laughing and whooping.

Colonel Spangler had come out the next day to investigate the incident. The culprits, who were under his command, had been confined to quarters, he'd said.

"That is hardly justice," she had scoffed.

"Please, Miss Dunbar, do not shoot at any more United States soldiers," he had said. "General Hurlbut is in a fury about the hostile activities of Memphis women. I wouldn't like to see you end up in the Irving Block Prison."

"Is it to be against the law for a lady to defend her honor, Colonel?" she had cried.

"I hope not, Miss Dunbar. But I would like to prove to you that all Yankees aren't beasts. Have supper with me tomorrow night. I'd like you to see we can be gentlemen."

She had understood that he was offering her

protection, and for the sake of Rachel and Robin Hill, she had decided to take it. He had been as good as his word about his conduct, and she had dined with him at several Memphis restaurants. She, the daughter of one of General Forrest's most able leaders, on the arm of a Yankee! She had been so humiliated she had wanted to die, but she had done what was necessary to save her home, just as the Rebel soldiers did. Since Colonel Spangler's interest in her had become known, Robin Hill had not been bothered—until tonight.

Somehow the single horseman frightened her more than the horde of drunks. They had been looking only for mischief. This man had a purpose. He hadn't lolled up the road singing and laughing as the others had. He had come at a hell-bent gallop. As he reached the house, there was an instant of weighty silence, then a sharp crunch that told her he had leapt to the ground instead of dismounting casually one leg at a time.

She waited, clutching her weapon, in the center of the dark house. What was he doing? Now the man's footfalls moved beside the slow pace of the horse. The animal blew out its breath, and she could tell that he was leading it through the boxwood arbor—intent on concealing it at the rear of the house.

Susannah trembled. He'd come to ravish her, just as she suspected. There could be no other explanation! She fought to get a grip on herself. She must be steady when she fired. She must not miss! She'd aim for his heart, because if she aimed higher and missed him altogether, she wouldn't get a second chance. If she were going to the Irving Block Prison, she might as well go for murder; the punishment would not be worse than if she merely wounded the man.

People called the Irving Block the Bastille; it was known all over the nation for its deplorable conditions. Women lived on the upper floor of the prison without any heat or any chairs or tables, only loose straw on the floor. They subsisted on crackers and cold potatoes and shared their lodgings with bugs and rats. Many didn't leave alive.

Few things on earth matched the Irving Block in vileness, but being violated by a Yankee within the very portals of Robin Hill exceeded it. Susannah felt no lack of resolve, but the lengthening quiet unnerved her. Suppose he broke into some distant part of the house and took her by surprise? Perhaps he'd pry off the lock to the cellar or quietly jimmy a window in the deserted rooms where household slaves used to live?

But instinct would cause him to check the front door first, surely, where the cut-glass sidelights had long since been boarded over to prevent their being broken by miscreants seeking a way inside. If the door were ajar, he might think the house deserted. He'd come inside, his guard down, and she'd be waiting in the shadow with the gun. The surprise would be on him!

Summoning all the willpower she possessed, she unfastened the door and set it open a crack. Then she stationed herself with her back against a wall and her arm braced by the top of a cupboard secretary.

Footsteps came onto the flagstone portico, and then the door swung open slowly. Even the breeze seemed to cease as Susannah tensed to fire, but instead of gunfire there was only her gasp of joy, followed by happy sighs and tears of relief as the soldier crushed her in his arms and covered her mouth with kisses. She responded eagerly, for the soldier's uniform was not blue, but stained and tattered gray.

"Cort! What in God's name are you doing here? I might have killed you!" New apprehensions seized her. "You're behind enemy lines, and there are patrols everywhere! If they find you—"

He shushed her with more kisses. "If they find me, I'll die happy because I've seen you, my love. I couldn't stay away any longer, Susannah. I had to know that you and Rachel were all right."

"All right? Of course we are all right! How dare you worry about me, Cort St. John, when *you* are tempting death every day . . . ?"

She had no breath to say more as his kisses moved from her lips down her throat. She threw her head back, her own lips parted, her breath coming quickly. "I would not value my life without you," he murmured, clasping her tightly to him, the material of his uniform pressing roughly against her satin wrapper.

He was thinner than he had been, but harder and more rugged. Nothing was soft about him, except the thicket of his beard, which he had grown since leaving. Its feathery touch made her skin tingle, or so she thought. She was tingling all over, though, right to her toes; and her fingers gripped his shoulders as though she were hanging on to him for her life, as though she might plunge over a cliff if she let go. A power seemed to surge through him, carrying her along like a rudderless ship on a swift Mississippi River current.

His lips went lower; her robe parted, leaving only her dimity nightdress to protect her pulsing body.

He had never been like this before, she thought, excitement and fear washing over her together. She had known him from childhood; his respect for her had always kept him within the bounds of propriety. She realized bewilderedly that she couldn't trust him now, and she couldn't trust herself. He was different. She was different. That bygone Cort and Susannah were unlisted fatalities of the war.

With a mighty effort she shoved him back. "You haven't told me how Papa is," she said with a gasp.

The mention of Susannah's father was enough to bring Cort to his senses. No officer in Forrest's army was sterner with his men or more formidable in battle. No officer except Forrest himself was more feared or more admired.

"Colonel Dunbar is well," Cort stammered as though he sensed his superior's presence in the rose-papered foyer.

"Thank God!" Susannah's voice trembled. She pulled her wrapper closely about her, her cheeks burning as the two of them tried to establish their normal relationship again. Where might all this lead if they failed?

"Susannah! What are you doing? What happened to the Yankee? I didn't hear a shot." Rachel was on the stairs. With a shriek of delight she recognized Cort and came dashing down to be swung in his arms.

"By heaven, can this be little Rachel?" he teased. "Why, you're a young lady, and as lovely as a bouquet of violets!"

"You see, Susannah? Cort thinks I'm old enough to put up my hair. Don't you, Cort?" She twisted up her curls to give him the effect.

Cort grinned, nonplussed by her appeal. Susannah's mouth tightened.

Rachel clung to his arm, gazing up at him in happy adoration. "You must be hungry. Come on, we'll find you something to eat."

He hung back. "No, Rachel. I have my own provisions."

Susannah took hold of his other arm. "What provisions? Hard biscuits? We've plenty of food, you needn't worry about eating some of it."

"You have—really? I'd heard . . . But there's no one around to fix it."

"Silly! We're quite used to doing our own work now. There'll be hot coals in the cookstove yet, if I'm not mistaken."

Cort allowed himself to be dragged toward the kitchen. "It's good to be home," he sighed, watching Susannah drop wood into the stove.

Tying on Aunt Caroline's checkered apron, Susannah set a big cast-iron skillet out to heat and threw fresh wood on the embers. Then she began to break eggs into a green crockery bowl, while Rachel, lighting the one lamp for which they had oil, seated herself at the pine sawbuck table with potatoes to peel. Susannah was glad to have her back to Cort so that he couldn't see that she was still breathless and agitated from his kisses. But she could feel the steady gaze of his blue eyes on her, and it almost seemed that she felt more heat from behind her than from the stove. For once she was grateful that her little sister had disobeyed her by coming downstairs, and she was grateful for Rachel's prattle.

Now it was safe to think of the sweet madness of Cort's embrace, the touch of hands hardened to the steel of guns and cannon so incongruously gentle on her skin. He had gone away an engaging boy and returned in a whirlwind of danger, excitement, and maturity. A slim, silvery scar gleamed like a medal from his forehead, and major's leaves had replaced the captain's bars on his shoulders. But had he ever been so purposeful against the Yankees as he had been at sweeping away her defenses tonight, the major's leaf would have been a general's star.

"You haven't told us how you came here, Cort," Rachel said. "Where have you been tonight?"

"Rachel! Cort is not going to give you military information."

"Oh, Cort knows I would never tell! Old Hurlbut is scared witless, Cort. And the rumor is that Sherman is going to replace him. Oh, it was marvelous when General Forrest whipped Sooy Smith's men and sent him scurrying back to Memphis! And when Colonel Hurst was chased back, he left his supply wagons and even his hat, they say. And then General Forrest fooled the Yankees into thinking they were going to attack Memphis by building the pontoon bridges at Wolf River, and attacked Fort Pillow instead. Get them scared and keep them scared, that's what old Forrest says, isn't it, Cort! We'll lick the Yankees. There won't be a stitch of blue left below the Mason-Dixon line."

"Certainly we will, Rachel, and then you'll have a new silk evening gown and put your hair up and ride to your first grown-up ball in a carriage drawn by four grays. Your very first dance must be with me."

"I'll save it for you, Cort," Rachel said, her eyes shining. She gave Susannah the potatoes, chopped to fry in the skillet, where ham was already sizzling, and beside it bread was toasting in the ham grease. The potatoes hissed angrily, and a cloud of steam shot up as they hit the pan.

Susannah felt the voluble potatoes rather expressed her own sentiments. She resented the rosy picture Cort was painting for Rachel, when it was quite obvious from his worn features and ragged uniform that things were not going as well as he said.

"We'll beat the Yankees," he'd said, but what he meant was: We'll beat them or die trying. In this August of 1864, it niggled at her that it might be better for the South to surrender before every mile of it was pillaged, to quit while some women's hearts might be left unbroken and something of the South's proud heritage left for future generations. These thoughts Susannah executed like traitors, stamping them from her loyal Confederate heart almost before she was cognizant of having them. But to see Cort and to be kissed as she had been kissed had made her yearning for the end of war unbearable. She had been living day to day, but his kisses had made her long for a real future. She felt herself blushing as she put the plate of hot food in front of him. Did he know she was thinking of a future with him?

"I've heard that General Forrest is ill," she said almost accusingly.

He looked up, startled at her disapproving tone. "He fell off his horse exhausted at Brices Cross Roads, and he received a painful bullet wound in his foot at Harrisburg, but it will take a great deal more than that to stop Bedford Forrest."

"He *will* attack Memphis, won't he?" Rachel demanded.

"Why, Rachel, Confederate troops have been in Memphis this very night!" Cort told her exuberantly. "While General A. J. Smith and his troops are being held down by snipers, General Forrest slipped around and has surprised the Memphis sentries in the fog. We rode over them before they could see us and knocked them senseless with our rifle butts. And then we rode straight to the Gayoso Hotel to capture General Hurlbut in his quarters."

"Oh, Cort, did you capture him?" Susannah said. They both waited breathlessly for his reply.

Cort grimaced. "The old reprobate wasn't there. He was out carousing. General Washburn was there, though. He fled out the back door and half a mile to Fort Pickering with Rebel yells splitting the air around him, and his nightshirt popping against his shanks. We did capture several hundred horses from the stables and a number of officers without any trousers. The telegraph wires were cut so the Yankees couldn't call General Smith, and our men rode over a battery and all resistance and retreated safely along Hernando Road.

"But it was the first time I'd been so close to home in two years. I couldn't resist taking another route. There were six or eight Yankees who rode after me, but don't worry, ladies. I know this country better than they do. I rode along Turner's Creek and took a path through the woods."

"You've lost them, then?" Rachel asked.

"Of course. Otherwise, they'd be here, wouldn't they?"

"You had better go, Cort!" Susannah said urgently.

"I'll catch up with General Forrest in good time. By heaven, this is the best meal I've had in months. Imagine your cooking it!" He gazed at her ardently. "Susannah, will you ride to Hazel Grove tomorrow and tell my mother I am well? I would like to go myself, but it's closer to Memphis and that road will be heavily guarded."

"Oh, she isn't there," Rachel said. "There are Yankees quartered at Hazel Grove now."

He froze, all the life in his body seeming to rush into fury in his face. This was how he could be in battle, she thought, shaken. Were all the men in Forrest's command so full of vengeance? No wonder twelve thousand soldiers allowed themselves to be bottled up in Memphis by Forrest's paltry numbers! She was almost frightened of him herself.

"Cort, your mother is quite all right. She's living in the town house in Memphis. She's better off there than alone on the plantation."

He seemed to hear her at last through the haze of his rage. "I'll leave now, Susannah; I don't want to put you in danger."

"Oh, Robin Hill is not in danger," Rachel said.

Susannah paled. "Rachel, go upstairs and keep

watch for any sign of a Yankee patrol," she commanded, glaring at her sister. "Hurry!

"Don't mind her, Cort; she's only a child," she said, stuffing the rest of the ham into his knapsack as Rachel rushed off.

But Cort was frowning. "Perhaps I shouldn't have come," he said. "I can't stand the idea of your being so vulnerable to the enemy." He seized her shoulders. "Why has Robin Hill been untouched, Susannah? Most Southerners don't have hogs to slaughter these days or chickens to lay so many fine eggs. What have you done, Susannah?"

"Stop it, Cort. I've done nothing but steal a bit from the Yankees in my own way. I'll give nothing in return, you may be sure."

"Cort! Someone's coming!" Rachel shouted from upstairs.

Cort clasped Susannah fiercely against him. She could feel the pounding of her own heart against his jacket. Instinctively she lifted her chin, and his lips again pressed deeply against hers. "I'll be back when we've won the war," he whispered. "I'll protect you then, the rest of your life. Will you marry me, Susannah?"

The suddenness of his proposal made her giddy. Surely she would say yes, but she wanted time to savor his declaration and to debate whether she would make him the happiest man on earth. In Susannah's experience, proposals were made on a moonlit veranda with waltz music in the background or in a garden of sweet william on a summer day. All the brides she had known had been proposed to in such situations.

"Susannah!" Hoofbeats of his pursuers' horses pounded outside while he waited for her reply.

"Oh, Cort, you know I care for you, but this is so . . . so improper!"

"You're quite right," he said with a shuddering sigh. "We've standards to maintain. Why, I haven't even asked Colonel Dunbar's permission. When I come back, I'll court you as it ought to be done. Just say that I may hope."

For answer she kissed him fervently, the cries of the approaching Yankees ringing in her ears. "Go!" she sobbed, and he bolted out of the house through the servants' entrance. She fastened the door behind him, trembling so much she could hardly turn the key, whether from fear or from passion. Knocking began at the front of the house.

"Susannah, has he gone? Are we going to let them in?"

"He's gone. We'll let them in to search the house, and that will give Cort time to escape.

"Who is it?" she called through the front door. "What do you want at this hour?"

"Miss Dunbar, it's Sam Spangler. There's no need to be afraid. My men were chasing a Rebel soldier and thought he might be hiding here."

"We've seen no one tonight, Colonel," Susannah called.

"I cannot take your word for it, much as I would like to, Miss Dunbar. Please open the door."

She unlocked it slowly, making every second count for Cort's sake. Sam Spangler was rocking impatiently on his heels by the time she admitted him.

"I suppose you want to search all the rooms, Colonel," she said.

"With your permission, Miss Dunbar."

"Very well. You'll do as you like, whether I give it or not. Pray do not miss the cellar or the attic, and be sure to give special attention to my bedroom. He may be lurking behind my bed curtains."

Colonel Spangler barked a command, and the half-dozen blue-coated soldiers dispersed. "Susannah, I do not like doing this," he said.

"Of course not, Colonel. It's your duty," she said mockingly.

"Yes, and I will do it. It is one thing to see that your home is left in peace and that you have food to eat, and quite another to wink at actions of yours hostile to the Union. I came along tonight to make sure than no harm came to you or your property, but if my men find that Rebel, I'll do nothing to prevent the consequences."

"Allow me to offer you a glass of sherry, Colonel." She took his arm and gazed up at him, teasing him with her eyes. Colonel Spangler wasn't a tall man. He was impressive, though, strongly built, with black wiry hair parted in the middle and swept out to the sides and a thick curve of mustache to match. He'd told her he was from Boston, and she'd wondered if all Boston men were like him. He walked as though he had starch for bone marrow, and his voice, with its clipped Northern accent, seemed starched as well. Many women might have found him attractive, even compelling, but Susannah did not. When a man wore that despised uniform, nothing else mattered.

She knew, though, that Sam Spangler was an intensely honorable man. In a way he was more honorable than she, because she did not scruple at taking every advantage of his honorableness. She knew, for example, that it was safe to tantalize him tonight. Color rose into his cheeks as she tormented him with the touch of her hand on his sleeve.

"Susannah, you know I cannot drink your sherry while I am on official business here!" he snapped. She saw he would like to steal a kiss from her upturned lips, but she knew he would not, even though he wouldn't have to bend over much to do it. Colonel Spangler wasn't given to bending at all.

"Why, Colonel, it's not really *my* sherry. It was you who brought it here last week as a gift."

He shifted uncomfortably. "Are you certain you've heard nothing tonight? Dogs barking perhaps? He was a wily Rebel, born around here, most likely, to give my men the slip the way he did. One of Forrest's men. That rascal Forrest!'

"Bedford Forrest is a brilliant general, as well you know!"

"Humph! I know nothing of the sort. He's a renegade who refused to serve under his superior officer, General Bragg, and raised his own command. Union officers obey orders. That is why we'll win this war!"

Susannah had not answered his question about noticing a disturbance during the night, nor had he expected her to answer. He had asked simply in an attempt to maintain his composure, and had been only partly successful. Southern women! If the Union did lose the war, it would be because of them. They took shameless advantage of their womanhood.

"Come, Colonel, there's no need to be cross, just because you've been outwitted by a Rebel," she teased. "Surely it's not the first time!"

"Colonel!" An excited shout came from the rear of the house. He rushed forward, his hand on his saber.

"Have you found him? Have you found the Reb?"

"No, sir. Only . . . look."

A belligerent Rachel was standing in the kitchen with a piece of Cort's toast in her hand. "They've been feeding him, sir. And not long ago. The fire's still going."

"Nonsense. It's getting daylight and my sister and I were only having breakfast. With so little help, we have to rise at dawn to get everything done," Susannah said.

"That's what little Miss Rachel said too, and we believed her at first."

"Well, then . . ." said the colonel impatiently.

"Then we asked her most politely to unlock the pantry for us, and she refused. So Joe here, wanting to teach her some respect, told her to get the key and pulled her up from the chair. And see what we found."

He brought out a Confederate hat, squashed flat from Rachel's having sat on it.

"That proves nothing," Susannah declared. "It belonged to our father."

"Then why did your sister sit on it to hide it?"

"Because you frightened her, you brutes. Breaking in on us this way."

Nobody believed her. Colonel Spangler barked

orders, sending his men racing out to search the grounds and pick up Cort's trail. Dragging Susannah into the library, Colonel Spangler slammed the door behind them.

"Let go of my wrist; you're hurting me," she cried indignantly. She was trying not to shake with terror. Colonel Spangler's face was livid.

"Dammit, Susannah! Is this how you repay my kindness?"

"Sir, the evidence that I have given shelter to a Rebel is highly circumstantial."

"It's quite more than that, given your temperament! Are you trying to make me compromise myself and place my career in jeopardy because of you?"

"I have not asked anything of you, Colonel. File a report if you must. There are fates worse than being convicted of such a crime."

"It would be hard to think of one. You would rot in the Irving Block with thieves and murderers, and you may not say I didn't warn you!"

"I would sooner die in prison than to turn away a Rebel soldier, a man serving with my own father under General Forrest. No, I would never refuse to help one of Forrest's marauders, no matter what the cost. The decision is yours, Colonel. Decide my fate according to that wonderful conscience of yours!" She was determined not to beg, and she had promised Cort she would give nothing.

She knew he had more than his conscience to wrestle. He was in love with her, and her defiance had deepened not only his anger but also his desire. In Boston he had been raised to protect women, but here in the zestier South he found himself torn between wanting to strangle

Susannah and his urge to subdue her with his passion. He hated her for the dilemma she had caused him and adored her beyond the limits of his judgment.

Forgetting his objections to the sherry, Colonel Spangler poured himself a glass from the decanter and drank it quickly. "I'll file no report, Miss Dunbar, though it may make me a laughingstock among my men."

"I'm very grateful, Colonel."

"I'm not interested in your gratitude, Susannah. Your friendship . . ." He sighed. He longed to tell her that what he wanted was her love, but now wasn't the time. She'd only humiliate him with her scorn, but someday he'd find a way to show her he was more than just a Yankee; he was a man apart from his uniform. He'd find the way or die trying!

Colonel Spangler suddenly looked as exhausted as though he'd just returned from a month's campaign. "Susannah, had there been more than the hat . . ."

"I know, Sam," she said softly.

"Nothing else must happen! I can't help you again, and I cannot bear—"

Triumphant in the aftermath of danger, she laughed at his discomfort. "Well, I shall try to stay out of trouble. After all, what else *could* happen?"

"Anything, since it's you," he answered ruefully.

"Would you care for another glass of sherry, Colonel, or shall I escort you to the door?"

He seemed to become aware of the intimacy of the situation, now that he had dismissed his men. "Of course I'll go," he told her, somewhat embarrassed. But at the door he paused. "Susannah, there is an officers' dance next week. Would you agree to go with me?"

"I think not, Colonel. Having dinner with you is one thing and allowing you to flaunt me before an entire crowd of Union officers is quite another."

"Susannah, I did not mean—"

"Good night, Colonel Spangler," she said, and closed the door.

"Is he gone?" Rachel's frightened face was in the shadows behind her.

"Yes, dear. Everything's all right now."

"Susannah, I'm so sorry!"

"Sorry? About what?"

"The hat, of course. I should have hidden it better. I couldn't think of any place that was safe and . . . Oh, if they catch Cort, it will be my fault!"

"Don't be silly, Rachel. Your idea was wonderful. And they won't catch Cort. He's far too smart for that. I should have seen the hat myself, only—"

"Only what? It's not like Cort to be so careless, or you either."

Susannah spun in a circle and hugged her sister. "Only Cort asked me to marry him! That was why he waited until the last moment to leave, and most likely why he forgot his hat."

"Susannah! Oh, how wonderful! How lucky you are! You'll wear Mama's wedding dress, and you could wear a wreath of flowers and a veil across your face to hide your blushes. It's the newest thing. I'll be the maid of honor— what a wedding it will be! Oh, now I really can't wait until this awful war is over! Tell me everything, Susannah! What *he* said and what *you* said and—''

Susannah laughed. ''Slow down, Rachel. Of course, I didn't accept him just like that. A lady has to show some reserve; I only let him see that I look on his suit with favor.''

''Are you crazy? How could you let a man like Cort slip through your fingers? You're not engaged at all, and some other woman may turn his head. Sometimes I think I ought to be the older one and in charge of *you!* Certainly I would have accepted him if he'd asked me.''

Susannah frowned. ''Well, he hadn't asked Papa, after all, and I just wanted our engagement to be perfect—with an announcement and a party and not at the back door in my night dress. Besides, the idea of losing Cort is silly. He's always loved me, and I think he'd have been disappointed in me had I not held to decorum. Even when there were dozens of girls fawning about him, he never noticed anyone else. But as soon as the war is over, I'll say yes, and then we'll have such a celebration . . . Come along, Rachel, I've a little cocoa and sugar saved back for a night like this. We'll make plans. It's certainly better than fretting over those wretched Yankees!''

A chilly dawn was breaking over Robin Hill before the two girls tumbled back into bed. Rachel was happy, her head filled with the stuff of lovely dreams. But Susannah was still restless. She remembered Cort's kisses, the strength of his body against hers, his voice choking with words of love which he had risked his life to ride to her to say.

And she! What sort of woman was she after

all, to put him off as she had? Rachel was right: she should have accepted at once.

Perhaps if her mother hadn't died soon after Rachel's birth, she'd have been better prepared for the moment a man would propose to make her his wife. Instead she'd been raised by Aunt Caroline, who'd loved and scolded her but who hadn't always been a perfect substitute for the mother she'd lost. Susannah remembered her mother only vaguely, or perhaps by now it was only the painting over the Adam mantel in the drawing room that she remembered—her mother in an old-fashioned pelisse with baby Susannah on her lap, round and rosy-faced in a smocked white dress and ruffled drawers. If the clothing had not dated the painting, anyone might now have thought that the woman was Susannah. What would Mama have done tonight? Susannah wondered. Whatever, it would have been the right thing. Oh, if he hadn't taken her so by surprise!

She wasn't used to being taken by surprise by Cort. He had kissed her before, but those had been polite kisses—not like tonight. And he had paid her pretty compliments, but nothing like tonight's passionate declaration. He was several years older than she and had had to keep his distance, for Papa had been determined that she graduate from Miss Pickens' school before she married.

Every winter the family had moved to its Memphis establishment so she, and later Rachel, could attend the academy for young ladies. Susannah always hated leaving Robin Hill just as the leaves of the sycamores were unfurling their autumn hues, but she loved Memphis.

There were friends to meet whom she hadn't seen since spring, news to exchange, and new laces and material to buy in the shops on Commerce Street.

In spite of her instruction in needlework, deportment, and diction at Miss Pickens', winter in Memphis had seemed a long holiday of parties, theatricals, and musicals. What could have been sweeter than Christmas in Memphis when candlelit trees could be seen through the front windows of every house; and pungent boxwood wreaths tied with red ribbons and lady apples decorated all the doors!

But the war had come, and Susannah had not yet received her diploma when Cort had gone off to war. By spring 1862 Memphis had been in danger. General Forrest had been home then, recovering from injuries at Shiloh. Susannah had joined the nursing group called the Southern Mothers to try to aid the wounded that poured into Memphis.

Federal troops were attacking Fort Pillow upriver then, and so many injured soliders came from there and from Shiloh that just burying those who died became a problem. Susannah held dying men in her arms and learned lessons never dreamed of within the walls of Miss Pickens' school. She had fainted only once; after that she'd held on with despairing courage. Then one day she'd looked up from her work to see her father standing there. She'd fled to him, weeping with joy, almost believing he could make everything right again.

"Come, Susannah," he'd said. "It's time to pack. I've only a short furlough, and I've come to move you and Rachel to Robin Hill."

"Robin Hill! But there's so much to be done here!"

"It's June, Susannah," he said gently. "The shooting star and the wood sorrel are blooming. I've been there and seen for myself."

At the Memphis house, Aunt Caroline was busy supervising the other slaves as the Hepplewhite furniture was loaded into big wagons. Paintings were being removed from the walls and silver teapots were being crammed into boxes.

"Papa, we usually don't take all this!" Susannah had protested. But he had simply directed her to go upstairs and make sure that her personal things were all being packed.

As they drove through town a flood of molasses was oozing down the bluff toward the river. Confederates had broken open the barrels waiting to be shipped rather than have them fall into enemy hands. The air was acrid with the fumes of thousands of burning cotton bales, destroyed by the Rebels.

Memphis had fallen the next morning, after an hour's battle among gunboats in the river. At Robin Hill the sound of the fighting was no louder than the thunder of a distant summer shower. The furniture from the Memphis house was stored away, and Aunt Caroline had set a dozen girls to scrubbing to get the sooty smell of the burning cotton out of all the clothing.

"Have you burned our cotton, Papa?" Susannah had asked.

"No, Susannah. Come, I'll have a pair of horses saddled and show you where it is."

They had ridden into the woods to an old barn which had been in use a generation ago, before the present house was built. It was dilapidated now, almost indistinguishable from the trumpet vine and Virginia creeper that covered it. Maple saplings grew on all sides and only a few had been broken down to get the cotton inside. Field mice were already starting to nest in the somnolent bales, and an old catalpa tree scattered purple and yellow blossoms onto the hastily patched roof.

"Nobody knows it's here," he told her, "not even any of our slaves, except Arthur. The Yankees need cotton, Susannah. Sell it if you must, but hold on to all that you can. We'll need this when the war is over to set Robin Hill to rights and plant new crops."

A day later he'd ridden away to join his regiment, and she hadn't seen him since. He'd been gone so long he sometimes seemed just a memory, like Mama. Perhaps that was all he'd ever be now. Perhaps he'd never come home again at all.

Cort had seemed like a ghost himself tonight. She had scarcely been able to believe it was he standing in the doorway. Was that why she had not promised to marry him? Because if she did, he would never come back at all? She shuddered in her feather bed, thinking of the boys from Shiloh who had murmured to her of faraway sweethearts, sometimes mistaking her for a loved one as they died. Was that the reason?

What a coward I must be, she thought. But she would find a way to set it right; somehow she'd send word to Cort that she would be his wife. As the sun rose higher, her thoughts melded into the sweetness of dreams.

2

She awoke to the sound of Aunt Caroline's rich voice bellowing downstairs. "Yankees! Got no more manners than a passel of pigs! Looks like pigs been in here! Miss Rachel, honey, help me roll up the rug. Got to take it outside and beat these Yankee footprints off it!"

"Oooh!" Rachel's voice drifted up in a wail. "It's so heavy. Couldn't we just sweep it? My back is still aching from churning the butter."

"Got to be perfect. What would Colonel Dunbar say? Yankee dirt on the rug?"

Susannah threw on her wrapper and hurried down. "Aunt Caroline, sweeping will be enough," she said. "We're shorthanded, and it's Southern dirt, even if it was brought in on Yankee feet."

Aunt Caroline shook a finger at her. Susannah was mistress of the house now, but Aunt Caroline wasn't yet used to abiding by the orders of the child she had raised. Aunt Caroline adored Susannah, but she was as used to being in command as a natural mother, and the war had only sharpened her commitment to domestic correctness at Robin Hill.

"Aunt Caroline, Rachel and I are going into town."

"Not today, you ain't. Arthur's down bad with the rheumatism and can't take you. You goin' haf to wait till tomorrow."

"We have to go today. We have to see Mrs. St. John to tell her that Cort was here. But I can hitch the carriage myself."

"Go without a man to drive you? If your papa heard of it—"

"He won't. He has much more important things to keep him occupied."

"That ol' horse don't like to be hitched, Miss Susannah."

"Well, if Rachel doesn't want to go, I'll just ride him."

"I want to go," Rachel declared quickly. Memphis was an adventure, but today she was especially eager to get away, with Aunt Caroline on a tear.

"Pack some teacakes and the sherry, then, while I get dressed. I don't like to go visiting empty-handed these days."

Aunt Caroline was still blustering when the carriage was ready to go. "There's a smudge on your skirt, Miss Susannah," she said.

Susannah glanced down. Grease had come off onto her clothing while she had been struggling with the harness. "There's no time to change it; sometimes I wish I could just wear overalls."

Aunt Caroline sniffed. "You might as well." She disapproved of Susannah's outfit, a walking skirt, which could be hitched up above the ankles for freedom of movement. Beneath it she was wearing only petticoats, without the benefit of crinoline. Rachel's demure princess gown, gored to fit at the waist, suited Aunt Caroline much better. A woman had to look proper in Memphis. There were too many females of the wrong kind there, and too many men primed to take advantage of any woman who seemed in the least approachable.

"You be careful!" Aunt Caroline called.

"I will. I can manage the horse," she said, tapping the bay with the whip. "Get up, Sultan!"

Sultan had not been used as a carriage horse before the war. He had been ridden more on steeplechases, and that by Colonel Dunbar. When it had been necessary to decrease the stable at Robin Hill, Sultan had been trained to pull. Being large and strong, Sultan had been the natural choice, when at last only one horse could be kept; but Susannah thought the situation left much to be desired, and so did Sultan.

By alternately balking and taking the carriage wherever he thought it should go, Sultan made his disdain known. Sultan also made his dislike of ladies plain. When he saw them approaching, he was likely to start off without them. It was just his way of saying he was still Colonel Dunbar's horse. Uncle Arthur could handle him better than Susannah, but even Uncle Arthur said that if Sultan ever heard the sound of a hunting horn while in harness, he'd jump over the next fence with the carriage behind him.

The drive into Memphis was made with a slight detour when Sultan refused to turn on the right road. What if he refused to stop when they passed the Union checkpoint? But as they reached it, the Union soldiers smiled and waved them through. Sultan became more cautious on the muddy streets, and they had time to study the rows of mostly closed shops.

The city, still so young, looked old before its time. Great cotton sheds loomed vacantly. The sound of the carriage echoed, and the only color to be seen was the blue of Union uniforms. They turned onto Beale Street, lined with brick mansions fronted with Ionic or Corinthian columns and wrought-iron balconies. This had been the finest neighborhood in Memphis, but now the balconies were rusting and shutters hung askew. Some of the houses were empty, and in some, runaway slaves had taken up residence.

Susannah halted the carriage and jumped down with relief to secure the reins to the hitching post. Even the camellias and oleanders in Mrs. St. John's yard seemed defeated, but the Yankee occupation hadn't spoiled Mrs. St. John's spirit. She greeted them exuberantly, exclaiming over the luxury of the teacakes; and when she had set them out on the last of her silver trays, the parlor, with its velvet settees and imported silk wall covering, took on a festive air. Her gratitude overflowed when she learned they'd come to bring news of Cort.

"Are you certain he got away, Susannah?" Mrs. St. John said fearfully, having been told about the Yankee patrol.

"Quite certain. We'd have heard shots if they'd sighted him. He's too fast for the Yankees."

Cort's mother sighed with relief, her soft bosom heaving.

"Susannah," Rachel said impishly, "tell Mrs. St. John the *important* thing that happened last night."

"Oh, Rachel!" Susannah cried, but she was blushing, and Mrs. St. John easily guessed.

"You and Cort are engaged, is that it? Why, nothing could be better. I've hoped for it for years! Come, let's pour the sherry and have a toast. Even Rachel is old enough on such an occasion."

"Please, wait . . ." Susannah said, embarrassed.

"Why, Susannah, dear, what's wrong?"

"It wasn't settled, you see. He quite took my breath away, and then the Yankees came—"

Mrs. St. John took her hand. "I understand, Susannah," she said gently.

"Do you? I'm afraid I really don't." Having Mrs. St. John was almost like having a mother. "I didn't accept him, and I don't know why." Susannah looked distressed.

"You were frightened of your own feelings, dear. It happens to every Southern woman, Susannah. We're raised to hold men at bay, to keep them in strict control. We're used to protecting ourselves with our very weakness and femininity. Men submit to our rules from a sense of honor, but there comes a moment in every man's life when he can no longer behave as a gentleman. He is overwhelmed by his desires, and that is when a girl learns that the world is different from the way she thought it was. If it is the right man, it may be a joy for her to discover how truly helpless she is before him; but remember, Susannah, the same desires lurk in every man. It's dangerous to push them too far. You can't imagine how frightened I've been that it would be that Colonel Spangler who would forget himself with you!"

"Colonel Spangler! Oh, I can handle him," Susannah said scornfully. He had been close to unleashing himself on her last night, she knew; and she shivered to think what it would have been like to be kissed by a man she hated. But she was surely more than a match for any Yankee.

"Please be careful, Susannah. These are dangerous times for two young girls with no father nearby."

"Yankees!" Rachel was peering through the lace curtains at a group of Federals who were riding by. "My goodness, they're dismounting! Are they coming here?"

Mrs. St. John remained unperturbed. "No, they're quartering in the house next door."

"And paying no rent, I suppose," Susannah said grimly.

"Of course not. I believe mine is the only house on the block still occupied by its owner. I imagine that's only because they've already commandeered the plantation. If anyone leaves a house unattended so much as a week, they declare it abandoned property."

"They've occupied our town house for months," Rachel sighed. "Oh, I wish we could *do* something! I wish I were a man and could fight them! Just look at them! Eating and drinking is all they have to do in Memphis. And those uniforms! They look as though they were issued yesterday!"

"Cort's uniform was threadbare," Susannah said.

"That's it!" Rachel declared, letting the curtain drop as she hurried back across the room. "Let's make Cort a new uniform! You'd have his measurements, wouldn't you, Mrs. St. John? Some old suit of clothes to judge by?"

"Well, yes, but—"

"Rachel, you know you have to submit a list of everything you want to buy to the Yankees for approval, and then you must go with the store clerk to the board of trade and swear it's for your own personal use. And as for gray cloth, why, that is contraband, of course."

"I do have a gray cloak," Mrs. St. John mused. "I'd forgotten about it. I'll go and get it." But when she returned with an evening mantle of soft gray wool, they quickly decided that there wasn't enough material in it.

"What a shame," Susannah said. "It must be the last piece of gray in Memphis. There ought to be a way to use it."

"I'm afraid there's not," Mrs. St. John answered, "and even if we could have turned it into a uniform, there's the matter of slipping it out."

"Oh, that would be no problem," Rachel piped in. "Everyone knows which guards are dishonest. Why, women are always carrying out supplies of medicine under their skirts. And the funerals that go out to the old country graveyards take coffins full of gunpowder."

"We would need money for a bribe in any case," Susannah mused.

"We could sell a bale of cotton," Rachel suggested. "That's what everyone does. They sell cotton to some Northern dealer, and then use the money to buy supplies from profiteers. You know that General Sherman says Memphis is worth more to the Confederacy now than before it fell."

"A bale of cotton is worth three hundred dollars in gold. It would be more than enough. But Papa did tell us not to sell the cotton, Rachel."

"Only one bale, Susannah! For Cort."

"Girls, girls, what a senseless discussion! There's no way to buy the cloth. I'll not have you dealing with the profiteers, anyway. It's far too risky. They're thieves and jailbirds, most of them, and you'd never know when one was a Yankee spy."

"Of course, you're right. It's a silly idea," Susannah agreed.

The conversation moved on to other things, but Susannah remained distracted, even when the talk centered on her wedding. The longer she thought about it, the more important it seemed that Cort have a new uniform. She wanted to do something special, to prove that she loved him. The nights would soon become chilly; the wind would cut right through his worn garments.

She smiled to think how proud of her he'd be, receiving the new uniform. Her stitching would be perfect; she'd learned that at Miss Pickens', but better than that, a letter would be sewn into the lining. Oh, he might not even notice it at once, but when he put the jacket on, he'd feel it; and when he pulled it out, he'd be in ecstasy. In the letter she'd promise once and for all to be his wife.

They stayed the night in Memphis, as they had intended, not wanting to be caught on the road after dark. But for the second night in a row, Susannah lost sleep, while Rachel slumbered unworriedly beside her. Perhaps it was only the unfamiliarity of the room that kept her awake. It was much smaller than her room at Robin Hill, and the ponderous sleigh bed, an American version of the elaborate French Napoleon bed, seemed to encapsulate her between its bulky head and footboards. The piece was a prize of Mrs. St. John's, having been brought upriver all the way from New Orleans, but Susannah thought she must be sure she did not receive it as a wedding present.

Thinking of sharing a bed with Cort made her flustered and warm, and tossing about, she flung off the light covers. Her imaginings quickly became too immodest, and she retreated in alarm to other thoughts.

It was the sound of Yankees passing in the streets that kept her awake, she decided. All residents were required to be indoors after dark, while the conquerors prowled the town, their boots echoing, their voices now and then boisterous beneath the window, which it was necessary to keep open in the sultry summer night. But it wasn't the noise itself that kept her awake; it was the knowledge that they had the run of the place. They were eating and drinking, gambling on waterfront casino boats, making merry with disreputable women. All this while Cort and her father suffered the hardships of exile.

Colonel Spangler was probably enjoying himself tonight. Oh, how she hated him! Oh, how she loathed him! She hated him all the more because he had been kind to her, and she had had to accept favors from him. She fumed at Mrs. St. John's worry that she couldn't manage him. Of course she could! The more she thought about it, the more it became a matter of pride to her that she could make him do anything that she wanted him to do. It was he who was helpless before her, instead of she before him. He belonged to the conquering army, but he, not she, would be the vanquished.

The idea of providing Cort with a new uniform was too pleasant to be forgotten. Before the sun rose in a weak haze over the dreary town, Susannah had hit upon a plan. What could be more perfect? She would make Colonel Spangler do something utterly against his principles. She would cause him to provide her with the necessary materials for Cort's uniform.

No one was stirring in the house as Susannah slipped out of bed, and having dressed in the same daring walking skirt that had drawn Aunt Caroline's comment the day before, she went quietly downstairs. The kitchen stove was cold, and nothing was on it but a pan of leftover cornbread. Susannah cut herself a chunk and carried it into the library.

Deep Aubusson carpets silenced her steps as she crossed to the flat-top secretary and took out pen and ink. She ate the cornbread while she wrote, pausing now and then to consider, yet hurrying with fear that someone would find her before she had had time to complete her task. Finally she put the pen away with a sigh of satisfaction, and completing her attire with a low-crowned sailor's hat, she went out to the carriage shed behind the house.

Mrs. St. John's stable man was busy mucking the stalls as she entered. Sultan threw back his head and gave a snort of displeasure at the sight of her.

"Reuben, will you please hitch my carriage?" she asked.

"Miss Susannah, you oughtn't be driving this horse. You go ask Mrs. St. John if I kin drive you."

"She's not up yet. Just hitch the carriage," Susannah said impatiently.

"Where you off to so early, Miss Susannah?" he asked curiously.

"That's my business, Reuben."

Now Reuben was really interested. "What'm I goin' to tell Mrs. St. John 'bout where you gone?"

"Say I'll be back soon," Susannah instructed him.

Mrs. St. John would have to know what she had done. As for Reuben, the less he knew about her activities, the better. Mrs. St. John didn't trust him. It was a wonder that he stayed on, she said. It wasn't family loyalty, she was sure. It might be just for the roof over his head and food to eat. Perhaps he was too much a coward to flee North or join the Union Army, but Mrs. St. John thought Reuben was into shady dealings. He'd be gone for long periods without permission, and once she had noticed that the earth of the carriage-house floor had been disturbed. Later there had always been straw covering the area, but Mrs. St. John thought he had gold buried there. He wouldn't be the only slave in Memphis to have an illegal nest egg.

"Lord knows how he came by it," she had said, "but if the North wins the war, he'll be a rich man."

Glad for the early outing, Sultan behaved himself as she drove south about a mile to Fort Pickering. The morning air was dank and foggy; the sun behind the mist made the sky look like a yellowed wedding veil, and the reek of mud came from the river. "I've come to see Colonel Spangler," she told a surprised sentry.

"The colonel is having breakfast in his quarters, miss," he told her.

"Well, go ask if he will see me," she said imperiously. "Tell him it's Miss Dunbar."

"Is it an emergency, then?"

Susannah considered. "Yes, in a way." What she'd come to do must be accomplished now. If she had to return to Beale Street without seeing the colonel, Mrs. St. John would surely try to prevent her coming again, and they had promised Aunt Caroline they'd be back at Robin Hill before dark tonight. A private was sent off with her request, and she waited impatiently until he returned with the news that the colonel would see her.

As she entered his quarters, Colonel Spangler rose from his chair at an oval Queen Anne tea table. The room was pleasant, with damask curtains tied back from the windows and a small fire to dispel the dampness. On another table, papers and maps lay beneath some shelves of books. Susannah's eyes went to the maps like a magnet.

Colonel Spangler laughed. "There're no secret troop movements for you to see, Susannah. It's merely a map of the county. I've been studying it to try to find how the Rebel escaped me the other night."

Susannah smiled at the confirmation that Cort was safe.

"Come here," he said, calling her to look at the map. "This is how he did it, I think," he said, and pointed to the route Cort had taken. "That road isn't on most maps, but I know about it now, so he'll not be so lucky next time."

"Dear me, how clever you are, Colonel," she told him. She knew he was warning her in case she had a lover who was slipping through the lines to see her. The Rebel's purpose at Robin Hill had occurred to him, and he was jealous.

She let her gaze shift to some photographs he had set out nearby. "Is that your sweetheart?" she asked about the picture of a pretty girl with dark hair puffed softly over her ears. She was sure that it wasn't.

"My sister," he said with a note of irritation in his voice. "Tell me your business, Miss Dunbar. I was informed that it was urgent. Is something wrong? Has someone annoyed you? Are you ill?"

"No, nothing like that." She felt a twinge of guilt at his genuine concern. "I'm sorry to have interrupted your breakfast, but it really couldn't wait."

She couldn't help glancing now at his breakfast table, laden with a plate of hot johnnycakes and sausage with a saucer of butter and a pitcher of syrup kept warm over a short candle. The aromas made her ravenous as she remembered the slab of cold cornbread that had been her breakfast.

"Won't you join me, Miss Dunbar?" he said, as though her discomfort were obvious.

"Oh, no, I couldn't. I've eaten already." She had dined with him before, but she had never liked the idea of his buying her meals, and this seemed entirely too intimate.

"At least have some coffee, then. It would be impolite of me to continue eating if you won't join me."

"Very well."

He rang for his orderly and had another cup brought. He asked for an extra plate and utensils as well. "In case you change your mind," he said with a smile. He poured the coffee himself and lifted the lid of a silver serving dish. "Perhaps just one johnnycake?" he suggested.

She gave in, dizzy with hunger. She did not stop him until he had loaded her plate with three of the fluffy golden cakes and had forked over a pair of sausages. The Yankees always ate like kings, she thought.

"That's better," he said with satisfaction. "Now, what is so important?"

"I have decided to accept your invitation to attend the officers' dance," she told him.

He was so startled he choked. "Well, this is good news," he said when he had stopped his sputtering with a gulp of hot coffee. "I'm delighted. But was it really so pressing that you had to interrupt my breakfast? You've not been so eager for my company before. What made you change your mind?"

"Oh, only that I love to dance, Colonel

Spangler, and I haven't danced in so long. It would be wonderful; and after all, it might do your officers a world of good to see how elegant a Southern woman is on the dance floor. It might make them more respectful and considerate."

Colonel Spangler looked bewildered. Her reasons didn't make sense to him, but he expected only to love her, not understand her.

"As for coming here so early, it's because I'll need a new gown for the occasion, and I thought you might save me time by approving my list of purchases yourself. I wouldn't have to go through channels, then. I could start right away. Even with Rachel and Aunt Caroline to help, it will be a lot to do."

She took out the list she had written and handed it to him. She watched breathlessly while he read it.

"Hmm, twelve yards of mauve glacé silk and fourteen yards of striped satin. Fifteen yards of green half-inch ribbon, and ten yards of lace." He stopped suddenly, and her hand trembled on her cup. "Egad, Susannah! What do you take me for? Ten yards of gray wool! Thirteen yards of gold braid! I cannot sign this, as well you know!"

"Of course you can. The gold braid is to go around the hem of the skirt, and the gray is for an evening cloak," Susannah replied with all the innocence she could muster. Could she fool him?

"Pick another color, and I will sign it. Tan is a good color for a cloak."

"Tan does dreadful things to my complexion,

Colonel. And navy or black is too dark. White is impossible to keep clean."

"Take the tan. I cannot imagine anything spoiling your complexion, but if it does, that is simply a sacrifice of war," he said grimly, exasperated.

"No," she said with a sigh. "If I cannot look my best, then I don't want to go." She laid her hand on his arm. "You stick to your rules. It's quite admirable. And I shall stick to mine." She rose to leave.

"Susannah!" She looked back as he stood up in an angry fluster. "You are the most spoiled woman I have ever known!"

Her smile told him she also knew she was the most intriguing woman he'd ever known.

"Dammit!" he cried, forgetting himself. "You know I can't trust you. You are the enemy!"

"You're right. Though Memphis has surrendered, I haven't. I'm sorry I came."

He groaned, almost beside himself with longing for her to stay. He *must* deny her, but how could he when he loved her? "I am a soldier, Susannah, but I only know how to fight men. If I were commander at West Point, I would insist on training in maneuvers against women. And I would put *you* in charge of it! What assurance can you give me that you are not going to turn ten yards of gray wool into a gray uniform?"

"Why, Colonel, there is the cloak itself. I'll be wearing it. And you will see that the braid is where it should be on the dress. You may measure, if you like."

"Perhaps you already have a cloak, Miss Dunbar."

She had to watch her expression carefully

then, for he had guessed the truth. She planned to put Mrs. St. John's cloak to use in her endeavor. "Don't be silly, Colonel," she said. "When was the last time you saw a woman wearing gray in Memphis? All the gray coats and dresses have been made into uniforms long ago, or used to patch them. And if I did have a gray cloak, why wouldn't I cut it up, instead of going to all this trouble?"

She had stumped him, she saw. He was only a man, and his grasp of sewing was minimal. Then he brought his fist down on the table so that the dishes jumped. "Aha! You nearly had me! You are going to wear the cloak and cut it up the next day!"

"Sir, I will give it to you the next day!"

He was entirely out of his depth now; he could not fathom why she would incur such expense for a cloak she could wear only once. But he knew he didn't understand women, especially Southern women with their fierce pride about everything from the Confederate Army to their nineteen-inch waists. His eyes took in Susannah's trim ankles, exposed below her walking skirt. Had she worn it to stay clear of the Memphis mud or to provoke his desire?

Her jaunty hat with its blue follow-me-lads ribbons down the back made her face small and delicate. It reminded him of a favorite china doll or the same sister whose picture he kept. As a child, when he had been angry with his sister, he used to tie the doll's hair in knots; and at times, similar behavior toward Susannah would have relieved his feelings. Oh, but no doll had ever gazed at him with such beautiful eyes, the color so pale and delicate he imagined no one could duplicate it in a painting, eyes that alternately teased and mocked and blazed at him, like an artillery position supplied with every sort of weapon from Gatling gun to cannon. He could read nothing in her eyes of her purpose and would have expected as much had they been dark, mysterious eyes. But how could she hide so much in those bright luminous orbs? She *was* hiding something. He was sure of it!

"I will have to see you home that night, of course, so there is no chance of its being stolen," he said meaningfully. But Susannah was undaunted by his implication that she might pretend a robbery.

"Of course I'll expect an escort home. I'll be staying with friends on Beale Street. If it's not too late, you may even come in for a cup of tea. You may take the cloak away with you then and keep it in case there is another dance."

Another dance! And she was saying she'd consider that, too! Crumbling, Colonel Spangler reached for his pen, even as his better sense told him not to do it.

"Oh, Colonel, there is one other thing," she said sweetly.

"What! What, for heaven's sake?"

"A pair of silk clockwork stockings. I forgot to add that to my list."

"I'll add it for you," he said with relief. "But, Susannah, if you get into trouble with your gray cloth, do not come running to me for help. I am endangering myself as it is."

"Of course, Colonel."

Susannah had long since dismissed Mrs. St. John's warning about pushing a man too far. She hadn't had enough experience to be fright-

ened of men. She wouldn't get into trouble, but
if she did, he wouldn't desert her. He hadn't
reported her for hiding Cort, had he?

Colonel Spangler signed Susannah's list, feeling tired before his day had even begun. It was
likely that somehow she was playing him for a
fool and that he was risking his career over her;
but deep inside, he cherished a hope that she
really wanted to go to the dance with him and
only wished to discomfit him as much as possible in the process. She'd been testing his devotion, that much he knew. Dared he hope she
cared for him a little?

3

Susannah forgot about Colonel Spangler and
the officers' dance the minute she left Fort Pickering. She drove back to Memphis along the
river, rolling with sluggish power in the summer morning. As she passed a ferry that led
across to Arkansas, the Yankee soldiers on guard
duty glanced up from mugs of hot coffee brewed
on a campfire. She felt a clutch at her stomach
and urged the horse faster, as if they might
somehow guess her errand.

Fog still clung to the water, blotting out the
view. It was a perfect day for illegal activity of
any sort on the river. It existed with impunity;
the river, however treacherous, always be-
friended those at odds with the law. Old men
and little boys, quiet and still as tree stumps,

were fishing for their breakfasts; they were all the male population now, except for the soldiers.

Oak and gum trees, along with chinquapins, ripening their chesnutlike fruit, gave way to wharves, and her progress was slowed by drays carrying away supplies brought down on barges from the North. Foghorns and whistles sounded, and she caught sight of a large steamboat, which perhaps had just come up from New Orleans, with a boatload of Yankees, no doubt, for that city was occupied as well.

Across the way, tired-looking women went back and forth, lifting their skirts to avoid the mud, while soldiers lolling outside cafés and taverns for an after-breakfast smoke stared at them or called disrespectful remarks. Some of the women answered with quick-tongued taunts of their own, arms akimbo, chins lifted. Others kept their eyes on the mud, as though mindful that symbolically they had already fallen into it. Spots of color on their cheeks were not blushes of embarrassment, but rouge they had not bothered to scrub off from the night before.

Susannah had heard of these women who served the soldiers in unthinkable ways, but she had never seen them before, and stared herself, almost forgetting the business that had brought her. She was so busy looking that she forgot she might be a sight herself, until she was startled by a long, appreciative whistle from a soldier she was passing.

"Hey! Where've you been hiding, my beauty? Are you free tonight?"

She gaped, looked about to see whom else he might be addressing, and turned crimson. Why, he'd mistaken her for one of them! Such inso-

lence! How dare he! Papa would call a man out
for much less. Papa would . . . She realized
that Papa was far away in Mississippi and that
even Colonel Spangler's protection would not
do her much good at the moment. She remembered Aunt Caroline's admonitions about the
short walking skirt and wished she had paid
heed. She dreaded the moment she would get
down from the carriage and give the men a
really good look at her ankles. For a moment
she was almost panicked to flight, but then her
good sense told her she would not be molested
on the street in broad daylight. The sight of her
destination steeled her.

A big frothy riverboat was docked with a gangplank extended and a sign that read "SLOANE'S
GAMING PARLOR." Susannah brought Sultan to a
halt and jumped down. The soldiers whooped
their approval of her ankles, but Susannah was
directed by a man in civilian clothes who was
crossing the street. He glanced at her for only
an instant, not leering, but appraising, his dark-
eyed gaze smooth and cool, as though she might
have been no more than a stray kitten that had
claimed his attention.

Everything about him seemed stern and aloof—
his complexion was dark like burnished pecan
wood. A finely cut nose lay between straight,
uncompromising eyebrows, and his mouth,
unshrouded by the beard or mustache most
men wore, showed no hint of pleasure. His tall,
lean body moved gracefully in trousers that fit
tightly from his waist to his smart Oxonian shoes,
and a dark wing of hair swept back beneath his
low-crowned muffin hat, worn at a rakish tilt.
She gazed back at him until their eyes met,

and a strange current of intimacy ran between them. She had never been looked at in quite such a way. She flushed, and he tipped his hat impassively as he went on.

He must be some sort of profiteer, since they were the only fashionably dressed men seen about Memphis these days, but somehow she knew he wasn't. Something about him was too magnificent to be contained by mere dollar signs. If he were an opportunist, he was after more than money.

The second after her feet hit the ground, he turned his back and disappeared into a café. She felt a stab of anger as she fastened Sultan's reins to a hitching post. Somehow she was more offended by him than by the simple lusty soldiers. When a man looked at her, she was used to seeing approval on his face. It was almost as though he had expected *her* to admire *him*, she thought. She did not, certainly. Her expression hadn't been more than casual—she hoped!

The incident affected her confidence as she walked up the gangplank and knocked on the cut-glass door of the gaming room. Disapproval would have been better than that unsettling look; that at least she understood. But why should his opinion matter?

A black man wielding a broom admitted her to the gloomy salon. He was a runaway, probably working for passage north on the river. His employer, Rudd Sloane, was no abolitionist. Rather, he lacked principles of any sort. Long before the war he'd used runaways to stoke his boilers. If there were an explosion, better to have someone else's property blown to bits.

Susannah recognized the former slave, who had worked on a neighboring plantation.

"Miss Susannah," the man cried in surprise. "You shouldn't be here!"

"Neither should you," she replied, "but these are strange times. I want to see Mr. Sloane."

"Miss Susannah, he's a bad man."

"Go get him," Susannah said imperiously. The man went off muttering, too used to subservience to protest further. Susannah hoped he would make it safely wherever he was going. Her own father, in the days before the war, had held the view that the system must change, and had supported changing laws that made it illegal to free one's slaves. But the change should have been gradual and through state legislation, not through this awful invasion of Southern rights, this cataclysm of war.

She waited, feeling choked by the fumes of stale tobacco smoke that permeated the heavy velvet draperies and the plush carpet. Amber-colored liquor stood abandoned in smudged glasses, and unlighted chandeliers tinkled gently with the motion of river waves against the boat. The place was so oppressive that Susannah was again tempted to flee. This dark, debauched room surely was more dangerous than the street had been. Could she even imagine the things that happened here?

"Good morning, are you looking for a job? There aren't any, I'm afraid."

Rudd Sloane, who had entered through a polished oak door at the rear of the room, didn't look as much like the devil as she had thought he would. He was slightly squat, with a bullish neck obscured by a wiry beard, a man who was strong and wily, but not imposing. He yawned, giving a snap to his suspenders, adjusting them. His shirt collar was open, as though he'd left off dressing to see her. "Everybody's looking for work. I've got lots of quality ladies like yourself waiting my tables. But waitresses is all I use, and I've got more than enough. Now, across the street at Mrs. Simpson's . . ." he added, naming a well-known house of ill repute.

"Mr. Sloane!"

"Don't get your dander up, dearie; I was only trying to help." Sloane noticed one of the half-empty glasses, and picking it up, emptied it down his throat, finishing with a resounding "Ahh!"

"It's a shame to waste good liquor," he sighed. "We don't use the cheap kind here. No, nothing but the best at Rudd Sloane's establishment."

"Mr. Sloane, I am not looking for a job," she said desperately. "I'm Susannah Dunbar and—"

"Miss Dunbar—of Robin Hill?"

"Yes," she said, relieved that since he knew who she was, she would get her due respect.

"So, what do you want, Miss Dunbar? Something to do with money, or you wouldn't have come to old Sloane."

"I want to sell a bale of cotton."

He nodded. "That's easy to do. But only one? There's a good market. I can sell all I can get. I hear that Robin Hill has been left almost undamaged. Surely you have more." His eyes had narrowed, as though he were concentrating; and Susannah, who had been somewhat lulled, felt new pangs of alarm.

"Only one bale, Mr. Sloane. You see, my father burned our cotton before the Yankees came," she lied. "But he saved one bale in case my sister and I should need the money. I don't like selling my cotton to the enemy, but I've already sold the silver and valuables."

"And yourself," he chuckled.

"Sir!"

He burst into merry laughter. "It's no wonder you don't need a job at Mrs. Simpson's. You've got your own private Yankee. Everyone knows about you and Colonel Spangler, but don't get all worked up now. You're a smart girl to save your plantation. You're a woman after my own heart, Miss Dunbar. I'll get two hundred dollars for your cotton."

"It's worth three," she said, trembling with outrage. She wanted to cry, but she wouldn't give him that satisfaction.

"My commission," he said, grinning.

"You'll pay two-fifty or I won't sell it," she declared.

"Two hundred. You will. You need the money badly or you wouldn't be here. But if you find you have other bales to sell, I'll give you two-twenty-five each on a hundred bales."

"Good day, sir," she said, stumbling toward the door.

"Same to you, Miss Dunbar. Send the bale anytime you like. Or the hundred bales."

The air outside was full of unpleasant odors, the smell of rotting garbage and old fish heads mixed with the reek of mud; but it seemed sweet after the foulness of Sloane's Gaming Parlor. Susannah filled her lungs as she hurried down the gangplank. She had held her composure while she was in Sloane's disgusting company, but now the tears began to flow. What a contrast that interview had been to her first interview this morning, with Colonel Spangler!

She wasn't afraid of Sloane, she told herself, though she was seeing the underseams of life for the first time. Was it true that her relationship with Colonel Spangler had destroyed her reputation in Memphis? Did everyone think—?

"Hello, sweetheart." The soldier who had insulted her was standing beside the carriage. He must have stationed himself there to wait for her to come out. "How about meeting me tonight? I'll buy you a nice dinner and pay you extra to boot."

She ignored him and climbed into the carriage seat. He reached up and squeezed her knee. Without a thought, she thrashed him with the whip. But the tip brushed Sultan's flanks as it passed over, and the horse took off at a gallop. Susannah, who had been half-standing, was thrown into the botton of the vehicle. She righted herself dizzily, trying to find the reins. Sultan jolted around a corner, and the carriage rose on one wheel. Susannah was spilled onto the floor again, clinging for dear life, terrified that the vehicle was about to turn over.

Suddenly she heard the sound of another horse, the squeak of saddle leather as the animal drew alongside. The carriage jolted as a man vaulted into it. A voice barked a command she didn't understand. Had it been in a foreign language?

Sultan understood, though—if not the word, then the tone, the skillful command on the reins, which even he had not the spirit to dispute. The carriage slowed and stopped. Susannah, on the floor, found herself eye to eye with a smart Oxonian shoe. In spite of everything, she had no difficulty remembering that such gear had already caught her attention once today, and she had no doubt that it was the same man wearing it.

"Are you all right?"

The voice, rich and warm, tangy with the accent of somewhere far more Southern than Tennessee, rang distantly in her ears. She felt a hand around her arm lifting her up. She tried to focus on his face, but saw only a blur. She swayed weakly and felt herself in his arms, her cheek against his worsted jacket. She drew in a deep breath, trying to recover her senses; and the heady mix of male aromas—wool, leather, shaving soap—melded by his own male chemistry, affected her like smelling salts. Her head cleared, and she pulled away from him so abruptly that she almost lost her balance again, and he had to grab her waist to keep her from tumbling into the street.

She glanced down and saw something that had escaped her notice before. The fine Oxonian shoe was squarely on top of her prized hat!

"Oh, my hat! You've ruined it!"

Following her gaze, he drew back his foot. She bent and retrieved the hat, studying it mournfully. It was the last nice hat she possessed, and with money so tight, she wasn't likely to spend for a new one. Saving it was hopeless; even the pretty ribbons were badly stained with Memphis mud.

"I'll replace it, of course," he said crossly. "At least you might be grateful it isn't your life that needs replacing."

"I . . ." Too late she realized she should have

been thanking him instead of complaining about a foolish hat.

"You should sell that horse for a calmer animal; you've no business going out driving behind that one. You've no business driving alone at all, as a matter of fact. Women in my country never do. But women in the United States seem to have forgotten how to be women." He leapt lightly down from the conveyance.

"This is not the United States, sir!" she cried furiously. "It is the Confederacy. And we Southern women take care of ourselves."

"As you were so aptly demonstrating when I saved your life."

"You did not save my life, sir. The horse has as low an opinion of women as you seem to, but I would have managed him."

"As you manage your men, no doubt. A girl like you should have no trouble finding a Yankee who'd keep her off the streets—and marry her after the war. Take my advice and do it."

"I don't want your advice, and I would never marry a Yankee!"

"Scruples! From a woman of your kind! But one never knows what to expect in the South." He took a roll of banknotes from his pocket and thrust it into her hand. "This should take care of the hat."

"I cannot accept your money," she said desperately, trying to give it back.

"Why not? Because it's only your hat I've sullied? Buy a new one. I should hate to think I was the cause of the sun glaring into those pretty eyes."

He swung into the saddle. Sultan took it into his head to start off too, and Susannah had to concentrate on the horse. "Whoa, Sultan!" she called, pulling on the reins, but the horse kept moving, this time at a gentle trot, while her rescuer moved off in the opposite direction.

She leaned out of the carriage, staring after him, longing to shout angry denials over what he had thought her into the growing space between them. But that would have created a spectacle worse than anything thus far, and he wouldn't have heard her anyway. She had ample opportunity to study his broad shoulders and admire the finely erect manner he sat the horse, for he never glanced back. Instead his attention focused on barges on the river, as though he had already forgotten the encounter.

Susannah couldn't forget it. Even after she was safely back at Mrs. St. John's Beale Street house, she couldn't stop thinking of him. She had never met a man so arrogant. Sam Spangler was a gentleman, even though he was a Yankee. This man was not. Who was he? Was she going to see him again? She would have to see him to give back the money. She couldn't take gifts from a man she didn't know, and it hadn't been his fault anyway that her hat had been ruined. What would she say to him, then? She wanted to put him in his place and make him take proper notice of her. She would teach him not to go about assuming that women were not ladies!

Her cheeks burned at the thought of her sojourn at the docks. It had been bad enough to go alone, but she had had to go in the walking skirt she'd worn for Colonel Spangler's benefit. Somehow the humiliation the foreigner had dealt her had been worse than what she had endured

from the soldiers and from Rudd Sloane. Those
men were cheap and vulgar. Whatever her rescuer had been, he was not that. What was he,
then? She still had no inkling, only that he was
such a stranger that he could call a piece of
occupied Confederacy a part of the United States.
He was a rich stranger, to judge by the amount
of money he had parted with so casually. It had
been more than enough to replace her hat.

Clearly he thought women were senseless,
dependent creatures, much inferior to the mighty
male. Did women in his country accept such a
view of themselves? Before the war, Susannah
had expected to be dependent on men, but she
had considered it a man's privilege to cater to
her. It had left women free for the gentler side
of life, but women had as much stamina as
men, as the Yankees had learned. Colonel
Spangler, for instance, did not underestimate
her. And why should he? In just one morning she
had inveigled his signature on a list that he
could be court-martialed for signing, and she
had invaded a masculine realm to arrange for
the sale of her cotton.

But it was not the stranger's disregard of her
abilities that bothered her so. It wasn't even his
notion of her morals. The thing that made her
livid was his indifference to her. And her infuriating inability to be equally indifferent to him!

But there was too much to be done to indulge
herself long in such reverie. She had first to
deal with Mrs. St. John's mingled horror and
delight as she learned of Susannah's plans.

"You did that, Susannah? Got Colonel Spangler
to sign a requisition for gray material and gold
braid? However did you do it? And you went to

Rudd Sloane's Gaming Parlor? If Cort or your father ever finds out—"

"They won't," Susannah said confidently. "Now, we must make decisions. There's not much time before the officers' dance, and we must make the gown. Of course, I'll wear the old gray cloak with some new trim sewn on. I'll go to Robin Hill this afternoon and arrange to have the bale of cotton delivered to Mr. Sloane."

"I'll send Reuben with you to bring it," Mrs. St. John offered.

"I suppose that's sensible," Susannah agreed. "I don't want to have to go to the gaming parlor again myself. But we should be careful that nobody learns where the cotton is hidden. We've several hundred bales, and Sloane suspects it. He'd do anything to get his hands on it. It's worth a small fortune, enough to refurbish Robin Hill and make it productive again after the war. We won't be ruined as so many will be."

Rachel was beside herself with excitement. "Oh, I wish I could have gone with you!" She pouted. "You've had all the fun of it."

"You sound like a child, Rachel. It wasn't fun. It was disgusting," Susannah said. But she didn't tell her sister about the compelling stranger.

"It was an adventure! And I want to have one too. Oh, I hate being the younger sister and always being told what to do!"

"Your turn will come, Rachel. I'll be an old married lady, and you'll be having the good times I couldn't have because of the war. In the meantime, there'll be plenty of sewing to do, if we're to fool the Yankees and get Cort his new uniform. It'll take the three of us working morning until night to get it done."

"Will we do it here or at Robin Hill?" Rachel asked.

"Well, I imagine it might be easier at Robin Hill. Aunt Caroline could help, and we'd have only the gray material to take out of Memphis instead of a uniform. It would save trouble, because we have permission for the material. Perhaps you could come to visit us there, Mrs. St. John."

Cort's mother shook her head regretfully. "I'm afraid you'll have to do without me. If I leave the house, the Yankees are sure to take it."

They were quiet for a moment, considering, Susannah and Rachel knowing that what she said was true. The Yankees were notorious for such seizures around Memphis.

"We can't do without you," Susannah said finally. "We'll come here, since Robin Hill will be in no danger from our being away."

"It will mean slipping out a finished uniform, Susannah," Mrs. St. John said. "Perhaps you should take the gray to Robin Hill unmade. We'll do the gown here, but there's no deadline on the other."

"Oh, I know nothing about men's clothes, and neither does Aunt Caroline. You're the only one of us who does. We'll do it here. Bribing the guard will cost a bit, but I want Cort's uniform to be perfect."

"Let me be the one to sneak it out, Susannah," Rachel begged, her eyes eager.

"You! Certainly not!"

"It's not fair," Rachel protested, standing with her hands on her dainty waist. "It's not even dangerous, and who would suspect me? You would be more likely to get caught. Colonel Spangler is suspicious."

"Colonel Spangler doesn't *want* me to be caught, Rachel, no matter how suspicious he is. And no one is going to get caught in any case. It will be as simple as a Sunday stroll. But I am going to do it, because Cort is *my* fiancé."

"She's quite right, Rachel," Mrs. St. John said. "Why, I would do it myself, but it will be a romantic story for Cort and Susannah to tell their children."

"Oh, very well. But, Susannah, when you tell your children, you must promise to say that it was their Aunt Rachel's idea." Rachel giggled, both at the idea of herself as an aunt and at Susannah's blush at the mention of children.

The drive home to Robin Hill was uneventful with Reuben to keep Sultan under control. Reuben, who was an expert with horses, dropped his usual surliness to whistle and sing most of the way, but Susannah doubted that his delight with the fiery Sultan was entirely responsible for his good mood.

In the morning, without being asked, he offered to help bring the bale from its hiding place. "Ol' Arthur, he shouldn't do it alone, Miss Susannah. I'll be goin' along, if you don't mind."

But Susannah did mind. "You stay here, Reuben; Aunt Caroline will find you something to do. Rachel and I will go ourselves with Uncle Arthur."

Susannah didn't trust Reuben. It wasn't like him to volunteer help, and she had no intention of allowing him to discover her hoard. So

Sultan was hitched ignobly to a small cart with Uncle Arthur to drive and Rachel and Susannah in riflecloth riding skirts walking behind. Aunt Caroline had strict orders not to let Reuben out of her sight. The path was overgrown and branches snapped under the weight of the cart. On the way back, the two girls obliterated the marks of the wheels with two sacks and tried to disguise the fact of their passage.

At Robin Hill Aunt Caroline had a hot meal of chicken and biscuits waiting. Reuben was asleep in the pantry. "I set him to patchin' windows, Miss Susannah, but he kept tryin' to wander off. I give him some refreshment that kept him around. Colonel Spangler's last bottle of sherry is all gone, but you were right. He kept tryin' to get me to tell 'im where the cotton was, once the liquor loosened 'is tongue." She gazed at the sleeping black in contempt. "Swine like that gives us all a bad name. Swine is swine, black or white."

The next day they were off to Memphis again with the cotton. Reuben was sent to deliver it to Sloane's Gaming Parlor. They counted on Reuben's being afraid to sell a bale so obviously stolen. It was something of a risk because some profiteers did deal with blacks, though the purchasing of stolen cotton sometimes resulted in boycotts from legal owners. By afternoon a messenger from Sloane arrived at the Beale Street house with the purchase price and a note from his employer again assuring Susannah that he was willing to buy a large stock of cotton.

"Why wait?" Sloane had written. "When the Confederacy falls, everyone who has been hoarding cotton to keep it out of enemy hands will flood the market with it and drive the price down. It's simply good sense to sell now and would profit us both."

"The nerve! To say the war is lost, when there are still such good men to fight it!" Susannah fumed.

"If Atlanta falls, Susannah, everything may very well be lost. Then you may need to think about this offer," Mrs. St. John advised.

"Atlanta won't fall," Rachel declared. "General Forrest will break the supply line."

"If he doesn't . . . Cort will need funds to restore Hazel Grove as well as to begin again at Robin Hill, in any case, and I do not see how we are to keep Hazel Grove off the auction block unless you bring enough to the marriage to save it. Cort wasn't as prudent as your father, Susannah. He *did* burn our cotton." She sighed at the rashness of youth.

Susannah merely smiled, remembering the sight of the cotton fires. The great stacks of bales had gone up in a magnificent blaze of patriotism and faith; the sun itself had faded in the clouds of sooty fumes. She did not share Mrs. St. John's regret that Cort had burned Hazel Grove's cotton. It only recommended him to her as a man of courage and conviction, the sort of man she wanted for her husband.

Thinking of Cort's burning the cotton made her more determined than ever not to sell her own to the Yankees after the one bale.

The three of them went shopping with Colonel Spangler's list in hand. None of the goods was easy to find, and they were forced to endure the company of a blue-uniformed soldier with a ring of keys to open private storerooms

that had been padlocked by the occupying forces.
The gray wool was the last thing to be found,
and they had almost given up when a bolt of it
was discovered beneath a box of whalebone
stays. Susannah unwound it critically, elated
that moths had not got to it.

"What do you think, Mrs. St. John?" she
asked, holding the material against her bodice.

"We might have wished for something a trifle
softer, but it suits you very well, dear," Cort's
mother replied, playing her part.

The amazed storekeeper cut off the required
yardage and signed papers that sanctioned the
sale. When they were home, they at last gave
vent to cheers and laughter, flapping the material up and down and taking turns wrapping it
about each other. After that the cutting and
sewing began, but not of the gray wool. Susannah's ball gown would be done first, since it
must be ready to be worn on her outing with
Colonel Spangler. The dining room, where they
laid out their work, was filled with the aroma of
crisp new material, and it had been so long
since they had smelled it that it seemed as though
bouquets of spring blossoms had been brought
into the room.

The bodice of the mauve silk was to be tight-
fitting, with a deep point at the waist, front and
back, and a décolletage of frothy ruffles. The
same material was looped up over the striped
satin skirt. It was impossible for Susannah not
to revel in the first ball gown she had had since
the beginning of the war; and though Rachel
sewed until her fingers were red and numb, it
was impossible for *her* not to be jealous. Once
when she had worked to exhaustion, she pricked

her finger and ran upstairs, where Susannah found her weeping.

"Are you hurt that badly?" Susannah asked in alarm. "What happened? Was it the scissors?"

"No, I am not hurt at all," Rachel said ruefully.

"Then what . . . ?"

"Nothing. Only, whenever you put the dress on, you look like a queen, even though it's just half-finished. I could never live up to you, even if I did get the chance."

Susannah kissed her sister's hair. "You'll be sixteen next month, and this should have been your season, your coming-out. I'm sorry the dress isn't for you."

"That isn't what bothers me. It's not that the dress is yours or how lovely you look in it. It's that you never complain; you're always cheerful about doing what has to be done. I know how distasteful it is for you to go out in Colonel Spangler's company, among all the Yankees. But you'll do it perfectly and without a murmur. I'll never be as beautiful as you, but what's worse, I'll never be as brave. I haven't your strength, Susannah."

"I'm just glad you aren't the one who caught the colonel's eye. I'd worry like an old mother hen. And you mustn't think I'm so brave. I was scared silly at the docks. I nearly turned and ran. A lot of people would say I've been foolhardy, and no doubt that is what I'd think if *you* were in my place. As for strength, why, you've been sewing all day. Look, there's a blister on your finger where you hold the needle."

Rachel dried her eyes. "I'll put a bandage over it. We have to finish the hem tonight."

The night of the officers' dance, Susannah felt like Cinderella, transformed from her worn wartime apparel. "I can't believe it," she sighed, gazing into the pier glass as Mrs. St. John arranged white roses from her garden in Susannah's *chignon à marteaux*, sausage curls carefully pinned and clustered, a labor that had absorbed hours with brush and rag rollers. A jet necklace added a sophisticated touch above the décolletage, and two-button white kid gloves, though a little old-fashioned, accented the smallness of her hands.

Mrs. St. John looked at her critically. "What's wrong?" Susannah asked. "You don't seem pleased."

"I'm afraid we've made you too pretty, Susannah. We should at least remove the roses. The scent of them will be intoxicating when a man is dancing with you."

"Oh, no, please!" Susannah raised a hand protectively to her hair. "Everything will come loose."

"Well, take the necklace off, then. Don't dispute me, Susannah. I'm older than you and soon to be your mother-in-law."

Susannah obeyed reluctantly. "I would like to look my very best in the company of the Yankees," she objected. "I wouldn't like them to say I lacked elegance."

"They won't say that, don't worry! Well, I am glad I don't have to conjure you up a coach from a pumpkin. I'm much too tired for that. I believe the colonel is here." She held up the gray cloak for Susannah to fasten about her shoulders.

"Do you think there's any chance he'll guess?"

Susannah asked, thinking of the uniform, now carefully cut and half-stitched in the closet.

"None at all, not with the shiny new trim. He's bound not to think it's old," Mrs. St. John said with satisfaction.

The August night was perfect for dancing. The air was really too warm for a cloak, but later the chill from the river might justify her having it to wear over her sleeveless gown. Moonlight dappled the plush cushions of the carriage as they rode through the town, and Susannah could almost imagine that if she turned her gaze from the window, she would find her father beside her, escorting her to one of the many soirees at the Gayoso Hotel.

In the ballroom familiar chandeliers cast the same patterns of glimmering light over the polished dance floor, and the same red cut-velvet draperies and swags hung over the arched windows. The coffered ceiling and the gilded paneling were unchanged, along with the Corinthian columns that flanked the great stair. Laughter and violin music swirled out from the room, but the illusion of the past was quickly shattered by the crush of blue uniforms. Leaving her wrap behind in the cloakroom, Susannah entered on Colonel Spangler's arm, opening her sandalwood fan with a snap, for immediately the air seemed too close.

Sideboard tables with marble tops supported serving dishes kept warm with spirit lamps, and the aroma of simmering sauces mingled with the cool tartness of pungent champagne. Butterfly shrimp and clams, no doubt brought up the river from New Orleans, lay on sparkling beds of crushed ice, sharing table space with cheeses and breads and sugared nuts. The sight of such feasting and bounty while so many of her countrymen were starving almost sickened her; she accepted only a glass of champagne and refused Colonel Spangler's offer of a plate.

"Can't I at least get you a petit four or one of the cherry tarts?" he asked.

She shook her head.

"Would you sooner dance, then?"

"Yes, I would like that," she said, though she had as strong an impulse to flee the place as she had had at Sloane's Gaming Parlor.

She had become inured to the reality of Yankees tromping through city and countryside, desecrating property and homes, but she was surprised to find herself not quite prepared for the sight of them enjoying themselves here. In her mind the Gayoso had been as before, even though officers quartered there.

Colonel Spangler swung her out in a waltz. He was an excellent dancer, and she allowed herself to be guided masterfully around the floor. Her heart wasn't in it, but at least her toes would not be trod upon.

"Susannah," he said.

"Yes, Colonel?" She realized she had not been paying attention to him. She had almost forgotten with whom she was dancing as she studied the other guests. There were several Southern women she knew among the Union wives and daughters, but she avoided catching their eyes, and they also looked away. They were here for their own reasons of survival or practicality, and none was proud of it. Some of the guests had come from St. Louis, but one woman with

a Southern accent and a flashy dog-collar necklace set with diamonds had come up from New
Orleans, a hotbed of female spies.

"Is it too much to ask that you might smile at
me when we're dancing, Susannah? It is supposed to be a pleasant pastime, and you look as
though you have a stomachache. You haven't,
have you?"

"No, Colonel." She flashed him a smile and
felt a quiver in his hand on her waist.

"Susannah, I wish . . . Do you think you
could call me Sam?"

"I doubt it; it's entirely too personal, sir. At
least I haven't complained that you address *me*
by my Christian name without my permission.
I suppose it's not your fault. It's the fault of
your Yankee upbringing."

His face went dark and thunderous; he looked
ready to explode, and she saw that she had said
more than was wise. Thankfully the waltz ended,
and a quadrille began. She was no longer required to dance so intimately with him, but
each time she glanced at him during the various
figures, his gaze was upon her heavily. She
could not understand how her small taunt had
upset him so thoroughly. She would need to be
more judicious.

She was so preoccupied that she failed to
notice who else was dancing in their square,
and suddenly found herself face to face with
the tall foreigner who had taken charge of Sultan. How could she not have noticed him? For
once she saw him, she could think of nothing
else. It wasn't only that his white cashmere
waistcoat and smart black frock coat made him
more elegant than any other man in the room.

He had a natural grace that made all the other men, even Colonel Spangler, seem no more skillful at the dance than trained monkeys; and other women kept glancing back at him, no matter which way their partners turned them, as though their eyes were held by magnets. His own partner was blissfully dazed and rosy, and Susannah felt a peculiar pang of envy as he guided her with haughty command. He gave a nod of recognition as they passed, and the corner of his mouth turned up in amusement as he saw that his presence disconcerted Susannah.

Susannah's legs shook so that she could hardly finish the quadrille, and she felt a telltale flush rising to her cheeks. It wasn't enough that he had seen her where he had and thought her a woman of low morals. That was only humiliating. What was worse was that he might come over to converse with her and Colonel Spangler. How easy it would be for him to mention where he had seen her!

Hardly had the fear formed in her mind than the music ended. "Colonel, I would like a breath of air," she started to say, but it was already too late. He was coming toward them, offering his hand to Colonel Spangler.

"Good evening, Colonel." He bowed to Susannah. "I have met this lady, but we have not been introduced. I hope you will do me the honor, Colonel."

"A pleasure, certainly," he replied. "Miss Susannah Dunbar, may I present Antonio Andrada, the Marquez da Silva, an envoy of the Emperor Dom Pedro of Brazil."

A marquess, a nobleman! Hadn't she felt it, though she had never met one before?

"Your servant, Miss Dunbar," he said in his creamy accent. "I hope you had no more trouble with the horse the other day. Fulton Street is a bad place for spooky horses—too much traffic to upset them." He spoke with a gleam of mischief in his eyes, for he well knew that it wasn't traffic that had caused Sultan to go on his spree. And then, before she could frame any reply, he went on, "Did you buy your new hat? And your lovely gown is so stylish, it must be new. Was the money I gave you enough to pay for that too?"

"I did not . . ." she began, but the room was spinning, and she had laced her stays so tightly she couldn't get her breath. She had been vain enough to want to be certain no Yankee woman's waist looker smaller than hers.

She felt Colonel Spangler's arm about her and from a distance heard him say coldly, "I must take Miss Dunbar outside. I will thank you to keep your distance from her in the future, or I will call you out!"

They were on the portico; Susannah could feel the fresh breeze and the coolness of the baluster against which he was holding her, but she didn't want to recover herself and face him. She wanted to sink deeper into her swoon, but a sensation she had never before experienced roused her. Colonel Spangler had slid his hands into her bodice. Her eyes flew open as his finger pressed lightly over her breasts.

"Oh!" she gasped, shocked to her senses.

Colonel Spangler's fingers worked on her laces. She drew a deep involuntary breath as they parted, and the colonel withdrew his hands. "There. I am sorry to have had to do such an indelicate thing, Susannah, but I knew what was the problem. I wasn't about to let you get by with fainting and being carried off to a bedroom with a lot of women to fuss over you and keep me out. No doubt that's what you would have liked. It was the most convenient swoon I've ever seen!"

She was still stunned by what he had done; and his face, close to hers, was strained by passion and fury. "So, Susannah! How does the Marquez da Silva fit into your plans? You bought a gown with money given to you by a man to whom you had not even been introduced? Did he pay for the gray material too? What plot did you hatch, using me as your gull? Tell me, Susannah. I swear I believe I am angry enough to kill you!"

Fainting having failed her, Susannah resorted to weeping. "Oh, Sam," she said, hoping the sound of the name he had wanted her to use would soften him. "Sam, I didn't buy the gown with the marquess's money."

"But he did give you money?" the colonel said, unsoothed.

"Yes. The morning I came to see you at Fort Pickering, Sultan ran away with the carriage. The marquess stopped it, and in doing so, he stepped on my hat. He gave me money to replace it. I tried to give it back—"

"On Fulton Street? What were you doing there, Susannah? No decent women has any business—"

"I did. I went to sell a bale of cotton. That's where I got the money for the gown." Surely truth would placate him. She was feeling stronger now, working up indignation which she hoped would gain her control of the situation.

"Don't expect me to believe that you sold a bale of cotton just to pay for a ball gown, Susannah! All Yankees aren't as stupid as you think! I know very well that you would dress in rags before you would help the enemy by supplying cotton. No, if you sold your cotton, you sold it to help your cause in some way. That is the reason most Confederates sell. To buy ammunition or medicine for the troops. Mark my word, if that's what you've done, I'll find out! It's something to do with that Reb that gave us the slip the other night, I'll wager. And something to do with that blasted gray cloak, but I'm damned if I know what!"

"Pray do not curse, Colonel!"

"I have been driven to it! You use me shamelessly for your own purposes and care nothing for the torment you cause me. What have I done to make you treat me so badly? I am always risking my neck to make you happy."

"You are a Yankee, Sam," she said gently, as if explaining to a child.

"That is only a name you give me. I am a military man fighting for a cause I believe in. I believe what Abraham Lincoln believes. I do not think that we can exist half-slave and half-free. And I don't think you ought to blame me for it. I think you know in your heart that slavery is wrong!"

"Perhaps it's not ideal, but it is what the South stands on—my home and everything I love. And neither are most Southerners the ogres they're made out to be. Most of our friends' slaves had plenty to eat, tight roofs over their heads, and the opportunity to work their way from field hands to positions of responsibility on the plantations. On Robin Hill the slaves were almost family. And what has happened to them now? They are starving and homeless, taken advantage of by Northerners, while an entire society lies in ruin. Is this the great good you've done?"

Colonel Spangler seemed almost beside himself. "It's what had to be done!" he cried. "Good will come from this awful war at last. Some good would have come from it already, if only you could care for me. I was wounded at Gettysburg and took a ball in the leg at Shiloh, but I would do it all again if this war could bring us together, if you could love me, as I love you. If you could swear to me that you sold your cotton only for a gown to wear dancing with me, then I could be content."

"Oh, I do swear it," she said, still wanting him to believe her story, not quite realizing the import of what she was saying.

"Then, if you would do that, you *must* care for me a little! Oh, my darling!" His mouth was on hers, kissing her. His beard pressed harshly into her delicate chin. She felt herself suffocating. The image of Cort St. John flashed into her mind, and she imagined what he would do to Sam Spangler if he were here. A Yankee kissing her! Choking, she fought free and, bringing up a white-gloved hand, struck him as hard as she could across the face. As she fled blindly, she heard a grunt of pain, and not understanding that it came from his heart, was surprised that the blow had hurt so much.

She ran into the ladies' cloakroom, knowing

he couldn't follow her there. Thankfully it was deserted. She sank onto an Empire sofa, resting her head against its lyre-carved arm until her trembling ceased. Only then did she begin to take stock of what she had done. Had she made an enemy of her protector? Oh, but how could she have responded differently? She went to the mirror and began to repair her dishevelment, replacing her stays, but not so tightly as before. It was impossible to restore her hair to its earlier perfection, but she did the best she could, discarding a crushed rose in the process. How would she face Sam Spangler again? Was he waiting for her beyond the cloakroom door? Voices outside the cloakroom warned her that other women were about to enter. She slipped out quickly through a door at the other end of the room and found herself in an empty hall. Music came from one direction, but she found herself moving away from it. Another door beckoned, and stepping through it, she found herself on the veranda again. Shivering, she fastened the cloak around her, grateful that she was still alone.

Then a figure detached itself from the shadow of a column and came toward her. It was surely Sam Spangler, and her heart pounded; but it thudded even more furiously as she saw that it was the Marquez da Silva.

"Are you feeling better, Miss Dunbar?" he asked sardonically.

"No thanks to you!" she returned. "Is it your custom to go out of your way to embarrass ladies?"

"On the contrary, I never embarrass ladies. And women rarely. But you deserved it. I did not misrepresent the situation. I didn't even mention your little sojourn in the gaming parlor. I may be a stranger in Memphis, but a person can't be in town a day without knowing its reputation. You really are no different from those other women, even though you are of good family. In fact, you are worse, since you ought to be better. But your gown *is* lovely, and you are lovely in it. Why don't you dance with me, Miss Dunbar, since your colonel has gone away in a snit?"

"Dance with you! Never! And don't flatter yourself that I'd buy a gown with your money. I don't want your money, and if you'd given me the chance, I'd have given it back to you."

He shrugged. "Very well. I apologize. I didn't understand then that you had no need of it," he said slyly.

She glared at him, hating him, horrified to realize that a part of her, some unfamiliar, incredibly rash part of her, desired to dance with him. She wanted to hit him as she had Colonel Spangler, to repudiate his insinuations; but somehow she was afraid to. Something told her there would be consequences . . .

"Where shall I send the money, please?" she said icily.

"Oh, don't bother sending it. I'll ride out to Robin Hill and collect it myself. It's a place I've wanted to see; I've heard a great deal about it from Colonel Dunbar. I want to see if my mental picture of it is as different from the real thing as it was of the daughter."

"You know my father?" she gasped.

"Don't worry; I'll say nothing of your shenanigans when I see him again. He's a fine officer, and it might break his heart. I had the privilege of camping for a few days with Forrest's army. They are a magnificent lot, and my emperor will be very pleased if I can recruit some of them to my plan."

"What plan?" she couldn't help asking.

"Haven't you heard of it? Dom Pedro is offering free land along the Amazon to Southerners who wish to rebuild there after the war. The land is some of the richest in the world, and the climate perfect for cane and cotton. And it would be hard to find anyone better qualified to develop it than Southern growers."

"There is land *here*, sir, when the war is over."

"Ruined land, Miss Dunbar. It will never be what it was after the Yankees have had their way."

"They will not have their way. And the South will be rebuilt."

He shook his head. "They've already had their way, have they not, Miss Dunbar?" he asked with a smile of innuendo. Then, in a more serious way, he went on, "No one who has traveled the South these last months can think there is hope. I have been to Richmond and New Orleans, Savannah and Atlanta, and the story is the same everywhere. Brave men from one end of the South to the other are beginning to face the truth. There is no reason left to fight. I am an impartial observer, and what I am offering is the hope of the future. Even slavery is still possible in Brazil, though the emperor's dearest wish is to find ways to phase it out. Brazil is a new world where the old may shine again. It's another chance to find solutions to the problems that caused its downfall here."

"You are spreading lies, sir!" Susannah snapped. "The war is far from over. You know nothing about the South, nothing about Southerners, and especially you know nothing about me! The South isn't giving up, and neither am I. A woman fights a war in a different way than a man, but that is what I am doing."

He laughed, amused at her ire. "You have a powerful arsenal, I'll grant you, Miss Dunbar. But pick a man who's a match for you. Colonel Spangler is too easily overwhelmed by a woman's charms. It's hardly fair."

"And you would *never* be susceptible to a woman, I suppose."

"My dear Miss Dunbar, I have been a bachelor long enough to develop an immunity."

"I hope you remain a bachelor, then. I wouldn't wish it on any woman to be wed to such an insufferable husband!"

"There are those who would disagree with you, Miss Dunbar. And in fact I shall marry when *I* decide the time is right, not because I have been tricked into it by a pretty smile and fluttering lashes. I shall choose my wife carefully, the way I choose a bottle of fine wine or as I select the choicest varieties of sugarcane to propagate on the Kiss Flower."

"The Kiss Flower?"

She was interested in spite of herself. She knew she ought to stop talking to him, but he didn't seem ready to end the conversation or abandon the veranda. Susannah had only the choice of staying or going back inside to a man whose company she dreaded even more.

"My plantation. It's up the Amazon past Santarém, near the mouth of the Tapajos. 'Kiss flower' is the native term for the hummingbird that comes to drink the nectar of the orange blossoms. No bird can match the beauty of the Amazon hummingbird, Miss Dunbar. In fact, you remind me of it, small and exquisitely plumed in that dress—a little American kiss flower."

Susannah frowned. He was altogether a bewildering man. They had been quarreling, and now he had paid her perhaps the prettiest compliment she had ever received. She was determined not to be pleased. She would not like him to try to charm her, for it was more than dread of meeting Sam Spangler that kept her from leaving. The same magnetism she had sensed on the dance floor held her, but now alarm at her own pleasure over his compliment gave her impetus.

"I'm going to look for Colonel Spangler," she told him. "He may be the enemy, but at least he is not a wolf in sheep's clothing. You pretend to admire Southern courage while you travel the Confederacy from one end to the other trying to persuade our men from their dedication. It is hard enough to endure without the foolish temptations with which you are trying to dazzle us."

"Do you think I am the devil, Miss Dunbar?" he asked with a chuckle.

She had not quite thought of it, but the comparison seemed to fit. He was dark, dashing—and destructive. Yes, if the devil chose to manifest himself, what better form could he choose than that of Antonio Andrada, the Marquez da Silva? The devil, yes, why not?

"That or a Union spy," she said acidly as she turned away. She was aware that the music had stopped as she braced herself to enter the ballroom, and vaguely she wondered why. It was too early for the party to be over; the musicians must be resting. She slipped inside, hoping no one would notice her. No one did. Everyone's back was to her, all attention riveted on the officer who was rapping for silence with the conductor's baton. General Washburn, she thought, recognizing him, the sucessor to the despised General Hurlbut.

"Ladies and gentlemen, I have just received a telegram—the news we've been waiting for. Atlanta has fallen! God bless the Union!"

Everything after that happened in a blur. She heard the general call for a toast, and the orchestra struck up "The Star-Spangled Banner." Jubilant soldiers contained their joy long enough to stand at attention for as long as the music played. Susannah, too, stood spellbound with horror and despair. Then, as whoops of joy and the sound of popping champagne corks broke her trance, she rushed outside, entirely forgetting both Colonel Spangler and the Marquez da Silva.

Someone called her name. She supposed it was one of them, but she didn't care. An hour ago she would have been frightened to make her way home through the Memphis streets. There was, after all, a curfew after which anyone caught on the street might be hauled off to jail. That, of course, was not what was most likely to befall a woman alone in the night with thousands of lonely soldiers. But tonight nobody paid any attention to her.

A group of Yankees almost ran her down as they galloped past shouting. Mud splashed on the new dress, which she had been trying to hold out of the muck as she crossed the street. Her square-toed slippers, trimmed with rosettes, were ruined; the ooze almost sucked them from her feet. Guns were going off all over town— from far off at the Auction Square at the north end of town to President's Island in the river, where a camp had been set up for black refugees. It would have been easy to believe it was a battle going on, except that there were church bells, too.

It was the church bells Susannah wanted most to blot out. Those at least should not be in the hands of Yankees, ringing so joyously the death knell of their own congregations. She ran down Gayoso Avenue to Third Street, then hurried down that to Beale, where here and there a frightened face, black or white, peeped from the windows of once-elegant houses.

White roses dropped from her hair as she reached the door and pounded for Mrs. St. John and Rachel to let her in. Later, when they had gathered their wits after hearing her news, Mrs. St. John noticed something important amiss.

"Susannah," she asked, "where is the gray cloak?"

Only then did Susannah realize she no longer had it.

4

Mrs. St. John would not hear of Susannah's going out again to look for the cloak; and Susannah, not really having the courage to face the night again, finally allowed herself to be put to bed and dosed with comforting herb tea. She drifted off to sleep wondering what had become of the cloak. She had had it when she left the cloakroom to go onto the veranda. Beyond that, she could not remember.

It must have come unfastened and dropped off on her way home. She had been so upset she hadn't even noticed, and now she felt beyond caring. Despair filled her dreams, and when she awoke, she thought she was still dreaming, for one nightmare was like the other, except for the sunlight glowing through the window, making honeyed patches on the oak floor. There at the foot of her bed, like the demon of her dream, was Colonel Sam Spangler.

She screamed, yanking the covers up around her bare shoulders. Colonel Spangler was gazing at her with a peculiar expression. He was furious, but he had stood watching the vulnerable sweetness of her slumber, and that had, in a way, softened him, aroused his longings, and made his anger deeper and more complicated. He seemed barely able to contain himself, but not quite certain what he would do if he could not.

"Susannah, where is the cloak?" he demanded.

"I . . . lost it, Sam," she replied in a small, frightened voice.

"Colonel," he corrected. "I don't want you to call me Sam anymore. It confuses the issue, and I'm tired of being confused by you. You've made a fool of me enough. I've been told that you lost it by Mrs. St. John, and I don't believe a word of it. My men are searching the rest of the house, but I saved this room for myself. Get out of that bed, Susannah. I've a good idea you hid it under the mattress. You thought it would be safe there with you in the bed, but I am through being a gentleman."

Susannah's pride blazed up through her fear. "I will not get out of bed with you in the room, Colonel Spangler! It's not decent, especially when I haven't even a wrapper at hand."

Her refusal sparked his certainty that his suspicions were correct, and his face went livid. "Get up, by God, or I'll haul you out myself!"

"You wouldn't dare!" she cried with equal rage.

"Why not? I have got nowhere by treating you with courtesy and respect."

Too late Susannah remembered that he had had the temerity to loosen her laces the night before. She felt a sudden chill as he jerked the covers off her and desposited them in a pile on the floor. Exposed in her thin silk gown, she drew her knees up to her chin in an attempt to conceal herself.

"Get up!"

"No! I've told you the truth, you Yankee swine!"

"If you have, no doubt it's the first time! There's no reason for me to believe anything you say, Susannah Dunbar!"

He took hold of her hand and tried to pull her up. Susannah resisted, and Sam Spangler, losing his balance, fell on top of her. She was pinned beneath him in her almost naked condition, and as she struggled to free herself, a strap of her gown ripped loose. Sam Spangler's breath came swiftly, strangely labored.

Somehow her very struggling beneath him was having an effect on him that she did not like. Her only other choice was to lie still. She took it, and felt her naked breast lying cool and smooth in the palm of his hand.

Colonel Spangler moaned. A queer sensation shot through her stomach, and she was paralyzed with dread of what would come next. He sighed passionately as he ran his hands over her.

"Susannah! Susannah!"

She had never heard her name whispered in such exquisite anguish, not even by Cort. As he drew back to take her face in his hands, the memory of last night's kiss fueled her determination. She was helpless; yet she must do something. Instinct rather than knowledge told her that if she did not save herself, he would sully her hopelessly.

As he lowered his lips to hers, she spat upon him. He fell back in horror as though he had been shot, tumbling off the bed onto the floor. This time Susannah leapt up without being asked, and wrapping herself in a quilt, stood cringing against a wall. Beyond her was the door, closed and locked. She was afraid to try to get past him to open it. She had no hope of winning, no possibility of escape. She could only try to shrink into the wall and make herself as small as she could.

He stared at her for a long moment, wiping his face carefully with his handkerchief. Then, with a savage cry, he threw the mattress off the bed. Nothing lay on the slats. He opened the bureau drawers and rifled the contents, tossed clothing from the chifforobe out in heaps. Finally he turned on her.

She waited cowering, her eyes filled with hate. Now he would wreak his vengeance on her. Nothing else was left. But Colonel Spangler did not approach.

"Are you satisfied?" he asked tersely. "If you are caught later with a gray uniform, it'll be prison for you! You've turned me into what you believed me to be—a beast! The South may have lost, but you've won. And all I ever did wrong was to love you!"

He unbolted the door and left it wide open behind him. She heard his boots on the stairs, his voice calling crisply to his men. She stayed where she was, afraid to move until the house reverberated with doors banging and horses' hooves clattering in the street. They were gone.

Mrs. St. John rushed up. "Susannah! Oh, my poor child!" she shrieked as she saw her huddled in the destroyed room.

Susannah wept in the older woman's arms, attempting to reassure her between sobs. "He didn't hurt me, really. It was the cloak he was after."

"Thank God! But the entire house looks like this room. His soldiers took care of that. You would think they might have a little decency. With Atlanta gone, surely it wouldn't hurt to leave us a bit of dignity."

"Did they find the uniform?" she asked, shuddering. If they had, would all of them be arrested? Did Colonel Spangler hate her now as much as he'd loved her? She had driven him too far, and though he had regained control of the beast she had unleashed, she wondered whether his feelings for her had transmuted into another, perhaps more dangerous passion.

Mrs. St. John shook her head. "No. It was in the false-bottomed trunk."

"It's safe, then. They won't be back to look for it again."

"No. But it's too dangerous to try to slip it out of Memphis now. I heard the soldiers talking about orders to close up all the leaks out of the city. The Yankees know the South is desperate now."

"Yes, you're quite right," Susannah agreed.

Susannah and Rachel remained with Mrs. St. John several days longer, helping with the enormous task of putting the house to rights. "It will never be the same," Mrs. St. John would say sadly, gazing at an ugly gash in a bow-front sideboard or an Empire chair.

It never would, but it was not just the damaged furniture that made it so. More and more runaway slaves were filling up the town, camping in houses abandoned by Southerners, who, finding the more stringent Northern rule intolerable, were heading for the ravaged countryside.

One day in the street, Susannah heard someone call her name and turned to see a young man who had once been a dancing partner of hers. It was difficult to believe that that had been only four years ago; he seemed a quarter of a century older, aged not only by sunken cheeks and drooping shoulders, but by the lifelessness in his eyes.

"I thought you were with General Lee," she cried when she had recognized him. To her astonishment, he was dressed in civilian clothes.

He shook his head. "Please don't think me a coward, Susannah. I'd fight to the death for the South, but it's foolish to die for a cause that is hopeless."

"Don't say such a thing!"

He shook his head and turned away, as though the sight of her beauty brought back memories that he couldn't tolerate. Never had she seen a Southern man look like that. The men she had known had always been ready for another round. Insurmountable odds had been only a challenge, whether in croquet, horse racing, or war. She had never before looked on the face of utter defeat, and until he was out of sight, she imagined his face as that of the whole South.

"Surely it's only a few who are like that,"

Mrs. St. John said when Susannah reported the incident. "General Forrest hasn't given up."

"No. Remember that Cort told us how he fell from his horse in exhaustion. And that he went on fighting after he'd been so badly wounded there was a rumor he had died."

"General Lee hasn't given up."

"No. And I cannot imagine Cort giving up, or my father."

"No." They were both quiet, telling themselves they had reassured each other, each secretly wondering what would happen to men like Colonel Dunbar and Cort St. John if the South fell.

Rachel had the strongest spirit of them all, Susannah thought. Not even Cort could be more determined to think the war wasn't lost. Every evening Rachel took out the gray uniform and stitched on it. Once they had all joined in, working feverishly, but now Rachel worked alone, while Mrs. St. John played the piano and Susannah looked on wearily.

"You're wasting your time," Susannah would say. "If you want to sew, mend something. Everything we have needs it."

"I'd rather do this," Rachel would reply. "Cort will have it someday. You'll see."

"I don't see how I'll see. You couldn't smuggle a hairpin out of Memphis these days."

"Things will change. They have to. We're going to best the Yankees yet, and we can't do it sitting on our hands."

Susannah tried to admire Rachel's faith, but it seemed more and more that her little sister was afraid to admit reality. What made her most angry at Rachel was that her attitude forced

Susannah to realize that she herself had conceded defeat. And that was what *she* was afraid to admit.

"We're going back to Robin Hill tomorrow," Susannah said one night. "Things need looking after there."

"You go alone, Susannah," Rachel suggested. "I still have all the braid to do."

"Will you forget that stupid uniform?" Susannah snapped. "Oh, I'm sorry we ever started it. It has been nothing but grief. I would like never to be reminded of it again!"

"Well, I'm not sorry. And I want to finish it. It's the first man's suit I've ever worked on, and Mrs. St. John is teaching me all about tailoring."

"Please let her stay, Susannah," Mrs. St. John asked. "She's wonderful company, and she has a real talent with a needle. Heaven knows, it will be more important to know how to do things oneself in the New South."

"The New South!" Susannah wrinkled her nose. "What a disagreeable phrase! And people are using it more and more. I suppose there's no reason why she shouldn't stay. I'll come back for you in about a week, Rachel."

The countryside, at the height of summer loveliness, was bright with goldenrod and black-eyed Susans. Brilliant trumpet vine wound over fences, and the crab-apple trees were laden with fruit. But Susannah did not see beauty. She saw chokeberry and buttonbush and buckthorn sprouting up where there should be nothing but the green and white of ripening cotton. Refugees of all kinds traveled the roads: homeless children, black and white; old people; and more soldiers like the one she had met in Memphis, ashen and bandaged, shuffling along the dusty road with a vision of home almost tangible before their eyes.

She was relieved to reach Robin Hill, but as she entered the foyer, she recoiled with horror, for the devastation had come even here. The old mirror brought from Virginia was smashed on the stairs, the frame shattered. The portrait of Susannah's mother lay nearby, marked with the footprints of a Yankee boot. The stair railing hung crazily from splintered balusters, and furniture was overturned and broken everywhere. Drawers and their spilled contents were strewn in a vast collage of desecration.

Susannah ran from one room to the other, upstairs and down. Each room held the same sights; each was more painful than the last, yet she was compelled to see it all. Each new loss brought forth only a choked whimper, for her misery welled up so intensely that it was bottle-necked inside. She could barely breathe for the pressure of it in her chest.

Savage holes chopped in the walls gaped like mouths open to scream, and wallpaper hung in shreds like flesh torn from the corpse of destruction. What must have begun as a search had turned into a rowdy free-for-all of hate, an orgy of unrelenting victory. The South was down, and what could be better than to bludgeon it from the face of the earth?

"Aunt Caroline!" she called. The sound of her voice in the stillness frightened her. Robin Hill had never been so quiet. She ran out through the back and stopped short at the sight of her chickens massacred in their pen. Was there no limit to Yankee killing? She rushed back inside to what now seemed the lesser wreckage.

"Miss Susannah!"

She saw Aunt Caroline on the cellar steps. "Thank heaven! I thought they'd killed you!" She ran to hug the old woman.

"I tried to stop them, Miss Susannah," Aunt Caroline sobbed. "Wasn't anything I could do. I told them to git. I told them this was Colonel Dunbar's house; he goin' to kill them all when he hears."

Susannah nodded. But for the first time she felt the defeat she had seen in the faces of the deserting soldiers. It was a contagion, like the yellow-fever epidemic in which she'd lost her mother. How much would she lose before *this* fever had run its course?

"Is Uncle Arthur all right?" she asked.

"When they tore down your mama's picture, he went for them with a pitchfork," Aunt Caroline said, her eyes bleak at the terrible memory.

Susannah felt an awful fear settle over her, changing to certainty even before Aunt Caroline went on.

"They shot him, Miss Susannah. Weren't nothin' but a pack of cowards, afeared of a sick old man. Colonel Spangler didn't like it. He put the soldier who did it under arrest and he sent out men with a coffin the next day."

"So Colonel Spangler was here! Did he order all this?"

"No'm, not in so many words. He told them to search for a uniform, but he didn't seem to care what they did. He just set on the steps drinking whiskey from his flask and saying words you wouldn't hear in church."

Susannah and Aunt Caroline spent the next week gluing pieces of furniture back together and trying to restore a semblance of order in no more than two or three of the rooms. A hammer and nails helped restore damaged floorboards, and short curtains were fashioned from ruined draperies.

Susannah worked from daybreak until it was too dark to see before dropping onto the remains of a feather bed that had been cut open with a Yankee sword. She worked wearing an old shirt and trousers of Arthur's, and even Aunt Caroline didn't object. There was no one to be shocked, and so much work to be done.

"Rachel mustn't see Robin Hill the way they left it," Susannah told Aunt Caroline. "She is very brave, but you know she has always been frail. This could be the one thing that is too much for her. You know how she has always loved Robin Hill. More than any of us. That is why Cort and I will probably make our home at Hazel Grove, so that Rachel can have Robin Hill someday, when she marries."

Rachel was her first thought each morning and her last thought at night. She and Aunt Caroline drove themselves beyond their normal endurance with their need to protect what they still thought of as the baby sister.

"I promised yo' mama, Miss Susannah," Aunt Caroline would sigh. "On her deathbed, she made me promise to take care of both of you. Couldn't nobody have known . . ."

"We'll get by, Aunt Caroline," Susannah said stubbornly.

It wasn't going to be easy to endure the approaching winter without Colonel Spangler's help. Wasn't it more for Rachel than herself that she'd taken it anyway? There were no longer any chickens for meat and eggs, and the cow was gone. She had not even a rifle to hunt for game—were she able to hit any. She had only a small pistol that had been overlooked in the secret drawer of the desk. She did have most of the money from the sale of the cotton. That would have to do them, she decided. Though she thought more than once about Sloane's offer to purchase all her cotton, she was determined not to part with any more of it. The cotton, hidden away as it was, provided her with something more important even than food. It gave them hope for the future. As long as the cotton remained safely in the barn, Susannah would not be entirely beaten. And so, as she struggled to repair the Yankees' ravages, she planned how Robin Hill would be beautiful and prosperous again when the war was over.

The cotton would not be worth as much then, when a great flood of hoarded cotton would inundate the market, but surely it would be enough. And in the meantime, she would suffer to keep so much as another bale of it out of Union hands. She would have to make do, because to sell so much as a bale was to risk having it discovered by thieves. Susannah had taken all the chances she wanted to, selling the first bale; and now, without Uncle Arthur, there was no trusted man to handle Sultan in the woods.

The remains of the garden would help, but though the canning kettle was only dented, many of the canning jars were broken. They would put up what they could, but it was necessary to begin at once, since much of the produce was ripening or had been bruised by the trampling of Union feet.

"We can't do all this, just us," Aunt Caroline told her. "You got to go for Miss Rachel to help."

"Oh, but nothing's ready yet. I don't want Rachel to know—"

"It's as ready as it's goin' to get, Miss Susannah," Aunt Caroline said grimly. "We 'bout run out of anything to fix it."

It was true. Susannah hadn't wanted to admit their supply of nails was running low. She wasn't sure whether there were any to be bought in Memphis. What thread was left was all the wrong colors. Should she try to buy more or save the money? Aunt Caroline was right, as she always was. The next morning the two women managed to hitch Sultan to the carriage.

On the outskirts of Memphis the blue uniforms of the hated Yankee soldiers were thick as they stopped vehicles going in and out of the city. Susannah was made to dismount while they searched the carriage. "Be careful, my horse is easily spooked," she warned.

"Yes, ma'am."

"What are you looking for going *into* Memphis, anyway?" she asked.

"Explosives. And gunpowder. There's been a threat made on General Washburn's life."

"Humph. I'm not surprised. And you Yanks are terrified, though you boast you have us beaten! But explosives come in on the river. Everybody knows that."

"That's what you Rebs want us to think. The river patrol has been doubled, and we're looking for it going out as well." The soldier handed her back into the carriage and saluted as he waved her past.

Memphis seemed to be more crowded than ever with Yankee soldiers and homeless slaves. Mrs. St. John's house was more an oasis than before.

Rachel brought out the finished uniform and showed it to her sister proudly. "See how well I've sewn it, Susannah. Even you couldn't have done as well."

Susannah smiled, realizing how important it was for Rachel to excel more than she in some endeavor. Ever since Rachel had been a toddler, she'd been racing to keep up with Susannah. Papa had been fond of telling that before Rachel could walk, she had crawled after Susannah as she played in the gardens of Robin Hill.

"This is really excellent, Rachel," Susannah said, inspecting the seams. "It's refreshing to see a gray uniform, even if there's no one in it."

"It will look marvelous on Cort someday. Oh, dear, I hope he hasn't lost weight. I hope it won't be too large."

"Rachel, stop this dreaming," Susannah said warningly. "There's not a chance we can get that uniform to Cort. They are checking everyone."

"Oh, I've heard. But when there's a will, there's a way!"

"Rachel! We have lost enough over that uniform already!" Susannah said sternly, and she began to tell her about what had happened at Robin Hill.

Rachel wept.

"I am sorry to have to tell you," Susannah said, "but you would have seen most of it for yourself, and I wanted you to understand how dangerous the uniform is."

Rachel looked up, her face dark with fury. If her rage could have been melted into bullets, there would have been enough to annihilate the whole occupation force. "We'll get even, Susannah. Oh, how I hate Sam Spangler!"

"No more than I," Susannah agreed. "And he had the nerve to say that I turned him into the monster he is!"

"It might have been worse," Mrs. St. John said evenly. "He didn't take the one thing you have that could never be replaced. He is not a complete ogre, and I hope you've learned something about men from what has happened."

"I have learned a great deal about Yankees."

"Other men are not so different when they are trifled with."

"I suppose you've seen nothing of Colonel Spangler since that day he came here?"

"No," Rachel said, "but another man called for you. A Marquez da Silva. He said he'd met you at the dance and wanted to return your cloak. So that was where it was, Susannah."

"On the veranda . . ." she murmured to herself. He'd unnerved her so much she'd left it there.

Rachel heard. "You were on the veranda with him, Susannah! He's devastatingly handsome! And you never said a word about him. In the moonlight, too! I remember there was moonlight. And you all but engaged! You had better be careful, Susannah!"

To her disgust, she felt herself blushing and

saw Mrs. St. John look at her in surprise. "Don't worry, Rachel," she said. "I could never lose my heart to anyone so rude and conceited."

"Well, I could! He seemed disappointed that you weren't here. I suppose you didn't even dance with him, and what would have been wrong with that? It would have been all right for you to have a *little* fun. Why, he's not even a Yankee."

"He might as well be a Yankee. They ought to give him an officer's commission for the work he's doing—advising Southerners to give up the fight and join him in his Brazilian boondoggle."

"Isn't it romantic? He makes his Kiss Flower sound like paradise. Antonio—isn't it so much more delightful than the names men have around here? Perhaps he'll choose some Southern woman to return with him to Brazil."

"He swears he'll choose his wife the way he chooses his wine," Susannah said with a scornful laugh. "He claims he's impervious to flirtation, but thank heaven Antonio Andrada's love life doesn't concern us. I have Cort, and you are too young to catch his eye."

"Perhaps I am not." Rachel danced about her sister, swirling her skirt impishly. "I'm almost sixteen. I'd be a—what would his wife be called—a *marqueza*? I'd be the toast of the court at Rio, and everyone would envy me."

"I wouldn't." Susannah yawned to show that she was bored with the subject. "Come on, it's time we went to bed. We want to get an early start in the morning. Aunt Caroline needs us at Robin Hill."

Susannah went to bed in a bad mood. Rachel's silly infatuation with the Marquez da Silva annoyed her a great deal more than it should. She supposed it was because she found him so sinister herself, in spite of his good looks; and it exasperated her to think of Southern women fawning over him and making fools of themselves while he was only amused by their machinations.

Sternly she turned her mind from the infuriating marquess and marshaled her thoughts to what was important—counting how much might be put by for the winter and how far she could make her money stretch. Would it come to a choice of selling the cotton or providing for herself and Rachel the way so many other girls had been forced to—on Fulton Street, or on some floating pleasure palace on the river? It was a measure of her love of Robin Hill and her hatred of Yankees that she hardly knew which would be worse.

She slept poorly as she always did nowadays in Memphis. When she had been a child, she had loved the sound of carriages in the night, life going on busily around her, the excitement of people coming and going to soirees and the theater. There had been nothing to dream about then, except whether her papa would remember to bring her a piece of almond pound cake, or when she would come out into society herself. Now she could not even smell the scent of roses that should have drifted up from below. Though the bushes still struggled and blossomed, she kept the windows closed to mute the sounds of Yankee revelry.

In the morning her eyes were ringed, and her mood hadn't improved. She was so eager to get away that she scarcely bothered with her toilette. A simple chignon, covered by a serviceable spoon bonnet, would do, and a plain merino skirt topped by a linen bodice added to the severity of her appearance. There was no one for whom to be beautiful.

Susannah was ready early, eager to start for Robin Hill, but Rachel irritated her sister by dawdling. At last she came downstairs in her best outfit, a bodice of shot silk with pagoda sleeves and rows of jet buttons down the high-necked front. A sash ending in a huge bow and streamers trailed over the frilly tiers of the skirt, worn over the widest of her crinolines. A tiny puff bonnet sat on her head like an elegant lace doily decorated with silk flowers. Her gloves matched her dress.

"You look as though you are going to a tea party," Susannah said, disapproving.

"Just because you've chosen to look like an old maid doesn't mean I have to," Rachel countered. "It's important to keep up appearances. General Lee hasn't surrendered, and neither have I."

"Is everything packed?" Mrs. St. John asked. "I'll send Reuben to bring down the valises."

They kissed their hostess farewell tearfully, not knowing when they would see her again. "We may have to sell Sultan when winter comes," Susannah sighed. "I don't know how we'll feed him when the grazing's gone."

"General Forrest will have stormed Memphis by then," Rachel said. "There'll be a Christmas party at the Gayoso, and all the uniforms will be gray."

They laughed at her spunk, and Rachel had

to grab at her silly little bonnet as Sultan took off at a rapid clip.

Rachel seemed nervous as they approached the Yankee guard across the street leading out of town. "Let's run the blockade, Susannah," she said suddenly. "I'll wager they won't shoot."

"Are you crazy? We've nothing to hide, Rachel . . . have we?" she cried in alarm. "Is there something in your valise?" Terror all but immobilized her hands on the reins. She couldn't manage to say "the uniform."

She tried to turn Sultan, but another carriage was approaching to block the maneuver, and Sultan half-reared and whinnied ominously.

"Susannah, don't be such a mollycoddle! There's nothing in the valise." Rachel grabbed the reins. "Gidup, Sultan," she called.

Sensing her inexperienced hand, the horse took off at a gallop. "Rachel! Pull in. Slow him down," Susannah shouted.

"Hang on! I can't. We're going through!" Her gleeful cry rang out as blue-coated soldiers scattered before them.

"Oh, fiddlesticks, they're coming after us," she announced, glancing back to see half a dozen soldiers racing for their horses.

"Of course they are, you idiot. Our horse is running away. Even Yankees aren't so low they won't try to help."

"Let's see if we can beat them, Susannah. Papa used to say Sultan ought to have been a racehorse."

"Rachel!" She fought her sister for the reins and almost lost her balance. The ground went by dizzyingly as she righted herself. "Rachel,

Sultan is not faster than horses without a carriage to pull!''

But for a breathtaking mile it seemed as though he might be. Sultan stretched out into a run, the bit firmly in his teeth as though he sensed and scorned the Yankee steeds behind him. The carriage lurched over the rough road, and Susannah feared every moment that the traces would break and they would go careening off to their death. Rachel, beside her, was pale but exhilarated, her doily bonnet bobbing from its ribbons. Rachel's fair hair, shaken loose from its pinning, blew in golden disarray.

Finally they heard the soldiers gaining. One leapt aboard, landing amid their crinoline, and seized the reins. Two others galloped to the horse's nose and took control of the bridle. "Oh, thank you," Rachel said as the carriage stopped.

"Glad to be of service, miss," the soldier replied, tipping his cap. Susannah, bruised and winded, gazed at Rachel and was unable to say anything at all.

"Sultan's awfully headstrong," Rachel went on. "He's the only horse we have, and he runs away all the time. Why, the other day my sister might have been killed if the Marquez da Silva hadn't stopped him."

Susannah felt a mild pang of surprise. Just how much of a conversation had Rachel had with the marquess? She seemed to know everything.

"You'll have to come back to Memphis with us, miss," the soldier was saying. "You've missed the checkpoint."

"Oh, but it's so far to go back!" She gave him

her most winning smile. "Couldn't you just go through the valises here?"

The soldier looked embarrassed, and Susannah wondered vaguely at his discomfiture. "It's the law now," he apologized. "You'll have to go back."

Groggily Susannah admired her sister's bid for the soldier's sympathy. She couldn't have done better herself, she thought. Rachel was more skillful than she would have given her credit for. She had a woman's wiles; the soldier was obviously struggling to be firm.

"I can't go back," Rachel's voice said pitifully. "I . . . feel very unwell. I need to go . . . out there." She pointed to a cluster of buttonbush and buckthorn as she scrambled down from the carriage.

The soldier, flustered, made no effort to prevent her. In fact, he put out his hand to help her down.

"Hold on!" Another soldier came around the carriage. He was older and had sergeant stripes on his sleeve.

"I *must* have some privacy!" Rachel said desperately.

"Get back up there!" The sergeant gave her a little push with the butt of his rifle. "You can have all the privacy you want after we've done with you back in Memphis."

The younger soldier looked appalled. On the carriage seat Rachel moaned and clutched her midsection. Susannah looked at her worriedly. Once she could have invoked Colonel Spangler's name and been sent on her way. That would do no good now. In Susannah's mind there was no doubt that Rachel was really ill. She was frightfully pale.

"At least let me give her a drink from my canteen," the young soldier said, his protectiveness aroused. "She looks very delicate, and a woman could faint after an experience like that."

"Quiet!" the sergeant barked, and the soldier subsided. Rachel was still a novice, after all. If only she could charm sergeants as well as recruits!

The carriage went back to Memphis. Rachel seemed to recover herself. "I suppose we'll get home before dark," she said cockily. "I guess Aunt Caroline will just have to do without us today. She'd take a willow switch to us if we were still little."

Rachel sounded as though she wished they *were* still small girls. There was a tremor in her voice that was unsettling. Exactly what had Rachel's motive been in running the checkpoint? Had it been only bravado? Susannah hoped so.

Finally they were back where they'd started, and the soldiers handed out their valises to be opened and searched. Susannah's heart pounded, even though she knew nothing contraband was in hers and that Rachel had declared that nothing illegal was in her case.

The soldiers went through the valises carefully, their hands on Susannah's camisoles and stockings making her wince with humiliation, as though the garments had been on her body. Once she might have had saucy words to say about men who had to win a war by examining women's underwear; now she stood tensely silent. Rachel, for all her previously rash behavior, did the same. Susannah worried about her sister, who was deathly pale and swaying on her feet.

"There, it's all over," she declared in relief, as the valises were snapped shut and tossed back into the carriage. "May we go now?" she asked with a touch of hauteur.

"I'm afraid not. You'll have to come inside." It was the young recruit who had to give the order, and his cheeks turned red with embarrassment. Susannah should have wondered why, but she was too angry to really even notice.

"Go inside? But you've checked the carriage, and you can see that my sister is indisposed. Why . . . ?"

"I'm sorry, but it's General Washburn's orders," the soldier said, and ushered them into the parlor of a house that had been occupied as abandoned property.

A black woman came to meet them. "Why, Sally!" Rachel cried, recognizing her as having belonged to the Bothwells' plantation near Robin Hill. The familiar face gave them both welcome reassurance. But the black woman didn't smile or return the greeting.

"Take off yo' skirts," she commanded, as if such searches were routine.

Susannah threw a quick look at Rachel. Why, after all, had she worn the crinoline? Was the uniform under it? Had she wanted to dispose of it in the buttonbush and buckthorn?

The black woman wasn't much older than Susannah, and as she'd been a housemaid, used to obeying women like them, surely she would obey Susannah now.

"Nonsense, Sally," Susannah said as calmly as she could. "You know us. Times are hard, but even so, you ought to be ashamed to be working for the Yankees like this, spying on women who have never harmed you. War is for men, Sally. Don't you remember I gave you a bonnet of mine when I was visiting the Bothwells?''

The woman hesitated. Susannah saw her wrestle with the problem, the past against the future. The past must win this battle at least, Susannah prayed, for a horrible certainty was coming over her, as though ice were being pressed to the small of her back.

But Sally shook her head. "You didn't have no use for that ol' bonnet, Miss Susannah. I wants me a new bonnet, anyhow, good as yours. Take off yo' skirts.''

There was nothing to do but call Sally's bluff. Susannah worked up every bit of authority she could muster. "We are not going to do any such thing. We are going to leave now, and you are going to tell the soldiers you found nothing. Either that or admit you didn't search us." She put her hand on the doorknob.

"Miss Susannah!" Sally's voice stopped her with a tone of command that Susannah had never heard in one of her race, not even from Aunt Caroline. Nothing of affection or respect lay in it, and nothing of fear.

Susannah turned to look into the eyes of a person who for the first time in her life held the winning card and knew it. *The New South*—this was the face of it, too, like the defeat in the eyes of the returning defenders.

"You take off those skirts, or I'll call the soldiers," Sally said. "You want Yankee soldiers to take them off for you?''

They were beaten, but before it could quite sink in, Rachel's voice came blithely. "Well, if we must, we must. Really, Susannah, that Southern pride of yours is going to make Sally think we've something to hide. Come on, let's get it over with. We're expected home." With a quick gesture, she unfastened the skirt and lifted her arms for Sally to remove it over her head. "Be careful not to wrinkle it, please," Rachel said.

"Yes, miss." Sally took the garment carefully. It might have been a scene from any Southern lady's bedroom a few years before.

Susannah followed Rachel's example, wondering if after all she had been wrong. Rachel, who had seemed so frightened before, now appeared nonchalant. "Do help Susannah with her cage, Sally," Rachel was saying. "I can do very well, but her fastenings are always in knots. That's what comes from being as old as she is and having to have such a tiny waist, since she's come out and everything."

The two crinolines fell to the floor, and the woman picked each up and turned it inside out and shook it. Nothing was there. Susannah breathed a fervent prayer of thanks.

"Well, give them back now," Rachel said.

"Just a minute," Sally said, scowling.

"What now?"

"Miss Rachel, you take down those pantaloons."

"What? You can't be serious! Why, I would be naked then!"

"Do it, Miss Rachel, or I'll call the soldiers. You want them to hold you until I undress you—and your sister?"

"They wouldn't!"

"That sergeant would, and enjoy hisself, too!" Sally's eyes burned again with triumph. "Take 'em down, Miss Rachel. They fit funny."

Rachel seemed unable to move. Even when Sally tugged at her fastenings, she stood like a statue.

Susannah gave a shriek of agony as the pantaloons fell, for underneath, Rachel was not naked. She was wearing the trousers of the gray uniform.

Sally, with a grunt of satisfaction, began to unfasten Rachel's bodice, and in a moment the jacket appeared from under its wide, loose sleeves. "Well, what have we here? A little Confederate soldier!" Sally crowed.

"Yes, that's what I am, a Confederate soldier," Rachel said. She refused to remove the uniform, and when they marched her away, she was still wearing it, her chin lifted bravely, her windblown hair streaming over gold braid.

"Where are you taking her?" Susannah demanded.

"To the Irving Block."

"But she's only a child!"

"We don't have any orders about children. And fifteen is not exactly a child, Miss Dunbar," the sergeant said. "You're lucky you are free to go. We've no evidence to prove you were involved, though no doubt you were."

Susannah raced outside to the carriage, knowing what she must do, and do unflinchingly. As she raced Sultan through the streets, she rehearsed what she would say, how she would beg Colonel Spangler's forgiveness, how she would pledge her eternal gratitude to him if he would save Rachel. She would offer to be his wife, if that was what he wanted, and find some way to prevent Cort St. John from dueling him to the death. She was through conniving and teasing. She remembered him in her bed, his body pressed to hers, his passion-twisted voice uttering her name. She would give him her virtue, as often as he liked. She would do what gossips said she had done already. Nothing mattered but saving Rachel from the torture of the Irving Block.

It's my fault, she thought. It wouldn't have happened if it hadn't been for me. If I hadn't been the one to arrange it all, just for the sport of tricking the Yankees. Just so I could send Cort a love letter in the pocket. How far away that all seemed now. Because of her silliness, Robin Hill was in ruins, and Rachel . . . Never again would she be so foolish, never again would she tease a man to see just how far he would go for love of her, if only . . . if only . . . She was willing to pay the price for her mistakes!

But Susannah still did not know the full extent of the trouble she had caused. She reined up before the gates of Fort Pickering and called down to the guard, "I must see Colonel Spangler."

"I'm sorry, miss, it's impossible," he answered.

"But I must! It's Susannah Dunbar. It's an emergency!" It had worked once before, but had she cried wolf and spoiled her credibility when the need was real? Had he really stopped loving her?

"No one can see him, emergency or not," the guard told her.

"But why?"

"He was taken to the guardhouse. There are rumors all over the fort. Something about his having authorized the sale of some gray cloth. They say he'll be court-martialed."

5

Susannah was placed under house arrest at Robin Hill. General Washburn regarded her as dangerous, she was told. He wished for an excuse to throw her into the Irving Block too, but she had had permission to buy the gray cloth, and so there was nothing with which she could be charged. But who knew what information she might have gleaned from her "friendship" with Colonel Spangler? Who knew what other friendships such a woman might form?

It was only sensible to prevent Union officers from contact with a potential spy. But the young privates who stood guard over her at Robin Hill seemed pleased with their duty. Susannah, deep in despair, would not so much as speak to them at first, but somehow they seemed to have no resemblance to the blue-coated mob that had ripped apart her home; and to relieve the tedium of their assignment, they began to fix windows and shutters and fill up the wood box each morning.

They asked nothing in return for their efforts, but hinted broadly for one or two of Aunt Caroline's hot fluffy biscuits or a piece of rhubarb pie. Susannah decreed it was out of the question. "They are the enemy, Aunt Caroline," she said. "We didn't ask for their help at Robin Hill."

"Mighty handy, though," the old woman said.

"Open the window a crack so they can smell what's cooking, Aunt Caroline, but don't leave anything on the sill. Remember, we're going to be hard put to have enough for ourselves this winter."

With the last of the garden almost gone, they were already having problems. Some potatoes had been dug, crowder peas dried, and apples put away, but the Yankees had ravaged most of the garden beyond saving. Only a little broccoli was left now in later October, and all the wild blackberries were gone. Meat, eggs, and cheese were distant memories, available only in Susannah's troubled dreams.

Susannah had lost weight, and her small waist needed no stays to make it fashionably tiny. But it was worry more than lack of food that had caused it. She had heard tales that there was nothing to eat in the Irving Block but rice and crackers, and rats were said to take their share of that.

Susannah had traveled to Memphis a dozen times in the company of her Union guard to try to obtain Rachel's release. She had written letters and filed appeals everywhere. She had even made a plea to General Grant and to President Lincoln, but she had no way of knowing whether her letters were even allowed to go through.

One morning a volley of rifle shots sent her racing downstairs. "Aunt Caroline, what's happening?"

"Yankees is shootin' out in the woods."

"At what? Did you hear any horses? Are there some Confederates out there?" She didn't know whether to hope there were or there weren't. If only General Forrest . . . But she was afraid, too, of Cort's having sneaked back again. She was afraid of seeing his body stretched out on the lawn of Robin Hill.

In a moment the brush moved, and they saw the guards coming up from the trees. "They're carrying something," Susannah said.

"Old gobbler turkey," Aunt Caroline said admiringly.

The Yankees brought the turkey to the kitchen door. "We'll be glad to share it, if you'll cook it," they said, grinning.

Susannah tried to say no. But she had been living like a Spartan for too long, and the thought of roast turkey trimmed with yams and cornbread stuffing overwhelmed her scruples. The Yankees were made to eat outside on the steps, but they didn't seem to mind. They declared it the best meal they'd had since leaving their mothers, and brought their plates back for seconds.

They didn't seem so different from the Southern boys Susannah had known, and the compromise was made. After that they often had game for the table as well as little gifts of flour and sugar. And so starvation was staved off for a while. "They's more than one way to skin a cat, Miss Susannah," Aunt Caroline said. Pie and biscuits were proving a substitute for the things Colonel Spangler had wanted, but Susannah felt guilty over every bite of Yankee food she ate.

"I wish Papa knew about Rachel," she would say every day. "If only I could get away and tell him, I'm sure General Forrest would raid Memphis and save her."

But there seemed no way to get a message through. No mail could reach the army, and Susannah's guard was always alert, no matter how heavily he partook of Aunt Caroline's cooking. Sneaking quietly away on the spirited Sultan would have been impossible anyway.

"Good morning, Miss Dunbar," said a man's voice behind her one bright November day as she searched the ground beneath the pecan trees for nuts.

"Go and fix the handle on the well pump," she said distractedly, not wanting to converse with one of the soldiers. "There'll be rabbit stew for dinner."

A soft laugh told her her mistake. Too late that musical Portuguese accent registered. She straightened suddenly and whirled about to see the Marquez da Silva standing over her, handsome as ever, with those dark, commanding brows over his critical, mocking eyes, and that exasperating twist of amusement on his finely formed mouth.

"You haven't changed, Miss Dunbar," he said. "You are still ordering men about, keeping them at your back and call."

"Yes, but don't worry. *You* are quite safe from me," she said coldly.

He laughed, his hands in the pockets of his Bedford cord breeches. His smile was easy and genuine, and his dark eyes flickered warmly.

"What a relief!" he joked sarcastically. "Especially with poor Spangler cooling his heels in the guardhouse. But perhaps it would not be so easy to order *me* hither and yon."

"That we will never find out," she vowed fervently.

She was satisfied to see a flicker of surprise cross his face. Undoubtedly no woman had ever snubbed him before. No doubt he was used to treating them however he liked and still having them fawn upon him. Brazilian women—and Memphis woman had been no more discriminating. Give a man good looks and a title and most women could not see beyond them. But she had more judgment.

"I suppose you've come for your money," she said.

"No, I'd like you to keep it for the hat I ruined. But I would like to see Robin Hill."

"Well, you are welcome to look. There is not much left of it. It might have fared better if you'd held your tongue that night. Or if you had returned my cloak that same night, it could have been prevented."

"The cloak? All this was over your cloak?" The marquess was entirely bewildered.

She realized that he really didn't know. How could he have known her devious scheme? She softened a little as she explained, "You see, Colonel Spangler thought I was going to turn the cloak into a Confederate uniform."

"Ah. But there *was* a uniform, wasn't there, Miss Dunbar? However did you manage it? It may be impossible for a man to understand you, but this much he can be sure of: you are always up to something outlandish. I heard the story in Memphis. Your little sister was apprehended trying to smuggle it out. What soldier was it for, Miss Dunbar? It would fascinate me to know what soldier is so brave and dashing as to capture your heart and cause you to risk a child's life to please him. But then, it's surprising to think you *have* a heart."

Susannah's mind went black with rage, and not the least of the reason for it was that he had touched on her own guilt over Rachel. If she had had her pistol with her, she might have shot him, and only the knowledge of his physical superiority kept her from lunging at him to claw his face. Her bag of nuts swung dangerously, like the twitching tail of an angry cat.

"I'll carry this," he said, saving himself from the likelihood of being hit with it.

But Susannah had had other thoughts through the heat of her fury. As always when Rachel came to her mind, she longed for a way to free her; and she had realized that the opportunity might be standing right before her in the loathsome person of the Marquez da Silva. Here was a rarity, a neutral who could move through the lines at will. If only he would take her message to General Forrest!

"Come into the house. I'll get your money, sir," she told him. "I'm sorry to have kept it so long. I expected you sooner, months ago."

"I've been away from Memphis, down to New Orleans to find ships and supplies for my expedition. It hasn't been an easy task with the city in such chaos."

She bristled at the mention of his expedition, but this time she refrained from lashing out at him for his plan to denude the South of what it needed most: its strong young people to rebuild it. Nothing was more important now than to placate him and charm him into doing her will. Perhaps, after all, he *would* see how well she could beguile him. She remembered how he had boasted of being immune to womanly wiles. How better could she punish him than to prove to him he could not resist her?

"I suppose it's quite terrible in New Orleans now," she murmured as she took his arm and steered him toward the house.

"Yes, much worse than here, and Atlanta is devastated most of all."

"You have been there too?"

"Yes, and I will never forget it. Nothing can be more terrible than a country divided, like two brothers set to destroy each other. War is bad enough, but this sort of war I hope never to see again. Someday slavery will be ended everywhere, even in my country, and I pray this is not the way it will end."

"It has not ended. There is still Richmond."

He sighed. "You will keep insisting, Miss Dunbar. But you're right. It hasn't ended, more's the pity. The suffering goes on. I do admire your stubbornness."

"La! You have found something about me to admire!" she cried, gazing up at him impishly.

"Stubbornness is not a particularly feminine trait," he observed. "In fact, I have never heard of a man who fell in love because a woman was stubborn."

"And yet you admire it in me."

"Perhaps your other traits are so thorny that it seems a rose," he mused, almost to himself.

"Well, maybe I will find something to admire in you," she returned flirtatiously, not bothering to take offense.

"Why, look all you like, Miss Dunbar," he said amiably.

She took him inside, half-abashed at the condition of her home, half-glad for the sympathy the gashes on the floors and walls might create for her.

Papa's study had been somewhat restored. The lithograph of early Memphis over the desk had been repaired with flour glue; and wild geraniums, potted on the windowsills, were still blooming in the light of a southern exposure. Susannah noticed his approval of her efforts, his appreciation of the short lacy curtains made of old tablecloths, and the cozy arrangement of the patched remains of the furniture.

"I'm afraid it will kill Papa when he sees it," she said, voicing a real fear.

"Colonel Dunbar will be equal to it," he assured her. "He'll rebuild Robin Hill, though I wish I could persuade him to come to Brazil."

"Brazil! That is all you think about!" Susannah could not stop her outburst.

"You'd understand if you saw it, Miss Dunbar. It's wild and beautiful, and no man has ever tamed it. I'm sure you'd like it; why, I might easily use the very same words to describe *you*."

She blushed in spite of herself. A few moments ago he had only admired her stubbornness; now he was paying her a dazzling compliment. He was a most confusing man. She wished he would be consistent—but consistently which way?

Susannah put her hand inside a desk drawer. "It's right in here in a little jar," she told him. Then, pulling the drawer open further, she feigned surprise. "Why, it's *not* here! Those Yankees took it! I should have known; they took everything else. Now what am I going to do? How am I going to repay you?" She slammed the drawer to prove her agitation, though she had already known that the money had been stolen. She glanced up at the marquess to see if he were fooled.

He was looking at her quizzically, only partly taken in, much as Colonel Spangler had been about the gray cloth. He knew her well enough to know she was full of tricks, and he was intrigued. But he clearly guessed that she had not really expected to find the money in the drawer.

"There's no need to do anything, Miss Dunbar," he told her. "I didn't want the money; it was you who wanted to return it."

"Oh, and I still do! I owe it to you, and I always pay my debts," she said heatedly.

The marquess drew in his breath sharply.

Susannah almost giggled, realizing he had a certain opinion of her and of the way she handled herself with men. He must think she meant a certain sort of payment which she was not in the least prepared to make. The idea seemed to unnerve him. Good! So much the better!

"My dear marquess, I do believe you're afraid

of me," she said coquettishly. "I only wanted to invite you to dine with me. Aunt Caroline is a wonderful cook, and I will ask her to make some hush puppies to go with the stew. You'll adore Aunt Caroline's hush puppies. They're crisp and sweet, with bits of onion and spices inside. Don't you trust yourself to share a meal with me?"

"Not trust myself," he said derisively. "What a peculiar thing to say."

"But I wouldn't blame you. Colonel Spangler's friendship with me earned him a court-martial. There's no telling what might happen to *you*!" she told him, wide-eyed.

He tossed back his head and laughed uproariously, seeming genuinely amused. "Well, now, I suppose I'll have to stay just to prove I'm not a coward."

"Wonderful. I'll tell Aunt Caroline." She spun away, out to the kitchen, where the old woman was preparing the meal.

"We've a guest, Aunt Caroline," she said mysteriously. "Set two places at the little pier table next to the garden window. It's a gentleman."

"A gentleman!" Aunt Caroline said suspiciously. "Not a Yankee?"

"Nobility, Aunt Caroline! The Marquez da Silva."

Aunt Caroline looked displeased. "We got nothin' to serve nobility, Miss Susannah. And I don't reckon Major St. John would like it much, either."

"Major St. John will be glad of it, and the rabbit stew will be delicious." She bent over the pot and added a pinch more of basil. "There! Now it's fit for a marquess. I'll have him so bewitched, he'll think it's roast pheasant. Bring us that bottle of wine Private Lewis gave us last week," Susannah called gaily as she pulled off her mantle and returned to the study.

Beneath it she was wearing a plain alpaca dress, but it would have to do. How could she have guessed when she'd gone out to gather pecans that she'd be having the marquess to dine? And how could she have guessed that it would please her so?

Perhaps the simple gown served Susannah better than her silks or her suggestive walking skirt, for the meal went very well. They fell into a sort of game, pretending that they liked each other and laughing at their great courtesy to each other, sipping wine until both of them were flushed.

The unassuming meal and the modest gown gave the marquess a different impression of Susannah, and he found himself more impressed by her grace over cracked dishes and mismatched silver than he had been by the glamorous show she had made in her ball gown.

She intuited his changing attitude as she drew him out about his homeland. And without having to pretend her interest, she listened to him tell about the black, rich soil of the Amazon plain, where sugarcane grew ten feet tall and two feet around. Near his house he was planting orange trees, so that he could reach from his veranda to pick them. And though his dwelling would be grand, he planned to make the roofs of palm thatch. "There is no sound as sweet as the patter of rain on palm fronds, Miss Dunbar," he told her. She saw that he loved the Kiss Flower as deeply as she loved Robin Hill.

"What about wild animals?" she said with a shiver. "Aren't there tigers?"

"Yes, and anacondas. Alligators and snakes, of course. But what is most fearsome of all is the . . . mosquito."

When they had laughed at that, he went on to fascinate her with tales of the prago monkeys that mischievously raided his cacao groves and the Amazonian otters that played in the channels.

"You would like the sloths," he told her. "They hang upside down while they eat the leaves of the cecropia trees. They are the laziest things alive and nearly tame. Why, many's the time I've nearly fallen over one. They like to feed with my horses and swin in the floating grass. No one bothers to hunt them except the Indians."

"You have Indians?"

"Yes, of course."

"But haven't the white men driven them off the land? There were Chickasaw here once, but they were forced to sign a treaty and go farther west because Fourth Chickasaw Bluff was considered a perfect site for settlement."

"I would try to stop anything like that from happening to our Indians. There are still more of them than whites, and in Santarém they live in a village that is almost a part of the town."

"Isn't that dangerous?" she said with a shudder.

"Oh, they aren't hostile. Except deep in the jungles, up the Tapajos, near Diamantina. That is quite different. The prospectors make trouble with the Indians, and even the missionaries are sometimes corrupt. Gold and diamonds do that to people."

"Gold and diamonds!" Susannah said with a touch of her former disdain. "I suppose you are telling all the starving Confederate soldiers that they are lying on the ground for the taking."

"They are, Miss Dunbar, if you can survive the jungle. But the last thing the Amazon needs is a swarm of prospectors who care nothing about the land and want only to get rich. Brazil doesn't need a Gold Rush, like yours in forty-nine."

He lingered a moment longer than necessary over her hand as he left. "I hope you are not going to vanish like the prospectors in the jungle," she said coyly. "I hope you'll visit Robin Hill again."

"But you've paid your debt, Miss Dunbar."

"Oh, but there was no dessert. The pecans I was gathering will make a wonderful pie. Next Tuesday? Unless, of course, your courage fails you."

He looked searchingly into her eyes. "It will not fail me," he pledged. "Tuesday it will be."

Susannah was giddy with success. Yes, she told herself, she was winning. Though he hardly trusted her, he was succumbing. He must be smitten! He must! It was her only chance to send a message to her father and Cort. Her only chance to rescue Rachel!

From that moment until Tuesday she thought of nothing but the Marquez da Silva. She planned menus and discarded them, walked into the fields for a bouquet of late-blooming asters and pretty fall weeds to decorate the table. At night she dreamed about him, peculiar dreams of a paradise carved from a jungle by a man at home in a wilderness more savage, primitive, and exotic than any her own country had to offer.

The Kiss Flower—the hummingbird. At Robin Hill she sometimes saw one in the summer hovering among the snapdragons. But where he came from, they flew in brilliant swarms. By day she could tell herself that he was only hypnotizing her with his tales, the way he was seducing Southerners to his colony. At night her defenses were left behind, as if in her dreams she knew that it was not the country, but the man it had produced, that held her spellbound.

She could hardly wait for his next visit, because, she told herself, it would put her that much closer to achieving the thing she required of him when she had chained him to her charms. I should have said Monday, she would chide herself. Or even Sunday. Then with a sigh she would scold herself for her impatience. It mustn't seem too soon. He must have time to anticipate their meeting.

But *did* he long for it? He had had the temerity to be indifferent to her before. But he must be thinking of her! He must! Thoughts and memories of their tête-à-tête must work on him like a potion to bind him to her will. It had worked before—with Colonel Spangler—but this time it was more important. Rachel's life was at stake. On Tuesday morning she was a frenzy of nerves, rushing here and there to see that everything was done, until there was nothing to do but sit and wait.

"Aunt Caroline, he isn't coming," she wailed when he was an hour late. "Do you think he forgot?"

"Ain't the man been born could forget about you, Miss Susannah," Aunt Caroline said loyally, but Susannah wasn't convinced.

"He's different. He's used to duchesses and princesses and—"

"Princess! Ain't nothin' but a name!"

"But he doesn't . . . approve of me! Ooh!"

Aunt Caroline chuckled. "Don't he, now! Well, not approving of a woman don't keep a man away, child. We'll just keep everything nice and warm in the oven."

Susannah leapt up at the sound of a horse; then, remembering herself, she ran upstairs instead. After Aunt Caroline admitted him, she kept him waiting a quarter of an hour—as long as she dared—to punish him.

"My dear marquess, how good of you to come," she said sweetly as she made an entrance in a bodice of shot silk worn with a velvet skirt and a broad belt that displayed the smallness of her waist. Her auburn hair, made shiny with a vinegar rinse, was puffed at the sides, accenting the delicacy of her features, making her little chin seem the point of a delectable heart.

"I would not have missed it," he said, though he almost had. She watched his eyes for his reaction and saw them dance darkly. The expressions in them were as quick and ephemeral as shooting stars, brilliant, but not lasting long enough for her to decipher their meanings.

"I've brought you something," he told her, indicating a bandbox beside him on the sofa.

"It would be improper for me to take a gift from you," she said. She was wildly curious to know what was in the box, but she didn't want him to know it.

He frowned. "Oh, come, Miss Dunbar, you needn't play the part with me. I know these soldiers bring you presents. Why should I be treated differently?"

"They bring food, a fair exchange for home-cooked meals. We could barely survive without it. It's a compromise we've had to make."

"A woman needs something beyond mere sustenance to survive; but this, too, qualifies as a fair exchange. It's a hat—to replace the one I ruined. Of course, though, I wouldn't want to insist, if you feel you shouldn't take it."

He lolled back, grinning, and Susannah felt a current of fury. But she wanted to know what sort of hat he'd chosen for her. His certainty that she couldn't resist his gift made her want to throw it in his face; but he was right. She couldn't resist.

She untied the string and lifted the lid, catching her breath at what lay inside. The hat was made of black silk, with a flowerpot and a narrow turned-up brim. A bright iridescent blue feather thrust up at a jaunty angle from the hatband.

"Why, I've never seen a hat like this," she said as she took it out.

"It's a Tyrolean hat," he told her. "I found it in a little shop in St. Louis some time ago. I was passing by and saw it in the window. I couldn't control my impulse to buy it. It made me think of you at once. The clerk said the style is all the rage on the Continent, but that not many American ladies had the flair for it. All the same, I wasn't dissuaded."

"I'm glad you weren't," she said, almost shyly.

The implied compliment, like his others, was surprising and unexpected.

"Put it on. I want to see if my judgment was correct," he urged her.

She obeyed with trepidation, wanting his approval and hating herself for wanting it. Her chin lifted and her shoulders straightened sharply to a stance of almost military precision as she studied her reflection in a cracked pier glass.

"It's perfect," he cried, "but the clerk was right, too. She said it would not sit right at all on a woman who was sweet and simple."

"Sir!" His approval had warmed her, but just as quickly he had followed it with the slap that was so characteristic of him, as though if he forgot himself enough to like her, he found it necessary to recant.

"Oh, come, Miss Dunbar! Your silly suitors may whisper to you that you are sweet, but surely you are too wise to believe them. Are you so clever that you even fool yourself? You can't fool *me*! After all, my business is sugar. Who should know sugar better than I?"

He was standing very close to her, adjusting the blue feather to suit himself, and she sensed with satisfaction the struggle raging within him as his judgment wrestled his attraction to her. Her breath came quickly, for if his judgment lost out, she was certain he would take her into his arms and kiss her. If he did, she would have won. He would be in her power. But Susannah felt not a sensation of impending triumph, but a dizzying fear, more incapacitating than the terror she had felt when Colonel Spangler had been in her bedroom. It was a danger she could not identify, but which ema-

nated from a battle of her own, akin to his. So
intense did the threat become that, without
knowing why, she reached up and removed the
hat, stepping back from him as she did so.

"Perhaps you had better confine yourself to
sugar, then," she told him. "You've no talent
for choosing women's clothing. Where in the
world would I wear a hat like this? It's much
too sophisticated."

"You'll find somewhere. I know you will."

The tension hadn't eased between them; the
new distance had only stretched it taut. She
wondered if she ought to take his retort as an
insult or another of his compliments. She remembered her purpose and told him pointedly,
"Perhaps you will provide it, then, since you've
provided the hat."

She had given him an opportunity to invite
her on some fine excursion, but the belligerence
of her voice and the rigidity of her body indicated she might well rebuff him. She held the
hat in front of her, its trembling feather betraying
the depth of her agitation.

"I'm afraid that won't be possible, Miss Dunbar. I'm leaving Memphis tomorrow."

"Tomorrow! But you can't . . ." She was too
shocked to cover her distress. He could not go!
Not when she had not got what she wanted
from him.

"I've important business in Chicago. There
was a problem with the train ticket. That's why
I was late."

She fought panic. "When will you be back?"

"Never, most likely. I've finished everything
I have to do here."

"Antonio, you have not!" she cried wildly,

hardly noticing that she used his given name for the first time. It wasn't really the first time. She had used it often enough in her thoughts. But in her thoughts he was never leaving, never going away to forget her. She had lost!

He laughed mockingly. "You mean I haven't done what you want me to do. You have been plotting for me to fall in love with you, like your foolish Colonel Spangler."

She flushed crimson. He had guessed!

"Maybe you're leaving because you're afraid you might," she taunted, determined to be as scornful as he. When she had accused him before of being afraid of her, he had thought it amusing. This time he obviously did not.

"I'll put an end to that stupid, conceited idea of yours once and for all, Miss Dunbar," he snapped, his eyes gleaming strangely.

The tension between them shattered. She was in his arms, as though she had been propelled by the force of an explosion. "I'll do what *I* want to do before I leave, Susannah! I'll do what you make men want to do!"

His lips were on hers, and she expected to be kissed bruisingly, the way Colonel Spangler had kissed her, but it was nothing like that. Neither was it the simple sort of kiss she had received from her girlhood sweetheart when he had asked her to marry him.

The Marquez de Silva towered over her, the power of his superb, muscled body making her feel small and helpless, like a magnolia petal on the Mississippi River current. And though she ached to fall against him in surrender, he himself held her from it, one hand at her waist, the other firmly beneath her chin, lifting it up to suit himself, so that he was in perfect control of her, even of her capitulation.

His kiss was exquisite, skillfully gentle, inflaming her with longing. But he held back, expertly gauging her need, drawing her slowly to him, giving always less than she wanted, driving her wild with her unprecedented desire. The hand that had been against her waist moved upward, caressing her back, leaving a path of warm, tingling excitement, tangling at last in the chignon at the nape of her neck. Hairpins, seeming to leap free of their own volition, clattered to the oak floor. And her tresses, seeming to conspire to twine about his fingers, gave the sensation of having nerves of their own as he stroked them.

Just as she thought she could bear it no more, he drew her tightly, but still softly, against him, pressing his lips to her mouth with such authority that her will seemed drawn out of her, absorbed into his. On some level of her devastated consciousness, she fought against his utter possession of her, lashing with gossamer remnants of resistance too frail for him to notice. She was as ensnared as a rabbit in a trap, but it was she who had baited it. And it was a trap without jaws, for he held her firmly but lightly, so that nothing prevented her breaking away, nothing but his own magnetic currents.

Colonel Spangler had had her at his mercy because of his brute force, but this man needed none of that. Some power of his, more profound than his superior male strength, held her in his sway, and she wondered where it would end. The question seemed beyond her imagining. Would he sully her as Colonel Spangler had come so close to doing? But "sully," though it was the word she had been taught for such a situation, did not strike her as describing what he might do to her.

Suddenly he stepped away from her. He was smiling at her with that same satirical expression in his dark, quick eyes. She was aghast that she had expected to be in control of him, as she had always been with men: with Cort St. John, even when he had risked his life for her embrace; and with Colonel Spangler, when he had been in her bedroom. She had failed completely with the Marquez da Silva, and it was she who had been defenseless. She reeled, still enveloped in the hapless dregs of her desire, as though half under the effect of a drug.

She remembered how she had seen women look at him at the officers' dance, misty and breathless. How many had memories of him like hers to keep? He was a mere charmer, and she had been swept into his web instead of he into hers! She felt fatally entrapped in its threads.

Antonio Andrada looked unruffled. Nothing but a quick intake of breath betrayed any emotion. He had done it to teach her a lesson, she thought with sudden fury. That was the only reason he had come today. He had felt nothing at all. He had proved himself immune to her charms.

"Well, good day, Susannah," he said softly. "I hope you find somewhere to wear the hat."

He was out the door before she had a chance to remember what it had all been about, why she had even asked him to Robin Hill to begin with. But as his kisses cooled on her lips, the image of Rachel rose to her mind. The marquess was her only hope, and he was leaving!

She dashed out the door after him, her hooped skirts, not made for running, gyrating, impeding her. Beneath the catalpa trees, he was already mounting his horse, gathering the reins to turn it down the lane.

"Antonio, wait!"

He glanced back, lifted his hand in a desultory gesture, and pressed his heels against the horse's flanks. But Susannah was fleeter of foot than most women. As a child she had loved to race about the woods, playing games of tag with slave children, who in a way had been freer than she. "Ain't what a lady does," Aunt Caroline had scolded, hoping to shame her.

Certainly Susannah did not make a ladylike sight speeding along the lane after him, but she looked compellingly beautiful; and Antonio, intrigued, reined up after all.

"Dear me, usually it is a hound dog I have trailing along as I ride," he remarked as she reached him.

"Don't make fun of me, Antonio," she demanded, and with a quick, unexpected movement, she kicked his foot loose from the stirrup, enabling her to thrust her own foot into it to reach up and snatch the reins from his hand. The animal half-reared; but Susannah kept the reins, and Antonio easily kept his seat.

"Do you intend to ride in that outfit?" he inquired in amazement.

"Antonio, you must help me," she begged. She had been gasping to get her breath from running, but now sobs began to come instead.

"So, Susannah, it wasn't my affections you

wanted after all! Why is it I'm not surprised? What is it, then?"

"Rachel. You could help her, Antonio. You're a neutral. You could ride to General Forrest's camp and tell my father that she is in prison. Then my father would bring his men to raid Memphis and save her."

Antonio seemed to consider. "So you wish me to commit an act hostile to the Union Army and to travel several hundred miles out of my way to do it, when I have urgent business elsewhere."

"I am only asking you to tell a father that his daughter is in danger, Antonio. I'll do anything, anything at all."

He frowned, and she saw that she had said the wrong thing. Sharply he twisted the reins from her hand, his countenance glowering.

"No doubt you would, Susannah, but you'll not have to. There are men who do not have to be lured into doing what is decent, and I am one of them. I'll go on your mission because it is the right thing to do, and not because you've dazzled me into it. You had only to ask, but you are too devious to have thought of it."

He pressed his heels into the horse's flanks and took off at a trot, which quickly became a lope and then a gallop. As he rode between the rows of bare-branched oaks, it seemed that his need to be away from her was a rapidly rising fever.

Aunt Caroline met her at the door as she returned to the house limping on a kid slipper that had broken its heel. "What happened, child? He's gone and didn't even have his dinner. I worked on it all morning!"

Little sobs still bubbled up as Susannah leaned against Aunt Caroline's soft bosom. "He's gone to General Forrest's camp," she murmured.

"He is! Why, that's just the best thing that's happened since the night Major Cort came back. Whatever are you crying for? Come have your dinner now. That quail the Yankees shot is roasted brown and pretty, and the potatoes and gravy are fixed just the way you like it."

"Let the guards have it, Aunt Caroline, I'm not hungry!"

"Miss Susannah!" Aunt Caroline looked after her worriedly as she ran upstairs.

Susannah closed her door and lay on her bed wondering why she wasn't happy. She should be. She had got what she wanted, and that was very important. Had there been something else important she had wanted?

She closed her eyes, and the memory of his kiss swam too close; she opened them and stared at the ceiling, which, untouched by the Yankee invaders, was nearly as white and pristine as before the war. How could even a ceiling remain unchanged? she wondered.

So much had happened that she could hardly get her bearings anymore. It was only her pride, of course, that was hurt. He was going to General Forrest's camp, and that was all that mattered. As for Antonio Andrada, he had never caused her anything but embarrassment and humiliation. It was only pride that made her wish he had gone on her errand from love.

I cannot bear him, she thought, even though he is helping me. It seemed unjust, but she didn't care. At least he was gone, and she'd never have to see him again.

$$6$$

Time dragged after Antonio left Memphis. Winter seemed endless, and no one seemed to even hope for spring. Spring meant renewal, the planting of crops, the sweet pale green of cotton plants. This spring only weeds would sprout in most of the cotton fields; and though the saxifrage and firepink might bloom, how could there be spring in the hearts of Confederates?

If, by some miracle, General Lee succeeded in the spring, it would be better than robins and flowers. But most people did not believe it could happen, and the gray horde of deserting Confederate soldiers moved through the countryside like dreary clouds over the landscape.

At Christmastime, under Yankee guard, Susannah took Aunt Caroline and went into

Memphis to spend the holiday with Mrs. St. John. She hardly felt up to a celebration, but she took along a small pine tree from Robin Hill to be decorated. Once there, she decided to stay for a while. The older woman was ill with a persistent cough, and all alone. Reuben had finally left and stayed away for good.

"Maybe he's gone North," Mrs. St. John speculated. "Probably with money in his pocket."

"I hope some Yankee opportunist takes it away from him," Susannah said. "It would serve him right."

"But Reuben is craftier than most of those who've lived in slavery. He has a talent for duplicity."

"I wonder where he got his money," Susannah said.

"Even before the war, the men used to ask Reuben for his advice on which horse to bet on when there were races. They'd pay him for it; Cort overlooked it because Reuben was so good in the stables."

"But there are no races now," Susannah mused.

They opened their presents on Christmas Eve, and though no one had gone Christmas shopping, each of them thought her gift was perfect. Mrs. St. John gave Susannah a pearl necklace hung with Arabian talismanic ornaments ending in turquoise. Susannah had never seen anything like it.

"Oh, such jewelry was all the rage fifty years ago," Mrs. St. John said, laughing at Susannah's surprise and pleasure. "The necklace belonged to my mother. It was to be for your wedding, but I decided not to save it any longer."

"I'm glad you gave it to me now," Susannah said enthusiastically. "I'll plan my wedding dress with a plain high bodice to wear it against. It'll be the most exotic wedding ensemble anyone's had in ages, and all the men will be envious of Cort, I hope!"

"And all the women jealous," Mrs. St. John agreed.

Though there were no more presents for Susannah to open, the two women whiled away a large part of the day dreaming up possible designs for Susannah's wedding gown, debating the advantages of silk or book muslin and whether the dress ought to be princess style or have an open overskirt. But as Susannah tried to imagine her wedding, it seemed like a childish fantasy.

"It doesn't seem possible that Cort and I will ever marry," she confessed. "I feel frivolous planning all this."

Mrs. St. John looked at Susannah sharply. "You must keep faith, Susannah," she reprimanded. "It's not frivolous for women to talk about gowns while the world is falling apart. It is a means of keeping the world together."

Susannah nodded. "It will seem real enough when Cort gets home," she said resolutely, but the strange feeling didn't leave her.

Susannah's gift to Mrs. St. John was large, flat, and rectangular and turned out to be a watercolor she had painted of the Memphis landing as it had been before the war, with crowds of people in fine clothing—women with bright dresses and small domed parasols, men in chesterfield jackets or raglan capes and top hats or brimmers. Steamboats sat like frothy wedding cakes on the river, and gum trees and water elms were depicted in full leaf. Susannah had fitted the painting into a chipped gilt frame, but there had been no glass to cover it. Mrs. St. John did not mind the lack of glass.

"Susannah, you always were the most talented artist at Miss Pickens'," she exclaimed.

"Oh, no. Miss Pickens always said I made my strokes too bold," Susannah said with a sigh. "She liked Becky Bothwell's flowers better. She did such dainty dogwood and pussy-willow."

"But you've done far more than paint a pretty picture! Why, you've put the world back as it ought to be. And, my goodness," she exclaimed, beginning to notice something else about the painting. There's Cort's face sketched and Colonel Dunbar's and Rachel's. I feel almost as if I'm really seeing them all again."

"Can you really recognize them?" Susannah said delightedly.

"Yes, of course," Mrs. St. John said, picking out face after face. "And not one Yankee in the picture!"

Or one Brazilian either, Susannah thought.

She wondered every day whether the Marquez da Silva had actually found her father and told him about Rachel. Perhaps he hadn't; perhaps he'd run into obstacles and abandoned the project, gone on about his business. Because surely if he had found Papa, there would have been a raid on the Irving Block by now. It had been over a month since Antonio had left, and Susannah fought down a dread that grew stronger every day, a dread that her father and Cort were dead, that there had been no one to find, that she was alone with no one left to snatch her sister from Yankee persecution. It was easier to hate Antonio; it was more satisfying to think he hadn't done as he promised.

"I wish I were a man," Susannah said as darkness fell on Christmas Day. "Nothing is harder than waiting." She was exhausted from the strain of their brave gaiety.

"That is why it's women's lot to wait, Susannah. They are the only sex strong enough to endure it. At least we were able to send some food to Rachel for Christmas."

"I wonder if she got it," Susannah said, in a mood not to trust anything. The guards at the Irving Block had relented a bit with the season, and though they had not allowed Susannah to see Rachel, she had been permitted to send a plum pudding and some meat pies. "I would not be surprised if the Yankees ate it all themselves."

"Then we had better hope they were too drunk to find the message."

"Rachel, Papa is coming," it had said, tucked deeply between the crusts of one of the pies. They had hoped it would give Rachel courage.

On New Year's Eve, they went to bed early, as they usually did, not wanting to waste firewood or lamp oil on staying up to see the new year in. They had expended all their celebration on Christmas and had nothing to give to a new year that promised nothing but hardship. The noise of Union revelry made sleeping more difficult than usual, but at least they were warm beneath the covers, lying together in the sleigh bed. A sprinkling of gunfire and the distant boom of a cannon at Fort Pickering marked midnight; then it was quieter, and Susannah dozed off.

Hours later, more gunfire awakened her. She sat up, her heart pounding. "It's only more celebrating, Susannah," Mrs. St. John said drowsily.

"No! That's all over. It's something else. It's fighting! I'm sure of it!" She leapt from bed and stood barefoot and shivering, trying to discern the location. "It's downtown around the courthouse, I think."

"That's where the Irving Block is." Mrs. St. John voiced what Susannah couldn't manage to say.

"It must be Papa with some soldiers!" Susannah was shaking so hard she couldn't move from the spot. Had she only initiated another disaster by sending the message? Would they all be killed? If only a small percentage of gunshots were hitting their mark, a lot of carnage was going on. She clapped her hands to her ears. "Oh, I cannot bear it! I must do something!" She began to throw on her clothes.

"Susannah, what are you doing?"

"I have a pistol. I'm going to help."

"Don't be an idiot! You won't get close enough to hit anyone with a pistol without getting shot yourself—or worse, perhaps, getting caught. You could be used to make your father surrender then. Have some staying power, Susannah!"

"But I have to do something! I'll just jump right out of my skin if I stand still any longer!"

Mrs. St. John pushed her to her knees beside the bed. "Pray, Susannah!" she commanded tersely, falling down beside her.

"I can't remember any prayers."

"There's the Lord's Prayer. It will come back to you. You've said it often enough in church."

Mrs. St. John pulled the quilts around them, almost over their heads, to dampen the sounds of the fighting. Numbly Susannah followed Mrs. St. John's voice, evenly praising God, asking for blessings and deliverance, through the popping gunfire. The shooting went on for what seemed forever, but so did Mrs. St. John's stalwart prayer. Finally the firing waned, and their strained, hoarse voices prevailed. Hoofbeats came down the street and stopped. Boots sounded on the walk, and knocking began on the door. The two women stared at each other in the nightglow, remembering what had happened the other time that the Yankees had come in the night, looking for Susannah's cloak.

"We'll have to let them in or they'll break the door down," Mrs. St. John said practically. "We'd be cold in January with a broken door."

Still wrapped in the quilts, they made their way downstairs and unfastened the locks. "Have you and your men gone mad celebrating the new year?" Mrs. St. John said. "Terrifying us with all that shooting, and now—"

"There's been an attempt on the Irving Block. Some Rebels killed or wounded at least two dozen Union soldiers and ran up a Confederate flag on Jeff Davis' home next to the prison."

"Did they get into Irving?" Susannah asked, breathless with hope.

"Yes, but only the first floor. They tried to rush the staircases, but they were well defended. I've orders to search this house."

"This house? Why?"

"To look for the Rebel leader. Some former

slaves recognized him, and General Washburn has set a special bounty on his head. Stand aside now; the man was Major Cort St. John!"

Rachel remained in the Irving Block. There was nothing more they could do, and now there was no more hope, except the ultimate hope that the war would end or that General Washburn would have a change of heart. Cort became a hero, as the news of his exploit spread through the city and through the South. He had no more than a dozen men with him on the raid, it was said; and there were twelve thousand Yankees in Memphis, odds of one to a thousand. He had waited for a foggy night; then, wearing a stolen Union cloak over his gray uniform, he had calmly approached the sentries and distracted them. A soundless attack with rifle butts had been over quickly.

Unmolested, Cort had slipped into the city with his men, he in his blue cape, they wearing gray. At the prison he had announced himself as an officer with prisoners to be admitted, and only when he was inside had he thrown off his cloak and given the spine-chilling Rebel yell.

It had been a clever trick, but it had been necessary to strike like lightning, and, as General Forrest would have said, be gone before the enemy heard the thunder. Cort, knowing the floor plan of the Irving Block, had designed a plan for the rescue, which would have succeeded, had there not been more soldiers in the building than expected. Cort had been wise enough not to fight to the finish. Exactly how the Rebels had escaped from the city was unknown, but the Yankees were not able to boast that a single one of them had been left behind wounded or dead. It was the best thing since the August raid, and Confederate Memphis took Cort to it heart. Even the Yankees began to call him Old Lightning, though Cort was still in his twenties.

"Lucky he's already proposed to you, Susannah," Mrs. St. John chuckled. "The girls will fall over themselves just to talk to him when he comes home."

"Cort was always popular at parties," Susannah observed.

"And never looked at anyone but you. Maybe you take him too much for granted," Mrs. St. John told her warningly. "Take care."

"Oh, it's just that it's difficult to think of love while Rachel is still in prison."

"Usually it's difficult not to think of it when a girl is in love. You do love Cort, don't you, Susannah?"

"Of course I do! No man could be kinder or braver or more dedicated. And I will be the wife he deserves. For heaven's sake, what man could be more worth loving than Cort?"

"Women sometimes have other reasons for love."

"I can't imagine what," Susannah said irritably, and went to help Aunt Caroline in the kitchen, banging the pans about so that the old woman complained.

"You in a stew, Miss Susannah!"

"Aunt Caroline, what other reason is there for a woman to love a man except that he is kind and brave?" She hoped Aunt Caroline would tell her there was no other reason; in fact, she expected it.

But Aunt Caroline stopped stirring her pot

and looked at her hard, hands on her hips. "Miss Susannah, ladies don't talk about that. They ought not even know about it."

"But I want to know," Susannah persisted, aware of sounding young and thirsty for life, like her sister Rachel.

"Wouldn't get you nothin' but trouble. Run along with you! You're gettin' in my way."

Susannah wandered out of the kitchen, leaving Aunt Caroline looking worriedly after her. Aunt Caroline had seen how Susannah had gazed at the marquess at Robin Hill. And time and again she had seen that expression cross Susannah's face as though at odd, unexpected moments she thought of him. Aunt Caroline wished Susannah's mother were alive to tell her whatever it was white ladies told their daughters about the perils of love.

Susannah spent the next hour lying on her bed contemplating a miniature of Cort St. John, thinking of his heroic actions, his steadfast love, the sweetness of their youth together. Yes, she cared for Cort; she would always care. But time and time again the fair features of the miniature darkened, and instead of his blond locks and blue eyes, she saw the marquess' dark features mocking her. She had challenged him with being afraid of falling in love with her, and he had met that challenge easily with a kiss. Oh, it must not be that *she* had fallen in love with *him*!

A Tyrolean hat and his effort to help Rachel were not enough to excuse all the trouble he had caused her. No, she would not forgive him for anything, least of all for kissing her and making her ecstatic in his arms.

She couldn't love him, but how was it possible to delight so much in the kiss of a man she hated? Could Aunt Caroline or Mrs. St. John have told her?

It must be only because the war would not end, because nothing was as it should be. It was because Cort wasn't with her, and she was afraid of losing him. It was because she was trying to escape all her frightening thoughts—of Rachel suffering through the winter away from fresh air and sunlight, of Papa. She knew that her father must be dead, else he would have led the raid on the Irving Block himself. She was an orphan, but when the war was over she'd start a new family with Cort. Children would be born who had never heard the sound of Yankee cannon.

But the war dragged on, and every day was another day she might lose Cort, too. A Union soldier who could kill him would receive a promotion and a special commendation. A civilian profiteer would do well, too, if he could bring word of a time and place where Cort was vulnerable to being taken. He had enemies everywhere; and if they found him, wasn't that her fault, too? It was she who had given Rachel her reckless ideas with her own rash behavior—she, the big sister whom Rachel had wanted to imitate, had been a model of irresponsibility.

Sometimes she thought she would never learn maturity. How could she possibly think of the Marquez da Silva when Cort was in such danger? Resolutely she put Antonio Andrada out of her mind. Tomorrow I will not remember his face, she told herself, and in a month I will forget even his name.

For several weeks in January she stayed in

Memphis while she visited other young women of her acquaintance, always setting them to giggling at the blue-coated guard who accompanied her and stood waiting by the door until she was ready to go.

They would gather around a piano and treat him to a chorus of "Dixie," but that was as far as Susannah's insurgency went these days. In fact, she often did not sing with the others. Patriotic songs seemed foolish now. She had bought embroidery thread and domestic and was hard at work on a set of tea towels for her trousseau, decorating them with a design of a robin perched on a branch to signify Robin Hill. So much needed replacing that the towels were merely a token, but an important one to Susannah, symbolic of her return to docile domesticity, a penance for her wayward spirit.

In February she went back to Robin Hill, fearful of leaving it too long unattended. There, impossible as it seemed, spring began to come. Redbuds and azaleas had softened the war-weary, paint-peeled walls of Robin Hill when, one day in April, a Union soldier galloped up the lane, shouting news of Appomattox. Lee's attempt to break out of Richmond had ended in defeat. The Yankees were no longer the enemy. There was no longer a Confederacy. Could it really be so?

"What will happen to the Rebel troops?" she asked. "Will they be allowed to return home?"

"President Lincoln has decreed pardons for all Southerners who will swear allegiance to the Union," the messenger told her.

"Thank God! What of the Southerners who are in prison already?"

The soldier grinned. "They are releasing all the prisoners whose crimes are only minor."

"When!" The word was a scream of joy.

"This afternoon. If you hurry, you may get there in time to meet your sister when she's released."

Her erstwhile guards hitched Sultan for her and drove her into town. The courthouse square was thronged with friends and relatives of inmates, hoping to see their loved ones appear. For a long time the prisoners trickled out, gaunt, ragged, and bewildered, dazed not only at freedom but also at the incredible spring, the leafing jasmine and allspice, the mockingbirds in the catalpas.

Slowly the square emptied, and Rachel hadn't appeared. A hard knot formed in Susannah's stomach. She clutched Mrs. St. John's hand and tried not to think the worst—that Rachel had died, and she had not been informed of it.

"Come, Susannah, we'll go to ask," Mrs. St. John said finally.

"No. Let's wait," Susannah said, afraid of the answer they would receive. "She may come out yet."

"I don't think so. It's been half an hour since anyone's left," Mrs. St. John said. "We have to know," she added gently.

Inside the gloomy foyer an officer checked for Rachel's name. "Yes, she's here," he told them.

"Then why haven't you released her?"

"She refuses to sign the loyalty oath. I'll have her brought down; you can see for yourself."

Rachel was barely recognizable, clad in a gown of coarse material, her once golden hair almost indistinguishable from the straw tangled in it.

"Susannah, have they arrested you, too?" she cried, flinging herself into her sister's arms.

"Oh dear, no. Sign the oath of allegiance, and you will be free."

"Pledge allegiance? To the Yankees? I would sooner die, Susannah!"

"You must! I have signed it."

"You have? *You*, Susannah?"

"Yes."

"Then if you have given up, we have really lost."

"Sign it, Rachel, dear, and we will go home to Robin Hill."

Rachel signed in a shaky hand, and then, as she walked away, her legs collapsed beneath her. A Union officer carried her out into the late-afternoon sun.

7

"I never want to leave Robin Hill again," Rachel swore, lying on a sofa beside a window from which she could see magnolia trees and a bed of blooming blue flag. If the condition of the house had shocked her, she had said nothing, only agreed with Susannah that it must be cleaned top to bottom for Cort's arrival.

"The bridegroom is coming!" Rachel declared happily. "Think of it! We are really going to have a wedding at Robin Hill. It ought to be a grand celebration, because the war is over. We can sell the cotton now, can't we, Susannah? And spend a little of the money on a pretty wedding? Oh, I know it will be nothing like it would have been, but it will be perfect just because it's you and Cort. Just because it's Robin Hill. Will Papa come with Cort, do you think?"

Susannah shook her head. "I am sure Papa is dead," she said, afraid her sister couldn't stand any more grief. But Rachel seemed unsurprised.

"I knew it already," she admitted. "You've said nothing about him." Death, even of a loved one, had lost its power to shock her. "I know there's a lot of hard times still coming, but it doesn't matter. I can stand anything as long as I'm home. Do you know how I survived the prison, Susannah?"

Her sister shook her head. She had been wondering how her frail sister had managed to live when so many stronger men and women had died. It seemed to her that Rachel had barely endured at that. She was too weak to walk more than a few steps. But Aunt Caroline was in her element, nursing her back to health with soups and hot buttered breads.

"I kept imagining Robin Hill. I imagined every little thing about it. The way the grape vines twist around the garden arbor, and the squirrels that come up to the steps looking for hazelnuts. The beans and carrots in the vegetable patch, the way the lace curtains in my bedroom look when they blow in the wind."

"Robin Hill is different now."

"But it is still Robin Hill. And I shall be happy as long as I am here!"

"That should be forever, then," Susannah said with a smile. "Until some beau makes you think that somewhere else is better—with him."

Rachel grimaced. "Oh, I've decided I'm not ready for serious beaus, after all. I don't want to grow up. I want to pretend I'm a little girl again."

"I know. Sometimes I do too. But it will pass."

"For you, when Cort comes home. Do you suppose he'll mind living at Robin Hill instead of at Hazel Grove?"

"I'm sure I can persuade him, Rachel. You had better get some sleep."

The Union guards were gone now. Every day she waited for Cort's arrival, braiding her hair in smooth twists about her ears, even when she was scrubbing floors or hoeing the garden. Her hands were callused, but that could not be helped. Peas and lettuce were already up, and she couldn't have the weeds take over!

There were debts that needed to be paid, especially years of taxes in arrears. A constable had come about it, but he had been kind enough to wait for Cort to settle things. When Cort came, she would have him sell the cotton, and they would hire former slaves to do the work. She would have the soft hands of a lady again, then. Oh, but she hoped he would not come while she was soiled and disheveled from her labors!

She had fallen asleep one night, too tired to brush out her hair or take off her clothes, when she heard a horse on the lane. She sat up with a start of fear before she remembered it could not be Yankees. Running downstairs, she lighted a lamp and tugged at the door latch. Cort's fair hair flashed in the lamplight as he vaulted up the steps.

"Susannah!"

"Oh, Cort! Is it really you?"

He took the lamp and set it aside, and taking

her in his arms, covered her with kisses—her lips, her cheeks, her eyelids. She sighed, loving the solidness of him against her, holding her so protectively that she felt she would never be in danger again. He was a dream that had become reality, instead of a man who had always existed. He was strange, yet familiar; and the strangeness was as disconcerting as the familiarity was comforting.

When they had gone into the house, she sat looking her fill at the man for whom she had waited during the long war, the man with whom she would spend the rest of her life, who would make those years both worth the wait and a distant memory. He was her past and her future, but the past and the future were not the same.

Before the war, Cort's eyes had glowed with laughter and the love of adventure. He had been capable of sternness with his slaves, but they had obeyed him more from love than fear. He had run his plantation efficiently, but his boyish energy had made the job seem effortless. Everything about him seemed heavier now, though the flesh was spare on his broad-shouldered frame. The boyish lightness was gone; the very gesture of his hand as he spoke was of more weight, more authority.

Perhaps she seemed different to him, too, for he stared at her as though he were discovering her for the first time. Dear heaven, no wonder he was looking at her so peculiarly! He had never seen her such a mess. Sprigs of her hair had escaped their coils everywhere, and her dress, worn with a single petticoat, was stained with garden mud. She raised both hands to poke at her hair, and seeing his eyes follow her graceful gesture, became self-conscious over her chipped fingernails.

"I cannot believe you are really home!" she murmured.

"Nor I." In his delirium of happiness, nothing could detract from her beauty, which represented for him love and peace. "Susannah, have you thought about what I asked you when I was here before? I . . . I cannot ask Colonel Dunbar, Susannah." He realized he might be telling her the tragic news.

"I know, Cort. I know he's dead," she said to ease his mind.

"You need a man to protect you, Susannah, you and Rachel; and I want to be that man," he said fervently.

"I have thought about it, Cort," she answered, with a blush worthy of a girl who had never flirted with a Union colonel or kissed a Brazilian marquess.

"Then, will you marry me? I haven't much to offer now, and I know I should reestablish Hazel Grove first, but I cannot wait. I would die of it! Waiting would be worse than a festering Union bullet. I have only love to give to you, Susannah, but my love is endless. I would have loved you even from my grave! I would have come home as a ghost to love you!"

"Oh, Cort, of course I'll marry you. I don't want to wait either!"

"I thought I couldn't be any happier when I saw your face tonight, Susannah," he murmured. "But now . . ."

He lowered his lips to hers, drinking in the sweet reward of his warrior's homecoming. She closed her eyes and sighed, her arms fastened about his neck, feeling his chest heaving with emotion. Her years of loneliness were over at last! The time had come to begin anew. The faith that had been so difficult to sustain had been fulfilled. Her mind was so busy with eager plans that she drew back from his caress to express them.

"We can have the wedding here, can't we, Cort? How soon do you think you could get the money for the cotton? There are four hundred bales, minus the one I sold to Rudd Sloane, but that is another story. Do you think some of our old workers could be hired for wages? It could be in June. That would give me time to plan everything, and you time to plant a new crop. We ought to paint the front of the house at least, and we'll simply have to have some new furniture. We're so fortunate to be able to start over, Cort!"

"Susannah . . ."

His tone held a note of warning, but Susannah chose not to hear it. She could not bear to be cautioned or held back anymore from her plans. "Oh, I know it will be a big job, having a wedding so soon when we've so much to do. It would be nice if Robin Hill were fully restored before our wedding day. But you said yourself you couldn't bear to wait. I've already designed my dress. And I'm going to wear a necklace of your grandmother's. Oh, I wish you could wear the uniform we made for you. It was a wonderful uniform, Cort. It caused so much trouble, but it would do Rachel good, even so, to see you wear it. We don't have it, though; and even if we did, I suppose the Yankees wouldn't let you wear it after you've signed the oath of allegiance."

"Susannah, that is what I want to tell you. We are going to start over, but not at Robin Hill."

"But, Cort, I was sure you wouldn't mind living at Robin Hill for a while. It's so important to Rachel." She searched his face, not understanding what she saw there, a steady resolve, strength mixed with bitterness.

"I would gladly live at Robin Hill, Susannah, but it isn't possible. It isn't even possible for us to be married here. I will ask someone I trust to sell the cotton, but I can't do even that myself. I wasn't exaggerating when I said I had nothing to offer but love, Susannah. I have decided not to take the oath of allegiance."

"Cort! You must! If you don't, they will . . ." She could not pronounce the grim thoughts she had hoped to banish with the end of the war.

"They'll kill me. At the very least, they'll sentence me to prison. I might be lucky if I were not drawn and quartered. Plenty of Yanks would like to boast they'd done it, and there are no stipulations that my body must be in one piece to collect the reward."

"Cort, stop! Stop!" She was beside herself, covering her ears with her hands. In a brief moment her happiness had turned to misery.

He took her hands in his. "I'm sorry, Susannah. I am used to speaking brutally. I have to remember I am with a woman and not battle-jaded soldiers now. Please understand. I can't pledge loyalty to those who have ravaged the South. I cannot be whipped into submission. I must live on my own terms, Susannah. I cannot live as a conquered man."

"I *am* trying to understand, Cort," she told him. But she could not grasp at all what it meant, what would happen to him and to her. "You asked me to marry you," she said dazedly.

"We *can* be married, Susannah, only not here. Not at Robin Hill, not even in Tennessee." His voice was charged with excitement now. "I met a man who offered me a new life," he told her. "New challenges, and a fresh new land where we can live in freedom and dignity. He came to General Forrest's camp to tell us what he could provide—Confederate settlement on hundreds of thousands of acres of prime Brazilian land, just waiting to be developed! Come with me, Susannah. We'll be married at the first opportunity—on the ship to Rio, if not sooner."

"Oh, Cort," she whispered in agony. If she had ever hated the Marquez da Silva, she despised him a thousand times more now; for he, not the Union Army, had been the means of depriving her of all that she wanted. "Cort, please," she begged, "don't ask this of me. I love Robin Hill; it's my home, and Rachel's home. I can't leave Rachel!"

"My mother will take care of her, and when she's well, she can join us."

"Oh, you don't understand! Being at Robin Hill is what is making Rachel recover. She couldn't bear the thought of leaving it forever."

"And I cannot stay here!"

"Don't make me choose between you! Rachel's all the family I have. And she needs me."

"I'd be your family, and I need you!" he said. "Come with me, if you love me!"

If you love me. How could he doubt her love? Oh, she knew that a woman should be willing to follow the man she loved to the end of the earth. But why did the end of the earth have to be the Amazon? Why must it be that following Cort St. John must lead her to the Marquez da Silva? Somewhere deep in her subconscious, she was afraid of meeting him again; and though she assured herself that she was as indifferent to him as he to her, the very thought of him made her warm and uncomfortable.

"I know I'm asking a great deal," Cort went on. "We'd be going to an untamed jungle. We'd have to hack out our future tree by tree, and past Santarém, there's no civilization at all, only an occasional trader's packet that might come along the river. But the challenge! And the adventure! Best of all, the chance to be my own man again! Please love me enough, Susannah!"

Susannah's head swam. The idea of the jungle, with its dangers, from alligators to hostile Indians, did frighten her. But Susannah had already lived through perils that would have vanquished many women. She refused to admit to herself that the danger that worried her most was one from which even Cort might not be able to defend her. "General Forrest has taken the oath of allegiance," she said, trying to reason with him.

"General Forrest is old and sick. I'm sure he'd go too, if he were a young man. I cannot bear to crawl before the Yankees!"

"Think of Robin Hill. Think of Rachel!"

"I *am* thinking of Robin Hill and Rachel. I'm thinking how both of them suffered, and I could not prevent it. Now I will not submit to those who caused it. I will not become meek and servile and endure the snickers as I walk by. "There goes Major St. John, Old Lightning. Just look at him now!"

"Cort, this is our home! We've fought for it. I, as well as you. We must have the courage not to abandon it!"

"The South is finished, Susannah. You are clinging to something that is dead."

"That is what *he* says—the Marquez da Silva! You've let him hypnotize you with those tales of his. I heard them, Cort, when he was here in Memphis. He is a self-serving scoundrel!"

"You can say that, when he was the one who brought word of Rachel's predicament?" Cort was genuinely surprised. "I found him impressive."

"Impressive! Yes, of course. What other sort of man would the emperor send to convince men to throw away their lives on a foreign wilderness? You will find out someday what he's really like, and then it will be too late. I know him, Cort. A woman can judge a man's character more easily than another man. Don't let the Marquez da Silva ruin our lives."

"Only you can do that, Susannah. If you don't come with me."

"Cort, I cannot leave Rachel."

"And I cannot stay here!"

"Then . . ."

They had reached the end of the argument, and reality lay bleakly before them. Cort was trembling, and Susannah's chest was tight with unshed tears. Words of farewell were all that was left; and then they would be parted, this time forever. They stood looking at each other numbly, each hoping for the surrender of the other.

Finally Cort spoke with a sigh. "I have to go now," he told her. "I'm going to New Orleans, and I must be gone from here before daylight." He put his hand into his coat pocket and handed her an envelope. "Take this. It's a steamboat ticket I bought for you because it would be too dangerous for us to travel together. The *River Belle* stops at Memphis once a week; the schedule's in the envelope. If you change your mind, I'll be meeting the *Belle* every time for the month I'll be in New Orleans." He clasped her hands. "You'd only grow to scorn and despise me if I stayed—you'd hate the man I'd become. But I will never love another woman, never!"

He kissed her, and a sob tore from her throat as his lips left hers. He strode away without looking back, as though he dared not or his resolve might falter. She stood miserably, not running after him or entreating him anymore to do what he believed would destroy him.

When he was out of sight, she took the lamp into her father's study, and setting it on the desk, took out piles of ledgers and began to read them. She was still there in the morning, still at her task when Rachel found her. Tears had made blisters on some of the pages.

"Susannah, what are you doing?" Rachel asked.

Grimly Susannah told her what had happened. "So you see, we will not have a man to run Robin Hill for us; we will have to do it ourselves."

"Run Robin Hill ourselves? Two women? Susannah, that is ridiculous!"

"No, it isn't. We've managed so far, haven't we?"

"Only barely. And we were only holding out until Cort came home. Susannah, you go after Cort. Use the ticket. You are giving up the man you love!"

"What would you do if I left?"

"What Cort thought I should. Go to live with Mrs. St. John. Don't use me for an excuse to punish yourself. That's what you're doing, you know. You think you owe it to me to stay because of what happened with the uniform. But it was much more my fault than yours." Rachel sank onto a sofa as though it had taken every bit of her energy to rebuke her sister. As she glanced out the window at the fields of her childhood home, tears welled helplessly.

Susannah flung herself down at her sister's knees. "I could never leave you, Rachel. I couldn't be happy."

"I'll get well, and we'll both go to Brazil, Susannah," Rachel promised, giving up her effort to convince Susannah to follow Cort.

Susannah smiled. "You'll get well. And then we'll see."

The next day Susannah drove to Memphis to make arrangements to sell her cotton. In the aftermath of the war, the city was booming. It was as though the cork had been pulled out of a champagne bottle, and froth was flowing everywhere—only the froth was cotton.

Wagons of cotton lined the roads into the city, many broken down in the mud. Contracts for new houses were being let, and hammers resounded. Memphis had been occupied early and easily, and now it was in better shape than most of the South. It hadn't been shelled to a shambles like Vicksburg, or sacked and burned like Atlanta. Ex-Confederate officers were flocking to the city, and there was a rumor that Jeff Davis would come home to open an insurance office. General Washburn, who had been a good administrator, was restoring city government, and the transition was going smoothly. Some Yankee officers, showing no interest in going home, were investing in cotton land.

Drays rumbled down the cobblestones in an endless line to Front Street, and the mountains of burlap-covered bales, matching the color of the bluffs, made the city seem almost to be built on cotton. Carpetbaggers were finding it worthwhile to keep moving past Memphis, for Memphis, unlike other Southern cities, had been a flatboat town and a jumping-off place for the goldfields and the West. Memphis knew how to rid itself of riffraff. Though Mrs. Simpson's house of ill repute still flourished on Fulton Street, Rudd Sloane's floating gambling establishment was no longer to be seen on the river. The discovery of a loaded roulette wheel had sent him scurrying downstream for safety. But Susannah didn't need Sloane these days to market her cotton.

The Cotton Exchange on Union Street was bustling. Wishing with all her heart that Cort were doing it, she went inside and struck a bargain for her cotton that included the buyer's sending his own drays to Robin Hill to collect it. That done, she returned home to report to Rachel.

"I imagine Cort would have done better," she said with a sigh. "But I did get a hundred and fifty dollars a bale, undelivered. The back taxes are two thousand, and then we will need new equipment and horses and mules."

"We should buy two nice mares for us to ride, and another for the carriage," Rachel put in.

"Yes. And the roof will have to be fixed before the fall rains start. That may not be easy. There is a terrible demand for carpenters."

"We'll have to hire field hands, too."

Susannah nodded. "When the cotton's sold, I'll go out to the refugee camp on President's Island and see whom I can find. I expect that seed is going to come dear, but we'll have to pay whatever is necessary. Papa would have had the crop sown by now."

"We'll need to paint everything, inside and out," Rachel enthused. "A new staircase. The floors will have to be refinished for our parties and dances. New draperies and furniture—"

"Hold up, Rachel," Susannah said with a laugh. "We can't build back Robin Hill all at once. We had better be content to bring in a crop first."

"But I'm ready for some fun, too," Rachel declared with her indomitable spirit. "Let's have new gowns anyway. You must have one to go with that wonderful hat the marquess brought you. We'll drive to Memphis to church on Sunday, and make everyone envious. I'm sure there's not another hat like that one in the whole city."

"If there is, it's sitting on some strumpet's head," Susannah replied. "The marquess has atrocious taste in women's clothing."

"You still don't like him, even though he tried to help get me out of the Irving Block, Susannah. Honestly, how could any woman dislike such a charming man? Why, let's see . . . if I didn't know you were in love with Cort, I'd think you hated him because he'd spurned you!"

"Rachel! Ooh!" Susannah flew at her sister with a cushion, as she used to do when they were children; then, remembering Rachel's weakened condition, she stopped herself.

Rachel giggled wickedly. "You ought to have hit me, Susannah. I'm really on the mend, you know. Perhaps I'll wear the hat myself and have sophisticated suitors."

"You'll do nothing of the kind. That hat is too old for you."

"Oh, you are still always saying something is too old for me or that I am too young for it."

"That's what big sisters are for," Susannah retorted. "You are supposed to respect them, Rachel." But at that instant her breath was knocked short by the blow of another cushion. With a cry, she attacked her sister with the one she still held; and in a moment they were laughing helplessly, their cheeks rosy and their hair askew.

The sound of their laughter was so unaccustomed that they stopped and stared at each other in amazement as the summer sun warmed the scarred floors and damaged walls. The war was over, and though it would take a long time, healing seemed to have begun. There was so much to heal—the loss of Papa and Cort, Rachel's health, and the memories that caused her to cry out in the night. Robin Hill itself must be healed. They would love the plantation even more dearly as it helped them to heal, and they it.

But the shadow of war was longer than they imagined.

The next morning Susannah walked down to the old barn, threading her way through Virginia creeper and wood sorrel, stopping to exult over a pink ladyslipper almost hidden in the tangle. She entered the gloomy ruin, grateful to her father for having been prudent enough to provide for them when others, caught up in the hatred of the moment, had rushed to set fire to their resources.

An owl flapped out, hooting noisily, barely missing her head as she intruded with her lantern, leaving only emptiness behind. The cotton was gone. There was nothing but strands of fluffy white clinging to the walls and sifting over the rocky floor like windblown snow. That was all that told her it had been more than a dream that the barn had once been filled with cotton.

Susannah dropped to her knees and buried her head against her lap. After a long, stunned moment, she looked up again, as if hoping to see the cotton miraculously reappear. After all she had endured, fate could not trick her so cruelly. But the shed was as vacant as before.

A groan forced its way up from the pit of her being, then another, then harsh screams that compressed the sides of her body in spasms and seemed to retch out her soul in a sort of death throe of the spirit. When she was exhausted, she lay for a long while feeling unable to move, faced at last with an obstacle she could not overcome. All the struggle and heartache had been for nothing. Convinced that all was lost, she felt her faith fail her. How could it have happened? Whoever had stolen the cotton must have done it long ago, for she had seen no fresh cart tacks or broken limbs to indicate that someone had recently visited the hiding place.

She thought of Mrs. St. John's Reuben, who had been seen recently in Memphis in an expensive worsted jacket and driving a four-in-hand. Had it been he? She had been used to thinking of those of his race as simple, and had thought she could deter him with no more than Aunt Caroline and a bottle of sherry. It was she who had been simpleminded! Or it could have been Sloane himself, or anyone. Hers wasn't the first cotton to be stolen.

We will lose Robin Hill. She could not prevent the thought from coming.

I can't tell Rachel, she thought. Rachel is just beginning to be better, and she won't be able to bear it. But how was Susannah to keep Rachel from knowing?

For the next few days she put up a brave front and spent much of her time in Memphis, appealing to banks to lend her money to plant a new crop. But no one had more than sympathy to give her. She was a woman alone, with a debt-ridden plantation, and even her father's closest friends advised her to give it up or at least to find a man to marry her and take over her affairs.

She thought of Cort, and sometimes she took out the ticket and looked at it. Perhaps she should have used it, but her decision had been to stay with Rachel, and she intended to stick to it. She tried to return the ticket for a refund, but even there she met with defeat.

Three weeks after Cort's departure, Robin Hill was auctioned at the courthouse. Even then, Susannah kept it from Rachel. The younger girl was becoming suspicious and worried, Susannah knew. No one had been hired to work in the fields, and the planting hadn't begun. Rachel guessed something was wrong, but Susannah couldn't bring herself to break the news. She paced the house all day, knowing that the moment had come when Rachel must be told, and wondering if it would cause Rachel any less suffering because she hadn't endured the weeks of waiting with her.

"It's so peaceful tonight," Rachel said with a sigh. "Did you notice that the yellow roses are blooming? You can smell them."

"Rachel—"

"Listen. Someone's coming," Rachel said. "Who could it be, do you think?" She jumped to her feet, eager for visitors to share the sweetness of the evening. Through the twilight they made out the form of a man on horseback coming at a trot up the lane.

Susannah clasped a porch column, as though that way she might keep hold of Robin Hill. Expecting some messenger of the court, she was surprised by the man who came into view.

"Why, Colonel Spangler!" Rachel said, astonished.

"Good evening, ladies." Sam Spangler dismounted and tipped his hat. In the dimness his expression was difficult to discern. "But it's no longer Colonel, as you can see." With a wry smile he gestured toward the insignia on his uniform, no longer that of a colonel, but a captain's bars instead. "That is thanks to you ladies, especially you, Susannah. I had several months in the stockade to reflect on the folly of having been in love with you. I suppose you haven't thought of it at all. I suppose you're not sorry."

"You were the enemy, sir," Susannah replied icily. Why was he here? Had he come to gloat over the demise of Robin Hill? Courtesy dictated she invite him to join them on the veranda, but Susannah was not feeling like a hostess.

Captain Spangler mounted the steps on his own initiative. "I'm glad you said 'were,'" he told her. "I am not the enemy any longer. The war is over."

"And you have come to set things right?" she asked with a sarcastic laugh.

"In a way."

"It would take you the rest of your life."

"So be it," he said.

"Frankly, I'd sooner never see you again," she replied, puzzled. She felt uneasy, wondering what he meant. "Please get off my veranda, sir!"

"Oh, but it's my veranda, Susannah. My veranda, my parlor, my stables, my smokehouse, my drive. I've purchased Robin Hill, my love, lock, stock, and barrel!"

His words exploded in her heart. So this was his revenge! She reeled, but not into a faint. Instead, a core of fury held her steady with its white-hot strength. Out of the corner of her eye she saw Rachel watching her, stunned and pale. Desperately, with no plan in her head, she turned and ran into the house. She paused in the downstairs hall, leaning against a door to try to think; but hearing the sound of his boots following her, she rushed on deeper into the house, into her father's study. Against her father's desk, she turned like an animal at bay.

"Susannah, don't you want to know why I bought Robin Hill?" he asked.

"Why should I give you the pleasure of gloating?" she snapped. "I know why you bought it. But why shouldn't you have? You're not the first Union soldier to buy up land around Memphis. It's wonderful cotton land, and with the demand so great, there's a fortune to be made. The victors exploit the vanquished; that's the natural order. I know you bought Robin Hill to torment me. You bought it because you hate me!"

Sam Spangler looked astonished. "I didn't buy Robin Hill to make a fortune, Susannah. In fact, since I know nothing about growing cotton, I may lose my shirt on it—unless you help me. Maybe that would please you; you'll have the last laugh then, Susannah. But we can help each other. I didn't buy Robin Hill because I hate you; I bought it because, God help me, I still love you!"

"Because you love . . ." Susannah's distress made her slow to understand.

"Marry me, Susannah! I will always love you. I bought Robin Hill to lay at your feet. Let's lay down our swords like Lee and Grant at Appomattox. Only this time it will be the North surrendering to the South, Susannah. I surrender my heart, my soul, my life, if only you can begin to care for me!"

But Susannah was not sympathetic to his plea. "You swine!" she said heatedly. "It's one thing for you to buy my plantation, but you cannot buy me. I do not come with the place, Colonel . . . Captain! I am not for sale! You cannot use Robin Hill to blackmail me into marrying you! What humiliation could be worse than marrying a Yankee—the very Yankee that wrecked Robin Hill? You have a great deal left to learn about the South! And no doubt it's beyond your grasp that we have surrendered our swords, but not our honor!"

"Susannah, please! Don't be so stubborn! We've caused each other enough pain. And I told you, I've come to set things right. You would love me eventually, Susannah. Only think! I'm offering you your old life—everything you want, everything you've struggled these last years to save. Cort St. John would not offer you that. Our intelligence says he's fled downriver to New Orleans, probably headed for Brazil."

He smiled at her gasp of surprise. "Oh, yes, my dear, I know that he was your sweetheart. I'm sure it was he who had been in the house that night; and it was for him that the infamous uniform was made. But how can you go on loving him, when he cares so little for you? When he will not swear allegiance and stay here with you? I will never fail you as he has. I will deserve you, Susannah!"

He moved closer to her as he spoke earnestly, almost desperately. She backed against the desk to avoid him, the handle of the center drawer boring painfully against her hip. "I would never marry you," she said in a choked voice.

"Susannah, what choice do you have? What will you do? Think of your sister. You'll have to take her away from Robin Hill if you don't marry me. Where will you go?"

Rachel! She had already given up Cort because of Rachel. Must she accept Sam Spangler for the same reason? What, after all, was the alternative? Losing her home might prove the final blow for Rachel, but could Rachel accept Susannah's marriage to Sam Spangler any more easily? Susannah saw Captain Spangler through a veil of hate. She hated him because he was a Yankee, she hated him for having allowed his men to sack Robin Hill; but that was all in the past. What she hated him for most was having the upper hand now. She hated him for the horrible choice he had put before her. Dare she spurn him? She struggled to hold her grip on her emotions; and then, as though sand were eroding beneath her feet, she felt her control sliding away, and she was enveloped in a tumultuous wave of loathing.

"Get out, Sam Spangler!" she shouted. "Get out of my house! Get off my land!"

"Susannah, it is not—"

She did not wait for him to tell her again what she could not bear to hear. The pressing of the desk-drawer handle had reminded her of the secret compartment containing her pistol. Suddenly she submitted to an urge, and yanking the drawer open, pulled it out and aimed it at his heart.

"Go, or I will shoot!"

He laughed. "Susannah, put that down. You wouldn't be so foolish. You're violating your Southerner's parole just by brandishing that weapon. I could report you, and you'd probably go to the Irving Block. If you shoot me, you'll hang!''

"Get out of here, Sam!" she begged. She knew, even in her rage, that she didn't intend to shoot him, though a part of her screamed that it would be wonderful to kill the man who, having robbed her of her home, was now trying to rob her of the only thing she had left—herself, her sovereignty over her own life and her own body.

Sam Spangler knew as well as she that she did not mean to fire; and brashly, he caught hold of her, attempting to twist the pistol away, while he pulled her to him in an embrace. She felt herself suffocating against him, knew he was going to kiss her and that she was helpless to prevent it. She fought uselessly, praying for that great friend of women, the swoon, to save her. She was aware of pain in her fingers as he tried to make her let go of the gun, but she tightened her hand around it as his lips came close. Though it would serve no purpose but to thwart him a little, the increased intensity of the pain seemed worth it. As she closed her eyes, trying to will her consciousness away, the room filled with the noise of an explosion.

Sam Spangler groaned, but not with passion. His head dropped intimately onto her shoulder, and as she twisted around to look, his eyes met hers with a stare of surprise and grief. His weight, perhaps twice hers, lay limply against her; her knees buckled with it, and her arms slid away from their entanglement with him. Captain Spangler crumpled to the floor, leaving a long stain of blood on her dress as he fell.

"My God, you've shot him, Susannah!" Rachel's voice told her what she could barely comprehend.

"No—I couldn't have!"

"Look, here is the gun." Rachel knelt to retrieve it. "It smells of powder. *He* wasn't holding it. He didn't shoot himself, did he?"

"No, he was trying to take it away from me. He must have . . ." The enormity of it began to sink in. "Dear heaven, is he dead?"

Bravely Rachel slid a trembling hand under Captain Spangler's jacket. "No," she reported as she felt the beating of his heart. Emboldened, she tore away the jacket, but the gore beneath it frightened and sickened her so much that she threw the coat back over him. The bullet, fired at such close range, had done a nasty bit of business.

A firm black hand pushed Rachel aside. "This ain't no work for you, child," Aunt Caroline's voice said. "Go and get a basin of water and some towels."

"Is he going to die, Aunt Caroline?" Susannah asked fearfully.

"Most likely. You go upstairs and pack, Miss Susannah. And take Miss Rachel to help you."

"Pack?" Susannah said, still dazed.

"You're in big trouble, Miss Susannah. Don't make no difference if he don't die. Somebody's goin' to come lookin' for him pretty soon. Maybe tonight. You got to be far away from here when they do."

"Where will I go, Aunt Caroline?" Susannah asked, glad to let the old woman give her directions as she had when she was a child.

"You goin' to Mr. Cort, where else? Didn't he give you a ticket on the *River Belle*, and don't she tie up at Memphis tonight? That's where you're goin', Miss Susannah!"

Susannah stared at Captain Spangler's unconscious form. "I don't want to be a murderess. We'll have to get a doctor—but how?"

"After you've packed, we'll saddle Sultan, and you can stop at the Bothwells' on your way to Memphis and ask them to send for one."

"Rachel—"

"I'll come with you, Susannah!" Rachel cried.

"You and me'll go to Mrs. St. John's like Major Cort wanted. Miss Susannah can get away better by herself, without you to slow her down. You ain't strong enough for it, and we only got one horse and one ticket."

Rachel looked stricken, but they both knew Aunt Caroline was right. When they had put what they could into a single valise and had saddled Sultan, they embraced on the steps of Robin Hill.

"I don't want to leave you," Susannah said. "Promise you will be all right."

"Of course I will," Rachel pledged. "I wish I were riding off to a handsome fiancé and a new country. You are still the one who has all the adventure, Susannah!" Rachel managed a mischievous grin.

"And you still are the one who cannot get enough of it. I should think you'd had your fill. Promise you'll behave."

"Oh, I'll behave. It's no fun when you get caught. Please don't get caught, Susannah." Rachel's courage gave way then, and she wept for a moment before pushing her sister away for a last hug against Aunt Caroline's ample bosom.

Susannah, wearing a divided riding skirt,

swung up into the saddle and turned down the lane. Looking back, she saw only a glimmer of light behind the windows. The forms of Rachel and Aunt Caroline were already lost in the darkness, and that was the last she saw of home.

8

At midnight the Mississippi rolled beneath a haze beside Riverside Drive. Above, stars shone like gems beneath a harem veil, and the scent of honeysuckle mingled with the familiar stench of the river mud. A light sparkled distantly from the far side, or perhaps it wasn't from the shore.

Perhaps it was on a barge, floating perilously in the night. Or it might come from a snag boat, with its forked hull and steam-operated derrick for removing the ever-present menaces: tree limbs or flood debris—swept into the water when land gave way by the acre, with barns, fences, and houses. But the worst hazard on the river was the sawyer, a tree floating on roots embedded in the river bottom, bobbing above the surface and then below, so that a pilot, rounding a bed, might see nothing at all as the boat bore down on it. Susannah wondered what dangers lay ahead for *her* on the river—dangers as swift and devastating, dangers no snag boat could remove.

She had had a doctor sent to Sam Spangler, and she hoped the doctor would be a Southerner, but even if he were, she could expect no more than a few hours' head start. The Southern doctor would run afoul of Yankee law if he failed to report the shooting, and the South needed the few physicians it had left. More likely the doctor would be a Yankee, an army medical man. She had instructed her neighbor to send for a Yankee, if need be. Major Bothwell, just returned from war himself, hadn't wanted to do it, but Susannah had insisted. She had refused, too, to allow him to aid her escape or even to tell him her plans. No one else must come to grief because of what had happened.

On the outskirts of the city she dismounted, and fastening Sultan's reins to the saddle, slapped his flank. "Go on, Sultan!" she commanded.

The animal looked back at her, startled at receiving his freedom. She slapped him again, and with an exuberant neigh he plunged down the road into the night. She hoped he might find his way home, but she could not leave him hitched somewhere along the river to announce the route her flight had taken. She watched as another part of her life disappeared. She imagined she was stripping it from her in layers, as a small boy might discard clothing on his way to go swimming. Soon she would leave Memphis itself, and then what would be left of her old identity? Only her valise stuffed with a few clothes and the necklace she had promised Mrs. St. John she would wear when she married Cort.

Clinging to the idea that she was running to the man she loved, she went on foot, striding purposefully to discourage any men who might think she was looking for companionship.

Along the wharves, cotton was stacked, and steamboats sat low in the water, loaded so high with bales that only the tops of the pilothouses showed. The cotton would be a fire hazard, exposed to any spark from the smokestacks above it, and she had heard of boats going down in watery conflagrations, the flammability of the cargo making any blaze difficult to bring under control.

The side-wheeler *River Belle* was easy to pick out, glowing with lights from its main cabin and its promenades. The hurricane deck, with its texas, the cabins for the boat's officers, and the boiler deck, with the staterooms and dining salon, gleamed with intricate scrollwork. Above the hurricane deck, the pilothouse sat like an ornament on a wedding cake, ending in a spire that looked as though it belonged on some Oriental mosque. The tops of the twin smokestacks flared like crowns, and a crescent moon hung between them, symbolic of the *River Belle*'s home port, New Orleans, the Crescent City. Red trim added dash to the fancy white woodwork on the decks; and paddleboxes, covering the side-wheels, were painted with magnificent sunbursts. People were wandering up and down the gangplank, having come to bid farewell to

the *River Belle*'s passengers and stayed to party
the night away.

Susannah's heart lifted at the sight of the
boat. She had been afraid it might not be here
after all. But she felt a wave of sadness, too.
She had traveled on this boat before, with her
papa and Aunt Caroline and Rachel, going down
to New Orleans for a holiday or up to Natchez
to visit. She had been a child then and had run
everywhere on the boat, inspecting gangways
and stairs and ogling the scenes painted on all
the stateroom doors.

Aunt Caroline had always been right behind,
afraid she would fall off the keel or get in the
way of the roustabouts who tended the boilers.
Then the *River Belle* had been the fastest boat on
the Mississippi, with the coveted deer horns
hung at its stern to prove it. Those days were
gone, but many a boat had been lost during the
war, and at least the *River Belle* was a survivor.
Susannah started up the gangplank, her ticket
pinned safely in her valise. Since she had come
so late, she imagined the staterooms had all
been assigned. She would have to travel as a
deck passenger with crude accommodations below the boiler deck on the main deck, next to
the kitchens and the machinery. But she hardly
cared.

Several people stared at her as she came
aboard, and she realized she was disheveled
from her ride and not dressed for the occasion.
Down a gangway, next to the paddlebox, she
found a ladies' lavatory and went inside to repair her hair and change into a brown delaine
skirt with double box pleats and a round-waisted
bodice of blue shot silk, worn with a broad red

velvet belt. It was a smart outfit, sewn by Mrs. St. John from some outdated garments, meant for Susannah's wedding trip with Cort, practical and elegant at the same time, and as the latest mode decreed, needing only petticoats beneath it. She changed her Wellington boots for silk slippers and added her necklace to look dressed for a soiree. In case someone should come looking for a woman who had just shot a man, she didn't want to look the part.

She stowed the valise in a utility room near the entrance to the ladies' cabin. Perhaps if the festivities went on all night, she would wait until morning to present her ticket and have her quarters assigned. It would be safer that way. Then the steward could not point out to Union soldiers a lady who had arrived late and alone.

Violins were playing inside the main cabin, and champagne was being served by black waiters dressed in crisp white jackets. Platters of fruit, cheese, and jelly cake were laid on a shining oak table. She accepted a glass of the champagne and drank it in a gulp, shuddering at the sudden stinging warmth it made inside her.

It was oddly fortifying, and she allowed the next waiter to refill her glass. The food reminded her that she ought to be hungry, but she wasn't, and nobody had ever bothered to tell Susannah about the effect of alcohol on an empty stomach. She finished the second glass almost as quickly as the first, noticing that the crystal chandeliers seemed brighter, the gilt of the French mirrors more golden, and the aroma of roses and asters in Tucker porcelain vases sweeter.

Men in velvet-collared dress coats were waltz-
ing with happy, fashionably gowned women,
and it seemed strange to Susannah to see so
many men not in uniform of either color. In one
corner of the salon a group of women was clustered around one of the men, and she let her
gaze rest there, wondering who he could be.
Then, as the gathering shifted, she caught sight
of a familiar head of dark hair.

The Marquez da Silva!

It wasn't so much that she recognized Antonio Andrada physically, for surely many men
must bear close resemblance from the back. But
her heart knew and started to pound. He had
about him that certain aura of excitement that
defied rational definition. Her eyes might tell
her it could be anyone, but her more subtle
senses knew it could only be he.

Susannah unwisely reached for a third glass
of champagne, glad to have something to seem
to be occupied with, as he turned and saw her.
His glance swept up and down her body like a
hot wind, making her feel as though she were
blushing from head to toe. As usual his eyes
were impassive; she looked in vain for the spark
of admiration that ought to be there, and was
furious at herself for wanting to find it.

He moved away from the group surrounding
him, excusing himself to those on both sides of
him as he came toward her. The envy on the
faces of the women left behind made up somewhat for the marquess's lack of expressiveness.
Just to attrack his notice, to be singled out by
him was enough to make the others jealous.

"Susannah!"

"Hello, Antonio. You should not let me interrupt your conversation. The ladies seem disappointed."

He grimaced. "Oh, they are a tiresome bunch. I heard about the raid on the Irving Block. Major St. John made an inspired attempt. Is your sister safe now?"

"Yes. The Yankees released her. I've had no opportunity to thank you for your help, Antonio."

His eyes seemed to laugh at her, and she was embarrassed to remember how she had tried to captivate him into doing her errand and how easily he had avoided her trap and turned the tables on her instead with his kiss. She had no more than taken the first step toward Brazil, and already she was face to face with the man she dreaded more than the country's wild Indians.

"I thought you weren't to be in Memphis again," she said accusingly.

"I'm only passing through. I'm on my way to New Orleans for the last time. The ship will be ready to leave for Brazil soon after I arrive. And what of you? Have you decided to leave your Robin Hill and come to Brazil too?"

"What an idea! A woman alone? Of course not. I'm merely going to New Orleans to visit friends." The lie came out before she thought. He would have to know the truth before long, and she wondered why she hadn't told him. She supposed she didn't want him to have the pleasure of gloating over her going to Brazil after all her resentment of his endeavor.

"I had thought of riding out to Robin Hill tonight to tell you good-bye," he admitted.

"Well, then, why didn't you?"

He shrugged. "What is the point of telling a

woman good-bye when it is forever?" he said.
"They are playing the 'Southern Rose Waltz,'
Susannah. Will you do me the honor? We have
never danced, you know."

She could not refuse; and though a part of
her told her she should, she floated into his
arms, giddy with champagne and with his
presence.

She forgot everything as they danced: the
inert body of Sam Spangler bleeding onto the
floor at Robin Hill seemed like a distant dream;
and Cort St. John, waiting in New Orleans. The
commanding touch of Antonio's hand against
her waist guided her as though she were a part
of him, and her ungloved hand clasped to his
seemed enveloped in a masculine strength that
was more than mere physical power. Leaning
too close, she felt the warmth of his breath in
her hair, a soft pressure that might almost have
been a kiss. She closed her eyes so that the
noise of the salon became a muted hubbub, and
all was shut from her consciousness but him
and the music.

She wanted it never to end, but the last chords
were played, and the dancers separated and
applauded politely. Reluctantly she parted from
him; and then, as the room came back into
focus, she caught sight of half a dozen blue
uniforms near the entrance. They had not been
there before! Without a word to Antonio, Susannah fled for the opposite door.

Once outside, she was out of their sight, but
far from safe. In fact, she might have done
better to remain in the salon, where she might
not have been recognized. Had her exit been
noticed? Where could she hide? She hurried

from the promenade to a gangway, where she tried the door of the laundry and found it locked. The next door was a barber shop, where a man was getting a shave, then the post office. The sound of footsteps came behind her on the front promenade, more than one man, hurrying.

Susannah ran on, the champagne clouding her judgment. Perhaps she could reach the storeroom where she had left her valise. But she heard footsteps coming from that direction too. She ran down to the main deck, among the boilers and machinery, the two great engines that turned the paddle wheels. Someone saw her and gave a cry. There were many places to hide, but Susannah couldn't decide on a safe one. With only a moment to spare, she jumped overboard from the shallow keel.

The muddy water closed over her head and cleared her senses. Groping through the dark water for the boat's hull, she surfaced deep in its shadow, near the paddle wheel. She grabbed it and held on, trying to keep from splashing.

The soldiers had heard the sound of her jump, and now they were peering over, calling to each other, trying to see her. "She couldn't have drowned already," one said.

"It must have been something else. She threw something overboard to fool us," another suggested. Susannah only wished it were so.

"Keep looking. Maybe she's still holding her breath under water."

"Let's search the deck. If she jumped, the guards will catch her when she tries to swim to shore."

There were sounds of agreement, and the voices grew more distant, but Susannah knew she was trapped. She could not hope to climb back onto the boat; and although the shore was only a few yards away, she could make out the forms of soldiers. They had not been alert enough to notice her jump; they were only watching the gangplank, observing everyone who left the boat. But she couldn't risk trying to swim in under their noses. She would be in the open, and if she discarded the petticoats that could drag her down, wouldn't they perhaps float ahead of her and give her away?

Teeth chattering, she clung to her perch. If she waited, they might all leave. But then how was she to get to New Orleans? Everything she had, including her ticket, was in the valise on the boat.

Footsteps came along the promenade again. They were coming back. But this time it was only one man. Susannah tried not to breathe. Maybe it wasn't a soldier. Maybe it was only a gentleman passenger who'd stepped out for a smoke. A rope dropped into the water beside her. She was so startled she lost her grip on the paddle wheel and floundered noisily to regain it.

"Be quiet, Susannah, and take hold of the rope," came an impatient voice from above. "They'll be back soon, and they'll hardly think I'm fishing with it."

Antonio! Why was it that *he* was always witness to her dilemmas? She seized the rope, and he hauled her over the side, catching her beneath her arms and helping her to scramble over. Susannah's terror of the soldiers was submerged for an instant in mortification at the ungainly sight she made, clambering aboard like an errant crayfish, her hair and clothes dripping, her silk shoes gone from her feet, floating somewhere in the river.

"I saw you from the hurricane deck," he said. "What have you done now, my little mermaid? Never mind, there's no time."

They could hear the soldiers, having circled the deck, returning from the opposite direction. Fear immobilized her chilled body. He had yanked her from the river to her doom! If she were to be dragged to prison, why must he be here to watch?

Antonio jerked open a door and shoved her inside a dark closet smelling of tar and oil. Boots squeaked and swords rattled in their scabbards as the Yankees stopped outside. Through the keyhole she could see that Antonio had lighted a cigar and was leaning on the rail.

"Have you seen a girl run by here?" one asked him. "Pretty, with sort of red-brown hair?"

"A girl? I certainly have. Only her hair was darker than that. Chestnut, I think. One could hardly tell under her mobcap. Pretty? Well, maybe, but she had the grace of a cow. She was carrying a bucket of water to mop the kitchen and spilled it everywhere. Look, it's all over my jacket. Do you know her name? I want to complain to the captain about her. I expect she'll be back soon with another bucket, if you dare to take your chances getting your clothes ruined."

The soldiers moved off muttering, glancing at the closet but not bothering to check it. Antonio let himself inside.

"Oh, thank you," she murmured gratefully.

"Save your breath, Susannah," he said tersely. "You're not safe yet."

"No. They'll be back. They'll think about the water again. They'll check next time. It's hopeless."

"Hopeless? It's out of character for you to say anything is hopeless, Susannah. How you fought for your cause! And how you hated me for knowing it was lost. Don't give up now."

"But you were right. Everything *is* lost, Antonio. There's nothing left to fight for. Nothing at all."

"This behavior is not appealing, Susannah," he said.

"I didn't think you found me appealing in any case," she replied huffily.

"That's better. A little spirit. Take off your petticoats."

"What!"

"Take them off. Otherwise we will have a trail of water straight to my cabin."

"To your cabin! Is that where we are going?"

"Hurry up!"

"Then turn your back."

"That's silly; it's pitch dark in here."

"Just do it."

He obeyed with a groan, while she divested herself of the dripping garments. Opening the door, he couldn't help smiling as he surveyed her, the delaine skirt now clinging as closely to her hips and thighs as the silk bodice was molded wetly to her breasts. Taking hold of the skirt, he wrung it out in his hands, twisting it so strongly she was nearly thrown off balance.

"That may do for a while," he said, "but nothing is so suited to holding water as a woman's clothes. Come on, now, before you start to drip again."

He checked the stairway and the gangway that ran between the stateroom and the big wheel box. Then, pulling her along the corridor after him, he took a key out of his pocket and opened his cabin door. She rushed inside without a thought for the intimacy of a man's bedchamber.

"Now! Take off the skirt. Take off everything."

"Everything! Are you insane? Of course I won't!"

"You certainly will! They will check the staterooms, if your crime is heinous enough to warrant it. What *was* your offense?"

"I shot a man."

"A Union officer, I presume."

"Colonel Spangler—Captain, I mean."

"Ah. Is he dead?"

She shuddered. "Probably."

"Demoted because of you, and now dead too. Well, when a man falls in love with a vixen like you, he shouldn't expect better. You wouldn't ever love a man without extracting your pound of flesh. You can undress behind that screen, Susannah. Quit dawdling! I cannot hide a woman in soaking clothes. Besides, you'll catch pneumonia."

She stepped behind the screen. "I have nothing to put on," she said.

He reached into a portmaneau and tossed a Turkish dressing gown over the screen. Naked, she tried to cover herself with the flimsy silk, finding it inadequate, with its broad rolling collar running to the waist and its wide sleeves so long that she could hardly get her hands free to try to cinch up the drawstring, which ended in large red tassels. She could not possibly show herself to him wearing it, but his voice told her he would brook no delay.

"Susannah!"

She crept out, blushing, trying to hold the robe together over her breasts. The very touch of the fabric on her skin seemed too intimate, and the faint aroma of his shaving soap clinging to it made her head swim.

"That will do quite well," he said sternly. "There's only your hair left to dry." He began to pull out the pins himself, running his fingers through her tresses to shake out the water. His touch was brisk, but still delicious. Maybe he did not mean it as a caress, but she began to tingle with a peculiar warmth. Antonio toweled her hair, and handing her a hairbrush, stood back to view the effect. "You look a bit tousled and a little anxious, but that will suit." He yanked down the covers on the low-post cherrywood bed. "Get in," he told her.

"I beg your pardon!" she cried in outrage. "You may have seen me at Rudd Sloane's gaming house, but no man can command me into his bed. Not even you!"

Antonio's dark eyes flashed with amusement. "You are going to get into bed, Susannah. Did you protest so with Sam Spangler? Or did you find that Yankee so much more attractive than I?"

"Oh!" She reached out to strike him, and had to retreat. The dressing gown had fallen open; and she had succeeded, not in punishing him for his audacious behavior, but in giving him a look at the creamy globes of her breasts.

"Get into bed, Susannah. Don't be such a ninny. It's the only way to save your life."

"You mean otherwise you will throw me out to be caught by the soldiers! I would sooner die than be saved that way!" Susannah broke off at the sound of pounding on some door down the corridor.

"It's your choice," he told her. "They're coming."

The knocking moved closer, and Susannah, overcome by panic, dived into the bed, pulling the covers tightly around her chin.

"Good," he said. "Now, throw out the dressing gown."

"Are you never satisfied? I will not!"

"Then I will come and take it. I need it, Susannah." He paused and considered, his hand pulling at the narrow bow of his string tie. He jerked it off and tossed it carelessly on the floor.

"What are you doing?" she hissed. The soldiers were beating on Antonio's door now, but he showed no inclination to answer it. His eyes burned into hers as he unfastened his fashionable open-behind pleated shirt and let it slide down his arms. With a lazy movement he discarded that, too, and was half-naked before her.

His massive tawny chest, as smoothly muscled as that of a jaguar, was adorned with an impressive mass of dark, springy hair. She had never viewed a man so nearly unclothed before, and the sight unnerved her almost as much as the insistent pounding on the door. Her heart was beating so hard she could scarcely separate it from the sound of the soldiers, and she hardly knew whether it was they or Antonio that caused its wild thudding. Why should it surprise her that he reminded her of a jungle animal? Hadn't he sprung from the untamed Amazon forests?

And like a beast of his native element, might he not be as savage when aroused?

He moved toward the bed, his eyes gleaming with feral light; and with a cry, she wriggled free of the dressing gown and threw it out to appease him.

"Ah, that's better, Miss Susannah. Now you have nothing more to do than to lie there and look frightened. That should not be hard."

It would have been difficult for Susannah to do anything else. She pulled the covers up to her chin and trembled, watching him don the dressing gown she had worn so recently that it must still be warm from her body. He gave a faint sigh, as though that warmth might have affected him, but he seemed totally in control, unperturbed either by her in his bed or by the soldiers at the door.

Flipping the tasseled sash into a knot, he flung open the door. "What is the meaning of this outrage!" he bellowed. "I will not have my privacy so rudely violated! I'll complain to the steward! I'll complain to the captain!"

The scene was familiar to Susannah, reminding her of the times the soldiers had come to Mrs. St. John's house, first looking for the gray cloak, and later looking for Cort. Like a recurring nightmare, she remembered Colonel Spangler bursting into her bedroom, accosting her in her bed. What would happen now? Memphis wisdom had been that it paid to be polite to Union soldiers; how dare Antonio be so audacious? She stuffed her fist into her mouth to prevent herself from screaming.

But his verbal assault seemed to have a beneficial effect. The sergeant in charge took off his hat. "I apologize, but we are looking for a traitor on this boat—a woman who shot a Union officer."

"Humph! A woman, eh? So you Americans are afraid of your women. Well, there's no woman here except my wife, and this is our wedding night. So kindly leave us in peace."

The sergeant glanced past Antonio and saw Susannah. His face reddened with embarrassment. "I beg your pardon, sir. We did not know—"

"Such incompetence! You barge in everywhere without asking. In my country even the savages have better manners! The captain would surely have told you not to bother the Marquez da Silva and his bride!"

The sergeant was clicking his heels and bowing, muttering protestations and apologies as he backed away. Antonio, still irate, started to close the door.

"Sir!" cried one of the soldiers, peering at Susannah. "That's the one!"

The sergeant whirled to stare at the soldier's earnest face.

"I'm sure of it. The light's poor, and I've never seen her with her hair down, but she's the one! I was with Captain Spangler more than once when he went to Robin Hill, and I know her!"

The sergeant's expression changed, transmuting from discomfiture to anger as he thrust his boot into the door. "Is that woman Susannah Dunbar?" he demanded.

Susannah's breath stopped as she waited for Antonio's answer.

"She is my wife, and that is all you need

know," he replied with equal ire. "Who she was before her marriage is of no consequence. In this country I am the official guest of President Lincoln and have diplomatic protection. How will it look if you drag my wife away to prison in the middle of the night? She may have been Miss Susannah Dunbar, but now she is the Marqueza da Silva, and any harm to her will create an international incident. The Emperor Dom Pedro will hear about it. Your superiors will not be pleased to be put on the spot, especially when it's shown that Miss Dunbar was provoked into shooting the officer. Be gone, if you value those stripes on your sleeve!"

The sergeant hesitated, intimidated, but suspicious. "Perhaps she's not your wife. Perhaps she's only your paramour. I'll not be made a fool, even by a marquess. Show the marriage certificate."

"Bah! Your insolence is beyond belief. You dare to demand papers at a time like this? I will not be treated this way! Do you suppose I keep my marriage certificate under my pillow? It's with my valuables in the ship's safe. I'll have it for you in the morning, not before! Now, get out! I have better things to do than waste my whole night on you!"

Antonio gave the sergeant's boot a swift kick that knocked it away from the door; and with a force that rattled the mirror and the gas lamp on the wall, he swung the door closed. For a moment he stood waiting, looking fierce; but no one beat on the door.

"They have accepted my terms, it seems," he observed, locking it. "They'll be watching the cabin, of course. A fine mess you've got me into. I suppose it's not even true that you were provoked into shooting Captain Spangler."

"Certainly I was!"

"He forced himself on you?"

"Not exactly. But he'd bought Robin Hill for the taxes, and he wanted me to marry him and . . ."

Antonio sat down on the bed wearily. "You mean he wanted to save your home for you and take care of you?"

"Yes, I guess—"

"You shot him for that. Well, my lady, I can see that the way out of this is not for me to marry you. I would most likely meet a similar fate for my efforts."

"It was an accident, but I wouldn't marry you even to save myself from prison or the hangman's rope," she said bravely.

"Then we are agreed on one thing at least. But we need a plan—"

"Have you a trunk? I could get into it and—"

"Be carried out? That's too old a trick, Susannah. Surely you've something newer in your bag of dupery."

"I . . ." Susannah began, and then forgot her jumble of thoughts. He was so close to her, and she was so aware of her own nakedness beneath the covers and his state of undress. A peculiar clutch in the pit of her stomach alarmed her, shooting tingling sensations down to her toes and upward to her trembling breasts. She tried to pull the covers more closely around her, but in the process her thigh grazed Antonio's; and as if by instinct, he stroked the part of her that had touched him. Even though the covers were between them, the caress made her weak and giddy. Could it still be the champagne she had drunk earlier? The dive into the river had cleared her head, but was it possible to become intoxicated twice from the same champagne? He stroked her cheek gently, turned up her chin, and drew her mouth against his, kissing her deeply; but as he pulled back, she saw that his eyes were not full of tenderness, but an angry lust.

"What a temptress you are, Susannah," he said. "How many men will you lure to their downfall before you're done? You'll drive them to madness and never love any of them; but why, after all, should I not enjoy you? Why shouldn't I have the same privileges as Sam Spangler? And how can I concentrate on a plan to save you, when you befuddle me?"

He tugged covers down to her waist. Susannah gave a shocked cry, but there was no time to protest before he slid down beside her. Holding her to his chest, he ran his hands over her body with the precision of a sculptor shaping his work. She shivered against him, no longer thinking of objecting; she could not. Her will had vanished into his, and she felt she had ceased to exist for anything except to savor the currents of exquisite pleasure that shot from him to her.

She heard a soft sound as he loosened the strap and buckle at the back of his trousers. Then came the sigh of dropping cloth. The covers lifted, letting in a cool breeze over her lower body, and closed over her again. The heat of his excitement pressed against her loins.

"Antonio . . ." She meant it for an objection, but instead it came out rapturously. His name hung in the air, the most beautiful word she had ever heard. Her cry seemed to spur him on. He ducked his head and kissed her smooth stomach, and then moved lower to her quivering thighs. She moaned helplessly and tangled her hands in his hair the way she used to twist them in Sultan's mane to keep from falling during a wild, swift ride.

Cort crossed her mind fleetingly. She knew that what was about to happen was the sacred act that should have been saved for her wedding night. Dear God, it was all *his* fault. She could not prevent it, and even with her passion rampant, a part of her cursed him for rendering her helpless.

His lips returned to her breasts, and she moaned, as all of her body he was not touching ached and screamed, jealous for his attention. A strange pressure came between her thighs, and suddenly she cried out in pain. The pain was over quickly, but she thought that she might have been mortally wounded and had traveled into another existence, for never in her old one had she experienced sensations of such ecstasy.

She had no choice but to cling to him while her body responded in ways she had never taught it. Finally another cry tore from her throat, but it was as different from the first as night from day, a ragged gasp of unbearable pleasure, a moan of deliverance.

The flame of her need sank to a sweet glow, and then the embers slowly faded, like coals from a dying fire. Reality became what it had been before. She struggled away from Antonio, who lay spent across her. Sobbing, she pushed him away.

The bed shifted as he left it. "My God, Susannah, why didn't you tell me? Why didn't you say something before?"

"I did!" she shrieked. "I told you from the very first, but you have always believed something else!"

"And you have shown me I was wrong. What sort of she-devil are you, Susannah? You bring out the beast in a man! To think that I, Antonio Andrada, could not recognize a virgin! But even in bed you were not what I'd expect a virgin to be. I swear I wouldn't believe it if the proof were not there on the sheets. But you are always full of surprises."

"You are trying to say I planned it?" she screamed. "Oh, I thought you despicable, but you are doubly despicable!" She was struck by the similarity to what Sam Spangler had said, that she had turned him into a beast, but at least Sam Spangler hadn't violated her.

Overwhelmed by despair, she gave herself over to her weeping, and at last, exhausted, slept.

9

She wanted to sleep forever. In her dreams she could return to Robin Hill, envisioning herself as Cort's bride, greeting her reception guests amid the summer roses with Rachel beside her. In her dreams there was no stain of blood on the oak floor of the study where Sam Spangler had fallen, no smaller stain on the bedsheets where she had lost her innocence.

In her sleep she waltzed with Cort in the white wedding gown she was no longer entitled to wear, but at last a weak gray light filtering through the window awakened her. For a moment she could not remember where she was, could not understand why the movement of the waltz seemed to continue even after the dream was over. Then she recognized the familiar roll of the river. They had left Memphis! Beyond the window, heavy morning fog blotted the view.

She remembered her need to escape. The fog could be a friend. But how? Starting to leap out of bed, she rediscovered her nakedness and blushed in shame at the memory of what had happened. Where was Antonio? He was wise to make himself scarce. She would punish him somehow for what he had done!

But perhaps he'd left the boat last night. Not wanting to share his cabin with a woman afoul of the law, he'd left her to fend for herself! Angry tears filled her eyes. He was an unspeakable cad to leave her, and what was worse, she would never be able to give him his due!

Gathering the covers around her, she crossed to the window and peeked out. On the promenade a blue-coated soldier, looking miserable in the chilly dawn, leaned against the rail, holding a coffee mug. Susannah noticed his eyes dart toward her as she closed the opening in the curtains. Bending to the keyhole, she checked the corridor. As she had expected, a soldier was on guard there, too. She could think of no means of escape.

Hoping providence would guide her, she washed from a pitcher and bowl on the washstand and dressed herself in clothes that were now only slightly damp. However she was to make her escape, she could not accomplish it naked; but nothing occurred to her. Her mind was a void of despair. Numbly she answered a knock on the door.

"Good morning, Marqueza." The sergeant's

salute came with a smirk. "Has your husband found the papers we require?"

"He's gone out. I imagine he will have them when he comes back."

"He's gone to get them?"

"Yes, I'm sure he has," she found herself saying. "The marquess told you he keeps all his important records in the safe. He cannot afford to be careless with documents for the emperor."

"We shall see how careless he is with his marriage certificate," the sergeant said with a smirk. "I won't wait much longer. And don't try any tricks. We're watching you, *Marqueza!*"

Momentarily defiant, Susannah slammed the door in his face, but she knew her position was hopeless. Antonio was definitely gone, she decided, looking over the room. Nothing that belonged to him remained, and now she hadn't even a pretend husband. But how would that have helped anyway, without the marriage document?

Susannah's eye lighted on one thing Antonio had left behind, a straight razor on the washstand. Had he forgotten it, or had he left it there on purpose to give her at least one alternative to the hangman's rope?

Whatever his intention, Susannah decided to make use of the razor. Picking it up, she tested its edge and drew blood along her fingers. She stared as the cut dripped onto her skirt. The razor was so keen that he must have just stropped it. Gritting her teeth, she pushed up her sleeve and put the razor across her wrist like a violinist readying his bow—for a finale, she thought, the finale of her life. But she must do it quickly and unhesitatingly. To outwit the

Yankees this last time, she must not botch the job.

A knock came again, softly. Susannah's heart beat more rapidly. Not a moment to lose now, no time for indecision. She closed her eyes and drew the blade down over her wrist.

But somehow the blade wouldn't move. She shrieked in fury at the Yankee who had got into the room and who held her about the waist, staying her hand.

"Susannah! What in God's name are you doing?"

Anotnio's voice. Antonio's powerful arm around her. She struggled as he twisted the razor away. "I don't want to be taken alive, Antonio," she begged.

"Better not to be taken at all," he replied blandly.

"I thought you'd gone," she whispered, leaning against him.

"Gone? Where would I go? Come along, now, what you need is a good breakfast."

"Breakfast! How can you think of food?" she said with a moan. "What am I to do, Antonio?"

"Eat. Even Rebels have to eat."

"You're giving the condemned woman one last meal. Will that ease your conscience when you turn me over to them?"

She let him guide her out of the stateroom past the guard to the dining room. The Union guard followed at a respectful distance.

"Please order," he said. "No, better I order for you. You'll have date muffins with currant jelly, a fruit compote, and tea. Hmm . . . I think I had better order rum in your tea. You need fortification. I have a plan, of course."

Her heart lifted. Had he ever let her down? "What plan?" she asked.

"You'll see. It can't fail, but it will do better if you don't know yet."

"Where have you been, Antonio?" she persisted. "What have you done with your luggage?"

Antonio merely smiled, so smug and self-satisfied that she became angry at him all over again and wanted to hurl the silverware at him as he began to consume an enormous meal of griddle cakes and ham, washed down with strong black coffee.

As the fog burned off and sunlight poured over the river, he glanced at her now and then, his dark eyes so intimately expressive she felt she had never dressed at all this morning, but was still as naked as when he'd so dishonorably used her. Oh, he was worse than the Yankees, she thought, quivering so much she could hardly lift her cup.

"Antonio, time is running out. They have demanded the marriage certificate already this morning."

"What did you tell them?"

"I said it was in the safe in the captain's cabin."

"Good."

"But it isn't!" she exclaimed, exasperated.

"The strawberries look delicious, Susannah. You had better eat; you'll need your strength. And try to act like a loving bride. The Yankees will think we're having a lovers' quarrel."

Susannah did his bidding and ate the strawberries, though she barely tasted them.

"Now the muffin, Susannah."

"I cannot!"

"Well, I'll have another helping of potatoes, I think. I'll need my strength, too."

Angry and frightened, she waited until he was done, and throwing down his napkin, came around to pull out her chair.

"We've something to attend to," he said, offering her his arm. He led her up to the hurricane deck, and then up more steps to the wheelhouse. She had never been in the pilot's cabin before, and the high, wide view of the river through its glass front left her breathless, but not so breathless as she soon would be.

"Ah, the marquess." Turning the steering over to an assistant, the captain greeted Antonio.

"This is the lady I told you about," Antonio said. "We'll be grateful for your help."

"Delighted, sir. Now, if you would stand over there—I haven't had much call for this, but I do keep a Bible up here, not a bad thing to have—a bit of God's help on this snag-infested river."

What had a Bible to do with Antonio's plan? Susannah wondered. Then the captain began to recite the familiar words: "We are gathered here to unite this man and this woman . . ."

Why, she was at her own wedding, and hadn't even known it! Who could believe that such a thing could happen to a woman? He meant to marry her!

The realization astounded her, setting off giddy shock waves of pleasure. Quickly she squelched her peculiar happiness. How dared he! How dared he bring her here this way to marry her without even asking her! What utter conceit! Did he intend this as a magnificent surprise? Did he expect her to fall into his arms in gratitude? The magnanimous Marquez da Silva, stooping to save her! She would not be humiliated this way! She ought to have finished the business with his razor before he'd found her, and she would sooner surrender herself to her pursuers than to him!

She tried to catch his eye, to let him know her feelings, but he wasn't looking at her. He was looking straight ahead at the captain as he intoned, "I, Antonio Andrada, take Susannah Dunbar to be my wedded wife . . ."

Oh, he did, did he? His face was going to be very red when *she* refused to take *him*! She waited impatiently for her turn, to put an end to this travesty. But as the captain asked for her vows, Antonio turned to her, and the memory of all that had happened the night before was in his eyes. Suddenly she could think of nothing else except his kisses, his caresses; and there was nothing on earth she would not have done to experience them again. "I, Susannah Dunbar . . ." The words were on her lips, and then his lips were on hers, kissing her with the masterfulness of ownership.

They were husband and wife, though she had not intended it. The captain, congratulating Antonio, wished her happiness. The needed document in Antonio's grip, they descended to the main deck, where Antonio paused to offer it to the Yankee sergeant. The soldier saluted as he handed it back, and Antonio flashed Susannah a triumphant smile. She wondered where he was taking her now, but she had learned he would tell her no more than he wished. She would only give him the satisfaction of her curiosity. She was subject to his whim and would be for the rest of her life, she reflected bitterly, as they strolled past staterooms with curtains still closed against the early-morning sun. He had done the noble thing, and no doubt he would never allow her to forget the sacrifice he'd made. He'd expect her to pay for it forever.

At the boat's stern, Antonio stopped at a door, and kicking it open with his foot, lifted her in his arms and carried her through it. He accomplished the matter so effortlessly that she felt as though she had flown into the room, her cheek cradled against his collar, her head resting cozily against his chin.

The cabin was twice as large as the one they had had before, magnificently appointed with a mahogany Hepplewhite sofa with satinwood inlay, a bed with an arched tester, and a crested Queen Anne mirror. The air was filled with the scent of roses from bouquets in three silver vases on little bead-edged pier tables, red and white blossoms mixed, their images from the mirror giving the impression of an entire bank of flowers.

"The bridal suite, my dear," Antonio said, setting her on her feet. "I moved here this morning and bribed the steward for the roses that were supposed to be for the dining room tonight. They serve much better here than there."

He stood smiling, waiting for her approval, but Susannah, fighting the spell of his presence and the beautiful room, seated herself huffily on the sofa and folded her hands in her lap.

Antonio scowled. "Have you nothing to say at all, Susannah? Some men appreciate silence in a wife, but I require a bit of conversation. We might as well make the best of it, you know.

Neither of us had any choice. I am aware that you would not have married me except that your life depended on it, and I could not in conscience do otherwise, especially after the wrong I did you last night."

"I suppose you think you've turned that to a right by making me your wife. Well, it will not happen again, sir!"

Fury flamed on his aristocratic face. "Indeed it will, Susannah. It will happen whenever I wish it to happen. I have appetites, and it is your duty to satisfy them."

"You lout! Doesn't it bother you at all, having a wife who was forced to marry you?"

He shrugged. "Madam, if anyone should feel guilty, it's you. It was *you* who put me in the position of having to rescue you, and the mistake I made last night was partly *your* fault as well. But in my country women do not choose their husband. Even the men marry for convenience. I am quite satisfied, Susannah. You are a troublesome woman, but you don't bore me. That is important when home is as much a wilderness as the Kiss Flower. And you are not mollycoddled like most women. You managed to live at Robin Hill under circumstances that would have undone many. You're resourceful, even if I cannot approve some of your methods. That will serve well where we're going. There will be much to overcome that an ordinary woman couldn't handle. You are wellborn, and have the necessary social graces for life at court, and your appearance is pleasant to the eye. It will work out very satisfactorily, Susannah, if you make the best of it, too, and do not dispute my authority. Life on the Kiss Flower will be far more pleasant than prison or hanging."

"Oh! So you've sized me up like . . . like a horse and decided I will serve your purpose! If I had not met the qualifications, you would have tossed me to the Yankees! What if I am not a docile mare, easy to catch and bridle? What will you do then?"

"Why, I'll teach you manners, Marqueza!" With that he seized her, and pulling her toward the bed, threw her onto it. She struggled to rise, but it was a deep feather bed and difficult to escape. Then his lips were on hers, and the endeavor became impossible, for she had herself as well as him to fight. His hand was on the buttons of her bodice, and she knew that in a moment it would be inside, exploring the warm, secret nooks of her body. His touch was like a drug that put her will to sleep, and her body, freed from all restraints but its own longings, moved in harmony with his, savoring the sweet rhythm of his desire as he took her.

Later, when he slept beside her, she remained within his embrace, telling herself that the only reason she did so was that by moving she might awake him and inflame him again. It was not to feel the smooth strength of his chest that she remained, nor to study his face, so classic and unguarded in repose, not to touch his lips and eyebrows with her fingertips, as though he were a new and treasured gift she had received.

During the afternoon, Antonio said he had some business to attend to and retired to the gentlemen's lounge. Susannah retrieved her valise and sent her delaine skirt and silk bodice to be laundered. She bathed in a tub located with a washbasin in a separate area of the bridal compartment and marveled at the hot water, heated in the ship's boilers, piped directly to the tub.

As she bathed, she was aware of her body in a new way, noticing its sensuous curves and roundings that had given Antonio such pleasure. Though she did not want to admit it the mere thought of his lovemaking made her ache to have it again. But it wasn't *she* that wanted it; it was only her mindless flesh, unleashed with no sense of anything but its own lusty need. Her body had played traitor, conspiring with Antonio to hold her in bondage. Antonio, who had wed her without courtship, with no more contemplation than he might put into buying a serviceable suit of clothes!

Serviceable! Yes, that was the word. He thought her serviceable. She would be serviceable on his plantation, at functions of court, and especially in his bed. She must regain control, now that the Union soldiers had disembarked at the *River Belle*'s first stop.

Beyond that, she could not bring herself to think what the future held. Even two days from now was too far, too impossible to consider— two days from now when the *River Belle* would dock at New Orleans and would likely be met by Cort St. John. Dear Cort, whom she should have married; Cort, who loved her, worshiped her, as a man should.

She tried to picture him, but his features whirled in the hurricane of her mind. Still trying to lay some sort of plan, Susannah dressed for dinner in a sea-green bodice of glacé silk, with gabrielle sleeves of puffs from shoulder to wrist, and a striped skirt with a scalloped hem. She had already almost exhausted the clothing she had been able to stuff into the one valise. In the very bottom she found the hat Antonio had given her, crushed by the weight of things thrown over it, but restorable. Rachel must have put that in; she had always admired it. Her heart ached as she thought of her sister. She would have to find some way to send word to her that she had escaped. But when would they ever see each other again?

In the rosewood-paneled dining room, Antonio ordered a meal of loin of veal with truffles and fresh vegetables and one of the two dozen red wines the ship carried. For dessert they chose white-raisin pudding à la Windsor with vanilla sauce, which was a favorite of Susannah's from childhood. But Susannah was a child no longer. Her childhood and her girlish innocence were gone. She knew as she waltzed the night away with Antonio how the evening would end. The knowledge made the music seem more brilliant, and every pressure of his hand at her waist sent rays of warmth along her spine and colored her cheeks, as though traveling the stem of a rose to its blossom.

Past midnight he handed her the key to their stateroom. "I'll have a glass of sherry in the gentlemen's lounge and then be along, Susannah," he told her. She knew what he was telling her: go and prepare herself, not to sleep, but for him!

She let herself into the suite and turned up the lamp, her heart beating rapidly. He was going to have his way with her just as he had last night and again this morning. So much had happened in only twenty-four hours! But now she wasn't in danger from the Yankees, only from him.

Her valise yielded a nightdress, a sleeveless white batiste garment with a bit of embroidery about the simple scooped neck. Susannah stared at the demure little garment. It hardly characterized the sort of night she could expect to have with her husband. Her hand trembled on the fastenings of her bodice as she imagined how unprotected she would be in the thin gown, how easily the winds of passion could buffet her.

Susannah drew a deep breath and refastened the bodice. Things could not go on as they had! Grateful as she might be to have been saved from Yankee clutches, she would not accept this arrangement for the rest of her life. He expected to master her with this terrible power of his over her. She had been robbed of her rightful marriage and her rightful home. She mustn't allow him to steal her very self! She must thwart him and his diabolical scheme.

She crossed to the door and locked it firmly. He had only one key, and he had made the mistake of giving it to her. Susannah sat down to wait, her hands cold in her lap. In only a few minutes she heard his purposeful pace. He hadn't tarried long conversing with the men. He was eager for his marriage bed. He turned the knob and muttered in frustration.

"Susannah!" he called.

Her tongue seemed paralyzed. But perhaps it was easier not to answer. Let him think she had fallen asleep and didn't hear him.

"Susannah, open the door," he demanded, still only annoyed, not yet in a fury. She could answer now and not have to bear the brunt of his temper, but she did not move.

"I know you are not asleep," he whispered angrily, and she felt as though he could see through the door. Did he already know her so well? Stubbornly she did not reply. He blew a long breath of exasperation, and his footsteps went quickly away. She had won!

She lay down on the bed, feeling tired and relieved. It seemed too easy, but it only proved that even a man like Antonio could be bested by a woman with a bit of gumption. What, after all, had she expected him to do? Had she thought the Marquez da Silva would cause a scandal by breaking down the door to his bridal chamber? Sam Spangler might have, but Antonio was far too aristocratic for such coarse public behavior.

Sam Spangler—was he dead or alive? She had been so occupied she'd almost forgotten she might be a murderess as well as a bride! In spite of her feelings about Yankees, she knew he had not deserved to die and that it was her fault, not for pulling the trigger, but for having toyed with him so shamelessly.

Antonio knew these things about her; he had reprimanded her long ago. It was no wonder that he didn't love her, or that, in spite of her innocence on her wedding night, he thought her the sort of woman whose body could be taken without love. But she would teach him she would not jump to his salacious bidding!

Exhaustion overwhelmed her. Her dreams last night had been too vivid for rest. Now, at last, she found oblivion. She felt she had slept no more than a moment when she became aware of voices in the gangway and a key scraping in the lock. Struggling to awaken, she saw Antonio standing over the bed, rage burning on his face.

"How—?" she gasped.

"I asked the steward to let me in with a master key. I said you had fallen asleep and I didn't want to wake you. What a tender bridegroom I am, Susannah! So the steward thought. But you were only up to another of your tricks. You wanted to punish me for taking my rightful pleasure with you, by making me sleep with the deck passengers next to the boilers. No doubt you hoped for an explosion in the middle of the night that would make you a widow! I warned you not to cross me, Susannah!"

Antonio yanked the covers off rudely. "Why, you are not even dressed for bed," he said in surprise.

"I was too tired," she said feebly.

"I will fix it," he said sharply, beginning to undress her roughly.

She dropped her head into her hands and wept. She hadn't the strength to fight him. What good had it done before?

She was aware of being naked to the waist, then of her skirt being pulled away, and finally of pantaloons descending over her ankles. An involuntary sigh of appreciation escaped Antonio's lips; and through her misery, she felt a twinge of triumph at the effect she had on him. He hadn't undressed her like this before; he had been too busy savoring her charms to indulge in mere admiration of his acquisition. He ran his hands lightly over her quivering body, causing her to moan with anticipation of an ecstasy she did not feel strong enough to endure.

"Susannah," he said suddenly, "how old are you?"

A new tone in his voice made her look up. He was staring at her as though he were seeing her in some new and unexpected way. Did her nakedness make her so very different to him? "How old are you, Susannah?" he asked again.

"Nineteen."

"How very young you seem tonight. I hadn't realized how young nineteen really is. I am nearly fifteen years your senior."

"Nineteen is a woman, sir!" she declared.

He smiled ruefully. "So I can see. It was a long war, Susannah, but it's over; and I am not the enemy, nor ever was. I am only your husband. It's all right to stop fighting me."

He took her little nightdress, and pulling it on over her head, smiled at her appearance in the prewar garment Aunt Caroline had sewn for her when she was only fourteen. Undressing, he got into bed beside her and pulled her close to him. She felt his feathery kiss on her forehead and waited, shivering. But nothing else happened, and slowly relaxing against his solid warmth, she slept.

In the morning she opened her eyes to find him propped on his elbow watching her. When he saw she was awake, he kissed her, this time with undisguised meaning, on the lips. Drowsily she opened herself to him, as though it were still a part of her dream, her pleasure mounting cozily, her spirit seeming this time to unite with her body instead of being undone by it; and in the moment that followed the explosion of her release, she experienced a blissful serenity. It was some time before she remembered that she had been coerced into marriage and did not wish to be his wife.

10

IO

Cort St. John reminded Susannah of her predicament. She did not see him at first when the *River Belle* docked at New Orleans. There was so much to distract her: tugboats blowing up and down the chocolate water, the casks of sugar being loaded, the oozing bales of cotton, the baskets of crabs set out for sale, the fishy odors mingling in the salty wind with the aromas of coffee brought from South America and the fragrance of bananas and mangoes from the Indies. People swarmed. Black women in bright bandanas, selling pralines, voodoo dolls, or camellias, blended with Union soldiers and gaudy men traveling with their belongings in valises made of Persian-style carpeting.

But as she came down the gangplank on Antonio's arm, wearing the smart black hat he'd given her, she couldn't help seeing Cort. He'd seen her first and was pushing his way through the crowd, gesturing and waving, wild with joy, his features bursting with smiles. He thought, of course, that her arrival meant she had changed her mind and had come to New Orleans to marry him.

"Look, Susannah," Antonio told her. "There is someone I believe you know, Major St. John."

"We . . . grew up together," she said, barely able to speak. "I—"

But before she could tell him what she should have told him days ago, Cort was beside her and had taken her in his arms and kissed her.

"Major St. John, I see I have no need to present my wife," Antonio said wryly, a hint of warning in his tone.

Cort released her, looking as staggered as though he'd been hit by a salvo of enemy bullets. "Your . . . wife . . ."

She put her hand on his arm. "We were married on the *River Belle*, Cort," she told him. With her eyes she tried to tell him much more— that rightfully she was still his—but he seemed too stunned with grief to see.

"Please accompany us to our hotel, Major," Antonio was saying. "I want to hear how our arrangements are progressing."

Cort demurred, obviously loath to join them. "We'll talk later," he said.

"I insist," Antonio said. "We've no time to waste before our sailing date."

Antonio hailed a hansom cab and gave the driver the address of a hotel on Rue Royale. As they drove through the narrow cobbled streets,

Susannah noticed how profoundly the elegant Vieux Carré had been affected by the war. Ironwork was ripped from balconies; archways had been bricked up; courtyards lay in disrepair, the fountains broken, advertisements tacked over hand-forged gates. She saw the opera house, where her papa had once taken her to hear Adelina Patti sing, desolate and forlorn; but she kept looking out the window. Nothing she saw beyond the cab could be half so terrible as looking at Cort. But even without looking, she could feel the pain of his heartbroken gaze.

"Major St. John is to have the position of vice-president of the new colony, Susannah," Antonio told her. "It's an enormous responsibility, but I cannot imagine anyone better the colonists could have elected to the task. It will be nice for you to have an old friend there."

"Yes," Susannah said numbly. She knew Antonio could not have missed Cort's shock at the news of their marriage, but he was going to great lengths to ignore the matter. She wondered if her own misery were as apparent. Now that she was near Cort, she wondered how she could ever have betrayed him in Antonio's arms. Perhaps, after all, she was really the sort of woman Antonio had first taken her to be.

Their suite of rooms had a view of the river and a wrought-iron balcony in live-oak design, shaded by a mimosa. In the sitting room a fireplace with a mantel of black African marble and a big Empire sofa with lyre-shaped arms kept company with a pedestal drop-leaf table. This Antonio and Cort expanded and covered with maps and lists, which they poured over for hours, while drinking coffee laced with chickory from a silver pot over a warmer.

"How many passengers now, Major?" Antonio asked.

"Two hundred and five, and four of the women are with child."

"Has a doctor been engaged?"

"Yes, a surgeon from the Confederate Army who has cut out too many Yankee bullets to want to stay in the South. And here is the list of medical supplies we've acquired."

"And provisions? How much flour? Have we a cook yet? Have you assigned new grants of land since I've been away? Has the ship been inspected? We mustn't have overcrowding or a lack of sanitation. I do not intend my ship to turn into a floating house of pestilence. It will be difficult enough settling the river with healthy men. We'll be going to Rio first to pick up agricultural supplies. The emperor wishes to meet his American colonists. This is a project close to his heart. Any women who wish to wait in Rio until their husbands build houses may, or they may stay in Santarém near the colony." Antonio glanced in Susannah's direction. "Of course, my house is already habitable."

Susannah busied herself unpacking their clothing, hanging her things side by side with his in the rosewood armoire and trying not to think about the huge Creole Seignouret bed, so large whole families sometimes slept in one. She did not want to imagine what a sumptuous field of love it might make.

Unpacking for him was altogether too intimate, though it was silly to think it after how they had been together. But it was terribly personal to handle his witney lounge jacket, his Wellington boots, his shirts with their turned-down Shakespeare collars, and his pearl studs and narrow ties. It was the first wifely duty she had performed for him, and though she might have waited for a maid to do it, she needed to keep herself occupied.

Antonio ordered the hotel's finest meal, remarking that the quality of the cuisine hadn't suffered in the war, perhaps because the Yankee commander, whom the residents called Beast Butler, had enjoyed bringing his wife here to dine. The very mention of General Butler made Susannah's blood run cold, for his "Woman Order" was famous, decreeing that any woman who so much as made a gesture of contempt to the Yankees would be treated as a prostitute.

The superb trout amandine, served with a good Chablis from Burgundy and a green salad with crepes Suzette for dessert, did little for Susannah's appetite; Cort didn't seem hungry either. At last café brûlot arrived, fragrant with brandy and spices, blazing in a silver bowl. Pleading fatigue, Susannah excused herself, but as she took Cort's hand in farewell, she pressed a note into his palm. "Meet me in front of the cathedral tonight," it read. "I'll come as soon as he's asleep."

She undressed, placing her clothes where they would be easily available, and lay in the big bed looking at the stars above the river and the gold lights of Algiers beyond, listening to the voices of the two men in the next room—dear Cort, the husband she had been meant to have, and Antonio, who from the very first had always been her undoing. What cruel fate had made them partners?

The fine bed soothed her, and she drifted off to sleep, telling herself all the while she mustn't. She mustn't risk sleeping through the night and missing her assignation.

But she needn't have worried. Antonio roused her, dropping his shoes heavily as he prepared for bed. She knew he had done it on purpose— but what purpose? Was he going to assert his rights tonight of all nights?

"So, Susannah," he said, when he saw he had succeeded in waking her, "apparently a guilty conscience doesn't disturb your slumber."

"Why should my conscience be uneasy?" she asked in genuine surprise.

"Why, over Major St. John. Don't you think I realize what has happened? You were running away to marry him when you boarded the *River Belle*. You didn't bother to tell me you already had a fiancé when I married you. Oh, there is no end to your dissembling, Susannah! I will never be able to trust you."

"Oh!" Susannah crouched on her knees in the bed. "What difference would it have made? You were bound to have what you wanted even that very first night! You thought so little of securing my consent that you did not even see fit to inform me of your plan to marry me. It's all your fault, Antonio. If it hadn't been for you, I'd be married to Cort. And but for you, I would never have shot Sam Spangler!"

"What!" Antonio was flabbergasted.

"It was easy for you to wander through the South, cavalierly filling the heads of our soldiers with your grand schemes. The consequences had nothing to do with you. If you hadn't convinced Cort St. John to join your glorious expedition, he would have remained where he belonged and we would have been married long before Sam Spangler had the idea of buying Robin Hill. It is all because of you!"

"By heaven, I have never heard such inventive reasoning! If you had told me, I would not have touched you, and we'd be eligible for an annulment. I suppose you'll have an affair with him, and that will be my fault too! I warn you, Susannah, do not attempt it. He is a fine asset, and I don't want to lose him; but I will call him out if I have to. I am skillful with both swords and pistols, and it will be you who's to blame if Cort St. John and I must test who is better!"

He removed his trousers and lay down stiffly beside her. She kept still, hoping to have it ended. In a moment he turned on his side away from her. Susannah was wide-awake now, her hatred of him pulsing in her veins.

Was it true he wouldn't have touched her if she'd told him about Cort? An annulment! In her naiveté, she never once considered the thing might be undone. Maybe it was still possible. He had only to agree to it, when they were away from New Orleans. Yes, that was it; she must make him agree to it!

It didn't occur to her that she was planning to manipulate a man again, as she had Sam Spangler when she had persuaded him to sign her shopping list. Only this time the man was more formidable and the stakes were higher than a uniform.

Eventually Antonio's soft, rhythmic breathing told her he was asleep. She crept out of bed quietly and carried her clothes into the sitting room to dress.

Jackson Square was only a block away. St. Louis Cathedral, with its three tall spires, was on the far side. Banana trees and palms rustled in the breeze as she passed the statue of Andrew Jackson in the center of the square. The Vieux Carré was becoming a slum, yet couples out for an evening still strolled the walks, many on their way to the French Market for coffee and square doughnuts dipped in powdered sugar. Many of the men wore Union uniforms, making Susannah feel as though she were still a fugitive.

"Susannah!"

Cort saw her while she was still some distance away and hurried toward her, taking her hand and leading her to a bench in the shadows. They flung their arms around each other for a long embrace in the jasmine-scented night.

"My darling!" he said. "I thought I might never see you again, but to see you as his wife! You do not love him—I cannot believe that you do!"

"I hate him!"

"He forced you, somehow! I'll kill him," Cort vowed fiercely.

"Cort, no. He saved my life." She began to tell him how it had happened, about Sam Spangler and how the soldiers had followed her onto the *River Belle*.

"I'm an outlaw like you now. And I have no choice but to leave the country as Antonio's wife. But once we are in Brazil, there will be an annulment. It should be easy for the Emperor Dom Pedro to arrange."

"An annulment!" Cort's eyes lighted with hope. "I should have known he was a gentleman. He has not . . . But that is what I would have expected of him. That is the sort of man I know he is! He knows about us, then?"

"Yes. You must be patient, Cort."

"That will not be easy. It is not easy seeing you as his wife. By heaven, if I thought he had taken advantage, I would call him out!"

Susannah felt ill. "Don't say such things, Cort." She put her fingers against his lips. "Everything will be all right."

"Yes. Thank heaven there is no reason for me to confront him. It's a difficult situation, but it's lucky that the marquess was there. We'll be together soon. You'll be *my* wife, as you should be, instead of his." He kissed the fingers she had pressed to his lips, and then kissed her fully on the mouth. It was a satisfyingly pleasurable kiss that did not stir the confusion of raw emotions that Antonio's did. It was the way a woman ought to be kissed, she thought. She was more aware of the current of his desire than she had been before her own had been stirred by Antonio, but it was well-mingled with devotion and respect.

He walked her back to the hotel, where she bid him good night at the foot of the stairs. As she opened the door, Antonio turned up the light. He had been waiting for her.

"Well, Susannah, you have been to see Major St. John, I expect."

"Yes, and I will not endure one of your temper fits about it," she said bravely. "I had to explain."

He nodded. "Yes, it was necessary for you to tell him good-bye."

"I did not tell him good-bye," she said, trying to hold on to her courage.

"What?" His voice was like a cannon round.

"I told him there was going to be an annulment."

"An annulment!" Merriment overcame Antonio's anger. "My dear, we have royally consummated this marriage," he told her, laughing uproariously.

Susannah blushed hotly, knowing how true it was. "Who is to say we have? Only you, Antonio. I want an annulment. I'm grateful to you for saving me from the Yankees, but you've had your fun of it, and Cort St. John is the man with whom I want to spend my life. It's the only honorable thing to do, Antonio, and you know it!"

"He would guess on your wedding night that you weren't eligible for an annulment," Antonio objected.

"I would see that he was too happy to think of it," Susannah declared.

"If he did think of it, I might have to duel him," Antonio sighed, "but I suppose you're right, Susannah. You had no choice but to marry me, so it's only fair I set you free again."

"You'll do it?" Her victory astonished her.

Antonio's face twisted sardonically as he tried to control his laughter. "You have only to convince me it's what you really want, Susannah. I have never forced you. You have only to resist me."

As he moved to take her into his arms, she stumbled past him to the bedroom door. "You'll sleep on the sofa tonight!" she cried. "You'll sleep there from now on!" Her heart pounding, she locked the door behind her, and leaning against it, heard him still laughing beyond.

I I

Susannah stood with the crowd of passengers jammed against the ship's rails as the vessel slid through the narrow passage that guarded Rio's harbor. The great rock on the right was called Pico, Antonio announced to everyone; and on the left was the famed island peak, Sugarloaf, fifteen hundred feet high.

A sob of relief welled in Susannah's throat as the calm green waters of the bay glinted welcome. It had not been an easy voyage. Five thousand miles from New Orleans, and no sight of land, except three of the Leeward Islands, where they had stopped briefly at St. Kitts.

Susannah had proved a poor sailor. She had been sick constantly; and when Antonio had insisted that fresh air and a turn about the deck

were the best antidote, she had been too queasy
to walk on its rolling surface without leaning
heavily on his arm.

Cort had been concerned over her loss of
weight and her gray, drawn face. Antonio's
reaction had been more complicated.

It had not been the sort of honeymoon he
had planned. In her condition she had not had
to resist him. Only an utter brute would have
asserted his husbandly rights. For a few days
he had been jaunty, assuring her she would
soon get her "sea legs." But Susannah never
had, and Antonio had slowly lasped into mo-
rose resignation. She had been nothing a bride
should be; she had been nothing but a burden.
Worst of all, Susannah knew Antonio resented
being cheated of the opportunity to prove to her
that she could not resist him. That was what he
thought of as she lay moaning in her bunk. Oh,
he had done his duty, bathing her forehead and
bringing her a cool drink or a particularly tempting morsel from the dining room; but she knew
he was annoyed. He wished to restore her health
only so he could savor his triumph. He was the
most insufferable man she had ever known!

Now this part of the journey was coming to
an end. Dom Pedro wished to receive his new
colonists at his palace in the city, and the ship
was to be reloaded with agricultural equipment
needed to begin the new plantations. It would
be wonderful to be on solid ground again, but
Susannah was in a way reluctant to leave the
ship. Once ashore, she would lose the refuge of
seasickness. And then what would happen?

She wondered vaguely why the rolling currents of the Mississippi had never bothered her.

The times Antonio had taken her had all been while traveling on water. Small wonder that at first he had openly accused her of feigning her discomfort to thwart him!

The idea had merit, she thought. She had at least managed to come all the way to Rio without succumbing to him. Now she would be without any defense except her own willpower. Would he be able to sweep that away as easily as he had before?

For two weeks before they sailed, she had kept her door locked, but Antonio hadn't challenged her. Each night he had worked into the small hours preparing for the trip. She would be in bed, her body pulsing with anticipation when she heard his step, and a shiver would race along her spine as his key turned in the outer door. As his steps came across the floor, she would tense, but each night she would hear him fling himself onto the sofa with a weary sigh. Filled more with frustration than relief, she would lie sleepless for hours, while he slumbered peacefully beyond her door. She told herself her restlessness was because he would not give her the opportunity to show her mettle against even such a man as he believed himself to be.

He was doing it on purpose, she thought, imagining that even through the heavy oak door he heard her pounding heart. He wanted her to admit she wanted him; but oh, she would not! How she hated him for ignoring the situation—or worse, for ignoring *her*!

As the ship crossed the smooth water of the harbor, the huge shape of Gavia, rock-capped and bald, swept above a backdrop of jagged peaks. Antonio, on a foredeck, pointed out to the passengers the peaks of the Two Brothers, the Hunchback and the Sleeping Giant of Tijuca. The colors of the mountains grew vividly green through a brilliant sunny haze as they drew nearer, as though the hue of the emerald water were merely a reflection from the jungle trees.

Then the city came into view, stretching along the shore between the foothills for miles to the north and south. Roofs of bright red or earth-brown, tile-topped walls of pastel or white so shimmering they hurt the eyes in the tropic sun. In spite of herself, Susannah caught her breath in excitement. The city looked like a collection of alabaster castles; she felt she was gazing at an illustration from one of the fairytale books Papa used to read to her.

Beside her Cort St. John clutched her hand as the weary passengers cheered and wept at the first sight of their adopted land. "It's even more beautiful than the marquess told us, Susannah," he exclaimed exultantly. "It's paradise!" And, unable to restrain himself, he embraced her. She ducked her head against his shoulder, her shirts flapping in the sea wind.

Some of the other passengers glanced at them, mildly curious. Most had heard something about the circumstances by which Susannah had become the bride of the Marquez da Silva. They admired her for her courage in defending herself against a Yankee, and they admired their leader for having so gallantly saved her. They approved, too, of the heroic Cort St. John, who had chosen exile over submission. Only a few, seeing Antonio's black expression, guessed the true scope of the situation.

Antonio's shining dark hair whipped in the breeze like a warning flag. His eyebrows were flown up in a scowl like wings. He looked as fierce as an eagle, ready to swoop upon them.

Susannah saw his look and, shivering, pushed away from Cort. She had not forgotten Antonio's threat to call him out. That, above all else, must not happen. A duel between them would be a catastrophe. Did she feel, deep inside, that as skillful as both of them were, Antonio would be a trifle faster, that he possessed a slightly superior accuracy that would be the difference between life and death? Cort had never dueled. Antonio hadn't told her that he had, but a coldness in his voice when he spoke of dueling made her certain he was a veteran of such encounters.

Poor Cort looked at her in surprise as she pulled away from his arms. He didn't understand how dangerous her embrace could be. Cort must think that since they were at Rio, where the annulment was to take place, they were far away from the need for Susannah to pretend to be the wife of the marquess.

Susannah shivered again, remembering the terrible consequences embracing her had had for another man, Captain Sam Spangler. She must be sure that Cort did not perish for love of her.

At Pharox Quay a line of conveyances stood ready for the passengers, and even Cort was painfully aware that Susannah still belonged to Antonio Andrada, at least in name, as they were separated. The marquess and his bride were to travel to City Palace in a gilded carriage driven by a black coachman in a royal uniform of green with gold braid and shining cavalry boots. The others were to go to quarters almost as lavish at the Emigrants' Hotel, which had once been the palace of a Brazilian nobleman.

Susannah's first impression of the city altered as they drove through narrow streets. Beggars squatted with their backs against the walls, wolfish-looking dogs slunk back from the horses, and horrible odors drifted in through the carriage windows. Susannah shot Antonio a resentful glance. "I knew you were lying about Brazil," it said clearly. He startled her by rising to the bait, beginning to tell her of the improvements the emperor hoped to make, how he hoped to erect a fountain at the quay in the midst of a handsome square with gardens, that he planned to level hills to relieve the congestion of traffic, that the marshes would be drained and a new sewer system constructed.

But as soon as he had expounded on these things, Antonio frowned. "I cannot imagine why I am telling you all this," he said brusquely. "It's no concern of a woman. I have no idea why I am talking to you about docks and sewers, when I should be telling you about theaters and shops."

"I would sooner hear what your precious emperor intends doing about the beggars," she said wryly.

Again Antonio could not resist coming to the defense of his emperor. "The poor are very much in his heart, I assure you," he told her, and he began to describe Dom Pedro's attempts to win appropriations from the Senate to establish primary schools throughout the country. "The gifted poor are already given scholarships to Dom Pedro II College," he told her, "and a few have been sent abroad to study at the emperor's own expense."

Susannah sighed. It was amazing that the mighty Marquez da Silva seemed to have a bad case of hero worship over the emperor.

"Does everyone think as much of Dom Pedro as you do?" she asked.

He laughed. "No, indeed. Many of the aristocracy would like him deposed. I myself am planning to win a seat in the Senate so that I may exert more influence in his behalf."

"I think, after all, I would like to hear about the shops," she said.

Antonio smiled—indulgently, she thought. Leaning back languidly, he stretched out his long, supple legs. His thigh was against hers in the confines of the coach, and even through her gown, she felt a warm rush. Antonio's eyes danced for an instant, as though he knew; and Susannah felt even more disturbed. Oh, why must he cut such a dashing figure in his smart roll-collar waistcoat and tight French-cuffed trousers! He knew his effect on her and was enjoying it.

"Oh, there is nothing like the Rue do Ouvidor with its fine old Portuguese buildings and its demitasse cafés," he told her.

"Perhaps it would be fun to go there. In Memphis it was always fun to shop before the war."

She remembered how excited she and Rachel had always been when they had moved to the city for the winter and could go out shopping whenever they wished. She had bought some new gowns in New Orleans, but there had been a scarcity of everything in that war-ravaged town. Would it be wrong of her to buy more clothing with Antonio's money? He would be willing to supply her wardrobe, of course. In his mind he would only be giving his wife what she needed to make a good impression at court. He gave no indication that he might have to make good on his promise to have their marriage annulled. No, he did not believe that any woman in the world would give up the privilege of being his wife, not even for the arms of Cort St. John.

"Well-bred Brazilian women do not go shopping," Antonio was saying, "at least not without an escort. Even then, the shopkeeper brings out the goods for them to see while they sit in their carriages."

"What! How absurd! But anyway, I am not a Brazilian woman, Antonio."

"Nevertheless, you must abide by the customs. I won't have people thinking my wife is a tramp."

"It would be nothing worse than what you yourself have thought!"

Antonio glowered. "I will have some gowns sent to the palace this afternoon."

"Don't bother," Susannah said heatedly. "I'd sooner do without. I will not be treated like a cloistered nun because I am a woman or because I am your wife!"

"Nun!" Antonio sputtered. "That would never describe *you*, Susannah!"

She barely refrained from striking him across his elegant mocking features. She controlled herself only because the coachman would see. Antonio's mouth tightened derisively, and his strong jaw set with infuriating determination. In such a state of discord, they arrived at the palace.

She would have never guessed it was the residence of an emperor from its barrackslike exterior. Only a few royal guards indicated as much, while around the basement area, men in tattered clothing lounged, smoking and talking. Gaunt-looking artists were laboring at easels, while an even scrawnier gray cat moved among them, hoping for scraps.

"Why on earth do they allow them there?" Susannah asked as the coachman opened the door, but Antonio offered no explanation. He seemed not to be on speaking terms with her at all, she thought, though he had had the last word in their argument. Inside the massive palace doors, Antonio was greeted with the news that the emperor was waiting to see him. An Indian servant girl was summoned to show Susannah to her quarters. Susannah would have liked to ask a dozen questions as she followed the graceful sway of her long calico skirt, but quickly she discovered that her guide spoke only Portuguese, so there was only the squeak of the girl's sandals to break the silence as they went along.

The palace was unlike anything Susannah would have expected. Most of the walls were simply whitewashed, instead of hung with silk wall coverings, and artwork and sculpture were liberally displayed, unlike any Susannah had ever seen—vivid landscapes, scenes of coffee or rubber plantations, featuring black or Indian workers, their bodies shimmering in the sun. Here was a laundress amid enormous red flowers, and there a carved ivory jaguar startled her as they rounded a corner.

The furnishings were finely crafted of shining Brazilian hardwoods, though they hadn't the pomp of an emperor, and chandeliers were far between. Only a huge portrait of Dom Pedro, strikingly handsome in gold braid embroidered on a general's uniform, stilled her doubts that she was in the right place after all. She stopped for a moment to study the portrait, noting the gentleness and intelligence in the emperor's face as he stood beside his sweetly smiling queen, Thereza.

The decor was, after all, airy and refreshing, and she was delighted by the suite of rooms designated for her and Antonio. The sitting room was white and rose, with sofas in morocco leather, damask chairs, and venetian blinds made of narrow strips of polished satinwood. Beyond the blinds was a vine-covered balcony with a view of tangled green mountain slopes where the tallest palms thrust up their crowns above the throng of trees and blooming vegetation, as though claiming recognition from the aquamarine sky. When she had admired this, there was her bedroom to see, with its ebony bed with white mousseline bed curtains held up by four carved gilded swans and its rosewood washstand with a bowl and pitcher of blue hand-blown glass. The Indian girl shook out Susannah's small wardrobe and hung it away in the wardrobe while she explored. Then, left alone, Susannah pulled off her travel clothes, washed in the cool water from the pitcher, and pulling back the wadded silk counterpane, lay down to rest.

She had expected to feel better as soon as she

left the ship; obviously it was going to take more time. As she closed her eyes, the bed seemed to sway. The whole room seemed to be moving, as though she had never left the boat. Reviewing her argument with Antonio, imagining the clever things she should have said, she drifted off to sleep.

An hour or so later, sounds in the sitting room awakened her. She lay too weary to move for a few minutes, but curious about the bangings and rustlings outside her door, the soft foreign exclamations that penetrated the bedchamber. Then, after a while, there was silence. Susannah, wearing only her wrapper, went out.

She gave an involuntary gasp at the transformation that had occurred. Exquisite gowns were draped everywhere—gowns of velvet, brocade, Japanese silk. There were bodices fastened with buttons of semiprecious stones and some trimmed in brilliant feathers. Boxes sat open, displaying large dangling earrings and necklaces of filigreed gold. Sandalwood fans, dainty leather slippers, and a fur boa! There was even a box full of unthinkably thin silk nightdresses in shades of blue and green, which Antonio had told her he thought best suited her fair skin and auburn hair.

Antonio! He was responsible for all this, of course! He had said he would have gowns sent. And she had sworn she would have none of them. Did he think that her simple feminine soul couldn't resist even clothes? The nightgowns clearly proclaimed his belief that she could not resist him either.

Everything shouted of Antonio's taste, sophisticated and daring, meant to cause a stir, like the hat he had brought to her at Robin Hill. If Brazilian women dressed this way, then perhaps it was no wonder that they blushed to be seen in the shops. But these were for occasions, she supposed, when the women were brought out to be displayed like fine silver and china. Antonio was planning on displaying her, she thought, like a bounty captured on his American journey. Well, she would thwart him.

A knock came on the sitting-room door. She was thinking so much of Antonio that she assumed it was he, though he would not have needed to knock. Flinging it open, resentful words springing to her lips, she found a pretty young women dressed in a linen skirt and bodice, holding a tray with a pitcher and two glasses.

"I thought you might like something refreshing to drink," she said.

Susannah stood back to allow her to enter. "How thoughtful! But my husband isn't here, so there's no need to leave the other glass."

"The other glass is for me! Did you think I was the maid?" She gave a soft laugh. "Of course you did, why not? But I am Princess Izabel."

"Oh, I beg your pardon . . . your highness!" Susannah stammered. She saw now that she should not have made the mistake. Princess Izabel carried herself with aristocratic bearing, and her clothes, though simple, were finely tailored. A small crown was embroidered in gold thread on the left side of the bodice, and an official-looking gold medallion was fastened beneath it, hanging from a striped ribbon.

"My name is Izabel; I don't like to be called 'your highness,' or even 'princess,' " the dark-haired girl said, "and I apologize for the position I put you in just now. It was just that I couldn't wait to meet you, and I was looking for an excuse. You see, I've just been married myself, and I haven't had the opportunity to know any other brides. Especially an American bride! Especially Antonio's bride. He has been a favorite of mine ever since I was a little girl. When I saw the gowns he was having brought in for you, I couldn't resist any longer seeing what woman he thought beautiful enough to wear them."

It was immediately easy to talk to Izabel, who was quick-witted and about Susannah's age. The princess moved piles of gowns from the sofa, and seating herself there, poured a drink for each of them. It tasted wonderfully cool and refreshing. Izabel said it was made from the pulp surrounding the cacao bean. Izabel was immensely interested in learning all about Susannah.

"Tell me what it was like being a girl in Memphis," she insisted. "And is it true that during the war you lived alone on your plantation and fought off marauding Yankees single-handed? Oh, I cannot even imagine it!"

Susannah found herself drawn out about everything from Miss Pickens' school and the parties at the Gayoso to Sam Spangler's unhappy fate. "So I have no idea what has happened to Robin Hill, and more than that, I am worried about my sister," Susannah finished.

"But all's well that ends well," Izabel said. "You had Antonio to carry you away down the Mississippi. Now you'll make your life on another river, even mightier than that, and you'll bring your sister to live there. Oh, it must have been romantic on the *River Belle!* I was half in love with Antonio myself, before I met my Gastão."

"Tell me about him," Susannah said, turning the conversation away from her praise of Antonio. Izabel was eager to describe her own romance.

"My aunt in Portugal suggested Gastão, the Conde d'Eu, and his cousin Prince Augusto, the Duque d'Saxe, for my sister Poldi and me. But Papa would not marry us in the old-fashioned way. He said we should see for ourselves whether we liked them. So he invited them to Rio without any betrothal agreement. Gastão was to be for Poldi and Augusto for me. But see what happened! Gastão and I fell in love, and so did Poldi and Augusto. It turned out perfectly, but not the way my aunt planned!"

"How fortunate that your father allowed you to choose," Susannah said, laughing.

"Yes. He is very progressive, you know. He believes in more education and more freedom for women, but even an emperor can't do much to accomplish it in Brazil. It angers the old aristocrats too much. They live by the old Moorish harem rules even now. So Poldi and I are exceptions among Brazilian women. It's wonderful to have you here. I wish you were going to stay in Rio. But you'll love the Kiss Flower, and you'll write to me, won't you? You'll tell me all the news about yourself and about the American colony. I find the idea fascinating, and I know you'll be equal to the Amazon. Now, tell me which of these incredible gowns you are going to wear for dinner tonight."

"None of them," Susannah said with a sigh.

"None! Dear heaven, I do have a lot to learn about American women!" Izabel exclaimed. "Don't you like them?"

Susannah explained her position, to Izabel's astonishment. "Do you think the emperor will be offended?" she asked.

"Oh, Papa will not mind at all. He thinks clothes are unimportant, and I've even heard him say they detract if they are too fine. He will not wear his uniform; instead he wears a black suit with a Prince Albert coat and a starched shirt. It took real courage for him to begin to do it. Most of the nobles and high officials would like him better in white satin and ermine, but he usually disappoints them. I predict he'll approve of you, Susannah. But perhaps I should warn you about Joaquina."

"Joaquina?"

"Joaquina is the daughter of one of the most influential men in the government. It's no secret that she and Antonio were intended for each other. It would have provided the perfect link between progressive and conservative forces on the Amazon. Joaquina couldn't have cared less about *that*, but she was—*is*—madly in love with him.

"Now the rumor is that her family will marry her to Conde Bernardo Marchado, who was Antonio's rival for her hand. The count's holdings on the Amazon are as large as Antonio's, and power there is almost evenly balanced between them. Joaquina's father will throw his own power behind the man who marries his daughter; he is very interested in expanding his fortunes through development on the river.

Conde Marchado opposes Papa's policies there, and I have heard that his slaves are brutally treated. I hope his wife fares better."

"Oh, that poor girl! How she must hate me!"

"Most likely. If you'll take my advice, though, Susannah, you'll waste no pity on her. She's very beautiful, and Brazilian men aren't noted for their fidelity. Joaquina will have plenty of opportunity to spoil things for you, if not in Rio, then in Santarém."

"Oh, but I can't help feeling sorry for her! I'm not afraid of her at all," Susannah told the astounded Izabel.

"You're very sure of yourself," the princess said, shaking her head.

But Susannah had confessed nothing about Cort St. John, or the fact that she expected her marriage to Antonio to be of short duration. Of course, she had nothing to fear from Joaquina, and Joaquina had nothing to fear from her.

Susannah appeared at dinner in the same outfit she had worn when she encountered Antonio on the *River Belle*. The box-pleated skirt and bodice of blue shot silk had been restored as good as new after their dunking in the Mississippi; and though Susannah was strongly tempted to add a pair of the large hooped earrings Antonio had had sent, that would have negated the point she was making. She decided against any jewelry at all, even the necklace Mrs. St. John had given her, which complemented the bodice so well. She did her hair as simply as possible, fastening it in a chignon with combs she had bought in New Orleans. She dusted a bit of pearl powder over her face, and wishing she owned a box of rouge, she pinched her pale cheeks to make them rosy.

She heard Antonio come into the sitting room and then go into his own bedroom to prepare for dinner. When he knocked on her door, she drew a trembling breath and stepped out to meet his displeasure. He stared at her for a long moment, his face growing blacker. She met his eyes with a steely look of her own, the same glare she had learned to use to intimidate Yankees who had invaded the sanctity of Robin Hill.

She half-expected that he would seize her and rip off the offending garments and dress her by force in the gown of his choice. And what persuasions might he use when he had her unclothed before him? How cataclysmic might his desire be, buffeted by the hot winds of his fury?

But finally he shrugged. "Well, if that's the way you want to appear before the emperor, Susannah, suit yourself. I will be busy all evening explaining that all American women aren't as eccentric as the one I married."

He offered her his arm, and trembling with her success, but somehow not quite happy, she took it. The minute she entered the dining room, she was overcome with mortification. Every head turned for a look at the Marquez da Silva's bride, and she blushed at the startled expressions she saw around her.

There wasn't a woman in the room who wasn't lavishly turned out in a gown similar to those she had rejected; and jewels sparkled everywhere from wrists, earlobes, necks, and elaborately coiffed hair. She realized at last with dizzying suddenness that although the palace had not met her preconception, she was really at the court of the Emperor of Brazil. Many of the men were as grand as the women, in white satin waistcoats and trousers with gold lace stripes down the seams. Antonio's velvet-collared frock coat of blue diagonal hadn't prepared her for such male splendor.

Only pride prevented flight. Certainly she had made a laughingstock of herself, but she would carry it off. She would not let anyone see how embarrassed she was—Antonio least of all. She smiled bravely, fighting the sting of tears that made the candelabra and rich colors swirl before her eyes. One face came out of the crowd. The others seemed to slip back as Antonio released her arm. Someone lifted her hand gently, and bowing over it, kissed it softly. She realized he must feel the calluses she still bore from her days at Robin Hill, and almost jerked her hand away. She recognized the handsome face from the painting—his royal highness Dom Pedro II. She looked for disapproval on his face and saw interest and admiration instead.

"Marqueza, you must do me the honor of sitting beside me tonight," he said.

She nodded assent, too dazed to form a reply, and was led to a cane-bottomed chair near the head of the table made of shining ebony inlaid with dozens of Brazilian woods, blending in color from pale yellow to deep purple. Antonio was placed across the table, beside Princess Izabel, who, wearing a peach-colored gown with a wide, lacy bertha, flashed Susannah an encouraging glance.

Susannah picked out Izabel's sister, Poldi, Princess Leopoldina, who wore a tiara matching Izabel's. Poldi wasn't as slender or as pretty as Izabel, and her mother, Empress Thereza, was stockily built and walked with a limp. It had been an arranged marriage, of course, but obviously the emperor and empress had been lucky in love, for he lifted his glass to her as she took her seat, and was regarded with a warm glance in return.

Susannah wondered if the gentleman next to Poldi were Prince Augusto, originally to be wed to Izabel. There was a gentleman beside Izabel also, but Susannah had no time to notice him as he spoke to Antonio across the princess, for the emperor engaged her in conversation, probing for information about the United States, much as Izabel had. They were much alike, this father and daughter.

Dom Pedro's special passion was astronomy, he told her, discoursing on his discovery of an important star in the neglected portion of the firmament where the Southern Cross takes the place of the Big Dipper. Then, laughing, he made light of it.

"It gives political cartoonists ready ammunition. They love to depict me in ridiculous situations, peering through my telescope. And to think I sponsored art lessons for some of them! I never seem to learn. I suppose you have seen some of the poor but talented artists and writers I allow to live in the palace basement?"

"So that is why they are there!"

"A good writer deserves a palace more than a king, Marqueza. How do you like Brazil so far?"

"I find it very confusing."

Dom Pedro chuckled, then grew serious. "It

is perhaps the most magnificent country in the world. There are eighteen provinces rich with fabulous resources—minerals, metals, gems. And the forests! Hardwoods, dyewoods, oil-bearing trees, balsa, rubber, chicle, and rosewood that makes the most beautiful furniture and the sweetest perfume on earth. We have tropical fruits, sugar, tobacco, chocolate, coffee, and cotton. We possess endless waterways and good harbors. Can you imagine, Marqueza, what it was like for a boy of fourteen to come into such an empire as I did? 'Confusing'—yes, that is a good word for Brazil. 'Overwhelming' is another. But 'exciting' is best of all. I am almost forty now, and I am still struggling to make my dreams for my country come true. There is one thing of which Brazil has never had enough, for all her bounty."

"What is that, your majesty?"

"Why, people, Marqueza! That is why I am so overjoyed that you and your countrymen have come. And I am especially delighted that you and Antonio have already united our countries in a special way."

The emperor was an optimist, she thought, to put such an interpretation on the loss of the advantages the match with Joaquina would have brought. Obviously Antonio had said nothing about the possibility of an annulment, Susannah thought. In spite of her awe of the emperor, it seemed the perfect opportunity to make sure he learned of the problem. "Your highness," she began, her face somber, "everything is not—"

The emperor interrupted her. "Ah, I know. Antonio has told me how the marriage came to be. But don't worry. I believe you have won his love already, even if he isn't certain of it himself."

The emperor chuckled. "I am an expert on such things, Marqueza. Why, when I first saw my Thereza Christina, I refused to go through with the wedding. I had fallen in love with a lovely miniature, you see, and I spent the entire night storming about the palace, while she, still on the ship that had brought her from Naples, wept the hours away for having seen *me!* But if two people are meant for each other, Marqueza, then there is nothing that will prevent the outcome, no matter how intense the grief or the polemics."

Then quickly the emperor changed the subject, telling her of his love of American ingenuity and describing his pleasure at having seen a new sort of cookstove when he had visited the colonists at the Emigrants' Hotel.

A knot settled in Susannah's stomach. The emperor seemed to like her, and that might be her undoing. He had made it plain that he considered her the right wife for Antonio.

Across the table a beautiful girl intruded on Susannah's vision. Diamond earrings sparkled, catching the candlelight and refracting it against her smooth olive skin as they danced with every little seductive dip of her head. Her wavy black hair was restricted only by a heavy ruby clasp at the nape of her long, fine neck, allowing any man to easily imagine how luxuriant it would be drifting loosely over her shoulders or over a lace pillowcase. Dark eyes were at once demure and overlaid with deep sensuality, made even more compelling by her seeming unawareness of it.

She had spent the first few minutes of the meal staring unabashedly at Susannah. Now, seeming to have dismissed her rival's presence, she was sending Antonio secretive smiles and glances, which were a secret to no one; and he, manipulated, was smiling back.

In the candlelight his expression seemed especially suggestive, the glow touching his mouth as if with the memory—or the promise—of a kiss. The deep tones of his skin were richly masculine, and amethyst buttons at the wrists of his silk shirt drew her attention to his capable hands, making her think of their skill on a woman's body. He lifted a crystal wine goblet, bobbing it in what seemed a gesture of admiration for the Brazilian temptress.

There could be no doubt that this was Joaquina, of whom she had been warned. This was the woman Antonio had been expected to marry. Once there was an annulment, he would probably marry her yet. Somehow the idea wasn't comforting. Why should she feel so possessive of him? It must be only that she didn't like being bested, and she did feel bested. She wished with all her heart that she had worn one of the feather-trimmed gowns flung uselessly about the sitting room. But even then, would she have been a match for Joaquina?

A knot settled in Susannah's stomach. The emperor was kind and charming, but suppose he refused to grant the annulment? She had known Dom Pedro less than an hour, yet she was already certain that no matter how much Antonio's marriage to this lovely creature would help him politically, that would not be the deciding factor in his decision. Oh, but he must understand!

She had not yet recovered from the voyage, she thought, unable to partake of much of the main dish of chicken and rice baked in a spicy sauce. The aroma of the strong Brazilian coffee that completed the meal made her woozy. After dinner they retired to a drawing room to hear a group of musicians that had caught the emperor's fancy. Izabel played a violin solo, but Susannah, feeling unable to endure the festivities any longer, excused herself. Antonio escorted her to their quarters, not seeming as angry as he had been before; but if she had hopes that he might stay with her, they were dashed before she could even admit them to herself, much less to him.

"I'm expected to return, of course," he told her. "It's my first night home."

She undressed, and putting on her old simple nightgown from Robin Hill, lay in bed listening to the strange night sounds of Rio: the sigh of the surf, wearing a ruff of lacy foam where it touched the starlit beach; the rattle of palm fronds, so much louder than the rustle of oaks; raucous birds, disturbing the night, perhaps parrots or macaws, with voices far less musical than the mockingbird that used to serenade the moon in Tennessee. Alone at last, she abandoned herself to weeping for home and for Cort St. John, with whom love had been an uncomplicated thing. Dear Cort, who was so close to her, yet seemed as long ago and far away as magnolias blooming beside the veranda at Robin Hill.

She fell asleep wondering if Antonio were

somewhere holding Joaquina in his arms in the moonlight.

Susannah slept poorly, and in the morning, the breakfast that was brought to her was no more appetizing than the meal the night before. Antonio was gone again, and his bed had been made. She wondered miserably if he had slept in it at all. Someone arrived to retrieve the gowns she didn't wish to buy; and Susannah, having stood on principle long enough to make her point, extravagantly chose six of them before returning the others.

"You may take all the lingerie," she said, holding out the pile. "I don't really need it."

But the woman pushed it back at her, protesting in Portuguese that needed no translation but a conspiratorial smile to inform Susannah that her husband had already purchased the entire lot.

Oh, he was so sure of himself, she thought furiously, trying not to imagine Antonio's lascivious thoughts while selecting them. There was no use trying to make the woman understand that she didn't want the nightgowns. She would have to keep them.

Susannah spent the morning watching frilly little pleasure boats in the bay. In midafternoon, Princess Izabel arrived to invite her for a sightseeing drive around the city in her private coach.

"But I'm still feeling ill," Susannah confessed.

"The fresh air would do you good."

"I'm so tired, I have hardly the strength to stand up; and I am still seasick, though I have been off the ship for a day and a half."

Princess Izabel suddenly began to ask questions, and having assessed the answers, clapped her hands.

"Susannah, perhaps . . . Oh, how lucky you are! To be married such a short time and already. . . ."

"Already what?" Susannah asked, mystified.

"Already with child. I think that may be what's wrong. You are going to have a baby!"

Susannah gazed down at herself in horror. "Do you really think . . . ?"

"Well, I don't suppose it's possible to be sure so soon, but before we were married, Mama told Poldi and me the signs. I could ask Mama if there is any way to know—"

"Oh, please, don't!" Susannah cried.

"But why not?"

"I . . . don't want anyone to know. No one must know!"

Izabel looked puzzled. "Oh, of course," she said after a moment. "You want Antonio to be the first to know. I suppose that's wise. He was angry last night, wasn't he? You and your dinner ensemble are palace gossip today, but you had your way about it; this news will heal the rift."

"Oh, but I'm not going to tell him until it's certain," Susannah declared.

"Well, wait another month, then, and if nothing tells you differently, you may be sure."

When Izabel left her to rest, Susannah wept bitterly and beat her fists against the leather sofa. "No, no, no!" she cried, as though that could make the difference.

Why had she never even thought this might happen? Even though she had had no mother to tell her, she had known vaguely the purpose of the intimacies of marriage. Only when Antonio had taken her, she had thought of nothing but him. No one must know! Not Antonio. Not the emperor. For how would she get her annulment then? And Cort! Dear heaven, she had told him the marriage was in name only! But Princess Izabel was only guessing; it simply wasn't true. She must get her annulment and marry Cort. No one must prevent it—not the emperor or Antonio or a baby! When her tears left her exhausted enough, she slept again.

Antonio was standing over her when she awakened, and she realized she had left the bedroom door unlocked. She drew the covers over her to hide one of her new nightgowns, which she had changed into to have fresh clothing.

"I knew that green would look lovely on you," he told her. "It was imported from Paris, you know, and on you it's worth every bit I paid for it."

Her anger flared. She felt like his chattel, his possession, in the gown he had bought her, and she would have thrown it off, except that then she would have been even more vulnerable to him.

"Antonio, when are you going to ask the emperor for the annulment?" she asked heatedly.

"Why, whenever you keep your part of the bargain, my love," he replied.

"Don't touch me, Antonio!" she warned.

"Prevent me, then," he said softly. He was already too close, and his hand was on the strap of the green nightgown. She shivered as his fingers crept beneath the thin material, his caress not demanding, but teasing, too tantalizing to need to command. A wave of dizziness washed over her, mingling fear and passion. "Antonio, no," she protested, but her voice was a moan of desire.

She fought for control, fastening her fingers around his wrist to pull him away. But he lowered his lips to her fingertips, and her hand fell helplessly back, her arm flung above her head as though tossed there explosively.

He kissed her lips gently, his eyes boring into hers. "Fight me, Susannah," he urged. "That's all you have to do to be rid of me forever. Imagine that I am that Yankee, Sam Spangler. What would you do then, *querida*? *He* would not take you unscathed. You would claw and bite and scream. That is all you need do. I won't take you by force; that's part of the bargain. I have never taken any woman by force, and I won't start now. It's your choice, my love. Kick! Scream! Just one good scream, Susannah! It would bring someone to help you."

As he spoke, he moved his kisses to her throat, his breath stirring warm currents, eddying along her collarbone. She felt the satisfying weight of his body against hers. The spicy aroma of his shaving soap mingled with his own masculine scent, making her dizzy.

She trembled uncontrollably, trying to hold herself tightly away from him, while at each soft, arrogant touch she almost convulsed with the urge to throw herself open for him. The gentle probings of his fingers threatened to turn the latch of her benighted resistance. She gasped, too breathless to gather the necessary scream of protest.

"Now, love, hurry!" he whispered as he slid

lower to her breasts. "It must be now, or it will be too late!" he crooned mockingly.

The force of passion gathered strength in the pit of her stomach, and she knew he was right. In a moment she would lose control. It would be too late.

She struggled to command her unwilling body, wondering whether, after all, he was in earnest in goading her to repulse him. The image of the exquisite Joaquina flashed through her mind. She remembered what Princess Izabel had said about the power Joaquina would bring him. And now that he was near her again, how could he be immune to her exotic charm? Joaquina surely was the wife he'd been meant to have, a perfect Brazilian woman, trained from infancy to submit to a man and worship him.

She tried to think of Cort, the man who had been meant for her, but Joaquina still intruded, the thought of her taking the place Susannah now occupied in Antonio's arms rankling. To think of another woman being touched this way by him! His hands stroked her intimately now, flames of passion licking hotly over every inch of flesh that met his caress, rising thickly, threatening to engulf her. The core of her being had become a molten ache of desire.

She felt she would die if it were not soothed, yet she mustn't give in! Neither must she delay to enjoy one more instant, though demons within her enticed her to hesitate just a few more seconds. A cool breeze sighed over her; a green cloud floated mistily by above her. Suddenly she was marvelously unencumbered; naked, she realized her gown was in a heap among the bedclothes.

The dark heap of trousers beside it told her Antonio's own state of undress. With all the will she possessed, she formed a scream and tensed her legs for a mighty kick that would knock his breath away and send her arrogant husband sprawling to the floor.

It was not because he loved her that he was determined to have his way with her; it was that he could not bear the idea of her choosing to be married to another man. But she would put an end to that, and he would have no choice but to keep his bargain.

The cry ripped from her lips, her legs flailing, as her fingers, bent like claws, reached for his face.

And then somehow the scream became one of muted rapture, her fingernails were digging into his back to hold him close to her, and her thrashing legs had not injured him, but fallen widely apart before the onslaught of his love.

She was lost, ecstatically lost! There was nothing to do but endure what was almost too blissful to bear; and then at last, in thankful oblivion, she felt the light pressure of his kiss on her forehead. "Don't be sad, *querida*," he murmured. "You were very brave, but it couldn't be helped. I knew it all along."

12

In the aftermath of his triumph, Antonio was even more infuriating. Futilely she begged him not to hold her to the bargain they had made. "It wasn't my bargain anyway, Antonio," she told him. "You made the rules."

"Ah, but if you had explained to me about Cort St. John in the beginning . . ." he replied. "I married you in good faith. What do you want? Another chance to repulse me? Would it end any differently?" He leered at her, and she blushed, having admitted to herself it would not.

Would there ever be any way she could protect herself against his caress? Somewhere a spark of her vanquished pride remained, which had not burned to a cinder in the flame of mutual passion. Oh, she did not want to admit that she had desired him as much as he had desired her! That would be the final humiliation—for a woman was not supposed to want and need as she did when his lips pressed against hers, when his commanding fingers stroked the secrets of her body, unlocking all that should be only hers.

He was like a conquering sea captain steering a fragile vessel through a storm, guiding her over each crashing wave of delight, his eyes inky as midnight with mystery, until they washed onto the shore of shared ecstasy.

Now he touched the softness behind her earlobe, tucking back a strand of her hair that had come loose. It was only an excuse to remind her, she knew, suppressing a shiver of pleasure.

Antonio smiled, as if he knew anyway. Oh, how had he any right to be so handsome, with his thick shining hair that always looked casually windblown, his high forehead and straight, fine nose, and his wide-set, prideful eyes? His features were all superbly classic, but it was more than the sum of these that made him so attractive. It was an aura—of excitement, of utter masculinity, even of self-assurance—that she could not resist.

"I'll explain it all to the emperor myself, then," she said. "I'll tell him how you've prevented me from marrying the man to whom I was pledged. He will be interested to learn exactly what you are like!"

"You would tell the emperor that?" he teased ruthlessly. "That would burn his ears, no doubt. But if you did find the nerve to appeal to him, do you think he would grant you an annulment against my wishes?"

"But why should it be against your wishes?" she persisted.

"Because I am quite content to be married to you. I told you that long ago."

"Yes, you explained that you choose your women like horses. But isn't there some woman with a better pedigree than mine to fit your needs?" she hinted.

"No, yours is sufficient. And there is more to it than that. A good mare must have some spirit, too. Come over here to the bed, Susannah, and I will remind you why an annulment is inadvisable."

"I will not. It's the middle of the day."

But in a moment she found herself on the bed nonetheless, unable to keep from laughing and enjoying herself as he unfastened her clothing and kissed her. Then the laughter sank to moans, and she opened herself to him shamelessly, begging him to hurry. Their excitement was such that they made love only half out of their clothes, getting all tangled in her petticoats and the suspenders of his trousers.

"Oh, see what you have done to my gown! It's hopelessly rumpled, and I am supposed to visit the princesses this afternoon."

He lolled back on his elbows. "Well, I will stay and watch you dress," he declared, "unless, of course, you wish the princesses to guess how you occupied yourself during siesta."

"Antonio, you are indecent!"

"Thank you, my love. Now, tell me, how are you and Izabel and Poldi going to occupy yourselves this afternoon?"

"With a sail, I think. The princesses want to show me a private beach where we can swim. They are in need of keeping their spirits up, now that there is all this talk of war and their husbands are planning to go with Dom Pedro to the front."

Antonio grew serious. "I am not glad to see the emperor go," he mused. "Dom Pedro is no soldier, but the country has never faced a more serious threat than the invasion of this murderous dictator of Paraguay, López. Even with Uruguay and Argentina as our allies, it's not going to be easy to defeat him. Dom Pedro hates military life, but he is determined."

The Paraguayan invasion of the Rio Grande do Sul had delayed Antonio's departure from the capital. The emperor had wished him to remain while he argued with his ministers to obtain permission for the trip to the distant border, even threatening to abdicate if it were not forthcoming. The war was more than a thousand miles away, where herds of fat cattle were being stolen on the immense Brazilian plains and ranches were being burned and the inhabitants butchered, but all Brazil was in a blaze of fury. Men were joining the army by the thousands, though it was poorly equipped to assimilate them.

The American colonists had been sent ahead to Santarém so that they would have time to establish themselves before the rains and floods of December and January. Cort had gone with them, in charge of the expedition, with Brazilian consultants to aid him.

It had at least put off the painful moment when he would learn that there would be no annulment, but Susannah worried every day about how she would tell him, and about what would happen when she did. Antonio had said that she must be the one to break the news. It was only right, for she had been the one who had promised the dissolution of the marriage.

Sometimes Susannah wished that Antonio would decide to go to the frontier with the emperor. There would surely be trouble when Cort found out he had lost her for good; and for the life of her, she did not know how blood-shed between the two men was to be prevented.

When she tried to discuss the problem with Antonio, he would shrug. "There is little I can do, if Cort St. John demands satisfaction, Susannah. He is entitled to it, and I cannot demean him by refusing."

"Then promise you will not aim to kill."

He snorted. "My dear, have you a yen to be a widow? I'm sure St. John is no poor shot. Are you going to make the same request of him? Do you suppose *he'd* agree? I've no wish to kill a man who hasn't harmed me, Susannah, but I've no desire to die, either."

She had no idea what she could do to prevent the duel. She had known Cort all her life, and she knew how strong his sense of honor was. Hadn't it been strong enough to drive him away from his home and country as an outlaw?

Antonio did not want to talk about it; the situation upset him. And if she pushed him, he would put an end to the discussion with a snappish remark. "I will do whatever I must; that is the fate of a man who becomes involved with a woman like you!"

Such comments cut her to the core, since she

was afraid they were justified. If only he would tell her that he loved her! But Antonio never had. She was sure of nothing about him, except that they had the capacity to drive each other wild in bed. She didn't think he trusted her. Did he even like her?

As the days passed, Susannah ceased to talk about the annulment. Antonio was determined to do nothing about it, and she knew in her heart nothing *could* be done. She could not ask for it herself, not only because the opportunity to speak privately to Dom Pedro would have been hard to come by, but because every day she became more and more certain that she was pregnant. She said nothing to Antonio about her suspicions. If she could not hide from him the immediate results of his lovemaking upon her, this she could conceal for a while longer at least. Perhaps it was a matter of pride that she did not want him to know that she was to be a mother because of him. She didn't want him to know how profound his effect upon her was. She hated to admit it, even to herself.

She had recovered from what Antonio still thought of as an indisposition of the voyage, and when they at last set out for the colony at Santarém, the ocean breeze seemed to bring a sparkle to her eyes, and the salty air gave her an appetite for the freshly caught fish that graced the dining table. Her waist was no longer nineteen inches, and her clothing began to be tight. She occupied her days letting out the seams in everything she owned. Still her condition wasn't really visible yet. Even when she was naked, it took a studious glance to detect the slight swelling. Antonio did not look at her that way. When she was undressed, the cabin was dim, and he was much occupied.

But some nights now, they didn't sleep in the cabin at all. Antonio had hung a hammock on the foredeck, and when the air was too close inside, he lay there for part of the night. The first time she had joined him, he had been surprised, as if he had never thought that a woman might sleep anywhere but in a bed. In a sweet intimacy their bodies rocked together closely in the hammock, swinging between the moon and stars and the glowing water.

During these nights the union of their love seemed celestial, his touch as dulcet and secret as the night wind on her smooth body, her moans mingling rapturously with the creakings of the hammock and the ship's rigging until bliss transported them close to the magnificent tropic sky.

At such times Susannah was tempted to tell him about their child. But those nights were dreamlike. The immense peacefulness she felt, protected by him, almost a part of him, never lasted long. With every day her fear intensified. She was going to a strange, wild place with a husband who was still much a mystery to her, a man who had not been raised to expect real love in marriage and who perhaps did not even think of love beyond the physical.

In this inhospitable place, with no mother or friend to guide her through, she was going to bring forth new life. She intuited that it was woman's business; she could not look to Antonio for comfort or help beyond the fetching of the doctor.

Sometimes she caught Antonio looking at her

quizzically and guessed that he, too, was perplexed by their relationship. Now that they'd left Rio, was he wondering why he hadn't let her have her way about the annulment? Did he regret forgoing the match with the seductive Joaquina? Beneath the appetites of the flesh, did he despise her for having caused him inadvertently to wrong a man he respected? At the end of the journey, the two would face each other; that terrified Susannah most of all.

Reaching Pará, they passed a little cheese-box fort with outsize guns, and red-sailed fishing boats appeared. Swamp forests closed in the tile roofs and yellow-washed warehouses as if threatening to reclaim the city, and turbid river water made the ship tug at its anchor.

The place was eerie and foreboding—the end of the world, it seemed. But enthusiastically Antonio told her they were half the distance from Europe they'd been at Rio and that the waterways connected Pará with the richest part of the continent.

His eyes shone with belief in the city's destiny, while Susannah accepted his ideas with uncertain faith.

The next night they caught the midnight tide across the Bay of Marajó toward the Breves Channel, which led to the mouth of the Amazon. In the morning a fairyland of palm forest towered over them, sweeping up from the water's edge. Soft, plumed fupatis drooped over the water below the gossamer fronds of assai palms and the light green vaselike bussus palms. Enormous fan palms rose to crowns a hundred feet high, and here and there a tree was draped with pendant mosses as if a green tapestry were thrown over it. By the edge of the water, flowering convolvuluses mixed with treelike caladiums and mangroves on stiltlike roots.

No other vessel was anywhere in sight, nor did they pass any other boat or sign of habitation hour after hour. The lofty forest made the wide channel seem narrow before it opened into the vast lakes and then cut away again through the intricate waterways. Susannah looked at Antonio for reassurance.

Simply seeing him there, his eyes shining with enthusiasm as he stood jauntily with one foot propped on the lower part of the railing, made her feel better. Just to be in his company gave her confidence. He had, as always, that easy confidence exuding from him. It was in his face, his stance, his voice.

She could not imagine how the pilot would find the way through all the islands and passageways, which were so confusingly alike. Once she caught sight of some sort of marker on a tree, but she had no way of knowing whether it was there to point the path or for some other reason. In fact she could not believe that anyone had ever passed this way before. The river was moody and exhilarating.

Antonio watched her, smiling, seeing her experience the thrill of remoteness for the first time. "What do you think, Susannah?" he asked.

"It's so serene," she replied; but at that moment an alligator, disturbed by the sound of the boat, slid off the shore into the water. Susannah gasped.

Antonio laughed. "They are difficult to see until they move. You could step on one."

He offered her binoculars to study the shore, and from then on she could scarcely be stirred from the deck as she perused the palms and rubber trees for signs of parrots and macaws or a busy little prago monkey.

Blue butterflies floated by, their wings so vivid that they cast bright reflections on the water. Once the boat's passage alarmed a flock of water birds, which flew up in a cloud of rainbow plumage.

"Oh, Antonio, I never imagined anything like this!" she cried, dropping the field glasses as the brilliant blanketing of birds soared close.

He smiled. "I am not a poet, Susannah. I couldn't describe it."

"I don't think anyone could. I accused you of exaggerating in Memphis, do you remember?"

"You were scathing. How could I forget? But now you see I was right."

He spoke with such satisfaction that her pleasure was marred. He was enjoying having been proved right, just as he had delighted in being right about her inability to resist him. His look told her he hoped she was learning not to question him. He, her husband, always knew best. Susannah sighed, wondering if in time she would come to defer to him in everything as she did in bed.

Soon there was evidence that all was not as uninhabited as it had seemed. They entered rubber swamps, gloomy and damp, where white sap dripped into pottery cups stuck to the tree trunks with clay. The Indians had come early in the morning and cut the gashes. In the evenings they would slip again through the wood like ghosts to collect the sap in calabashes to take to their huts to process.

"But where do they live, Antonio?" she asked, unable to imagine any village in this wilderness.

"You'll see," he promised. He suddenly sounded irritable.

Before long the dwellings came into view. Susannah didn't even recognize them as houses at first. Then what had appeared to be merely piles of old brush became thatch huts, sagging half-ruined with brightly blooming vines climbing over them, in and out through the holes in their roofs. Women were working over outdoor fires covered by odd clay chimneys which poured a thick smoke, and the air was heavy with the reek of hot rubber. Ill-kept children stopped playing to stare or wave or run into the huts to hide as the boat went past. The boat's whistle tooted a greeting, and the children jumped and chattered in reply. Susannah gazed at the scene in horror. She knew that now she was seeing another facet of Brazil, one Antonio had never included in his glowing account of his country.

"I have never seen anyone in such poverty; I don't see how they survive," she said accusingly. "In the South, even the most mistreated slaves lived much better."

"They are none of your concern, Susannah," he said sharply.

She had touched on a sore point, and she knew she should drop the subject, but somehow she couldn't. Maybe the war had honed her dislike of injustice, or perhaps she merely was pleased to feel him on the defensive for once.

"Why are they so poor?" she persisted.

He gritted his teeth. "Because the traders to whom they sell their rubber cheat them."

"Well, surely it ought to be possible to put a stop to that."

"You know nothing about it!"

"Then tell me, and I will know."

He looked at her for a long, angry moment. She was on his masculine turf, and he didn't like it. "It's not anything a woman needs to know about. You wouldn't understand."

"Try me," she challenged.

He blew an exasperated breath, and she felt a twinge of fear; but she was determined not to be afraid of her husband, and stood her ground. He could dominate her utterly in bed, but that was the only power he had over her, and until night she was safe.

"The traders have to borrow money from wealthy rubber princes to buy their goods, and they are hopelessly in debt. The rubber magnates cheat the traders on everything."

"Then that is what must be stopped."

"It is never easy to stop the rich from doing as they like."

"But laws—"

"Laws do about as much good as mosquito netting against a tiger out here, Susannah," he said with finality, his patience giving way. "I told you you wouldn't understand."

And he was right again.

The next morning they emerged into the Amazon proper, five miles of yellow water from bank to bank. Great trees lined the shores that sloped so deeply the steamer almost brushed the foliage at times, but the forest was only a narrow band hiding a flood plain of meadows and shallow lakes that would be flooded several months of the year.

These rich lowlands were the farmlands of the *váreas*, preferred by the Brazilians for their plantations. Here where forest trees did not grow, the land was rich and easy to prepare, and crops that took a year to mature on the highlands sprang to maturity in the six months of the dry season.

Cotton fields again! They were as sweet and green as the finest she had ever seen in Tennessee, but how different, mixed with the tall dark foliage of cacao plantations. Antonio was jubliant now, grinning with pride, happy to explain to her everything about the miles and miles of luxuriant cotton and cacao, sugarcane and tobacco.

They passed a planter's white house, perched on a hillock just above the reach of the highest floods. Tears came to Susannah's eyes. "Oh, it's beautiful, Antonio. It's like home, but in another world."

"There are no Yankees here to take it away from you, Susannah. Brazil is not divided North and South like the United States."

"But it *is* divided, Antonio. Princess Izabel told me that the emperor's wedding present to her was the freedom of the slaves that would have been her dowry."

"Yes. An unusual gift and an expensive one. But we must find some way to develop Brazil without slavery. The emperor believes, and so do I, that no country can really be great built on slavery. It has been illegal to import slaves for decades, and we must find some way to do without them altogether." He looked grave for a moment, and then went on in a lighter vein. "You'll like Santarém, Susannah. It's not like Memphis, but it has a gracious social life. We'll buy a weekend home there someday if you like. Many planters do. Then you'll not be without civilization."

It was several more days before they passed from the yellow Amazon to the black water at the mouth of the Tapajoz River. She was fascinated by the dark, mysterious current, for she remembered that Antonio had told her that up this river gold and diamonds had been found.

White beaches and clumps of javary palms edged the banks, the sky was cloudless, and the air sweet and cool as they approached the harbor at Santarém. The rows of whitewashed houses and the big municipal building reassured her. Surely this place could supply enough of the amenities, and she was grateful that the colony had brought its own American doctor, who would take care of her when the time came. If only Santarém was where they would be living, instead of somewhere in the middle of the jungle!

She wanted to go ashore on the first boat, but then again, she didn't want to go at all. Surely Cort would be waiting for her there, just as he had been waiting in New Orleans. She couldn't stand a repetition of that scene, but this time it could easily be worse.

This time Antonio and Cort were each aware of the other's claim on her. Antonio had been moody and brusque as the steamer approached the town. He was caught in a trap of masculine honor, and he would have to depend on her, a woman, to get him out. He had confessed to her angrily that once in his youth he had challenged a man and killed him and that the experience had disgusted him with that way of settling things. Susannah knew Cort would not share that view; she would have to explain things to Cort so that he believed it was her own decision to stay with Antonio. It would not be easy, since she assumed that Cort held the common opinion that a woman could be mindlessly seduced by an unscrupulous man.

Had she been? Was she merely a love slave? She was never at peace when she was near him. His slightest smile made her giddy, and his flashing eyes could violate her with a casual glance. She loved him wildly, but did he love her? There was something about him that compelled her adoration, something utterly male, yet finely developed, with nothing of the crudeness or roughness of most men about him. His sexuality emanated from him with every step he took. His slightest gesture was infused with his magnetism. He seemed certain of himself about the outcome of the duel. Wasn't he always certain about everything? He never told her he was willing to die for her love, if need be. Indeed, she knew he was not! For when he spoke of Cort's probable fate, he never forgot to infuriate her with a reference to Sam Spangler.

She waited nervously while he went ashore without her, passing the time watching washerwomen slaves spreading the beach with lines of brightly colored laundry and women of all hues going back and forth, carrying jugs of dear river water on their heads. Bathers appeared, one by one, on their way to a certain part of the beach below town.

Through the binoculars she saw clerks carrying towels over their arms; and now and then a well-to-do gentleman followed by a slave carrying a chair, a sponge and soap, and slippers. Indians shot in and out in canoes. A few approached the steamer, hoping to trade produce or pottery. A cattle barge went past, and pretty little pleasure boats drifted about.

In the afternoon Antonio returned with the news that Cort was not in Santarém. The Americans had set up camp on a portion of land grant some miles out of town, and Antonio thought he must be there. Antonio had taken rooms for them in the town's tiny hotel.

Santarém was clean and shadeless, with only a wide, grassy square in front of the twin-towered church and half-wild gardens behind the one- and two-story houses. From the window of their room Susannah could see shops with big green doors where the proprietors sat in the breeze, and at the far end of town were palm-thatched huts along little winding lanes, half-hidden by bushes, the original village, the Indian town.

There was a pile of mail for Antonio, and as he occupied himself reading it that evening, he paused suddenly and handed a letter to her. "This is for you."

"For me? But who . . . ?" She took the envelope wonderingly, the first she had ever seen

with her new name, the Marqueza da Silva. But
the handwriting was as familiar as the address
was strange. "It's from Rachel!" she cried, rip-
ping it open. She had written to her sister from
New Orleans, describing what had happened
and giving her destination.

*Dear Susannah—or must I call you Marqueza, or
are you still a marchioness?*

*Probably by this time you've had your marriage
annulled and are about to marry Cort. Oh, I have
always said that you have all the adventures! Imagine having to choose between two such men! I would
be hard put, I can tell you. Cort is wonderful, of
course, but you know I think the marquess is devastating! I cannot imagine the pair of you sharing a
stateroom, you feeling as you always did about him.
No doubt I won't stop laughing for a week when you
tell me all about it. Do you suppose Cort will mind
if we giggle all day like a pair of schoolgirls? I am
much recovered now, and hope to join you, whenever Cort can spare the money for my fare. In the
meantime, I am living in Memphis with Mrs. St.
John and Aunt Caroline. Do you remember how
expert I became at tailoring while I was making the
uniform? I have put that skill to good use at last.
Mrs. St. John and I have begun a business as
seamstresses. Everyone needs new clothes, and we
have more work than we can handle, making gowns
and even shirts and frock coats for men.*

*Recently we made up a very smart Tweedside
lounge jacket for Captain Spangler. Only he isn't a
captain anymore. Everyone has gone back to calling
him Colonel, though he's left the army now. As soon
as he was well enough, he had the charges against
you dropped. So you ran off and married the marquess for nothing. But isn't it strange how fate
works? If our cotton hadn't been stolen, and if Sam*

Spangler hadn't bought Robin Hill, you would not be where you ought to be—with Cort. Colonel Spangler has put in a new crop at Robin Hill and has repainted the house—

Susannah put the letter down with a gasp. Antonio looked at her sharply. "Not bad news, I hope?" he asked. She flung the letter at him to read.

"So, Susannah, you gambled badly," he said, when he had finished. "You chose me instead of prison, when you could have had neither. Well, at least I have a sister-in-law who approves of me. You may write to Rachel and tell her to make arrangements to join us. You'd like that, wouldn't you?"

"Yes, Antonio. Thank you. Antonio, there's another favor I'd like to ask. I want Aunt Caroline to come too."

Antonio frowned. "Aunt Caroline is free, Susannah. And the Kiss Flower is run with slaves. I'm not sure that mixing them is a good idea."

"Oh, Antonio, that's silly. Rachel will need a chaperon. Who else is she to get? And I want Aunt Caroline." She gazed up at him seductively.

Antonio grinned. "So, my dear, are you willing to pay a price, if I let you have your way?"

"If you are, sir," she said cagily, then lost her dignity as he yanked her into his lap and pushed up her skirts wantonly, his hands circling her thighs.

Laughing and shrieking, she tried to free herself, pushing against his shoulders, enjoying the ripple of muscles beneath his soft shirt, even as she struggled. She failed to realize that she was leaning so that her bodice hung away from her breasts, exposing her creamy skin to his lips. At the tingle of his first intimate kiss, she sighed, giving away a secret that was no secret at all to her husband.

"You shall have your way, though it may well be a mistake, Susannah," he told her. "Now keep your part of the bargain."

"I suppose I must," she murmured happily, glad for the excuse to end her resistance.

With a small grunt he rose, draping her over his shoulder, his hands clasped about her buttocks as she clutched his back, blood rushing to her head. He carried her away to the bedroom to satisfy her desire.

In the morning he surprised her by handing her a list of household items which they required. "I've brought china and linen from Rio, and I've commissioned the largest pieces of furniture. In fact, we have slaves capable of making almost anything you could want, and hundreds of acres of fine hardwoods from which to make it. But we are in needs of utensils and sundries. Buy anything else that catches your eye. The house still needs a great deal to make it seem furnished. Merely give the shopkeeper my name to send the bills to."

She was agog. "Do you mean, Antonio, that I am to do the shopping? Alone and on foot?"

He scowled. "Yes. I suppose I cannot expect to turn you into a Brazilian woman. The other American women will be shopping here, and since we are involved in the colony, it will be better for you to do the same. It will have my mark of approval then and help the Americans to be accepted. But don't expect to behave this way in Rio."

Though he had had the last word, she had won a victory. It would be a long time until they were in Rio, and she did not intend this to be the last instance in which she'd prevail over her prideful husband. They were not so unevenly matched—out of bed!

13

Susannah enjoyed the morning. The air was soft and cool from the river, the sunlight turned the whitewashed buildings golden, and the town, with its unfamiliar shops, was hers to explore. She was scarcely bothered by the startled looks she received from storekeepers and from the gentlemen who seemed to lounge over coffee in every shop. There was too much to see, and after all the penury of the war, she was thrilled with Antonio's instructions to buy anything at all she wanted. In addition to the necessities Antonio had listed, she fell in love with an inlaid table that reminded her of the one in the City Palace, though smaller and round instead of rectangular, the woods arranged by color in a sunburst pattern. She purchased an enormous china clock, a pair of oil lamps, some native pottery for the kitchen, bolts of softly flowered material for curtains and bed hangings and more material for making light, simple dresses. It was odd to be buying for a house she had never seen, and now and then a wave of homesickness washed over her as she thought of Sam Spangler refurbishing her home to suit his Yankee taste.

She was relieved not to be a murderess, but after all, Colonel Spangler had received the lesser wound that night. Hers would never heal, and another life might be lost before the consequences were complete. Susannah made purchases at a furious rate, both to keep her mind off the impending confrontation between Cort and Antonio and to punish Antonio for his insistence on possessing her. If she must be his wife, then she would be an expensive one. She ordered all her purchases sent back to the hotel, where he had told her he would be loading wagons to travel to the Kiss Flower. She had just finished buying a necklace crafted in gold from the Tapajoz and was starting back to the hotel when a voice with an American accent called out to her.

"Hello! Miss Dunbar! Miss Susannah Dunbar!"

The man might have been one of the colonists, but he would have called her Marqueza. She turned in amazement and saw Rudd Sloane coming toward her.

"Bad apples keep turning up, eh, Miss Dunbar?" He smirked as though to say he meant both of them. "I had a bit of a hassle with the law back in Memphis, and this seemed a good place to come. Just like you, eh?"

"I'm married now, Mr. Sloane. I am the Marqueza da Silva."

"So *you* are his wife! Well, there are a hundred ways for a man like me to make a fortune out here, but you have bested me and made yours already!"

Susannah lost her temper. Since she had never expected to see him again, her guard was down, and in spite of the scene it would cause, she wanted nothing more in life than to thrash him senseless with the handle of her new silk-brocade parasol.

"Sir, you are annoying this lady," another voice growled, intervening as she snapped her weapon shut to ready it. Susannah saw Sloane seem to shrivel, even before she turned to see who had arrived to help her.

He wasn't as tall as Antonio, but he was broader, so solid and determined that she couldn't imagine a blow fazing him. His panama hat sat evenly but casually on his head, as though even that would not be dislodged in a fight. His eyes glimmered as though he enjoyed his own strength; and his iron-gray beard stirred in the breeze, the only thing about him in motion, seeming to give impetus to his aura of impending danger.

"Let me know if you have any more cotton you want to sell." Sloane called the parting shot over his shoulder. By the time it was out of his mouth, he was a dozen yards away.

"I am in your debt, sir," Susannah said. She could see Antonio now in the doorway of the hotel and felt a stab of apprehension.

"Allow me to introduce myself. It's not quite proper, but under the circumstances . . . I am

Conde Bernardo Marchado, a friend of your husband's, and if you are in my debt, then I am a fortunate man. Allow me to escort you, Marqueza."

It wasn't surprising that he knew who she was, she thought, taking his arm. But why was *his* name so familiar? As they crossed the street toward Antonio, she remembered suddenly. He was the man who had been Antonio's rival for Joaquina, the man she would now marry. Susannah jerked her head to see if she could find any sign of the brutality of which Princess Izabel had spoken. His face had a ruddiness which came perhaps more from rum than weathering, and his arm was like a thick iron rod where her fingers touched it through the fine worsted of his coat. He was the man who opposed Antonio and Dom Pedro in Santarém!

In alarm she tried to withdraw her hand from his arm, and received a first impression of how demagogic he might be. He simply clamped his arm against his side and squeezed her fingers bloodless. There was no time to think of protest or struggle before he was delivering her to her husband as though she were a lost puppy.

"Welcome back, Antonio," he was saying. "Such a lovely creature you've brought us from the States. I congratulate you. But do you really intend to allow her to wander about alone? The town is filling up with riffraff like the one I've just sent scurrying. Santarém is turning into a den of scroundrels since the river has been opened to foreign navigation. Americans are the worst offenders; I think that colony of yours is attracting them—like flies to a heap of refuse."

"If refuse is attracting them, it is not my

colonists, Bernardo. I wouldn't complain, if I were you. Santarém seems to agree with you. You're looking fit. I thank you for your gallantries to my wife."

The count chuckled, obviously enjoying the innuendo in Antonio's tone. "It was my pleasure," he said so suggestively that Antonio gave up his pretense of equanimity and scowled. "I have to speak to you, Antonio, on business," he said, seeming pleased at having goaded Antonio into an expression of displeasure.

"Go inside and change into something suitable for travel, Susannah," Antonio said. "I want to leave as soon as the wagon is loaded. We've a long way to go tonight."

Susannah did not dispute his command. She was glad to escape the scene. She was ready and waiting an hour later when he arrived to fetch her. She was wearing her riding habit and a smart riding hat with a feather and a wide brim to keep off the sun. But Antonio was still frowning, not seeming to notice how attractive she was in her outfit, and his mood didn't improve as they left Santarém, Antonio driving the first wagon, laden mostly with supplies from the steamer and provisions of dried fish and manioc meal. A second wagon, driven by an Indian in loose white trousers and shirt, carried Susannah's purchases.

She sat quietly beside Antonio on the wagon seat as they left Santarém behind, traveling through sandy hills scattered with low, gnarled trees. Bushes and grass clustered about the tree roots, but there was no real undergrowth, and the horses struggled to pull the wagons along a road that was only a track in the sand.

It was getting dark when they entered the forest. The branches, almost blotting out the graying sky, made the darkness seem sudden. Susannah screamed as a great arm seemed to swing out of the branches and snatch off her hat. Antonio halted the wagon with a sigh and retrieved it.

"It's just a grapevine, Susannah. Their roots have been cut to make the road, but you must watch out for the top parts."

As they drove, he slung the vines left and right into the bushes with great crashing sounds. She began to tremble, not knowing whether it was the forest that frightened her or her husband's foul mood. The wagon jounced in and out of ruts and finally jerked to a halt, entangled in a liana root. Muttering, Antonio got down to chop it away. With the wagons stopped, she was aware of a weird sound all around, like a low growl.

"Antonio, what is that noise?" she said fearfully.

"Tree frogs."

"Oh." She laughed with relief. "They sound different from Tennessee frogs. I thought it was a wild animal."

"Don't worry about night sounds out here, Susannah," he told her. "The dangerous animals like the jaguars usually keep quiet if human beings are close. When you hear them, it's probably too late to run."

Susannah was far from comforted. A peculiar glow beside the road ahead of them claimed her attention. "Antonio, are there ghosts out here?"

"The Indians would say so. But surely you don't believe in ghosts!"

Susannah thought briefly of Robin Hill and the games she and Rachel used to play, making believe they were afraid of the ghost in the old hall mirror. How innocent and long ago! "Then what in the world is that shining up ahead?"

He laughed, his first hint of good humor all evening. "Anthills, my dear, white anthills. They are phosphorescent. There are a lot of them, but at least you won't step on them by accident in the night."

Encouraged, she decided to ask his forgiveness for the incident with Conde Marchado. "I'm sorry about this afternoon, Antonio," she said. "I didn't want assistance from the count, and I know that you and he are adversaries."

"How do you know that, Susannah?"

"From Princess Izabel."

"Really? What else did she tell you?"

Susannah hesitated. "Nothing," she decided to say.

He gave a sigh—of relief, she thought; and she was glad she had not brought up the subject of Joaquina and her probable union with the count.

"Don't worry about this afternoon, Susannah. It's nothing you did that has me upset."

"Then it's something Conde Marchado has done. I knew you must be thinking of him when you said that law did not control rich men out here."

She couldn't see his face in the darkness, but when he spoke, she felt his respect for her insight. "Conde Marchado is not only the wealthiest man in the province, he is intelligent, unscrupulous, and addicted to power like a drug."

"But what has he done, Antonio?" she asked softly.

"He is bent on making mischief in the colony," Antonio told her. "He is bringing in a shipment of a thousand slaves and hopes to sell most of them to the new American growers."

"But what is wrong with that?" she asked, wondering if she sounded foolish. "The growers need slaves."

"They need workers. And it is the emperor's plan and mine to import labor—immigrants from Europe or even China. But the Paraguayan war is causing delay—"

"And the slaves are available now. Perhaps it can't be helped. The Southerners are used to a slave society. They prefer it. I'm sure many of them came to Brazil because it was the only place left to live as they had. It's legal, even if you don't like it, Antonio."

"Legal!" he said furiously. "Conde Marchado will bring the slaves from Ceará, from the slave breeders. They grow them there like stands of timber, and when they are ripe, they cut them away from their families and bind them in chains. They float them away over the treacherous surf on rafts to ships, while their mothers weep. And if the raft capsizes, they drown in irons. There are still some blacks who come in from Africa over that same surf, half-starved themselves and followed by hungry sharks. Maybe it's the lucky ones who fall off the rafts. Importation is illegal, at least, but slave breeding is not."

Susannah was deeply shocked. She had heard of slave owners in the South who separated families or who offered incentives to the parents of slave children, but even that had been rare in her experience. "I don't think the colonists would want to buy slaves that way," she said. "I know Cort wouldn't."

"Perhaps they'd prefer more civilized purchases, but these are the only slaves available at the moment. And what is even more disastrous is that most of the colonists would have no way to pay for them. The count would give them credit against future crops, and then if the harvest fails, he'll have the colonists at his mercy. That is what he's after. He wants control of the American colony. He'd like to develop it into his own empire, with the colonists enslaved to him like tenant farmers on their own plantations."

The night seemed eerier now than when she had merely thought the frogs were some fierce animal and the anthills supernatural spirits. "It won't happen, Antonio," she said. "You and Cort will be able to prevent it."

"Do you really think Cort St. John and I will be able to work together after this?" It wasn't really a question. Antonio seemed more tired than angry now, after confiding his troubles. "We'll be home before long," he told her. "You won't really be able to see it until morning, of course."

In fact she did not see it at all that night. She fell asleep with her head against his shoulder and slept so soundly that she was hardly aware of the wagon creaking to a halt. As if in a lovely dream, she was lifted into his arms, carried up a stairway, and deposited into a soft bed. She smiled in her sleep, certain of what would happen next. She felt a feathery kiss and stretched languidly, wishing for more. But nothing else happened. She slept on, dreaming lovely dreams of Antonio. When she awoke, she almost believed herself still dreaming.

The room was big and airy, its low ceiling making the handcrafted rosewood furniture seem large and more dramatic against the whitewashed walls. Her valise sat beside an armoire of fine *moiracoatidra*, striped black and yellow, polished to a glossy sheen. The beautiful hardwoods never failed to excite her admiration, and she was beginning to recognize most of them.

Wide louvered doors stood open to a balcony, seeming to bring the outdoors in. The bed was so near the doors that she felt she could step out of it into the trees, from which a chorus of birdsong serenaded her. From the balcony she beheld masses of green, glazed gold with morning sun. Cacao and lime trees, banana trees, and coffee bushes climbed the slope. Not far from the house a giant Brazil-nut tree towered two hundred feet, its branches so high above the earth she had to crane her neck to see.

The trees rolled up to a plateau, where she could just make out stalks of waving cane. A burst of color flashed over blossoms below the balcony—a hummingbird in the lantana, followed by another, brighter than any she had ever seen.

The Kiss Flower, she thought exultantly. She was home at last in that place Antonio had fabled.

A knock came on the door, and she called out permission to enter. An Indian girl appeared, carrying a large towel and soap. "Do you wish to bathe, Marqueza? Your husband said I should ask."

"Oh, that would be lovely! And I am so glad you speak English."

"I learned from missionaries. That is why I was chosen to be your maid, Marqueza." She smiled shyly, happy with what must have been a coveted appointment, and apprehensive at the same time to be in the service of the exotic foreigner the marquess had brought home.

"Tell me your name," Susannah said.

"I am called Olinda," she said. "I was named for a spring where my mother gave birth to me. She had gone there to dig for sarsparilla root."

A scene flashed into Susannah's mind. A woman alone in the jungle, helpless in childbirth. But nothing like that would be required of *her*, she told herself sternly. She smiled at Olinda, who was looking worried, afraid she'd displeased the marchioness somehow.

"I would love to bathe," Susannah said enthusiastically, and Olinda sprang into action this time, searching the portmanteaus for a wrapper and a change of clothing. Still in the garments she had slept in, Susannah followed her through the house, down a shining stairway into a long center hall, where a cool breeze swept from one end to the other. It wasn't as large an establishment as Robin Hill, but it sparkled with newness. As Antonio had told her, it was practically unfurnished.

In the dining room a pair of slave women, working at unpacking boxes of silver into an ebony sideboard, looked up and smiled, chattering greetings in Portuguese. *"Bonsdias,"* Susannah returned, for she had been trying to learn the language of her new country. In the drawing room the tables and lamps she had bought in Santarém sat awkwardly before uncurtained windows, waiting for her to arrange them. This house had belonged to no other woman, she thought with a surge of excitement. It was hers to put her own mark upon.

Olinda led her out through an arched doorway, onto a portico flanked by slender Ionic columns. "Where are we going?" Susannah asked as the girl went nimbly down the brick steps onto a walk lined with luxuriant caladiums and pink begonias. Beyond the walk was a long drive lined with little palms which she knew would soon grow as tall and magnificent as the surrounding forest into which the avenue marched and disappeared. The house itself sat on a small hillock in what seemed a natural clearing, but Olinda left the brick walk for a little path which quickly became narrow and weedy. Insects and butterflies flew up at their passage as they entered the edge of the woods.

In a moment she heard the trickle of water and caught sight of the pool. A low rock wall surrounded its clear water, in which were reflected tree ferns and palms, bending over it as though to observe their own beauty. Orchids trailed among the branches of the shady arbor they made, and wild roses were rampant over the walls of a little thatch-roofed bathhouse. A spring gurgled, making the reflections ripple over the water. The jungle growth made her privacy complete; nonetheless, Olinda sat not far away, ready to ward off any intruder, and for a while Susannah shared the place only with a monkey that scolded her from a branch.

She refreshed herself gloriously, then knelt in the shallows while Olinda washed her hair with a sweet-smelling soap she said the Indians made, and then rinsed it in lime juice.

Finally, clad in only a chemise, she drowsed in the filtered sun, drying her hair spread over the rocks, while Olinda picked oranges from a nearby tree to squeeze for her breakfast.

She roused with a start, now knowing why. She had heard no sound; yet as she lifted her eyes, wondering why she was suddenly afraid, she met the gaze of a savage looking down at her. He was no more than two yards away, his shadow across her shutting off her sun, his body naked except for a leather loincloth. All of his bronze skin, from his sandaled feet to the plume of bright feathers in his hair, was tattooed in incomprehensible red and blue symbols. Olinda was nowhere in sight, and as the Indian stretched a hand toward her, it flashed into her mind that he had already murdered her.

Susannah screamed. But the Indian held his ground, speaking now, in an unintelligible language, gesturing at her, threatening with his powerful outstretched arm. Susannah screamed again, scrambling to her feet, trying to find a loose rock to throw at him. But the rocks were all too large and too well seated.

"Go away! Go away! Oh, what do you want?" She was shaking, almost sobbing. She wrapped herself in her towel to hide her undress. Heavy footsteps raced along the path, and Antonio came crashing through a clump of banana trees, taking a shortcut in his haste. "What's the matter?"

She pointed wordlessly.

"That is only Jamunda," he said, panting.

"He is a Mundurucús chieftain, and to be respected. The Mundurucús have been friends to us ever since they overcame the Tapajoz tribe almost a hundred years ago, and without them to guard us, we would still be subject to the attacks of hostile Indians. To think I ran all the way from the top of the bluff! I would have thought you'd have better sense than to scream like a mindless female." He sounded disgusted, and she remembered that one of the reasons he had thought she'd be a suitable wife was her experience at self-sufficiency.

"I didn't know he was friendly," she shot back.

"You could have asked Olinda."

Susannah glanced about and saw Olinda standing by the door of the bathhouse. She must have come out at the beginning of the commotion, but Susannah had been too riveted on the Indian to see her. It had all happened quickly, and now that her terror had vanished as quickly as it had come, Susannah felt foolish.

"What does he want?" she asked.

Antonio spoke with the Indian in his own tongue. "He has a message for you. See, he is offering you a pouch."

Susannah was even more chagrined that she hadn't noticed the little bag in the chief's hand. She took it and opened it gingerly, half-expecting something grotesque inside, but there was only an envelope addressed to her.

"It's from Cort," she said.

"Olinda, take Jamunda and get him some refreshment," Antonio ordered. The next moment they were alone.

"Open the letter, Susannah," Antonio commanded.

"Oh, Antonio!" This was what she had been dreading.

"You can't put it off," he told her sternly. "The time's come, and I won't do it for you. You know what's in it already."

He was right on both counts, as he always seemed to be. She had been pretending all morning, enjoying the beautiful place, delighting at having become its mistress, making believe that nothing was wrong.

But, of course, it couldn't last. Perhaps that was why Jamunda had frightened her so badly. She had been expecting trouble. She broke the seal and took out the letter.

Dearest Susannah,
   Please come to me at once and tell me when we can be married. Jamunda can show you the way. I cannot wait, my beloved!

"He has sent the Indian to bring me to him," she told Antonio, who was watching her impassively.

"Then you must go."

"Antonio, I—"

"I have thought about this, Susannah. You must tell him the truth as only you know it. Don't try to protect me, Susannah. Let me take the consequences for whatever I have done. Whatever advantage I took of you, report to him. Though it may cost one of us his life, we are both men of honor, and neither of us can live in peace until this matter is resolved."

"Antonio—"

"I will have a horse saddled for you. It's no more than an hour's ride, and you will be very safe with Jamunda."

At Antonio's insistence, she choked down a breakfast of fish, fresh orange juice, and corn muffins, and sooner than she wished, found herself clad in her rather wilted riding skirt and a fresh blouse, trotting along a pleasant path beside the silent Indian. The trail led down a forested slope and into a valley where the vegetation was thick and high. Then they passed into an old clearing, luxuriant with flowering vines and young trees. Later they stopped at a clear brook overhung with acacias and scarlet passionflowers. Around the brook dozens of paths led back to little thatched Indian houses built in small clearings. Finally they arrived at a larger cleared expanse where a log house had been started. Though the spot was as lovely, with huge palms arching over the half-finished veranda, the contrast with the Kiss Flower struck her forcibly.

As she dismounted, suddenly there was Cort in the newly framed doorway, lean and sun-browned, his hair as much lighter in the blazing day as his skin was darker. He hurried toward her joyfully in his rough trousers and shirt rolled high over work-muscled arms.

A wave of pleasure washed over her; he was no longer the battle-weary wraith who had come home to her after the war, no longer ravaged and hopeless. Brazil had done this for him, as Antonio had promised, but she was about to disinherit him again.

Cort misunderstood the look of despair on her face; perhaps he wanted to. "I know it isn't much, Susannah, but someday we'll have a grand establishment here. We've wonderful black loam two feet deep, and plenty of water power.

I've already bought fifty slaves and begun the crop. Oh, but I don't want to talk about crops, my darling. I want to talk about us. About how much I love you. And about when we can be married. When, Susannah?" He reached to take her into his arms, but she moved away.

"Cort," she said grimly, "we can't be married."

The light went out of him. "Why not?" he asked. "Wouldn't the emperor grant the annulment?"

She wanted to blame it all on Dom Pedro, who was far away on the Paraguayan frontier and out of reach of Cort's retribution, but she remembered what Antonio had told her. Nothing but the truth would do.

"The emperor never heard of it, Cort."

"Never heard of it! Why?"

"Because . . . because . . ." She dropped her eyes from his, burning with pain and anger. "Because it was not in name only."

"What, Susannah? I cannot believe . . ." His voice was a croak, almost as inaudible as hers.

She looked at him. "It was not in name only," she said strongly.

"Then I will kill him, Susannah!" The simplicity of the statement made her shudder.

"Oh, Cort, it won't change things to kill Antonio," she pleaded.

"Certainly it will. You have been dishonored, and I will make him pay for it. We will be married, and after a time, we'll forget all this and be happy. I don't care what's happened. I love you."

"Cort, please don't duel Antonio!"

"I suppose you think that husband of yours would kill me instead. He will not, I assure you. Must I prove to you that I am the better man? I will do so with pleasure."

The truth. Tears came to her eyes. "You will be murdering the father of my child, Cort. I am going to have his baby."

Cort was so staggered he collapsed on the porch step and put his head in his hands. She waited, hoping that somehow he would accept the situation, knowing all the while he wouldn't. He stood up, went inside, and returned, bringing with him a flat rectangular box.

"Do you remember these, Susannah?"

She felt ill. "Yes, the dueling pistols from Hazel Grove."

"They've been in the family for generations. My grandfather defended his honor with these. And now it's my turn. When I took them with me, I thought I was only saving a memento of the past."

"Cort, don't use them! They *are* the past. *We* are the past, you and I. It's all gone—the time and the place where we were meant to spend our lives together."

"No, Susannah. Nothing's gone. We came out here to save what we had. We are only rebuilding."

"It's gone, Cort! I was willing!"

But Cort, staring at the pistols, didn't seem to hear. "Tell the marquess, I shall be at the clearing near the Indian village at one o'clock. I shall expect him to meet me there."

"Cort, I was willing! I love him, Cort!"

He turned and went inside.

If he had heard her, it didn't matter. But *she* had heard, and it mattered very much. The truth, Antonio had said, the truth as only she could know it. And in telling Cort St. John the truth, she had learned it herself. She could not help loving Antonio. She would love him forever.

She jumped back on her horse without waiting for Jamunda. She knew the way now, and she galloped for the Kiss Flower as rapidly as the terrain would allow.

Antonio came out onto the portico at the sound of the horse on the lane. She saw him as she never had before, and her heart caught at the sight of his dark, graceful figure in the sunshine.

How heartbreakingly stalwart he looked, his eyes set with purpose, failing to mask the pain in his task. Manliness exuded from him, vulnerability mixing with honor and courage. Oh, how handsome he was, his proud head lifted, the athletic shoulders squared. He was everything she would ever want or need; and because she might lose him, she saw him in a golden light.

"Well," he said, reading the results of her encounter on her face as she slid down from the saddle, "when and where is it to be?"

"Antonio, don't go! Don't fight him!" She flung herself at him, arms around his neck, sobbing into his chest.

"This behavior is unbecoming, Susannah," he said irritably, disappointed in her again. "You know I must go. St. John and I cannot live on the Amazon together without resolving our differences."

"Then resolve them some other way!"

He laughed shortly. "Do you think fisticuffs or a wrestling match would suffice in a matter of this magnitude? Perhaps you'd like a fencing exhibition. Cort St. John deserves his duel, and

I would be a coward for suggesting anything else."

"Antonio! There is more than yourself and your pride to consider. You have a family. Antonio, I am going to have your baby!"

The desperate words tumbled out. She had told him at last! She waited to see the difference that the knowledge of impending fatherhood would make. But Antonio's expression didn't change.

"I know you are pregnant, Susannah."

"You know!" She flushed with anger and embarrassment. "How long have you known?"

"I knew on the ship on the way to Rio. It wasn't seasickness, love. Did you think I was too stupid or ignorant to figure it out? That is all the more reason, of course—I can't have a child who thinks his father is a coward."

"You knew then, when even I didn't know!" Her grief turned to sudden fury. She realized miserably this must be the reason he had refused the annulment. He had been interested in the child, not her! Overwhelmed with humiliation, she thought of how she had succumbed to him. She had been powerless to resist him, but she had hoped, surely she had hoped that he loved her. He was a practical man, and she had already proved herself a good brood mare. That was how she had got the advantage on the lovely, wealthy Joaquina!

"Oh, go and fight your duel if you must! But if you live and Cort St. John doesn't, I will make the rest of your life miserable. I swear it. Do you think I will let you in my bed again after you have killed him?"

He pulled away from her flailing fists and

gave her a mocking look to tell her he wasn't worried by her threat. "Well, my dear, do as you wish. I'll have no trouble finding someone to warm my bed if you leave it!"

"Oh, I hate you!"

"You are married to a fool, Susannah. Were foolishness grounds for an annulment, you would have it at once. God, does the man exist who doesn't play the fool for you? There was a time when I thought myself superior to Sam Spangler. Now I only hope I am as lucky as he!"

He shoved her away from him. "When and where, Susannah?" he demanded.

"In the clearing near the Indian village at one o'clock," she said tonelessly.

"Then I've no time to lose," he said. He gave a shout, and a slave brought up a horse he had had saddled and waiting. Antonio mounted and galloped off down the lane of fledgling palms.

As he disappeared, her anger changed again to terror. He had ridden away, perhaps to die because of her, and the last thing she had said to him was that she hated him. Was he right about her? Was she destined to lead men to their doom? Sam Spangler and now Antonio or Cort? Cort, whose only crime had been to love her. Antonio, who held her with a fascination undimmed by his many transgressions.

Dear God, whom was she to hope to see remain standing? What could she, a mere woman, do about this intensely masculine event?

But Susannah wasn't a woman to accept the role of female helplessness. The war had taught her that there was always a way—only, a woman must use her head more than a man, and she must not be afraid of risk.

Suddenly she knew how to stop it. She might have thought of it before, but it was so drastic it could not have occurred to her until the time was imminent.

I will throw myself between them on the dueling field, she decided. They will have to shoot around me if they are to kill each other. And if they remove me by force, they will have to bind me hand and foot to prevent my returning.

Cort would never do that, although Antonio might. And either of them might be capable of locking her in a room. She would see that it took both of them. She would become the common enemy, pitting herself against them and their male code; and perhaps when they had subdued her, their fire to murder each other would dissolve into something less.

Without calling a groom, she unhitched her horse and mounted from a huge stump where a tree had been cut down; but the horse, from the morning's exertion, refused to go as fast as she wished. She dug in her heels and applied the crop, cantering where she should have trotted and trotting even where the terrain was too dangerous for anything but a walk. More than once the horse stumbled over a liana root and Susannah was almost thrown over its head. But she was a good rider and hung on, knowing that it would be her fault if the horse broke a leg and had to be shot.

Overhanging branches grabbed at her hair and slapped at her face. She endured the punishment for the sake of speed, but when they came to the brook near the Indian houses, the horse stopped to drink and would not go on. She shouted and hit him with the crop and kicked him bruisingly, but the animal merely turned its head and gazed at her blankly. Tears streamed down her cheeks, the salt making the scratches on her face burn. Finally an Indian came into the clearing. A few hours ago she would have been afraid of him, but now she only begged him to help her, speaking in a confused jumble of English and Portuguese which she hoped he understood. But the problem was easily understood in any case, and the Indian took some sugar out of his trouser pocket and lured the horse away from the stream. Once started, the horse kept moving, but at a leisurely pace. She supposed that Antonio had chosen one of the Kiss Flower's least spirited mounts for her. Hadn't he been privy to her troubles with Sultan in Memphis, though she could ride as well as anyone?

As she approached the clearing, she saw Antonio's horse tied to a palm tree. Snapping open the cover of her little pendant watch, she saw it was several minutes past one, and she jumped down and ran as hard as she could toward the edge of the woods.

They were already on the field: Cort with sunlight on his hair, his suntanned face and arms looking almost as golden, poised like a bronze statue; Antonio like the shadow of a tall tree in the afternoon. Across the field, between them, one of the colonists was ready to give the command, and there were several others who must have come as seconds or witnesses.

She opened her mouth to scream, but she

was so out of breath that the sound was only a gasp. And then she heard the cry. "Fire!"

It happened so quickly she could hardly grasp it. One shot, and somehow both were standing. Inexplicably, Antonio's pistol was pointed toward the sky. Into the sound of the first shot came a second, so quickly it could hardly be distinguished from the first. Antonio jerked backward and fell to the ground. Susannah burst through the brush and ran to his side. As she knelt, she looked into the stunned eyes of Cort St. John, who knelt on the other.

"Susannah! He could have killed me! He fired into the air, and then it was too late. I was already squeezing the trigger and . . . Is he dead?" Cort, unfastening Antonio's jacket, was pushed aside by one of the spectators, who, she saw now, was the colony's doctor.

"Move aside, young man," the doctor said disgustedly. "He's alive; I'll save him, if I can. I thought I was done with this sort of thing, but the Yankees made me an expert, at least, on gunshot wounds."

Antonio opened his eyes and saw her weeping over him. "I guess my luck's as good as Sam Spangler's," he said, and lapsed into unconsciousness.

14

For weeks Antonio hovered between life and death, while Susannah remained by his side, wondering if she were to be a widow. It was impossible to imagine marriage to Cort now, even if Antonio died. If he died, in time he would be only a distant memory, except that she would have the child to remind her. But the idea of doing without him forever appalled her. She had learned the truth for the first time when she had told it to Cort, and now as she bravely changed bandages and pressed fluid between his lips, she never doubted that she loved him.

Did he love her too, in spite of everything? She had told him she would never warm his bed again if he killed Cort. Was that why he had fired in the air?

When Antonio was finally on the mend, she asked him for his reason. "Because I was too vain not to fire at all and have people say he was faster than I," Antonio confessed.

"But why didn't you shoot him, Antonio?"

"Because I had wronged him. I didn't want the blood of a man with whom I had no quarrel on my conscience."

Susannah believed him. What had happened had had nothing to do with his feelings for her.

She was growing large with his child and could no longer hide it from anyone. A room near hers had been set aside for a nursery, and a craftsman slave set to making the cradle. But Antonio was constantly in a foul mood. He was unable to attend to the plantation or the affairs of the colony, and when he tried to get up in spite of doctor's orders, the pain was so sharp that he fell back with a cry. When she tried to calm him, telling him to rest and get well, he would fly into a rage.

"What is to become of this place, Susannah? I had not hired an overseer, and there is a crop to bring in. If we do not have it ripe and harvested by the time the floods come, our future will be swept down the river!"

"Perhaps you could tell me what to do," she said tentatively.

"What nonsense! You, ride herd on the slaves? A woman, in your condition! Why, you are going to be a mother and are supposed to confine yourself to sipping tea and crocheting little garments."

His tone always diminished her. "There are no crochet needles out here," she retorted once, but this made him even angrier, since he thought she was complaining about his failure to provide the niceties of life.

"There may soon be nothing out here but jungle again," he stormed, "and your St. John will be the ruin of me. He is buying slaves and encouraging all the others to do so. Soon everyone will be in debt to Conde Marchado; and then, if anything happens to the crop, he will have the entire colony at his mercy. Of which he has none!"

"Do you mean he will foreclose?"

"He'll do whatever suits his schemes. He will have the power in my colony."

"But there was no choice but to buy slaves, Antonio. You've said yourself that the Indians are too unreliable."

"Yes, when an Indian gets a day's pay, he's likely to go to a rumhouse—probably one that belongs to Conde Marchado—and forget work for the next week. Ha! That is one thing the count wants to keep as it is—the duties on sugar, so that we cannot afford to export it and have to turn it into rum instead. But Cort St. John prefers slaves, Susannah. He wants to rebuild the old system, while I want something new. And when you combine that with his dislike of me, he is the count's natural ally."

"Antonio, are you sure that Cort hates you? He . . . admired you so much once. He's had his satisfaction now. He's nearly killed you. He'll make peace someday with the fact that I am your wife."

"He may forgive me someday for marrying you, but he'll never forgive me for humiliating him by not taking my shot in the field of honor."

"Then why don't you replace him as vice-president of the colony?"

He shot her a scoffing glance. "Replace him! He was elected to his position by the colonists and probably has more influence with them than I by this time. And there is no one half as competent as Major St. John."

She sighed and went to throw open the shutters to the cool evening air.

"Susannah . . ." His voice had a softer tone. "Have *you* made peace with being my wife?" As she passed close to him, he stretched out his arm and touched the swell of her body tenderly. "I know you would not have given up on the annulment if you hadn't been pregnant."

"I suppose I am . . . used to it." She looked away from him, not wanting him to see how much she loved him. She was certain that he regretted the impulsive actions that had led him to marry her. Hadn't he married her after having taken her as a virgin and when she was in dire need of a husband to protect her from the Yankees?

In spite of his blusterings, would he have resisted the annulment in Rio if he hadn't guessed she was carrying his child? Now that he had nearly met death because of her, surely he hated her. Every stab of pain must remind him of all the misfortune he'd suffered because of her. The trouble with the plantation, the direction the new colony was taking—how different these things might have been if he had been well and strong.

Though he had discouraged her, she took to riding about the plantation, learning all she could and trying to stamp out inefficiency where she saw it. It was hardly an easy task, and one Antonio would never have allowed had he known it, since the doctor had told her to give up riding until the child was born. But Antonio slept for long periods, and she was always there when he wakened and called for her.

The amazed slaves resisted her at first, but slowly she won them with her fairness and praise and her concern for their well-being. Even so, Susannah knew she couldn't go on for long; each day it was harder to climb into the saddle, and the jolting seemed worse. She was becoming exhausted, and though some of the slaves did well with limited authority over others, these slaves needed direction themselves. In spite of Susannah's progress, there was still a lack of discipline and a great deal of carelessness. Susannah hardly knew why the slaves simply didn't vanish into the jungle without an overseer riding herd with a shotgun. But the slaves seemed to feel lucky to be on the Kiss Flower. A runaway, if caught, could expect to be sold, and Conde Marchado was the major slave dealer in the area. No one wanted to risk falling into his hands, she discovered; the notion frightened them far more than the thought of jaguars and tigers lurking in the jungle.

Meanwhile, the colonists had built a blacksmith shop and a tile-roofed millhouse and had imported an American sugar mill made of iron, turned by water power. They had dammed a stream for the water wheel, and the cane was to be fed into the mill down a long chute, five hundred feet of hand-hewn boards leading to the grinders. The new sugar mill, located on Cort's plantation, Twenty Palms, was more elaborate than the wooden mill owned by the count, which in turn had superseded crude rollers which the Indians turned by hand.

The work was slow and often discouraging. Those who had bought slaves were ahead of those who tried to depend on Indians, but everyone was suffering the privations of pioneers.

Susannah heard the news of the colony from those of the men who stopped on their way to or from Santarém to see what she needed or to bring her goods. Sometimes a wife came along, and then Susannah, desperate for companionship of her own kind, would insist they come inside and share a glass of native wine, made on the Kiss Flower from *caju* fruits. The husband might be impatient, but he could at least enjoy himself smoking away Antonio's cigars, and the air of the veranda was filled with the fragrant aroma of fine local tobacco while the ladies talked.

The women of the colony hardly knew how to relate to Susannah. The two most important men of the expedition had dueled over her; and in a way, it was difficult not to be envious. Some women believed the marchioness to have been at fault; others, putting together what they knew, found her innocent. Some denounced her for deserting Cort St. John; others, still suffering in tents and longing for civilization, did not blame her for becoming mistress of the beautiful Kiss Flower and the wife of a charming nobleman. Those who visited carried away impressions to be shared. The marchioness, they said, did not choose a leisurely life, and her foolishness was likely to be the death of her in her condition. Already one of the women had died giving birth in a thatched hut, and another had had a sickly infant that had succumbed in a few days to a fever.

A few praised her for trying to keep things going as well as she could, but most agreed that the marchioness had forgotten she was only a woman.

In spite of her visitors, Susannah really had no friends in the colony. She had been too ill to get to know anyone on the voyage out and now that only added to the sense of distance between her and the others. Olinda was too unworldly to offer much companionship. She had never even been to Santarém, and sometimes Susannah wept from sheer loneliness.

But one day an elegant young woman alighted from one of the colonists' wagons. Her smart dark serge walking dress was trimmed in white braid, and her little "Japanese" hat, flat and round, with a knob in the middle, was worn tilted forward, while her blond chignon rose up behind. Susannah stared for a long moment, until a more familiar figure, black and rotund, descended, carrying a silk pagoda-shaped parasol and fussing noisily at the blond lady for having left it behind in the wagon.

"Rachel! Aunt Caroline!" She raced awkwardly down the path and hugged and kissed them both while happy tears ran down her cheeks.

"Oh, Rachel, how beautiful you've become! But . . . oh, didn't you get the second letter I sent you? I wanted things to be perfect when you came, and they certainly are not! Why, I haven't done a thing with the house yet. Even the drapery material is still in bolts. Antonio is

. . . and I am . . ." She gestured helplessly at her distended body.

"Dear me, Susannah, I'm not a guest, you know. I'm your sister. Of course I got your second letter, and that's why I took an earlier boat that I intended. A good thing, too, by the looks of you! Had I been any later, I might have missed the birth of my niece or nephew, and I want to be in on everything from the beginning."

Rachel stopped and laughed wryly. "Well, of course, I have not been in on everything. You've kept secrets from me, Susannah. Otherwise I shouldn't have been surprised to learn how things have turned out. So this is the Kiss Flower. What a wonderful place, just as he said it was. And Antonio is recovering. We heard that news in Santarém. My goodness, Susannah, you could never have resisted him for so long if it hadn't been for Cort. To think you used to say you hated him. And he thought you were—"

"Things haven't changed as much as it seems, Rachel," Susannah said as she led her sister into the house. And when they were alone upstairs, she said trimly, "I am carrying his child. That is why we have remained husband and wife. He would tell you the same thing."

"But he . . . and you let him . . ."

"Passion is not a simple thing, Rachel," she sighed.

The last words she'd spoken to Antonio before he had ridden off to duel for her had been words of animosity. He'd never known that she had ridden after him to throw herself between him and Cort St. John. She had confessed her love for her husband to the wrong

man, but perhaps it had been a good thing.
Better for Antonio not to know how much she
loved him. She would only be humiliated all
the more. And though Rachel was bound to see
how strained their marriage was, she needn't
know the full extent of her sister's pain.

To Susannah's surprise, Rachel took over the
house like a windstorm. She had bloomed into
a self-confident young woman, and her health
had bloomed with her. Her old spunk had not
diminished, and she bustled about giving orders, enjoying having her older sister depend
on her for the first time.

"Susannah, your hair has become dull. You
must brush it a hundred strokes each night as
you used to do."

"Oh, I'm too tired."

"Then Olinda will do it for you. You mustn't
let yourself go out here. Are you drinking milk?
I'm sure I've heard that mothers-to-be should
do that. Is there a cow?"

"It's too hot for milk, Rachel!"

"I'll put it in the springhouse and make it
nice and cool."

She was every bit as tyrannical with Antonio,
plundering his care from Susannah. Somewhat
to Susannah's dismay, Antonio seemed to like
her energetic dominance. It was a change, she
supposed, to have someone so bright and spirited after her own weary ministrations. What
man would not prefer to be nursed by the vibrant, laughing Rachel, graceful and petite in
the finely tailored gowns she'd made herself?
Rachel had always admired Antonio and had
never made a secret of it. Now, as his sister-in-
law, she made him simple little gestures of af-

fection, patting his hand as she smoothed his sheets, mussing his hair as she plumped his pillow, and calling him her "dear brother" when he ate his dinner for her.

His face lighted up every time she came into the room, and in the days following Rachel's arrival he improved dramatically. Soon she was taking him for walks about the grounds, holding onto his arm to make certain he didn't stumble, smiling up at him all the while, as though he were the one giving support.

From her bedroom where she was trying to rest, Susannah could see how handsome they looked together, and she was furious with her own clumsiness and exhaustion. If she were not pregnant, she thought, wild with jealousy, if he had not done this to her . . . But he and she had never been so easy and carefree together.

To make matters worse, he began to notice changes she had made on the plantation, and approved of none of them.

"Where is the white mule, Susannah?" he demanded.

"I lent it to Mr. Anderson. His mule died, and he couldn't plow without one."

"You ought to have lent the gray one. If Mr. Anderson had one mule die, he's likely to work another to death as well, and the white mule was the best I had."

"Then if it's the beast, it'll be harder to kill," she countered.

"Blast it, you ought to have asked!"

"You would only have ordered me to keep to the house," she retorted.

"Yes, and with good reason," he said, eyeing her midsection. "What is that I smell? Molasses? We are making molasses? We always make rum."

"There was a problem with the distillery, and there's been no one who could repair it, so it was either molasses or take the cane to Conde Marchado's distillery."

"We'll make less from molasses."

"But the count would have charged us too much, and this way he will not profit."

He strode off in the direction of the distillery, noticing as he went some children headed for the stream with cane poles. "Why are those boys going fishing in the middle of the day when there's work they ought to do?" he growled, his mood now completely foul.

"They'll work better for the fun, and their parents will work better for the fine meal they'll bring home," she said strongly, but with courage waning.

"Susannah, I do not want you giving any more orders around here. You're turning the place upside down. Thank heavens you'll have a child soon to keep you out of mischief. You may give *him* all the orders you like until he's old enough to come with me. Imagine a woman running the Kiss Flower! How will I ever set it straight?"

Susannah fled to her room and wept. Had she been hoping to win his approval with her activities? Even a declaration of love? She should have known better, of course. Antonio could not cope with loss of control, especially to a woman. He could not accept the notion that any of her ideas might be worthwhile outside of the normal realm of a woman.

That, she had almost entirely neglected, and

it was left to Rachel to enthusiastically begin the decorating. Unlike Susannah, she seemed delighted to deal with only feminine endeavors, which, when Antonio noticed, drew his praise. And when Rachel wished something of him, she charmed and cajoled, much the way Susannah used to do with Colonel Spangler. Susannah had changed, she realized. Her girlish flirtatiousness had vanished. It was no longer easy or natural to be coy. Was it her pregnancy? Or the duel? Or was it because she cared too much?

Almost without willing it, she challenged Rachel about her attitude toward Antonio. "You must be careful not to fall in love with him, Rachel," she said one day.

"Fall in love with him? What an idea! Why, he is my brother now."

"Brother! That is only a relationship on paper."

"Like husband?" she countered. "Have you made up your mind yet whether you want him, Susannah? I am not the one with the reputation of betrayal and violence. Don't blame me if you've lost him."

Tension between the sisters grew; it was even more painful to Susannah than the tension between her and Antonio. At least she was glad to have the comfort of Aunt Caroline, who would be with her when the baby was born, just as she'd been with Susannah's mother.

Aunt Caroline had been overjoyed to accompany Rachel to Brazil. She was back with her two "children," and all was right with the world, even if her pies were sometimes stolen from the windowsill by tattooed Indians, and monkeys scolded and pelted her on her way to do her wash.

But even Aunt Caroline was different now. Every evening when the work was done, she disappeared from the house. Had she been a younger woman, Susannah might have guessed she was meeting a lover, but Aunt Caroline was white-haired. Though she didn't know her age, Susannah simply couldn't imagine it. But Aunt Caroline was going somewhere, and secretively. Sometimes she slipped out of the kitchen with a basket and hid it beneath the leaves of a big philodendron. Then, later, she would retrieve the basket before she slipped into the woods.

Susannah, confined more and more to a rocking chair on the veranda, was sure she was the only one who had the time and interest to notice Aunt Caroline's strange treks. One evening Susannah had gone down to the bathing pool to pick some little yellow *janitá* berries, for which she'd developed a craving, when she saw Aunt Caroline's bright calico skirt go past on the path. The old woman hadn't seen her, kneeling behind dense foliage. Susannah gave in to an impulse to follow her.

Moving as quietly as she could, Susannah kept the old woman in sight, watching as she turned off the main trail onto an overgrown footpath into a grove of banana and castor-oil trees. For all her age, Aunt Caroline was sprightlier than Susannah, and as the brush grew thicker, Susannah fell too far behind to see where Aunt Caroline was going. She was a little frightened, alone in the woods and afraid of losing her way altogether. But suddenly she came to a tiny clearing in which stood an old hut, leaning, so covered with vines it seemed to have grown there. On second glance, she saw that it *had* grown there, after all. The sides were buttresses formed of great tree roots, spreading out a yard or so wide and rising against the tree to twice that height. Someone had long ago thatched a roof across to make a shelter. Curiously Susannah approached it.

Inside, Aunt Caroline whirled as a branch cracked under Susannah's foot. On her face was a hostile expression Susannah had never seen before. In the corner of the shelter sat a black man, thin and tattered, eagerly consuming cakes of manioc meal from Aunt Caroline's basket. His wrists were bound in chains, which he had managed to break apart in the middle.

"Aunt Caroline, you are hiding a runaway slave!" Susannah said, shocked.

"Ain't no slave, Miss Susannah. This is a free man. I been both and I know the difference."

"Why, Aunt Caroline, it hasn't been any different for you. You've stayed with Rachel and me just like before the war. You've been loyal."

"Miss Susannah, you're a white woman and cannot know the difference freedom means to all of us."

This, astonishingly, came from the manacled man, in a precise British accent. Susannah simply stared.

The black man smiled. "It surprises you that I am educated, Marqueza. Let me introduce myself. My name is Simon, and I studied at the missionary school in Africa. I learned quickly, and when I had learned everything available to me in my native country, the church arranged for me to go to England to study. I hoped to return to minister to my people, but I never reached England. I was kidnapped and put onto a slave ship headed for Ceará."

"And then sold to that Rudd Sloane," Aunt Caroline put in.

"You know Rudd Sloane, Marqueza?" Simon asked.

"Indeed I do. He stole all the cotton my father had hidden for my sister and me to sell after the war. I was left penniless, while he outfitted himself in style. I'm sure it was he. No one is more despicable!"

"Unless it is Conde Marchado."

"What has he to do with this?"

"I kept my ears open, Marqueza. Conde Marchado merely pays Rudd Sloane a commission on slaves he brings from Ceará. And it's not just the legal slaves from the breeding farms Sloane is selling. The count finances slave ships, like the one I came on."

"Why, that's what Antonio has suspected. He'll be delighted to have some proof!"

"Miss Susannah, don't tell your husband!" Aunt Caroline said in just the tone she had used to order the little girls to stay out of her buttermilk cookies.

"Not tell Antonio!" It was difficult for Susannah to disregard the old woman, but she was a married woman and had new allegiances now. Antonio was already furious with her over the things she had done while he was ill. How much angrier would he be if he found out about this?

"Aunt Caroline, he is really opposed to slavery; and he hates the idea of illegal slaves most of all. You cannot expect me to have secrets from Antonio."

"Marqueza, it will be Conde Marchado's word against mine, and there are too many planters who want to keep the illegal slaves coming. I don't dare trust him. Your husband knows my word is worthless; and anyway, there's no need for him to know. Bring me a little money, and I'll be gone. I'll hire an Indian guide to take me to Pará. I can hire myself out there, like other free men of color. I have even heard there are some tradesmen of my race in Pará."

"It's true. But suppose I don't bring you the money. Suppose I tell my husband, as a wife ought?"

Simon gazed at her with intense sorrowful eyes. He impressed her in a way that few men of any race had. His face was gentle, but deep within it was determination, molded into his features like the creases of tree bark, a certainty of purpose, the knowledge of some destiny, some sacred mission from which he would not be swayed. His soft dark eyes intruded into hers. "Then whatever happens, I'll be on your conscience, Marqueza."

Susannah turned and ran back down the tangled path. When she reached the bathing pond, she was aching and out of breath. Pausing, she took a drink of spring water from a dipper made of a calabash and straightened her hair and clothing. Why, after all, should this man upset her so? She'd tell Antonio at once, of course. She must try to be the sort of wife he wished her to be; and as a wife, she had not any doubt of her duty to tell him about the runaway slave hiding on his property.

It was almost dark, and the crickets were serenading loudly from the woods when she reached the house and found Antonio in his study, working at his desk by the light of an oil lamp around which flitted a dark-winged moth with bands of pale blue.

"Where have you been, Susannah?" he asked.

"To the pond. I wanted some berries."

"Then you should send someone for them." He eyed her speculatively before returning to his work. "There's a rip in your gown."

Susannah hadn't noticed it herself and pulled a fold of material over it as though he hadn't already seen. She seated herself in a nearby chair.

"Antonio, I have been thinking about Conde Marchado," she said, drawing a deep breath.

He frowned. "Why should you let him sully your thought? You should be reading sonnets or planning menus. We've had baked chicken twice this week."

Susannah ignored his admonishments. "Antonio, what if a slave came to you and said that he'd been taken illegally on a slaver financed by the count?"

"How preposterous! That would never happen."

"Why not?"

"Because it would be only a slave's word."

"You wouldn't believe it?"

"Good heavens, Susannah, this is a ridiculous conversation! How do I know whether I would believe it? Do go to bed now."

He was getting angry, but so was she. "Would you think he was lying just because of his color?" she demanded.

"No, of course not. But if one slave got his freedom on his own say-so, then half the slaves in the province would follow suit, and a lot of them would be justified. We would have a rebellion, and the entire economy might collapse. There'd be bloodshed on both sides, plantations ruined . . . You do remember your war, don't you, Susannah?"

"What would you do, then, send him back to the count?" she persisted.

"By heaven, Susannah, I am working for legislation to have slave breeding made illegal. And I would like to see Ceará's coasts patrolled for slave rafts. But I must keep friends in my district. Otherwise I cannot get my appointment to the Senate. The emperor can't appoint an unpopular man. Do you want me to take on the whole province? What has got into you, Susannah? Don't we have enough problems without hypothetical ones? If this is some game of yours to get my goat, you are succeeding very well!"

"But what would you do?"

"I . . . don't know, and thank God, I do not have to decide!" he shouted. "Go to bed, Susannah!"

She fled the room, her heart pounding. She slept poorly, the face of Simon appearing, sad and intense, in her dreams. The next morning she sent the money with Aunt Caroline, along with directions obtained from Olinda as to where an Indian with a canoe could be found. After that she was uneasy but calmer. He would not be on her conscience anymore.

But guilt remained with her; there was no way she could escape it, since she hadn't told Antonio. Trying to quell it, she remembered his suggestion about planning the menus and ordered a dinner she knew he would like—freshly caught fish, fried in cornmeal as only Aunt Caroline knew how; a salad of tropical fruit; and for dessert, a wonderful chocolate pie with a rich meringue.

When it was ready, candlelight gleamed softly over the silver and china they had brought with them from Rio, and a breeze through the French doors stirred the curtains Rachel had just had hung. On the wall over the sideboard was a painting framed in gilt of a hyacinthine macaw, which Susannah had done from the veranda. Antonio was proud of the painting and told her so.

"The Kiss Flower is beginning to seem like a home, and I am lucky to have two such beautiful and talented women to grace it. Soon there'll be a child! I can hardly imagine how happy I'll be to hear my son running and laughing at his play and to know that he will grow up to be the master of the Kiss Flower. What a different world the Amazon will be when our child is grown! Santarém will be a city, filled with every kind of luxury and opportunity; and the plantations will reach for hundreds of miles. Did you hear that there is a Chinese colony beginning further on? And there are Germans. The whole world will come to share the treasure of the Amazon. How fortunate I am to be beginning a family at the dawn of an era! To think how one night on the *River Belle* changed my life!"

The touch of his lips thrilled her as he bent over her hand. She studied the way his hair lay against the arch of his neck, like a dark rippling current down the stream of his neck, inviting her caress. As though he felt her intimate gaze, he glanced up at her, his eyes brighter than the candle flames with promise. He smiled roguishly.

Susannah, a hibiscus blossom in her upswept hair, was radiant and happy. How little it took to please him, after all! And by now the runaway slave was gone, never to be heard of again.

But before the wonderful dessert could be served, Susannah was proven wrong. A knock came at the door, and the housemaid who answered it appeared to inform Antonio that Conde Marchado wished to see him.

Antonio frowned. "I'll not have my dinner spoiled by that man. Offer him refreshment and tell him I'll receive him as soon as I've finished."

"There are others with him, sir. I don't think they'll like waiting," the girl said diffidently.

"What others?"

"Senhor Gracilano, Senhor Murat, and Senhor Vinagre," she replied, naming three of the largest growers in the province.

"Then I suppose it's important," he said, throwing down his napkin.

Susannah knew it was. It might have been wise to seek sanctuary in her room, but Susannah was driven to follow him and stand in the shadow made by the arch of the sitting-room door.

"My dear Marquez, I've come to return some money of yours that was stolen by a runaway slave of mine," the count said, tossing down a little purse, which Susannah had sent to Simon.

"You're mistaken, Conde. I'm missing nothing," Antonio said, puzzled.

"Oh, it's a small amount, but it's the principle of the thing that matters, isn't it, Antonio? There's no doubt it's yours. Your crest is on the purse, there in the corner. The slave was caught not a mile from your property. I've had men and dogs looking for him for days. Unusual fellow—knew how to read. I didn't realize, or I'd never have taken him, of course. Slaves that can read are natural troublemakers. I thought perhaps you'd seen him."

"Are you accusing me of something, Conde?" Antonio said dangerously.

"Of course not. All of us accept your word. But we have come to voice our concern about your abolitionist tendencies, Andrada. We will not tolerate runaways seeking asylum on the Kiss Flower."

"You are trying my patience, Conde Marchado. I know about your operations, and I don't doubt that you had no right to the man! But I did not see him, and the Kiss Flower does not harbor runaways, as you ought to know."

There was a babble of heated voices amid which finally came the languid assertion, "Well, it doesn't matter now, at any rate. I'll have him punished. I'll have him thrown into the middle of the river where it's most infested with piranhas and alligators. If he lives, he'll be without an arm or leg or both, and I'll make up in the fear he'll put into the other slaves what I can't get out of him in work. A fine specimen, that Simon, but too stubborn to be useful."

Feeling her stomach lurch, Susannan ran for the stairs. Near the top a pain struck her with paralyzing force. She grasped the railing, her breath knocked away, unable to call for help.

After an eternity the agony lessened, and she stumbled on, as though she could run away from it, as though it were a demon chasing her from below, following her like the men's angry voices. At the top of the stairs it caught her again, and she collapsed, forgetting Simon and Conde Marchado and everything else.

It was there Antonio found her, and shouting for Aunt Caroline, lifted her in his arms. "I'm sorry, Antonio," she murmured, knowing how furious he must be. No doubt he knew how Simon had come by the purse.

"It's all right, love," he whispered back. "I've bought the man, though the count did charge me a pretty price. But it must never happen again. You must not meddle in slave escapes. Nothing is more dangerous. Promise me, Susannah."

"I promise," she whispered gratefully, and then again was aware only of pain.

The strain of her months of pregnancy took its toll, and for an endless time she gave herself over to her struggle, aware now and then of Aunt Caroline crooning encouragement, and of Antonio, who, defying orders from the doctor, refused to leave her side. She knew they expected her to die, and for a time she thought she would. She drifted away, home to Robin Hill, where, to her delight, everything was just as it had been before the war. Rachel was a child, setting tea for her dolls in a puff-sleeved dimity dress, and Papa came prancing up the lane on Sultan.

But something was wrong at Robin Hill; she wasn't happy there. Something was missing. She'd lost something important. Antonio. It was his voice that called her back to the Kiss Flower, his sweet voice murmuring like a song the words she had waited so long to hear: "I love you, Susannah."

She decided that she would not die just now. She would not allow herself to die—not until she had done this one duty correctly as his wife. She thought she saw Joaquina standing at her bedside, smiling, ready to whisk him away; and the vision made her fight harder. She might be doomed to die, but at least he would have the child to make him think of her always.

He would look at his son and think of the great gift she had given him, and Joaquina would never be able to entirely wipe her from his heart. But the shadows shifted, and sunlight fell on the woman beside her bed. It wasn't Joaquina, but golden-haired Rachel, pale and frightened. Rachel. Why shouldn't it be Rachel who was the next mistress of the Kiss Flower? Rachel was in love with him too, she thought.

A hazy darkness closed over her; she lost herself in the cataclysm of birth. An infant's cry came weakly, far away. Her baby, she thought, longing to hold it in her arms. But the sound grew more and more distant, and instead of her child, she embraced the darkness.

15

Susannah's child was a week old before she opened her eyes and saw it, a dark-haired little bundle in Aunt Caroline's arms. A flock of canaries was singing among the branches of the Brazil-nut tree outside her window, and the fragrance of blossoms wafted in on a warm breeze.

"Why, he looks just like his father!" she whispered. "May I hold him?" she asked, and felt her baby solid and squirming beside her. Only one thing marred her rapture.

"He is a she, Susannah," Rachel told her.

So she had not done this right either. She had not given Antonio a son. But oddly, Antonio didn't seem to mind.

"I'll have a boy next time," she promised.

"Next time!" he said with a shudder.

"I'm sure it will be easier next time, Antonio."

"Don't think of next time, Susannah. The emperor hasn't a son to inherit his crown, and I do not require one either. I am well content with our daughter."

They easily agreed that her name would be Izabel, after the crown princess.

The season's crops had been harvested, and the rainy season arrived. The skies remained dark, and day by day the water rose until the house was marooned on an island; but it had been built that way, on a knoll to protect it. It was the silt deposited by the floods that made the rich loam, where crops grew so quickly and abundantly, so Susannah endured the weather in good spirits, secretly pleased with this final isolation that kept Antonio inside much of the time with her and the baby. It was hard to imagine now that she had ever stepped outside her woman's role. Now that she had the baby, her life was too full for her to give thought to anything else. She was settled and content. At last she would be what he wanted. At last that was what she wanted as well. He'd been right, just as he always was, but Susannah was glad to have it that way.

But not all the colonists had been as lucky with their crops as the Kiss Flower. The flood caught some of them before they could finish the harvest, and now hard choices were being made. Some of the colonists were leaving, but more were borrowing again from the count. Antonio begged everyone to wait until he could apply to the emperor for funds.

A meeting was called at the Kiss Flower, and Susannah could hear Cort's voice complaining that there wasn't time to wait for an appropriation of funds from the government. "We'll lose everything, just as we did before," someone else put in. Later Antonio's strong, persuasive voice drifted up, and finally there was a shuffling of feet and furniture and murmurs of accord as the men began to leave.

Antonio came upstairs. "Well, it's settled. They will wait for funds from Rio."

"Oh, that's good, Antonio! I'm so glad."

"But they can only wait until April. I am going to the capital myself to speak to the emperor and make a plea to the legislature."

"But, Antonio, we can't take the baby all the way to Rio."

"Of course not. And you can't leave her. That's why only I am going to Rio."

"I am to stay alone on the Kiss Flower? In the jungle?"

He laughed. "Why, Susannah, the Kiss Flower is your home now, and you will hardly be alone. You have Rachel and Aunt Caroline and Olinda. If a jaguar bothers any of the livestock, call Jamunda, and he will have the hunters track it and kill it. Best of all, you'll have Simon. He's been worth every bit of Conde Marchado's outrageous price. He's the best overseer I've ever had. Things will go smoothly with him in charge."

Susannah knew it was true. A black overseer was highly irregular, but Simon's intelligence and education were a tremendous asset. Antonio had allowed him to borrow books on everything from agriculture to history from the Kiss Flower's library. Simon would take them away to his thatched hut to read; and when he brought them back, if he could find Antonio with time to spare, the two of them would have a lively discussion. But more than that, Simon had a way with the other slaves. They obeyed him with a willingness they would never have shown a white overseer. They loved to please him; his words of approval fell on them like cool rain. They seemed just to like to be near him, as though a canopy of dreams hung over him, shimmering like rainbows where the sunlight struck the jungle mist.

"I suppose you're right, you must go to Rio," Susannah sighed.

"And you shall have the last word about everything here," Antonio told her. "You are to be master and mistress of the Kiss Flower while I am gone."

"You trust me so much, Antonio?" she asked happily.

"You didn't do such a bad job before, after all. Mr. Anderson brought in his entire crop because you lent him the best mule, and we made a decent profit on the molasses in Pará. I knew all along I'd married no ordinary woman, but it took me a while to realize just how extraordinary a woman can be."

"I don't want to be extraordinary, Antonio," she murmured. "I only want to be your wife."

"Indeed you shall always be both, Susannah," he declared, kissing her tenderly, pulling her gently to him so that their bodies met and caressed. "You could never resist me," he told her.

"Or you me," she replied, having realized this truth.

But after he told her his plan, her nights were

sleepless. Lying in the crook of his arm, nestled against him, she worried about his leaving the Kiss Flower. It wasn't that she was so much afraid to be alone or afraid of any danger that might befall him. She was afraid that when he reached Rio, he might not remember that he loved her.

When he saw lovely Joaquina, who had been raised only to please men, and him in particular, whose dark eyes mirrored nothing but love and desire—would he think then that he had made a good bargain marrying her? What might not happen during Rio's exotic nights? There would be concerts, dances, excursions on the graceful little galleons that darted about Rio bay, while passengers luxuriated in prettily curtained cabins and watched flying fish dive into the moonlit lace-and-velvet waves. Joaquina would be soft and sensuous as the tropical breeze, her sighs as intoxicating as the sigh of the surf.

Brazilian men were not expected to be faithful. Marriage was only a form, and women were not important enough to command fidelity. What resources did a woman have if her husband proved disloyal? Only to be more provocative than her rival or to counter with affairs of her own.

She wanted to give him nights of love to remember while he was gone, but the doctor had told him she wasn't well enough. One night in their bed, she could stand it no longer, and reaching out for him, inflamed him with her touch, running her fingers over the muscled ridges of his chest and down his cool, muscular thighs. He moaned, and turning his body against hers, kissed her deeply. She pressed against him, almost unable to breathe from the desire, feeling a sharp painful ache of need.

Furiously he threw back the covers and stood up. "Isn't it enough that I must control myself, without your making it more difficult?" he cried.

"Oh, but just tonight! You'll be gone such a long time, Antonio!" she pleaded shamelessly.

"It's indecent for a woman to touch her husband first," he fumed. "It's my prerogative to decide when I'll make love to you."

"Then perhaps you were right long ago about the kind of woman I am! What a fool you are, Antonio!"

He stormed away to sleep alone, and left her sobbing with humiliation and frustration.

When he had sailed away from Santarém, she turned all her attention to the baby, thriving on goat's milk, since Susannah had been too ill to nurse her. As for the Kiss Flower, it was easy at first to keep things going as they had been.

Many evenings Simon came to the kitchen, and they would sit at the table while he discussed plans for the next several days' work and tell her what provisions needed to be approved for purchase. When Antonio had been gone two weeks, she made her first big decision, sanctioning a plan of Simon's to build a mill to process cane fiber to be fed to the cattle when the floods forced them to abandon the lowland pastures. She was proud of her easy resolve and confident with Simon; but soon Simon himself gave her a problem that was not so simple.

"Marqueza, I wish to work for my freedom," he told her.

She nodded. She knew Simon had already discussed this matter with Antonio. "The law allows it. Of course you may, on your own time. But the marquess paid a high price for you, Simon. I don't see how you can ever earn it."

"By working for Conde Marchado. I am good with horses, and the count has purchased a fast mare he wishes me to train to race in Santarém."

"But how can you work for that man, Simon? Think what he would have done to you if it hadn't been for the marquess!"

"I can do it because I must, Marqueza. Senhor Vinagre offered me the same kind of work, but Conde Marchado will pay twice as much, because he wants his horse to beat Senhor Vinagre's. There are things I intend to do with my life, and I can't do them as a slave, so I will work for the count."

"I don't know, Simon. You can't trust Conde Marchado. Maybe it's a trap. Maybe he'll accuse you of some crime and hold the marquess responsible. He'd love to discomfit Antonio, and I'm sure he doesn't approve of the things you'll do when you're free."

Simon laughed. "Conde Marchado is greedier than he is wise. And he doesn't really think I'll earn my freedom, not at that price. He doesn't dream that a slave could ever be as dangerous to him as I may one day be."

"Oh, I wish Antonio were here!"

"He did tell me that the decisions were to be yours, Marqueza," Simon said quietly.

"I will consider it," Susannah said. She struggled with Simon's request for a week before she gave her permission. She wasn't sure at all that it was best or that Antonio would have agreed to it; but she thought Simon should have the chance. Thereafter, the eager Simon spent his one day off each week in the count's employ and returned to the Kiss Flower sometimes long after dark, only to rise at dawn to take up his duties again. Susannah never worried about Simon's running away, but someone else did.

One morning Susannah's housemaid came upstairs to tell her that Major St. John wished to see her.

"Major St. John? Here?" He had not been to the Kiss Flower since Antonio had left, and she herself hadn't seen him at all since the day of the duel. Trembling, she checked her appearance in the mirror before she went down.

She had not paid much attention to how she looked since Antonio's departure, but now she noticed how much she had changed. She was a woman now, fully bloomed, not the girl that Cort had fallen in love with during her coming-out season in Memphis. Her breasts were fuller, her carriage more stately and confident, her expression serene with the knowledge and fulfillment that love and motherhood had brought.

But she needn't have bothered with the mirror. Cort's hungry eyes reflected her beauty well enough. "Susannah!" he said, taking both her hands in his; and then, to cover his feelings, he more familiarly seized Rachel and spun her around.

"Cort! Cort! Do stop!" she squealed. "I'm not a child anymore."

"No, I suppose you aren't," he said, releasing her with a sigh. He seemed to wish she *were*

a child still and all else was as it had once been.
But then he smiled.

"How very beautiful you've turned out, Rachel. I suppose you didn't save your first dance
for me as you promised."

She gave him a coy glance. "No, but you may
have as many as you like now."

"Well, then, I am invited to a ball in Santarém
next Saturday. Would you be so kind as to
accompany me?"

"Oh, Cort, really?"

He looked at Susannah.

"I suppose it's all right," she said. "It's a
debt, after all." She invited him to take refreshment on the veranda, and with Rachel's gaiety
to alleviate the tension, they partook of tea
cakes and an iced chocolate drink. Finally he
expressed an interest in seeing the baby, and
Aunt Caroline came out with Izabel to be cooed
over and admired. Susannah wondered what
Antonio would think of it, but shouldn't old
wounds be allowed to heal? And Antonio no
doubt was being treated to the company of his
old flame, Joaquina.

Finally Cort explained why he had come. "I
wanted to make sure you and Rachel were all
right. Is there anything you need, Susannah? I
would never have gone off and left you in this
wilderness."

"I did very well in Memphis," she reminded
him, "and here I have Simon."

"Simon! That is the very thing I wanted to
talk to you about. You've given him too much
liberty, Susannah. What's to keep him from
leaving altogether? He ran away before. He's a
troublemaker."

"He'll stay, Cort. He owes Antonio his life. Simon's loyal."

"Loyal!" Cort snorted. "That was what we thought about our slaves during the war. The idea of freedom takes them like madness, and once they are in its grip, they care about nothing else—not about those who have protected them and been like family, not even whether they themselves live or die."

"Yes, I've seen it," she said with a shudder.

"Then why do you allow this Simon to stir up your slaves?"

"He is not stirring them up, Cort."

"Aren't you aware that he is teaching them to read? I heard a rumor of it; I could scarcely believe it."

"It's quite true. He is teaching them a number of things."

She had seen them in the dusk, trekking down to a grove of fountainlike Inajá palms, carrying lanterns toward a bonfire that blazed in the dusk, signaling men, women, and children to hurry away from their suppers to feed their minds instead.

"Dear heaven, does Antonio know about this?"

"He thinks it's a good idea, Cort."

"What a dreamer you've married, Susannah! What a fool! You and I know perfectly well that slaves should never be educated. It makes them discontented. The reason Simon isn't leaving isn't loyalty. It's because he's preparing his people for a rebellion! Can you imagine what that could be like, and you without even the master home to protect you? Give the word, and I will put a stop to this nonsense."

"That would be dangerous, Cort. Besides, Antonio says that our slaves need to be prepared to fend for themselves when slavery finally becomes obsolete."

"Obsolete! What a notion!"

"Antonio sees the future, Cort. He was the reason you came to the Amazon. You came because he made you share his dream. And now that I'm his wife, I share it too, all of it, from the new colonies and new prosperity to new equality and justice."

Susannah paused, surprised at herself. She hadn't realized before that it was true. Gone was the time when she resented the rhapsody of his hopes; she hadn't noticed that they had become hers as well. She was growing to be one with him, and wryly she remembered what Dom Pedro had once told her, that if two people were meant for each other, then nothing could prevent it.

Cort St. John began to visit the Kiss Flower regularly. His reason—or his excuse—was always the same: he wanted to make sure there was nothing they needed. In Antonio's absence it was his duty as vice-president of the colony to check on them; he would do it for any of the colony's families in which the man was absent. Susannah was sure that was true, but she also knew that he still loved her. She ought to tell him to stop coming. She could send word if anything were wrong.

But Susannah was lonely, and she enjoyed his visits. She enjoyed his admiration, though he hadn't Antonio's fiery intensity. Cort's gentle conversation, laden with memories of their past life, could make her feel as though she were home again. His visits both heightened and soothed her homesickness; and when he left, she sometimes wept for Robin Hill, for the life she had known and expected to live, and for all she had loved and would never see again.

She supposed she would never stop thinking of Robin Hill and wanting to return to oak trees and mockingbirds instead of palms and macaws. Cort was her link. He was not building a new world like Antonio, but the old one again. She stepped into the sweetness of the past when she was with him, and sometimes she wished she never had to return.

She was careful not to be alone with him, and she kept the visits short by excusing herself to tend to Izabel. But Rachel always wanted Cort to stay, and they would walk together in the gardens, their fair hair shining like two glowing blooms amid the pendulant blossoms of the banana trees and wine palms with long tassels of crimson flowers. Susannah was happy to see them together, though wistfully she sometimes thought of the time when she had been the girl by his side, younger than Rachel now. Rachel had always worshiped him like a wonderful big brother, and now Susannah was glad Rachel had him to squire her about Santarém and give her something of the glowing social life she should have.

Rachel's future was a problem Susannah and Antonio had discussed. Among the Americans there were only a few prospects for a suitable husband for her. Several of these had paid calls on her and were smitten, but Antonio didn't really approve of any of the likely matches. Rachel's suitors had just begun their plantations, and there would be years of hardship ahead. Worse, most were indebted to the count, and Antonio had told Susannah he would withhold Rachel's hand until the groom was clear of it. But Rachel had not returned anyone's affections. How could she when she had a man like Antonio with whom to compare them? But only Susannah guessed Rachel's secret.

In Santarém Brazilian women mingled very little with the men, attending only occasional dancing parties, such as the one to which Cort escorted Rachel. There was some possibility here, but Susannah worried about Rachel's becoming the wife of a Brazilian. Antonio had suggested they might spend some time at the court at Rio in a year or so, where there would be many possibilities of every kind, but Susannah didn't like to think of it. Such a marriage would take Rachel too far away, maybe even across the world. Cort kept Rachel content, and that was enough reason not to discourage his visits.

But Cort never left without chiding Susannah again about her slaves; and after he had gone, she would gaze down toward the slave quarters at the lights in the misty dusk, where Simon unveiled to his people the mysteries of reading, history, and geography. Sometimes a bit of song floated up, something Simon hadn't learned in the missionary school, but a chant, a bit of Africa to remind them of a faraway heritage. Susannah felt a twinge of empathy then, remembering the painful stirrings of her own heart when Cort would come up the Kiss Flower's lane whistling "Dixie."

Sometimes she would hear a chant from the school in the palm grove, which, when she listened carefully, turned out to be, not savage

African words, but the English alphabet. It had a strange, almost militant sound. She would shiver, wondering if Cort were right after all. Just as quicky she would be abashed. How could anyone be afraid of the alphabet?

Nonetheless she took to riding about the place every day, looking with a sharp eye for any sign of something amiss. "Simon, who is that man?" she asked one day, noticing a strapping young fellow she had never seen before.

"His name is Pedro, Marqueza."

"But where did he come from?"

"He was a herdsman, but I decided he would be more useful in the field."

When Susannah returned to the house, she got out the slave records and searched for the entry of a purchase of a slave named Pedro. There was none. Had the man's name been changed later and the matter overlooked?

Several days later Pedro was gone again, and Susannah asked Simon what had happened to him.

"I sent him back to the cows, Marqueza," the overseer said. "He was too lazy in the field after all."

Susannah couldn't ride over every inch of the Kiss Flower's hundreds of square miles, but she had a feeling that if she did, she would not find Pedro. She had noticed how Simon looked away from her as he spoke.

Susannah's suspicions were aroused, but for a while she saw nothing else unusual. She changed her custom and went riding before breakfast and saw a strange young woman with a child taking laundry down to the stream. She didn't bother to ask their names; the furtive look the woman gave her was enough.

Susanah knew now what was happening, though she didn't know how the clever Simon was accomplishing it. And she knew, too, why Simon had been dishonest with her. Illegal slaves were escaping routinely through the Kiss Flower, and it was her responsibility to stop it. If she had been confined to ordinary female pursuits, she would never have learned of it; if she had been a man, perhaps she would have been suspicious sooner. The men would be talking about the escapes over coffee in Santarém, but being a woman, she was cut off from this major network of information.

Susannah wished Antonio would come home and do the deed himself. Athough she understood how disastrous the situation could be to Antonio, she could not quite bring herself to do what her husband would wish. The faces of the escaping slaves, mingling hope and terror, haunted her dreams. These were not the family slaves of her girlhood, but human beings captured for sale or raised like cattle for the market. She was beginning to understand the horrors of slavery for the first time. Ending the escapes was not for someone with the heart of a woman. It was a job for a man.

Susannah stopped her early-morning rides, but one day as she was breakfasting on the veranda, she caught sight of Simon coming up through the palms toward the slave quarters. Why, he had been out all night and had had the temerity to come home in broad daylight, even though he had tried to hide it by coming through the woods. Susannah remembered what

Cort had said about her giving Simon too much freedom. It was time to take action, she thought, and sent a boy to tell Simon to come to the house.

He stood before her, hat in hand, head bowed in the proper slave stance. "I cannot believe this behavior, Simon. You are setting a bad example for the other slaves, and if you continue, I'll have you punished."

Simon's eyes flickered. He didn't need to backtalk her. She knew what he meant. Who would she find on the Kiss Flower to flog Simon? She realized suddenly that the slaves were more loyal to him than to her, and, her stomach knotting, she thought again of Cort's warning.

If Simon weren't handled correctly, he could cause the others to revolt. Suppose there was an uprising on the Kiss Flower? Certainly if the other growers had any idea about the escapes through the plantation, they would hold back and allow the Kiss Flower to be destroyed—especially Conde Marchado. No doubt he wouldn't mind seeing his adversary suffer.

"If this happens again, Simon, I will have to prohibit you from working for your freedom," she said, knowing she had an ace. Who knew what mischief he had been up to in the darkness? But her threat would put an end to it. Even the count, who valued Simon's services, would have to respect her decision. She had only to let the other planters know, and no one would offer Simon work again.

Simon sighed. "Marqueza, I was going to speak to you anyway. I am a man, and I can't promise it won't happen again unless you allow me to marry."

Susannah gasped. It was the last thing she had expected him to say! So he had been abroad not on matters of rebellion, but of love.

"Why, Simon, I have no objection. The marquess always gives permission when any of our slaves wish to marry. And you needn't worry, either, that he would ever separate your family."

"It isn't that simple, Marqueza. It isn't one of the Kiss Flower's slaves I want to marry. She belongs to the count. We met on the way from Ceará."

"An illegal slave?"

Simon shook his head. "She was born in one of the breeding camps. I want you to buy her for me, Marqueza."

"Buy her! That is a big decision. Wait until the marquess comes home and let him deal with it. I know nothing about buying slaves; I don't know what is a fair price, and I don't know if the marquess would approve."

"But it can't wait, Marqueza!"

"You will have to be patient, Simon."

"Patient! She is very beautiful, and the count is paying too much attention to her. That is why he didn't sell her along with the rest of the slaves from Ceará." Simon hesitated and then plunged on. "Conde Marchado has no mercy on women who draw his attention. I have seen the scars on some from his lusty attentions, and there is one who still screams with nightmares, even though it's been a year since he touched her. I don't like to say such things to a gentlewoman, Marqueza, but several have had a child of his—and he has sold his own children away!

Please, Marqueza, use the money I've already earned toward my freedom to help buy her. I will repay every cent the count charges you for her, as soon as I can earn it. Her name is Maria Rosa. Please try."

"He will demand a good price, Simon. You will never free yourself, if you make this bargain. It would take you a lifetime to earn enough for both of you. I am surprised you haven't simply stolen her," Susannah said in a voice heavy with meaning.

"You've found out, Marqueza," Simon said flatly.

"You thought I wouldn't because I am a woman, Simon. You underestimated me."

"And you underestimated me, Marqueza. You thought I could ignore my brothers and sisters in trouble."

Susannah sighed. "Perhaps you're right. You must not underestimate me again because I am a woman, and I will not underestimate you because of your color."

Simon grinned. "Agreed, Marqueza. I didn't steal Maria Rosa because I am a man of honor, after all. I would not run away from the Kiss Flower and repay the marquess that way for saving me. I will remain on the Kiss Flower until I'm free. If I must, I will send her on the railroad, though it will mean we may never see each other again."

"The railroad?"

"Surely you've heard of the idea, Marqueza. I read of it in a magazine in the marquess's library. The underground railroad that helped slaves in the South escape to the free states of the North. Only my railway is made of canoe paths and jungle trails, instead of wagons and roads. I have established a network of Indian guides all the way to Pará."

"And how do you pay these guides, Simon?"

"Sometimes with a bit of my freedom money, but mostly with rum from the Kiss Flower's distillery," Simon admitted. Now that the plan was discovered, there was no use in keeping anything back.

"I suspected as much! Simon, you must stop this operation at once, before someone else discovers it."

"If I don't, Marqueza?" he asked softly.

"I will tell the marquess, of course, and he will have you sold." Susannah hoped the slave couldn't see she was trembling. Was there anything Simon couldn't do with the Kiss Flower if he decided to? Antonio could handle it, but Antonio wasn't here.

A savage expression crossed Simon's face, then faded. "Buy Maria Rosa to be my wife, Marqueza. I will do anything you say to have her."

Susannah visited Conde Marchado the next day. There was really no other way she could be certain of keeping peace on the Kiss Flower. But Susannah had no objections to buying a woman away from the count's sadistic pleasures. She only wished Antonio were here to handle the dealings.

Conde Marchado's house was more palatial than the Kiss Flower, shaded by a marble-columned porch that made it darker inside. It was furnished with heavy leather sofas and oil paintings brought from Portugal. Persian rugs made the rooms seem a bit close, and they gave

off a mildewed odor. The estate, Casa Rio, lacked
the charm of the Kiss Flower, and its spirit of
newness as well. Sitting amid its lawns of huge
old palms and mossy ponds, trickling fountains,
and Greek statuary, the house reminded her of
an old alligator dozing in the sun, lazy and
stately, but nonetheless dangerous.

In the hallway a young slave girl watched
Susannah from the shadows. "Maria Rosa?" Susannah called. But Susannah had only a glimpse
of her winsome form and pretty face before she
vanished at the sound of the count's footsteps.

"Well, Marqueza, how may I be of help?" the
count said, greeting her. "I hope you've had no
more trouble with that baggage Sloane, in spite
of the rumors he's been spreading about you in
Santarém." He chuckled wickedly, and Susannah was immediately aware she would have to
be very careful of him. He had come in from
the distillery to see her, and his shirt collar,
unbuttoned in the heat, displayed wiry black
hair like the legs of spiders. She shook the idea
away and made herself smile at him. She hadn't
been aware that Rudd Sloane was spreading
rumors about her, but she had a good notion of
the nature of them.

"Why, Conde Marchado, the rumors are true.
I shot a man, you know."

Susannah rather wished she had brought a
pistol with her today, or at least not left Aunt
Caroline outside with her driver. Conde Marchado had made no advances, but her skin
seemed to burn from the heat of his lustful
gaze. The count was noted for his sexual adventures, and she was a woman whose husband was far away. No doubt it would appeal

to the count to add Antonio Andrada's wife to his conquests.

"I'm sure you had cause to defend yourself, Marqueza." The count made his remark a lascivious compliment.

Susannah frowned, impatient at fencing with him. "I've come on business, Conde. I wish to buy a slave."

Conde Marchado was genuinely surprised. "Why, Marqueza, your husband doesn't approve of anyone buying slaves from the traders whose expeditions I finance."

"I am aware of it. And I know that you wouldn't be half as wealthy or influential as you are except that you keep the growers supplied with the slaves they need, legal or not. And I know that another portion of your wealth comes from keeping the rubber-growing Indians in poverty. It's a wonder that you bother to grow cotton or cacao at all, Conde. Nevertheless, I need a slave, a particular slave, and since you are her owner, I have no choice. Her name is Maria Rosa, a girl you recently brought from Ceará."

Conde Marchado's face darkened. "Maria Rosa is not for sale. Why should you want her, anyway? There are a hundred other girls who haven't been settled on any plantation yet. I will give you your pick before they are auctioned."

Susannah had been afraid the count would balk. Hadn't Simon warned her? "Oh, but I was depending on your help, sir! I need a nurse for Izabel, and I've heard that Maria Rosa is wonderful with children. I can't have just any girl taking care of my baby. It won't be easy raising a child out here." She overcame her revulsion and laid a hand on his arm. "I would be forever grateful," she told him.

She saw him take stock of what her gratitude might mean. If he believed the things Rudd Sloane was saying about her, perhaps he'd believe the slave wasn't the main reason for her visit. If he were conceited enough, he might think he appealed to her. But should she disillusion him? What might happen on the Kiss Flower if she did? And it might be hard to sleep nights, knowing she'd refused to help another woman in such peril—a woman who was a slave and whose skin was a different color, but a sister in the kinship of the vulnerability of their sex.

"Let us talk further, Marqueza. Perhaps we'll reach some sort of agreement. Would you like a glass of wine?"

"It would be delightful," she replied, making her smile flirtatious. He rang for refreshments, and sitting beside him on the leather sofa, she sipped her rosé from a goblet of hand-blown glass. The wine made her hotter. She would have preferred fruit punch.

"You see, Marqueza—Susannah—I have special duties for this Maria Rosa to perform. She is very necessary to me."

"And she is necessary to me, too, Conde. Surely you have a price," Susannah said.

He refilled her glass, which in her nervousness she had emptied. "Please call me Bernardo," he said silkily. He had taken the opportunity of pouring the wine to move closer to her, she noticed in alarm. Pretending to adjust her skirts, she scooted away.

"It's not the price; it's the discomfort her leaving would cause me. Surely you agree that a man needs some comforts out here."

"Of course," she had to say.

"Perhaps, if you could think of some . . . substitute for her services. If you could think of someone who might give me enjoyment, it might prove pleasant for us both."

"My dear Conde, I can't trade you one of the Kiss Flower's slaves for her. Antonio would be furious. We are very cautious about selling our slaves. They are like family."

Susannah knew what he wanted, but she had to pretend she didn't. She did not have to pretend shock; she could scarcely believe his audacity. She had hoped to flirt her way into a bargain, but what he had in mind was no bargain!

It was time to leave, she thought prudently, and stood up. But she had drunk the wine too fast. The room spun, and she almost lost her balance.

Susannah cursed her foolishness, remembering the time on the *River Belle*, when champagne had almost cost her her life. Had she learned nothing? If she weren't careful, there would be a cost now.

"I will pay a hundred dollars for Maria Rosa, Conde. I assume that's more than fair. Please send word to the Kiss Flower, if you decide to sell her."

"But, Marqueza, you're not leaving yet, surely!" He was in front of her, blocking her path. "I haven't even told you what Maria Rosa's duties are."

"It . . . doesn't matter," she almost pleaded.

"Oh, but it does! If I don't tell you, you can't understand how much I would miss her."

She thought of screaming. That would bring Aunt Caroline and the driver. But then Antonio would hear of it, and there might be a another duel. Two duels is less than a year. Being her husband might be too much for any man!

She held back her screams, and then his lips were on hers, heavy and demanding, welding hotly, as though they would remain forever. His arms held her like tentacles, one hand skillfully probing her bodice. She pushed against him uselessly.

"Come, Marqueza, don't be so coy," he told her, drawing back at last from kissing her. "I will give you the slave girl. I'll give you anything you want."

"Let go of me!" she cried.

"Marqueza, such indignation! I'll wager you wouldn't behave so badly if I were Major St. John!"

"He is a gentleman!" she replied dazedly, not realizing what he was insinuating.

"A gentleman! A gentleman who visits a lady twice weekly while her husband is away. Major St. John is making hay while the sun shines, and I would like a few bales myself!"

"I would sooner be thrown to the alligators, like your runaway slaves!"

"Oh, come, Susannah. I'm sure you have a soft spot in your heart for me. Just as you have for Major St. John."

"Oh . . . I have not . . . Oh, you beast! Cort and I have not—"

"Then it would be a shame for your husband to think you had, Susannah. He would believe it if certain stories were to each his ears. It could happen, Susannah, but you can prevent it."

Susannah's mind whirled. If she did not give in to him, he would see to it that untrue stories about her and Cort reached Antonio's ears. But she would not, could not, give in! She recoiled inwardly, drawing herself tight, as if she could protect herself that way.

Conde Marchado touched her cheek, caressing her neck behind her earlobes, drawing his hand sickeningly along her little chin. But as he came close to her mouth, she gave a moan and sank her teeth into his hand with all her might. Conde Marchado released her with a cry of pain, and Susannah raced for the door.

As she ran, she glimpsed Maria Rosa again. Susannah did not need to be told it was she. Their eyes met, and the expression of mutal horror they exchanged was enough. It was all Susannah could do not to grab her hand and pull her along with her to freedom for what no woman should have to endure.

At the Kiss Flower she sent for Simon and told him the impossibility of the mission she had undertaken. Simon's expression frightened her, but his rage was not directed at her. "I understand, Marqueza. You did everything you could," he said.

"You must try to forget her, Simon; don't allow yourself to think about it."

But she knew he *would* think about it. He would not forget. He would have his woman one way or another, she thought, and was terrified what way that might be. And she really had no way to stop his activities. Any punishment she dealt out, including not allowing him to work for his freedom, might actually bring what she dreaded closer.

If only Antonio would come home. But now she was half-afraid of his return. What if Conde Marchado made good his threat? Perhaps she should tell Cort, she thought, but what could Cort do about it? Antonio was no more likely to believe Cort than her.

During Cort's visits, she made herself totally absent and left Rachel to entertain. Once, looking down from the nursery window, she saw them kissing beneath the Brazil-nut tree and wished for the time when her romance with Cort had been so simple and innocent. But this newfound romance wasn't like that at all. Was it really romance? Susannah knew that she was still the one Cort loved; and as for Rachel, she too was in love with someone she could never have.

It seemed that nothing would ever be as it should. She did not even know whether Simon had ceased to operate his "railroad." She hadn't the nerve to try to find out and confront him with the issue again. She had tried to run the Kiss Flower and felt she had been inadequate. What would Antonio make of things when he returned? In how many ways would he accuse her of failing him? There was nothing to do but wait.

16

When Antonio's boat was due, Susannah and
Rachel took the baby and Aunt Caroline and
went to Santarém to meet him. Neither of them
could stand waiting at home; and after all, it
was time for a holiday. But it bothered Susannah that Rachel was as eager as she to see
Antonio.

"Do you think he'll come ashore in the first
launch?" Rachel asked a dozen times, practically jumping up and down at the dock to try to
see who was getting aboard.

"You can't make out a thing at this distance,
Rachel," Susannah answered. "We'll just have
to wait and see."

Susannah was nervous herself, wearing a new
gown of sky-blue silk looped up over a satin

petticoat short enough to show off her little patent-leather boots. A smart sailor hat set off her waist-length jacket of rough white material studded with big jet buttons. But Rachel had worn her red merino blouse and a striped silk skirt fastened with a wide velvet belt. "So that Antonio will be sure to see me from the launch," she explained.

"Rachel—" Susannah said warningly.

"Oh, for heaven's sake, Susannah, let me have the fun of having him for a brother. Honestly, if you go on being jealous of every woman who finds him attractive, you'll go mad. He adores you. A person would think you weren't sure of him."

"Of course I am sure of him! It's you I worry about, mooning over a man who is married."

"Oh, look, Susannah. Here comes Cort." And Rachel ran off to meet him, hooking her arm in his. Then they caught sight of Antonio riding toward them in the launch, and Susannah and Rachel waved wildly.

"Do you suppose he got the grant, Cort?" Rachel asked. Cort merely sighed, pacing. "Why, look, there is a woman with him!" Rachel was looking through opera glasses now. Oh, she seems very beautiful!"

"She must be Conde Marchado's bride," Cort offered. "He's been expecting her to come from Rio."

"Poor thing. Who would want to marry *him*?"

"She probably isn't doing it because she wants to," Cort speculated.

"But if she's his bride, why isn't he here to meet her?"

"He's gone away on business."

Susannah, borrowing the opera glasses, saw Joaquina looking anxious and holding on to Antonio in the boat. To think she had been with him all the way from Rio!

What might not have happened? she thought, remembering the delights that voyage had held for her. She had been worried about Antonio and Joaquina in Rio, but she had not expected this; and Antonio hadn't bothered to tell her. Traveling with Joaquina thousands of miles on her journey to marry a man she didn't love, there must have been ample time for regrets, time to make memories to last a lifetime. Joaquina was talking earnestly to Antonio now, while he listened and seemed to be reassuring her. Was he telling her he would always care for her? If only Susannah could hear what they were saying! Them came ashore, and Antonio embraced her.

She clung to him shamelessly, drinking in the wonderful male scents of his ribbed melton frock coat, the mysterious aromas of the ship and the great river that spoke to her of adventure and distance. With her cheek against his velvet collar, she felt his energetic body set with determination, electric with purpose. But his purpose seemed not to be to provoke her desire, for it seemed to her that his kiss was constrained. Or was it only that she wanted so much from it, much more than could be expected in public?

Rachel received a chaste peck on the cheek, and then Antonio shook hands solemnly with Cort.

Susannah watched fearfully. The two men appeared to have achieved a truce of necessity, though their differences over the running of the colony had become as acute as their differences over her had been. That quarrel was finished, she hoped, unless Conde Marchado made good his threat to see that rumors about her and Cort reached Antonio.

Susannah understood that the count had more to gain from spreading them than punishing her for having rejected him. He might accomplish what even the duel had not—an irreconcilable rift between Cort and Antonio. Then, if it were impossible for them to manage the colony together, it would be easy enough for Conde Marchado's influence to prevail there.

For the present at least, Cort and Antonio realized how vital it was for both of them to work for the colony. With the welfare of so many at stake, they could not indulge in rancorous feelings for each other.

"Have you brought the funds, Antonio?" Cort asked anxiously. "There's not much time left to buy slaves and supplies before we plant the new crops."

"I've brought aid from the emperor, but not in the form of money to buy slaves," Antonio replied.

"Not money? My God, what else is there that can save us? We are almost all in debt up to our ears!"

"Manpower. I have brought you several steamer loads of workers from the slums of Rio. Men and women who will labor from dawn until dusk for what would seem to them paradise—enough to eat and a roof to sleep under. They have all agreed to work for no more than that, and a small cash payment after the crop is harvested and sold. Now it will be possible for the colony to sell its slaves and use the proceeds to extricate itself from its debt to Conde Marchado. We'll be able to set an example to all Brazil. We'll prove it's possible to succeed without slavery."

"Without slaves? You dreamer! You'll ruin us all! All except you, of course. You're too wealthy to be affected. What a fool I was to think you care about the people of the colony. It's just as Conde Marchado says. You're trying to get ahead politically by toadying to Dom Pedro and his silly intellectual ideas! Well, let the 'Light of San Cristavo,' as they call him, come out here and try it himself for a while. I'll wager he wouldn't last a week. And you, Andrada, are twice the fool he is, because you've been here and seen it! Or, you're twice the traitor—selling out your responsibility for political influence in Rio!"

The women, privy to what would usually have been a males-only dispute, stood united in fear. "Cort, I am sure Antonio has done his best," Rachel said. Her hand was on his arm, and for an instant it seemed as if he would shake her off. It was as though she had stepped into the middle of a dogfight and was likely to be bitten herself. Then, surprisingly, he looked down at her, and his face softened.

"Rachel, dear, this doesn't concern you. Take Susannah and go into the hotel."

"Cort! Please listen to Antonio!" Rachel cried. Susannah hoped it wasn't as apparent to everyone as it was to her that Rachel thought anything Antonio said or did couldn't be wrong.

"Brazil is at war, St. John," Antonio said evenly, "and there is a deficit in the treasury. Dom Pedro has only recently returned from the front, where he held a council with our allies, Argentina's great president, Mitre, and Uruguay's Flores. It's obvious that Brazil must carry the main burden of defeating the Paraguayan tyrants. Argentina is depleted from its own struggle with its deposed dictator, and Uruguay is suffering from civil war between the Colorado and Blanco factions. Paraguay has a disciplined army of eighty thousand; and we, at the beginning, had only seventeen thousand, scattered from border to border. Dom Pedro has made a fourth of his personal fortune available to meet war costs, and there is not much left for anything else."

"It sounds like another of the emperor's pipe dreams, Andrada, one that will cost thousands of lives. How can Brazil win such a war?"

"We'll win because we must. The Paraguayan, López, is a beast who commits atrocities on his prisoners that I cannot mention in front of these ladies. He must be ousted from influence in South America, or he will terrorize the entire continent. And you are not the one to cringe at the odds, St. John. You are a man who fought for what you believed in when everything was against you. And you struck like lightning to rescue Rachel from the Irving Block. You're a man who does what needs doing, St. John. There is no possibility of money from the treasury this year, and probably for several years to come. The solution the emperor and I decided upon will provide some relief to the colony as well as ease the poverty of those who've made the journey out here to work the plantations."

After Antonio stopped speaking, there was a

long pause, during which Cort stared at the sky, scowling and silent. Finally he drew a deep breath. "Well, Andrada, I have no choice but to do the best I can with what you've brought me. It will take training to teach slum dwellers how to farm. And no doubt they'll not take orders as well as the slaves. When they get a little money in their pockets, they'll get ideas about going off to Pará to set up fruit stalls or shoeshine stands. I'll support you, since there's nothing else for it, except mortgaging ourselves completely to Conde Marchado. I'm not sure that wouldn't be better in the long run, and I'm not sure the other planters can be convinced to go along with it. Our job is cut out for us, Andrada."

"Susannah"—Antonio turned to his wife—"Major St. John and I have things to tend to. Please start for home without me. And take Joaquina and her chaperon with you. They'll be staying with us until the count returns so that the marriage can take place. The emperor has made me responsible for her until then."

"I hope it's not inconvenient," Joaquina said when Susannah and Rachel had taken her to their rooms at the hotel to rest and refresh herself.

"No, not at all. We're delighted, aren't we, Rachel?"

"Oh, yes," said Rachel, no more truthfully than her sister.

Susannah knew Joaquina must have seen her stunned look when Antonio had told her Conde Marchado's bride would be staying at the Kiss Flower. And Rachel, who had heard of Joaquina from Susannah, wasn't pleased to be sharing her brother-in-law's attention with a third woman.

Joaquina's duenna, muttering in Portuguese, took down her charge's tresses to redo, and Susannah and Rachel caught their breaths at the shining length of Joaquina's wavy black hair. Susannah thought of the count wrapping his fingers into it on the wedding night and gave an involuntary shudder.

"Have you brought your wedding dress from Rio?" Rachel asked to make conversation.

"Oh, yes, and my entire trousseau. Antonio will arrange for it to be sent to the Kiss Flower, and we will have fun unpacking it all."

And they did enjoy themselves, opening trunk after trunk filled with wonderful silks and brocades, hats and Empire bonnets, silk slippers in every color with ribbons or rosettes, little boots of morocco leather, tiny handerchiefs with embroidered corners, exquisite sandalwood fans, and jewelry—strings of filigreed silver beads, dog-collar necklaces studded with diamonds and pearls, earrings of gold plates with dangling pendants. The fact that Antonio was rarely at home lessened the strain among the women. Seeming to hold no grudge against Susannah for having wed Antonio, Joaquina made herself agreeable. Maybe, Susannah thought, Joaquina did not blame her because she could not conceive of the choice of a husband being a woman's prerogative.

But sometimes Susannah caught Joaquina looking about the Kiss Flower wistfully, and every time she remarked to Susannah about the beauty of some aspect of the house or grounds, Susannah thought Joaquina was wishing it might have been hers. When she played with little Izabel, she would mention how much the baby favored her father, and Susannah would guess that Joaquina longed to be the mother.

Joaquina's bravery shone through the fog of sadness that seemed to surround her. When Antonio was home for the evening, she was always eager to play on the grand piano and sing ballads in Portuguese, which Antonio seemed to love to hear. He would smile at her or at the music as he sipped his coffee or a dark-colored drink made from the berries of assai palm.

"Doesn't it seem peculiar to you, having her here?" Susannah couldn't help bursting out one night as he was preparing for bed.

"Peculiar? No, why should it?"

"Because you once loved her, and now she is about to marry your enemy."

Antonio laughed uproariously, a thing he rarely did these day, with the colony's many problems to burden him. "Is that what you've been thinking, Susannah? She is a beautiful woman, but I never loved her. Who told you that?"

"Princess Izabel. She said that you would have married her if it hadn't been for me."

"Oh, well, that's true. I probably would have. She would have made an excellent wife. But love wouldn't have been the reason."

"What, then?" she persisted. "Her dowry? Izabel said you would have been wealthier than Conde Marchado then."

"My goal is not be richer than Conde Marchado, who, incidentally, is only my adversary, not my enemy. I have always been willing to depend on the rightness of my position and my power of persuasion to best him. No, if I had married Joaquina, it would have been for her fine character. Joaquina knows what a wife should be." He chuckled. "She would not be headstrong and disobedient like you!"

"What, do you regret having married me, then, sir?" she said, bristling at his teasing.

Antonio did not answer. Instead he unfastened her bodice and slid his hands inside. "Decide for yourself, Susannah," he murmured as he undressed her, his kisses more urgent as he fumbled with her feminine lacings, torn between the task of removing her clothes and savoring the delights he found beneath them. But Susannah made the choice for him, beginning to unfasten her own petticoats, her hands and his crowding each other in their different endeavors.

When she had finished with her own clothes, she began on Antonio's, removing his narrow tie and then unbuttoning his shirt, running her hands blissfully over his chest, the hardness of muscle contrasting with soft, springy hair.

Antonio sighed with pleasure, and lifting her lightly in his arms, carried her to the bed. In another moment she lay open to his embrace, filled with the purest rapture of wedded love, her breath coming quick and hard with passion.

She struggled toward paradisiacal delight, helpless and consumed, transported at last into reverberating ecstasy.

When the crescendo of their lovemaking had subsided, she lay beside her sleeping husband, wondering whether, if he had married Joaquina, this part of the marriage would have satisfied him less. He had told her he would have married Joaquina for her ability to be a good Brazilian wife. And she knew why he had married *her*! It has been for these exquisite nights. Had he merely chosen a woman to fill one need instead of another? Did he love her? Love was what she felt when he took her in his arms and pulled away her clothing, making her shiver with anticipation. But could she be sure what he felt wasn't simple male lust?

Joaquina loved the Kiss Flower. It was a treat for her simply to be allowed to walk anywhere she chose. She had led a cloistered life in Rio, with only the family garden, walled from prying eyes, where she could be in the fresh air. She was amazed that Rachel and Susannah were free to come and go as they pleased; and provided they took a trusted slave with them to protect them, they could do all their own shopping in Santarém. Joaquina had never even learned to ride horseback. There'd been no reason in Rio, where ladies went about in curtained coaches.

Rachel and Susannah undertook to teach her. Though she was terrified at first, she soon got the hang of it, and the three of them went exploring during the cool hours of the morning and evening, riding along paths and cart tracks in the forest, stirring up parrots and monkeys, pretty green lizards and ugly crested ones. Joaquina loved the butterflies: flocks of blue ones; others with red and yellow markings; the long-winged Heliconii, which hovered about tangles of morning-glory blossoms, lovely, but with a disagreeable odor that kept it safe from birds and human collectors. Under the leaves of arum bushes they searched for its cousin, the Helicopi, creamy, spangled silver, the most delicate and breathtaking of all.

"Susannah, who is that?" Rachel asked one morning, catching sight of a pair of dark faces almost hidden in a clump of lantana.

"Where, Rachel?"

"Why, there," she said, pointing, but the faces were gone. "I'm sure they were slaves, but whose? I don't think they wanted to be seen, and they didn't look like any of ours."

"You must have been mistaken, Rachel. Maybe you saw monkeys. They can look quite human sometimes, you know, especially when you don't see them clearly."

"But I'm certain, Susannah. One was wearing a kerchief."

But they had disappeared, and Rachel let the matter drop. Susannah felt a clutch at her stomach. Simon had not ceased his operation. She should make good her threat to tell Antonio, she supposed. Then Simon would be sold and forgo the chance to work for his freedom. He would be sent away from the woman he loved, and the Kiss Flower would lose an excellent overseer.

But perhaps these weren't the reasons that Susannah said nothing to Antonio. She was more afraid that he would discover that she had allowed it to go on, when she had known he would disapprove. Headstrong and disobedient—that was what he had called her; he would call her worse, if he decided to blame the "railroad" on her negligence.

She thought of confronting Simon again, but she knew she had no evidence, only Rachel's word. Simon would only deny it.

Joaquina was especially entranced by the nests of the japim bird, which hung like mossy socks by the dozens in villages that were noisy all day with the song of the glossy black-and-yellow inhabitants. Susannah kept a pair of the young birds in the house at the Kiss Flower. Olinda had caught them for her and told her that it was common to tame them. Now the half-grown birds flew about the house at will, in and out the windows, always returning to the cage, where food waited and where they felt most secure. Joaquina didn't understand why the birds didn't just fly away.

"It's because this is their home," Susannah said, lifting a bird onto Joaquina's finger. "It's what the Kiss Flower is all about" she added, the thought occurring to her. "Slaves have the chance to work for their freedom here, and woman aren't kept caged any more than the birds. Someday I hope all Brazil will be like the Kiss Flower. When little Izabel is a woman, her namesake will be on the throne. And then perhaps Brazil will be different for women."

"I do wish I could stay on the Kiss Flower, Suannah. You've been so kind. I suppose the count will return soon, though, and we'll be married."

"Don't you mind, Joaquina?" Susannah was emboldened to say.

"Mind? Why should I mind marrying the count?"

Susannah was baffled. "Well, because . . . I mean . . . you don't love him, do you? I thought you . . . well, cared for someone else."

Joaquina laughed. "Oh, what does it matter whom I care for? I am only a woman and can't expect to have my way. My father decided for me to marry Conde Marchado and that is what I'll do, of course. I'll take pride in trying to be a good wife to him, so that my father will have no reason to be ashamed."

"Joaquina, have you met the count?"

She nodded. "In Rio. He is . . . a rather handsome man. I have never liked the expression in his eyes, but I will have children to distract me. A lot of them, I hope. It will be best when they are little, because the boys will pay no attention to me when they get older and the girls will be sent anywhere the count wishes to marry them away. I know already how heartbroken I'll be to see them go. I had a mother and sisters I had to leave in Rio. So I hope I will always have one in the cradle."

On impulse, Susannah promised Joaquina one of the japin birds to remind her of the Kiss Flower and was rewarded with a smile. They were almost friends, but not quite.

Joaquina might seem naive and docile, but Susannah could not forget the way she had looked at Antonio in Rio, and sometimes still did, when she thought Susannah did not notice. There was another side to Joaquina, sultry and dangerous. She had been trained to acceptance, but such unrelenting commitment to duty couldn't be easy. To marry Conde Marchado with equanimity must take a steeliness every bit as powerful as Susannah's outspoken rebellion. They were opposite sides of strong character, and each of them dismayed and fascinated the other.

Susannah understood only the facets of Joaquina that were like herself. Susannah thought of Conde Marchado, remembering what Simon had said about the way he treated slave girls, remembering the indecent advances he had made to her, his mouth disgustingly on hers. She had felt death would claim her if she hadn't been able to escape from his caress, and she would have been satisfied with death instead of him. Could Joaquina really be so different? Could she be strong enough to endure a lifetime of the count, while the man she loved was only just beyond her reach? If Joaquina reached the limit of her submissiveness, what might happen?

Carriage wheels in the drive one morning announced the count's arrival at the proper calling hour. Dressed formally in a black superfine frock coat with a silk serge collar and close-fitting black trousers, he waited in the drawing room for his bride, who was sent down to meet him, but still in the protective company of her duenna.

Susannah, loath to be in the same room with him, excused herself on the pretext that the baby needed tending and sent Rachel to play hostess until Antonio arrived. Nevertheless, Susannah couldn't resist peering over the stair banister to catch a glimpse of the proceedings. Seated on the sofa, Conde Marchado rubbed his hands on his knees as though he could barely control himself. He inquired how Joaquina's trip had been and hoped she would be happy on the Amazon; but his eyes, those eyes Joaquina had never liked, said something else.

"How beautiful you are, my dear," he kept telling her, his voice heavy with anticipation. And he chuckled like a man congratulating himself on having made an excellent bargain. Not many men had a bride so lovely and so wealthy to boot.

The wedding would take place in a week, he told Antonio, and the two of them disappeared into the library to discuss the technicalities of the settlement, which were too complicated and indelicate for feminine ears.

Joaquina fled upstairs and shut herself into her room, missing the midday meal and refusing to answer Rachel or Susannah's concerned knocks. But in the evening she reappeared, calm and cool with no trace of redness around her eyes. It must be frightening, now that the date was actually set. But Joaquina brushed away their attempts to comfort her and aloofly asked that her wedding dress be brought out the next day for a final fitting.

Rachel made the needed adjustments herself, chattering away about the wedding dresses she had designed in Memphis while she had worked with Mrs. St. John.

"So many girls were marrying their sweethearts who were coming home, and most had little money. We'd redo an old family wedding dress, or if the Yankees had burned it, we'd use muslin. Muslin's quite nice, if the gown is kept simple. Of course, those who were marrying Yankees always had new silk dresses."

But Joaquina wasn't interested. She didn't blush and laugh the way those brides had. Finally Rachel fell silent and worked wordlessly on the most elaborate wedding gown she had ever seen, all heavy satin, its skirts liberally puffed and set with lace and crustings of pearl. The train lay in long, elegant folds behind it, so wide and heavy that three young girls had been designated to carry it. Instead of a veil Joaquina would wear a mantilla of handmade lace that nearly touched the floor, held secure by gold combs set with emeralds.

Joaquina walked down the aisle of the big, showy Santarém church, proud and serene on Antonio's arm, her face pale, without the smile of a bride. She had no family of her own to see her on her wedding day. Her father, a general, was far away at the Paraguayan front, and her mother and sisters weren't able to make such a journey without him. Her brothers were with her father.

But perhaps it was just as well that Joaquina's mother wasn't here, Susannah thought. Would she really be able to rejoice in the life on which her daughter was embarking?

The Catholic ceremony was long and tedious. One of the young attendants fainted in the heat, and there was a pause while she was revived and led away. Joaquina, in the immense weight of her gown and train, swayed, but as though by sheer willpower, she did not disgrace herself and her bridegroom by swooning. As he led her back up the aisle as his wife, she even smiled at last. At least it was over. But there was more to come.

It was scarcely cooler on the grassy square, where a party with music and dancing went on until after midnight, one of the few occasions when women mingled freely with the men. Joaquina could at least have a cold drink and a bit of wedding cake, though she could hardly rest a moment from the dancing. And even when he carried her away, just before the clock struck eleven, what Susannah was sure was another ordeal was just beginning.

Having heard of the custom from the American women, Joaquina tossed her bouquet of orchids and roses. Rachel, at whom Joaquina aimed it, caught it and blushed furiously. Susannah was surprised; it really wasn't like Rachel to react so strongly.

"So, you'll be the next one married," she teased as the other unmarried girls gathered about to admire the flowers.

"I suppose I will, Susannah," Rachel said solemnly, and then smiled brightly as a Brazilian planter claimed a dance.

The bouquet was wilting on Rachel's bedside table the next morning when Cort St. John rode up to the house and asked Antonio for Rachel's hand.

"Are you sure, Rachel?" Susannah asked anxiously when they were alone.

"Of course I'm sure. How could I do better? He's a wonderful man, gentle and considerate. He'll do everything in the world to make me happy. And we share a past we both hold dear. You're only jealous, Susannah. You haven't any hold on him now; you can't expect him to spend his life pining away for you."

"Rachel, do you love him?"

"Of course. Haven't I always?"

"No, not that way."

"Well, perhaps I haven't the luxury of marrying a man for . . . for passion. I am in Brazil now, and I am grateful that Antonio hasn't tried to marry me off to someone like Conde Marchado!"

"Oh, balderdash! They would have to drag you kicking and screaming."

"That's true. And I don't want to be a spinster, either, growing old and shriveled, dreaming of what I never could have. Some is better than nothing. I'll have some, Susannah!"

"So Cort will keep you from shriveling! Does he know how you feel?"

Again Rachel blushed. "Yes, and we are a good match, because *he* will never have what he wants, either. We are lucky to have each other. We understand each other. After a while that will be better than the physical thing."

The physical thing that you have with Antonio, she really meant. Perhaps it *was* appropriate that the two of them join forces. Susannah remembered what the emperor had told her about his own marriage. In time Cort would lose his pain in Rachel's tender care; and Rachel, with Cort for her own, would surely forget her girlish infatuation with Antonio.

They were married several months later on the grounds of the Kiss Flower beneath a natural orchid bower beside a little stream that ran through the well-tended palms and mango trees.

Slaves in crisp white served the banquet that followed, replete with enormous bowls of fruit—pineapples, melons, bananas, and oranges, all grown on the plantation. There was native *caju* wine, as good as any grape, and game brought in by the Kiss Flower's hunters—vension, wild boar, and, though Susannah couldn't bring herself to taste it, tapir, which the Brazilians enjoyed as a delicacy.

Rachel had chosen a gown of thin silk, sleeveless, with a square ruffled neckline, above which she wore the necklace Mrs. St. John had given Susannah that Christmas in Memphis. It might have been a hundred years ago, Susannah thought with a stab of longing. Familiar waves of homesickness engulfed her. Would the Kiss Flower ever really be home? Who could ever have imagined it would turn out this way when she had first been old enough to go to dances and be squired by Cort St. John?

I wonder if I will ever see Robin Hill again, she thought as she watched the bride and groom waltz together in the dusk, to the music of violinists that had had to be brought all the way from Pará.

Rachel's veil blew in the breeze, and petals of orange blossoms scattered from it, as if to remind Susannah that all of life was ephemeral. Then Antonio was beside her, and she smiled up at him to thank him for the magnificent wedding he had given her sister.

Conde Marchado attended the wedding, and Susannah hadn't been able to avoide dancing with him, but she did so with a bit of triumph. Cort's betrothal to Rachel had put the lie to any stories that could have been started about him and Susannah.

"I would still like to have Maria Rose for Izabel's nurse," she told him. "Perhaps you no longer require her services."

"She isn't for sale, and I wouldn't deal with a woman in any case," he retorted, feeling her barbs.

"Ah, I see. But if you change your mind, do speak to my husband. He indulges me, you know." She had the satisfaction of seeing how irritated her certainty of Antonio's affection made him.

The count was too interested in dancing and flirting to notice Joaquina leave the gathering and disappear down a path, but Susannah saw, and tired of smiling through her own confusing emotions, followed. She caught up with the countess at the bathing pond, where she sat dabbing her face with a lacy handerchief dipped into the cool spring water. She looked worn, now that she had dropped her party pretense. She was thinner, and her eyes seemed dull.

"Susannah," she said, "I was just thinking of the good times we used to have riding about the Kiss Flower—you and Rachel and I."

"You make it sound so long ago, Joaquina. It's only been three months."

"Sometimes days and weeks aren't an accurate measure," Joaquina sighed.

"Yes, I know," She was thinking of Robin Hill.

"Oh, how would you know? You are happily married! *You* married Antonio! And Cort St. John will make Rachel's life sweet. My misery is your doing. I don't know why I should even be on speaking terms with you!"

"Joaquina, I never intended to steal Antonio from another woman."

Joaquina burst into tears. "Oh, I know. You had little more to say about your marriage than I did about mine. It's just that I'm so desperate. I don't have anywhere to turn."

"Tell me about it," Susannah said softly. It was a while before Joaquina could gather herself, but her tears told everything. In such a short time, the bravery had crumbled; Joaquina, strong as Susannah had believed her, had broken.

"He comes every night," she said finally. "There are no locks anywhere. I can't shut him out; not that I ever dreamed I would shut my husband out. But he is never satisfied; I can never sleep, or it seems so, because when I sleep, I dream he's still touching me. And when I wake up, he's right there, and I find my dream is true.

"There is nothing tender about him. He doesn't care if he hurts me, or if it is torture for me. I didn't expect to find pleasure, but oh, it is so much more terrible than I imagined."

Not knowing what to say, Susannah simply put her arms around Joaquina, who sobbed against her shoulder.

"The worst thing is the slave girl," Joaquina said.

"Maria Rosa?" Susannah guessed with a shudder.

"Yes, the one you wanted to buy. He is always laughing about that, telling me she is the last slave he would consider selling. He keeps her practically a prisoner because he is afraid she may try to escape. He's lost other slaves, and he won't take a chance with her. He takes me to her room and makes me watch while he does awful things to her, and then he tells me he is going to do the same things to me."

"Does he?" Susannah said with a gasp.

"No, not the worst of it, and he doesn't beat me the way he does her. But I know he will treat me as badly as he can someday. For now he is enjoying making me afraid. It pleases him to think I am imagining what he may do to me,

more than actually doing it; but he will tire of
that. Susannah, you cannot guess, and I would
never tell you what things men are capable of
doing to women. No one should have to know!"

"Or endure it, much less! Something must be
done!"

"Nothing can! I am his wife."

"But that doesn't give him the right to mis-
treat you so. Antonio—"

"Oh, please don't say anything to *him*. He
can't help, and I don't want him to know. I feel
so ashamed!"

"You, ashamed?" Susannah said, but she saw
that Joaquina was right. Antonio could hardly
interfere between the count and his wife.

"Your father, then."

"He's too far away. And he would only say I
was a hysterical bride who must get used to a
man's way. He and Bernardo are deeply involved in business ventures together, and trouble might cost him dearly. I am nothing but a
part of their agreements."

"Dear heaven, what is to become of you,
Joaquina?"

"I don't know. I'll endure as long as I can. I
told the priest when I was allowed to go to
confession, and he gave me a penance for un-
christian feelings against my husband. But he
said, too, that it might be different if I became
pregnant. I am praying for that, because it's not
a sin, like praying for someone to die."

Susannah drew a deep breath, deciding on a
risk she must take. "Joaquina, you could escape, like one of his slaves. I know how it can
be done. You could go all the way to Pará
without his discovering you."

Joaquina was so astonished she stopped weeping to stare at Susannah. "You know how the slaves escape?"

"Yes, but don't tell anyone."

Joaquina laughed weakly. "Whom would I tell? Him—Bernardo? Why would I do that?" For a moment she seemed to consider the outlandish notion of escape. Then she sighed. "What good would it do, Susannah? Where would I go? I'd disgrace my family. I couldn't go home. If I did, I'd probably be sent back."

Footsteps and laughter echoed not far away. Other wedding guests were on the path, and Joaquina, in a panic, jumped up and rushed away to keep anyone from seeing her discomposure. Susannah was caught where she was and had to remain, making conversation and accepting compliments on the splendid wedding celebration.

Later, when Susannah returned to the festivities, Joaquina was dancing with Antonio, looking as poised and regal as a countess should and smiling as though she were the happiest woman on earth. Susannah marveled. How long could it go on?

17

Cort and Rachel moved into his almost finished house on his plantation, Twenty Palms, in a stand of trees that had been too pretty to cut down. Although the palms dwarfed the house, they also gave it an air of importance, nestled among them while they stood like an honor guard with tall plumed helmets.

The house was small, but the inside was a surprise, all plastered sparkling white, the windows framed with damask curtains, and a pretty staircase of native rosewood leading upstairs. It was a cozy honeymoon cottage, and someday, Cort promised, it would be enlarged. Of course, it would need to be, when children came along.

But the newlyweds hadn't much time to enjoy their new life before the colony was hit with an infestation of fire ants. Suddenly they were everywhere, and there was nothing anyone could do about it.

At first they seemed only a dreadful nuisance. Anywhere outside, one might be stung by the vicious quarter-inch beasts. Little Izabel was bitten in her bed and screamed for half an hour; and women began to wear divided skirts or even their husbands' trousers to avoid having the things nest in their petticoats. The legs of chairs had to be rubbed with bitter copaiba balsam to repel the ants, and everyone sat with feet propped on stools, which had also been treated. But nothing overcame the menace. The ants seemed to bite from pure malice, and anyone who stood even for a moment anywhere near a nest would be severly punished. The instant an ant touched flesh, it secured itself with its jaws, doubled its tail, and stung with all its might.

As the infestation grew, the soil was undermined with their subterranean tunnels, houses were overrun, and food supplies became difficult to defend. Susannah and Rachel, like the other American women, lost some of their favorite gowns to the voracious ants, before discovering that the starch was what attracted them.

"We are literally losing our shirts," Cort told his bride, examining the remains of a favorite garment.

"How long can it go on?" she asked worriedly.

"Years."

"Years!"

"Antonio says there is a town called Aveiro up the Tapajoz that has been deserted for years because of the fire ants."

"Oh, Cort, surely that can't happen here!"

"It's already happening," he told her grimly. "The workers are leaving. Why should they stay and be bitten fifty times a day in the field and more at night in their beds? I knew I was right. If we had slaves now, they wouldn't dare to run away."

"But where are the workers going, Cort?"

"Anywhere they can away from here. Santarém. To Pará, if they can find a way. All of them had something they did before to try to survive, even if it was only begging. And that is what they'll try again. Oh, perhaps I should have put my bullet where it counted when I had the chance to dispense with the Marquez da Silva. This is all his doing."

"Cort!" she cried fearfully.

"Oh, don't worry, Rachel. I am not going to do violence to Antonio. And neither am I going to see this colony abandoned. We are not going to be beaten again the way we were by the Yankees. We are not going to be driven out by an army of ants! I swear it, Rachel!"

"What will you do, Cort?" she asked. Once she had thought he could do anything; she had thought he and the Forrest raiders could not be vanquished. But where were the Forrest raiders now?

"We will have to have slaves to harvest the crop," Cort said. "I believe it's still possible to save the cane, if we hurry."

"But how will we buy them? By mortgaging the plantation to Conde Marchado?"

"I don't approve of him, Rachel, but it's only a business transaction. It's the only way."

Most of the colonists followed Cort St. John's

lead and increased their indebtedness to the count to pay for slaves. Antonio still opposed it, advising the colonists that it would be difficult to make enough this year to repay their loans, which the count insisted on making short term, for the season. The marquess hoped to do business with a slave contractor in Pará who would lease slaves to bring in the crop. It was a fairly common practice, but the contractor refused, claiming he couldn't send his slaves into such terrible conditions. Antonio knew better. It wasn't that the contractor was a humanitarian. It was that Conde Marchado supplied him with most of his slaves.

Antonio himself might have secured bank loans for some of the colonists, but he wasn't wealthy enough to provide collateral for everyone. Only Conde Marchado, backed not only by his own wealth but also by Joaquina's dowry, could invest so freely in loans.

But lack of funds wasn't the main reason Antonio didn't make loans. It pained him to see the colony return so rapidly to slavery. He didn't want to give up his dream. He recruited Indians, who were less afraid of the ants, to work the colony's fields. But Indian labor was undependable at best.

Cort was quick to point out to the other colonists that the Kiss Flower wasn't being worked by Indians. The marquess still had slaves. Why not? He could afford them. All this antislavery talk was nonsense, mere politics. Antonio Andrada wanted only to use his influence with the emperor to maneuver himself into a seat in the Senate. The appointment would be due before long, and Count Marchado was his main opposition.

There was some truth to these accusations, Antonio told Susannah as he paced the Kiss Flower's veranda.

"I've been a hypocrite," he told his wife, having long given up the idea that business shouldn't be discussed with a woman. He had never thought, when he married, that one of the greatest benefits of having a wife would be the privilege of unburdening himself to her. "I shouldn't have kept my slaves. Perhaps I should set them free."

"It's no use, Antonio," Susannah sighed. "The colonists would continue buying slaves anyway. It would only put the Kiss Flower in danger as well."

"Surely I must take the chance!" he cried.

"It's your pride talking, Antonio. If you are going to free our slaves, do it when it isn't so likely to destroy us. You are a family man now, and can't afford irresponsible behavior."

He frowned. "There *is* Izabel . . ." he said.

"And in a few months, she won't be your only child," she said, smiling as she told him the news, that she was pregnant again. "This time it will be a boy," she promised. "And he will need the Kiss Flower."

"But I don't want my son to manage slaves," he protested as he kissed her. He knew, though, that she was right. This was not the time to free his slaves. When he did that, he wanted to offer them jobs on the Kiss Flower and have everyone prosper. That couldn't be done now, when they would be so tempted to run away from the fire ants. Instead Antonio settled for working with a skeleton force of slaves and sending as many as he could to help on other plantations.

But nothing saved the crop. Aided by confusion, disorganization, and the conflict between Antonio and Cort, the ants won. If the cane were harvested, the ants ate it in the cane carts on its way to the sugar refineries. Sugar, too, was consumed by ants, before it could be shipped away. Rum fared better, but it was far from enough. Many colonists would be unable to repay their debts.

Some families packed what little of their possessions remained and set out for the States, but that wasn't Conde Marchado's plan. He wasn't interested in mere land. He wanted the colony intact, an empire that would encompass all the vast area of the plantations as one. And so, each owner whose land was mortgaged was given the alternative of remaining as manager of the plantation he had pioneered.

The incentives were attractive. A handsome salary would be paid, and a bonus when the crops were good. But independence was lost. A man who accepted wasn't his own man anymore; he was subject to the count's every whim. He would have to be careful to stay in the count's good graces. He could never dare to oppose him, politically or otherwise.

Still, many settlers accepted the conditions gratefully.

A few, having had especially good fortune with Indian labor and labor from the Kiss Flower, repaid their loans, but Cort St. John was not among those.

Rachel was frantic. Cort wasn't the kind of man who could compromise, certainly not with a man like Conde Marchado. The count had offered Cort a better proposition than the others, a merging of interests, which might have Cort involved in projects of which he didn't morally approve. Rachel thought the count was especially eager to take advantage of what he considered a natural animosity between Antonio and Cort.

Antonio visited Twenty Palms and offered to make good Cort's loan. "It's because my wife's sister is involved," he explained.

It galled Cort to accept Antonio's offer, but he had little choice; and Rachel begged him to borrow the money from Antonio to repay the count. For weeks after that, Cort sat about the house morosely, as if the humiliation had robbed him of the spirit to go on.

"He has lost respect for himself," Rachel told Susannah.

"How foolish. He tried as hard as any man can."

"Susannah, I'm frightened. He's going to do something rash. I'm sure of it."

"Nonsense, Rachel. He may not like borrowing from Antonio, but it's an honorable debt, and he'll simply work hard to repay it."

Rachel shook her head. "He's thinking about something quite different. I can see it in his eyes. He seems so far away, and he hardly concerns himself with the plantation. Sometimes when he looks at me he seems to be imagining he may never see me again."

"Rachel, how ridiculous! How can that be?"

Before long they found out. Having arranged

with another planter to oversee Twenty Palms, Cort outfitted himself with a canoe and supplies, and with the Indian chief Jamunda to guide him, set out up the treacherous Tapajoz to search for diamonds or gold.

The floods came again, and most of the fire ants were destroyed. Some climbed onto the tops of grasses, nesting there in balls, but even then they were doomed because the planters sent out boats and knocked them into the water with sticks. Next season the fire ants would be gone. Susannah was relieved to have the infestation over, for at this stage of her pregnancy she had no choice but to wear loose clothing that invited their crawling inside the hem. Her second labor, as she had been determined it would be, was easier than the first.

She was getting the knack of it, she thought proudly, as she watched Antonio take his first look at his new son, named Josiah, for her father. They would have a large family, she thought happily as she drifted off to sleep.

After the floods had subsided, she was able to visit Rachel more freely again, riding the forest trails instead of having to take a canoe or go the long way on the high ground. Susannah missed her sister. Still, in her secret heart, she was glad that Rachel hadn't taken her invitation to return to the Kiss Flower after Cort's departure. Rachel had not wanted to close the house. She wanted to have it ready for Cort when he returned, she said. But Susannah thought Rachel was really too wise to subject herself to being in the same establishment with Antonio again.

Rachel came frequently to visit, though. Alone

on Twenty Palms, she battled loneliness and despair. Cort had been gone nearly a year.

One sweltering day in March, Susannah was surprised by another visitor, Joaquina.

She came alone, which in itself was daring for her. She had not been raised to travel about unchaperoned. But the duenna, who should have come with her, had never been on a horse and was too old anyway; and had they taken the carriage, slipping away would have been difficult.

"I need your help, Susannah," Joaquina said. "Thank heaven you taught me to ride! Thank heaven I've a friend out here!" She wore a wide-brimmed straw hat with a veil that didn't quite conceal a deep bruise on her cheek. It was impossible to read her eyes, obscured by the netting.

"What can I do, Joaquina? I'll try, of course." Susannah felt a pang of guilt. If she hadn't married Antonio, this would not have happened to Joaquina.

"The escape route, Susannah. Can it still be used?"

Susannah caught her breath. "Have you decided to run away from him, then?"

Joaquina threw back her veil, and Susannah gasped, not only at the angry mark on her face but also at the anguish in Joaquina's eyes, which seemed to burn like a fever from the disease of her marriage.

"There is nothing left to do," Joaquina said dully.

"What happened? Why did he hit you?"

She smiled ruefully. "Hitting me was the least of it. What hurt most doesn't show. He hit me bacause I refused to allow him to do everything to me that he wanted to do. Can you imagine, I, who was taught that pleasing my husband was the highest of duties. I resisted him." A sob struggled out. "But he had his way in spite of it, and he will always have his way. Until he uses me up and is done with me. It's my turn. Maria Rosa just sits in the shade now. He hasn't even bothered to send her back to the fields. Sometimes that seems the most unbearable thing—to have her around to remind me of everything that is in store for me."

"You're right, you must go, Joaquina!"

"And you'll help me? You can arrange it?"

"I'm sure I can. Meet me day after tomorrow at the pond where the Indians draw their water. Can you come in the morning? Perhaps about nine?"

"He would be away from the house then," Joaquina said, nodding.

"Antonio, too. He mustn't know about this either. I let the escape plan operate while he was away in Rio, you see. Oh, I did try to put a stop to it, but I couldn't, and I have never told him what I know."

Joaquina's eyes flickered. "We will both be careful, Susannah."

Susannah sent for Simon on the pretext that some repairs needed to be arranged in the kitchen. The overseer frowned in displeasure as Susannah outlined the problem.

"I don't like it, Marqueza," he said. "It's too dangerous."

"It's dangerous when it's a slave, too, and you don't seem to mind then," she said meaningfully, letting him know she was aware that his ventures had continued.

"But I am very cautious and take someone only now and then. A countess is a very different matter. A countess cannot just disappear like a slave."

"But she must. And she is a slave, Simon. It's no different because her skin isn't black."

"I can't do it, Marqueza. I'm sorry."

Susannah grew determined, both because she shared a woman's sisterhood with Joaquina and because she still felt blame over the situation. "Simon, if you don't do this, I'll tell the marquess what you've been doing. I should have done so long ago anyway. He will punish you severely, and not with the whip. That would be too easy."

Susannah saw that dangerous look in Simon's eyes and was reminded again of Cort's misgivings about him. For a moment she was almost frightened, but then his expression became obedient again. "I will do what you want, Marqueza," he said.

She conveyed the news to Joaquina when they met at the Indian pond, and a date was set for the escape.

Susannah was nervous during the few days it took to make the arrangements, but she needn't have worried that Antonio would notice anything amiss. The new Senate appointment was due to be made during the next month, and he was busy talking to planters and businessmen to secure their backing. It was going to be difficult. Antonio was well liked, but his new ideas worried them. Some were sure to stick with Conde Marchado and his support of slavery. The effort claimed all his attention.

The evening of the escape, Susannah wan-

dered down to the tree-root hut beyond the bathing pool, where she had first seen Simon. It
was there Joaquina was to arrive to begin her
journey. Conde Marchado, also preoccupied with
winning the Senate position, would be dining
away from home, so Joaquina wouldn't be missed
for hours.

At the appointed time a woman slipped
through the banana grove carrying a bundle.
She appeared to be a slave, and Susannah assumed Joaquina had disguised herself that way
in a calico dress and a bandana, her face darkened with ashes. But when the woman reached
the hut, Susannah discovered there was no disguise. Maria Rosa rushed into Simon's arms,
weeping with joy at the sight of him.

Immediately she suspected that Simon had
arranged the switch, but he was as puzzled as
Susannah.

"Why are you here?" he asked her. "Where
is the countess?"

"The countess?" Maria Rosa was bewildered.
"She told me to come. She said you wanted me
to run away with you." Too late she realized
Susannah's presence—the Kiss Flower's mistress!
She cowered in terror.

"It's all right, I won't hurt you," Susannah
told her.

Susannah could not imagine what had happened, and Simon, with Maria Rosa in his arms,
hardly seemed to care. Painfully he was telling
her that he did not want to leave the Kiss Flower
a slave, and she would have to go back to the
count or go alone. "If I send you, we'll be
separated forever, Maria Rosa," he told her.
"But I will, if you don't want to wait for me.
You can be free now, without me."

Maria Rosa clung to him and wept, shaking

her head. Susannah felt tears in her own eyes as she realized that the girl loved Simon enough to remain in slavery for his sake. Perhaps it would be more possible to buy Maria Rosa now, she thought, since the count had tired of her. She left them their privacy and went back to the house, her heart filled with dread. What had become of Joaquina? Why had she sent Maria Rosa in her place? Antonio seemed preoccupied during dinner, but tonight at least Susannah didn't mind. She was grateful not to have him notice her own distraction.

Had the count changed his plans and made her flight impossible? And had Joaquina thought it better not to waste the effort that had already been put into the escape by sending Maria Rosa? Susannah remembered that Joaquina had been bothered by the slave's presence.

Knowing Antonio was to attend a political meeting in Santarém later in the evening, she asked whether Conde Marchado would be there too.

"Of course. Would he miss the opportunity to contradict everything I say?" Antonio looked at her quizzically, wondering why she wanted to know.

Susannah covered with a discourse on her confidence in her husband to carry the debate and announced there was a choice of chocolate or coconut pie for dessert. After dinner Antonio kissed her perfunctorily and set out for his meeting.

After he had gone, Susannah waited only a moment to send to have her own horse saddled. During the meal an awful possibility had occurred to her—Conde Marchado had beated

Joaquina so badly that she had been unable to leave. She had either hidden her injuries from Maria Rosa or forbidden her to tell. Or, if Joaquina were only frightened, Susannah might be able to restore her courage. But whatever the reason, there was no time to lose, if the escape were to be completed.

Riding faster than was wise along the root-laced path in the darkness, Susannah became aware of another rider not far ahead. Antonio! She was catching up with him, for this was the trail he would take to the main road to Santarém. Having glimpsed him through the trees, where the path made a wide loop, and moonlight filtered through the palms, Susannah reined in and kept back, glad for the noise of crickets and frogs, which covered the sound of hoofbeats. In another mile he would turn off, and she could gallop again.

But Antonio didn't turn off. Instead, a third rider came toward him, and when they met, both dismouted. Susannah, hearing nothing but the crickets, and unable to see through the forest tangle, was almost upon them before she realized they were there, locked in an embrace. Her husband and her sister, Rachel!

18

Susannah turned her horse in a panic and rode for the Kiss Flower. The pair of them heard the racket of her departure. She heard Antonio call out, but only dug her heels in harder against her horse's flanks. Antonio might know someone had seen them, but he would never know who.

Susannah forgot about Joaquina. Now she could think of nothing but the image of Antonio and Rachel twined together as lovers. She had been betrayed twice in one swoop, by her beloved sister and by the husband to whom she had recklessly and helplessly given her heart. She lay on her bed unable even to weep. Which one of them was more to blame? Antonio, after all, was a Brazilian man. Hadn't she known that such men thought little of having affairs? But Susannah was an American and had counted on fidelity. No, it wasn't because she was American, entirely. It was because she loved him so much she could not endure the thought of sharing him, not even if the affair was casual and meaningless. Casual—was it that? Or did Antonio's feelings for her vibrant little sister run deeper? Had he fallen deeply for her seductive worshipfulness, cloaked in the innocence of a family relationship?

Had he been the "victim" or had it been he who had made advances to a lonely young woman who was desperately in love with him and could not possibly resist? She hated first one and then the other, then both at once. To think she had worried that it would be Joaquina with whom Antonio would someday stray! All in all, that might have been easier to take, she thought ruefully. Her own sister! Where a man was concerned, a woman never could guess from where a threat might come.

When Antonio came home, she thought wildly, needing to scream and beat upon him. But mad with frustration, she realized she couldn't. Otherwise he would know she'd been out in the night. He'd want to know why.

She wept herself into a tortured sleep, from which she was awakened by Aunt Caroline shaking her. At first she thought it was part of a dream. It was like so many dreams she had had.

"Miss Susannah, there's men outside. Must be twenty or thirty, yelling and hollering just like a passel of Yankees. They say they goin' to break the door down if we don't let them it. It's just like Colonel Spangler at Robin Hill, Miss Susannah. What do they want?"

"I don't know, but we have had experience defending ourselves. We'll deal them them. Go and send Olinda to hide in the pantry with Josiah and Izabel."

She could hear the commotion outside the house as she went downstairs. The banging on the front door was so loud it seemed to rattle the house, and through the windows she could see horsemen trampling the flowerbeds. Fear overcame her anger, and she wished Antonio were home. In his study she removed his hunting rifle from its rack and loaded it. A few months ago Antonio had brought down a marauding jaguar with this weapon. And he had taught Susannah how to use it before he had left on his trip to Rio.

Trembling slaves huddled in the foyer. She ordered the door unbolted and took a stance before it with the rifle leveled at the brass knob. As the door swung open, the besieging men halted their forward rush at the sight of her.

"What is the meaning of this?" she demanded.

"Your husband, Marqueza. Step aside. You won't get hurt. Our quarrel isn't with you."

Susannah recognized Conde Marchado's voice and pointed her weapon at his chest. "You are the one who will be hurt, Conde! I am not afraid to fire in self-defense. I've done it before. I've yet to kill a man, but there must be a first time. Perhaps tonight, Conde. The marquess isn't home. You'll have to deal with me." As her eyes adjusted to the fragile moonlight, Susannah began to recognize other faces—mostly those of planters, some colonists who had sold their

farms to Conde Marchado. Not a few were men
whom Antonio had counted upon to support
his Senate appointment. Now, here they were,
an angry crew, seething to tramp across his
hearth. Susannah knew why they had come; she
was as guilty as she had been the night Colonel
Spangler's men had come chasing after Cort St.
John and Rachel had sat on his hat to hide it.
They had got wind of the escape route, though
she couldn't fathom how.

She was guilty, and Antonio would surely
guess it. She had been involved with Simon's
escape, and he had told her it must not happen
again!

"We intend to search the property, Marqueza,"
Conde Marchado told her. "A slave of mine is
missing, the very slave you took such an interest in, and it wouldn't be the first time I've
found a runaway slave of mine at the Kiss
Flower. Where is that slave of yours, Simon?
He'll be behind it! I warned Antonio he was a
troublemaker! He'll hang this time, with the
marquess's permission or without!"

Susannah tried to remain calm, though her
mind was in pandemonium. She remembered
the night the count had found Simon. Antonio
had solved that matter, but this was different.
Simon had been an illegal slave, and the count
would not have liked that made public, but
Maria Rosa had been born in Ceará. Even more,
there was the Senate appointment. What better
time to embarrass Antonio, to accuse him of
being a rabid abolitionist, willing to break the
law for his purpose? How sour would Antonio's plans for growth and freedom along the
Amazon ring in the growers' ears then! And

Antonio's vision of a booming river society with opportunity for people of all nations—Portuguese or American, Chinese, German, or Indian—might be lost along with his Senate seat.

Why should she care after what he had done to her? But she did care. She realized miserably that his rendezvous with her sister hadn't diminished her love for him; instead, it had only made her feel its immensity measured by the immensity of her fury and grief. His dream had become her dream too. It was her dream for him, for their children, for the colonists, and for all the other settlers who would come to build new lives along the river.

And what of Maria Rosa? If she were found, Conde Marchado would deal her a horrible punishment, and it would be Susannah's fault for ever having allowed Joaquina's escape attempt.

"I will allow two of you into the house, provided you wipe your feet," Susannah said haughtily.

"Very well, Marqueza. But we don't expect to find the slave sitting in the marquess's parlor or in his bed." Conde Marchado chuckled at his lewd suggestion. "We'll have to search thoroughly."

"Search anywhere you like, Conde. You won't find a runaway being harbored on the Kiss Flower," a voice barked. Antonio strode onto the veranda. Susannah almost fainted with relief at seeing him, but immediately wasn't relieved at all.

Antonio went past her, his anger like a black wind blowing trees and leaves in a storm. Ignoring her, he went into the house and pushed the door shut.

Bravely she followed him into his study, where he stood towering with hostility while he poured himself a glass of wine. The sensuous lips that had thrilled her with so many intimate kisses were tight with fury. His eyes were darker than usual, but angry lights jumped within, like explosions on a moonless night. A tingle ran down to Susannah's toes. Fear, of course, but fear mixed with something else as well. Some demon in her hoped he would vent himself in mastering her in bed. How exciting that would be! But first she must tell him the truth.

"Antonio, she is hiding in the banana grove," she managed to say.

"No, Susannah, she is not. She is back where she belongs, no thanks to you!"

Again she felt relief and again knew it was premature.

He turned on her with an anger unlike anything she had ever seen. She had witnessed the jaguar just before he had shot it, fierce with power and savage grace, poised to strike, with the light of its brutal strength shining in its golden eyes. She was reminded of the jaguar now, except Antonio's eyes were dark as whirlwinds.

"Do you have any idea what you almost caused, Susannah? All because of your headstrong disobedience! You allowed your sentimental concern for one slave to endanger the hope of all!"

"But, Antonio, I—"

His voice boomed over hers. "That is why women are not fit to make their own decisions. They let their foolish emotions get in the way. That is what husbands are for! You did the one thing you knew I could not tolerate! You cannot learn a wife's duties, which you should have been taught from the cradle!"

"You are the one who doesn't know a husband's duties, sir!" Susannah shot back. "You did the one thing *I* cannot tolerate!" Deep inside she knew it would serve better to collapse weeping and plead forgiveness, but her own pride and hurt would not allow it. Instead, her own reckless wrath came bursting forth. "Perhaps if you had been at home, instead of amusing yourself at my expense with my sister—"

"Have you gone mad!" He seemed stunned, but that was only because she had dared to accuse him.

"Do you deny it?"

"Deny it? Deny some female delusion of yours? I am not on trial, Susannah! I don't care; think what you like. It's clear to me I made a terrible mistake when I married you. You are nothing of what a woman should be, and it is not your place to attempt to censor me. You don't know how to be a woman, Susannah!"

"You are not the only one who made a mistake, sir! There is more to being a woman than minding one's master! In fact, that's not it at all! You pretend to care about ending slavery, but what you really care about is your own political glory. You care about being a power close to the emperor. Otherwise you could not blame me so completely for trying to help poor Maria Rosa. Oh, I would have been better off in prison! Better even in the hangman's noose than to suffer marriage to you!"

Beside herself, she seized the decanter of wine and hurled it at him. It shattered at his feet as he jumped back, splattering wine over him as it broke.

With a cry, he sprang toward her. She whirled and ran up the stairs, barricading herself behind her door, sliding the lock shut, terrified that he would follow her inside. If he did, she knew how it was likely to end. And she would not have the strength to resist. She never had.

As his footsteps hurried close, she felt the rush of overwhelming desire, and without waiting for him to force the door, opened the lock again.

Dizzy with anticipation, she waited for him to burst through to assert that mastery of her which so excited them both. Anger, fear, and heartache could never follow them to the paradise to which they ascended in each other's arms. Passion would dwindle all else; his rage would be but the kindling of the fire of their love.

The footsteps stopped. She heard his quick breath beyond the door, and her heart beat faster. Then, in disbelief, she heard the footsteps going away.

She had lost her hold over him. The magical charm that had drawn him to his heedless marriage no longer bound him. He saw clearly that Susannah was not the woman he needed as a lover or even as only a respected wife. And though, in the days to come, she tried to appear proudly beautiful before him, she felt herself fade, her luster dimmed by its failure to reflect from his eyes.

Susannah did not confront her sister about Antonio, though she wondered whether, during his many nights away from home, he enjoyed himself with her. The thought was too painful to bear, so Susannah buried herself in caring for her children, remembering ruefully that Joaquina had told her that children were destined to be the comfort of a Brazilian marriage.

Joaquina herself seemed to have survived the crisis easily. Less than a week afterward she was seen at a party in Santarém, smiling and now without evidence of physical injury. Susannah still did not know exactly what had happened to Joaquina's escape plan, but the tale came to Susannah that Joaquina had spent a great deal of time with Antonio, who had dropped in on the gathering without bothering to return to the Kiss Flower for his wife. How unfair to take advantage of their estrangement, when she had been responsible!

Antonio made a trip to Pará to talk to influential men in that part of the state; and after he had gone, the days seemed emptier. She had been lonely before, but then at least she had listened for his footsteps late at night. She could only guess whether he was returning from a political gathering or a romantic rendezvous; and though now and then he had paused near her door and made her tremble, it was as though he did it by accident while searching for something in his pockets. Would she have let him love her, had he tried? Would she ever forgive him?

With Antonio gone, she noticed how large and endless the forest seemed, how eerie the call of birds and monkeys through the trees. Most of all, she missed Rachel, whom she had not seen since she had spied on her and Antonio.

One evening she heard a tapir's cry and shuddered, wondering if Indians had killed it to roast as it came down from the high ground to wallow in some river pool. Storm clouds gathered. Heat lightning exploded silently behind the lofty palms, silhouetted against mauve, green, and deep violet as the sun sank like a gem into the batting of clouds. As she stood on the veranda, a sudden breeze brought the cool smell of rain, and the aroma of burning jetahy bark, over which someone in the slave quarters was glazing pottery with copal.

Olinda came to the door and begged her to come inside.

"It's so pretty," she protested, gazing out at the wind-tossed jungle, realizing how much she loved this wild place. When had it happened? This was home now, not Robin Hill.

"It seems far away, but it strikes without warning, Marqueze," Olinda told her. "Beware of jungle lightning."

"Look, here comes Simon. Why is he riding so fast? Is it to beat the storm?" Susannah waited curiously as Simon galloped down from the bluff on a big white mule, his wide-brimmed straw hat blowing on its string behind.

"Marqueza!" he called.

The wind whipped her hair and skirts as he halted near her. His dark face roiled with fury as though he were a part of the oncoming storm. Had she not know him so well, she would have been frightened.

"Marqueza, you must go to the count and ask to buy Maria Rosa again," he cried. He wasn't making a request; he was giving her an order!

"No, Simon. I can't go back there," she said, feeling uneasy. "Wait and ask the marquess."

"It can't wait. You must try again. He is about to sell her to Rudd Sloane!"

"You do not know the price he would ask of me!"

Simon regarded her for a long moment and then sighed with resignation. "Perhaps I do."

He paced the veranda with a ferocious gait. "The marquess is away too much. It will be too late. Most likely Conde Marchado will not consider disposing of her to a kind owner anyway. He is punishing her for trying to escape, even though he has no real proof of it. She was only missing a few hours, but that is enough for him to make an example of her to the others. Besides, he'll enjoy it. Sloane will dispose of her as a prostitute. That's what happens to the very prettiest."

"Simon—"

"Oh, it's true, Marqueza," he said bitterly. "There are plenty of white men in Pará who'll pay to debauch themselves with a beautiful slave—those who don't have the luxury of owning their own whore. But I have the same feelings all men have about their wives!"

"Your wife, Simon!"

"The Christian slaves at Casa Rio have a chapel. It's only a hut with a slave minister who works in the cane fields, but that's how all the slaves are married. Maria Rosa and I were married six months ago."

Six months ago. Had that been when the count had ceased to entertain himself with Maria Rosa? Had she waited for his lust to burn itself out before consenting to marry the man she loved? Simon must know or have strong suspicions about what had been done to her. He had had to accept it, but now . . .

"It's not a real marriage. You didn't have the permission of your owners," she said a little desperately, sensing the temptest bursting in his soul.

"It is real in God's eyes, Marqueza. Maria Rosa is carrying my child."

His child! Could anyone be certain that it wasn't the count's? Maybe not even Maria Rosa could be sure. But Simon obviously had banished any such doubts. She was his wife, and the child was his to protect.

"Simon, you did promise to stay at the Kiss Flower until you were free," she reminded, intuiting what he had in mind, guessing how Antonio would view Simon's flight with Maria Rosa.

Simon pulled a bag out of his pocket and spilled money onto a wrought-iron table. "I was waiting to have the marquess come home and sign the papers, but I'll go without them. I am a free man. I do not belong to the Kiss Flower and you and the marquess cannot be held responsible for whatever I do."

"Maria Rosa is not a free woman!"

"She shall live as one!"

"You're going to steal her! Simon, the planters are just looking for a reason to kill you."

"I know, Marqueza. And I intend to give them reason. But we shall see who is killed. You had better put the children in the pantry tonight, in case there is trouble when they come here looking for me. They'll be disappointed. I won't be found on the Kiss Flower."

With a quick step he jumped from the veranda, mounted the mule again, and galloped away.

It was past midnight when, lying awake, she heard the shout from the slave quarters. Until then there had been only the patter of rain, the soft dripping on thatch, the second movement of a symphony that had begun with thunder, wind, and a lashing downpour.

The rainy season was beginning, the time of quiet isolation. This year the colonists had almost completed their harvest. Big wagonloads of cotton bales rumbled into Santarém every day to be loaded onto barges for their journey downriver. The rain, then, should have been lulling, signaling a time of rest approaching. But the peace was fraudulent with Simon out in the night.

Susannah leapt from bed at the first indication of commotion and summoned Olinda to go to find out what the trouble was. She had no compunction about sending the girl. If Conde Marchado were there, searching for Simon and Maria Rosa, Olinda wouldn't be bothered. She was only an Indian, not a part of the society of slave and master, more a denizen of the jungle like a deer or paca. Olinda went quickly and was soon back, her hair streaming rainwater.

"What's going on? Are there planters? Are they looking for Simon?"

Olinda shook her head. "Someone from Casa Rio brought news that Simon and Maria Rosa have escaped and are being pursued. The slaves are going to help them."

"Help them! But I haven't given permission

for anyone to leave the Kiss Flower! And I cannot!"

"It doesn't matter, Marqueza. They wouldn't listen to you if you tried to stop them. Let them go. It won't be only the Kiss Flower's slaves. There are already slaves from several other plantations with them. They are going to ride from plantation to plantation, burning and looting, until the planters have to turn their attention from Simon to save their homes."

"And then?" Susannah asked, barely able to breathe.

"They are talking about freedom, Marqueza. Simon filled their heads with it. He gave them hope. If he dies, they'll lose that, so they say now is the time, and Simon must lead them."

From the window, Susannah could see torches waving, heads of fire trailing tresses of bright destruction. She shuddered, remembering again that Cort had said it was a mistake to allow slaves to learn to read and write, to develop a sense of self-worth and unity.

"Are we to be ravaged, then? Will they burn the house? And the cane. There are fields that haven't been cut, and sugar and molasses that haven't been shipped . . ." She thought of Memphis, the sticky river of molasses pouring down the bluff, and the stench of burning cotton.

"It's revolution, Olinda. It's like the war again, only without armies to give it form. It's only them and us."

"They won't hurt the Kiss Flower, Marqueza," Olinda told her. "Don't be frightened."

But Olinda could not understand how deep Susannah's fear ran. She had never been through war as Susannah had. Susannah ran down to the pantry where Aunt Caroline was sleeping with the children and flung herself into the comfort of her old mammy's arms.

"There, now, it ain't like the Yankees with no respect for white folks that's been fair," Aunt Caroline told her.

Susannah began to stop trembling. "We'll just stay right here, Aunt Caroline. Of course I trust the Kiss Flower's slaves."

But suddenly Susannah thought of a danger even Aunt Caroline couldn't soothe. "Rachel! Rachel isn't safe. The slaves may burn and loot on Twenty Palms, and the planters may be rough with her too, since she is related to Antonio and me. I'm sure some of them will be blaming the Kiss Flower. I've got to go and warn her!"

"Don't you go out there, Miss Susannah!" Aunt Caroline cried. "Send somebody else! Send Olinda out again."

It was a sensible suggestion, but Susannah was too overwrought to take it. She told herself she wasn't sure of Olinda's commitment, but actually she had a complusion to go to her sister. Memories of other treacherous times engulfed her, memories of Rachel's being taken away to the Irving Block. No mere man must come between her and her sister. They must face tonight together.

Nothing Aunt Caroline could say would dissuade her. Having changed into her riding habit and Wellington boots and borrowed a waterproof poncho of Antonio's, she saddled a horse herself, grateful that it stood patiently, not like the irascible Sultan.

Her mount was surefooted on the muddy path, along which banana leaves and palm fronds loaded with rainwater like dippers spilled onto her as she brushed against them. But deep into the woods she came to a turnoff amid assai palms, their slender trunks, twined with philodendron, moving restlessly, as such trees always did, even in the lightest breeze, like an impatient crowd among the low fern and arum. The palms seemed like intelligent presences in the heavy night shadows. The lantern she carried made all the familiar jungle shapes large and grotesque. Somewhere a monkey chattered; a bird fluttered noisily, disturbed by the light. But it was the sighing palms that whispered to her, as an impulse seized her and solidified into determination.

She must do better than make sure Rachel was safe. She would go to Casa Rio instead, no matter how dangerous. She knew better than anyone what was beginning to happen; and if action came quickly enough, it might still be stopped—if Simon and his wife were allowed to go free to make their escape along the canoe route to Pará.

She chose the fork that led to Casa Rio, and before long the forest opened onto its broad lawn. The magnificent house, trimmed in banana trees and huge castor-oil plants, shone palely ahead. She left her horse tied to a lion's-head hitching post as she dashed to demand entrance, swinging the knocker with all her might.

The house was dark, and there was no answer, though she was certain someone must have heard her. She shouted her name shrilly and finally was rewarded by the glow of a light moving inside. A salve woman's dark face looked through the narrow diamond-cut panes of the sidelight that distorted its shape as much as the jungle had been by her lantern. Then the door opened, its creak rising like a question. Behind the slave woman stood Joaquina in a satin robe, her black hair flowing.

"Susannah! What are you doing here?"

"I must see the count, Joaquina!"

"Why, he's not here. He rode away hours ago. He didn't say anything to me, but he never does when he goes out late. I know better than to ask. What's wrong?"

Susannah knew her distress showed on her face. She had wasted valuable time coming here. She should have known the count wouldn't be here. "Please think, Joaquina. Which direction did he go? You must remember something. It's about the girl Maria Rosa. My Simon has run away with her. The count intended to sell her, to punish her for her escape attempt. And you cannot say you know nothing about *that*, Joaquina!"

The countess pulled Susannah into the drawing room, taking with her a lighted candle from a hall table. "That will be all," she told her slave. Go back to bed now." Joaquina slammed the French doors behind them. Susannah's poncho dripped onto the Aubusson carpet.

"It's no wonder you don't want her to hear," Susannah declared in sudden fury. "It's your fault! Why did you send Maria Rosa in your place, Joaquina?"

"Susannah, don't be angry," Joaquina pleaded. "I was too frightened to come. Where would I have gone? My family wouldn't have taken me back."

"You should have thought of that before," Susannah snapped.

"Oh, but I wanted to come so much, and then, when I lost courage, I thought how wonderful it would be for Maria Rosa. She had suffered so much."

"She'll suffer even more now. Who knows how many will be hurt or even die, regardless of their color of skin! There is an uprising of slaves. Perhaps they'll come here, looting and burning. And you are far from innocent! How did it happen that your husband found out that night you sent Maria Rosa to the Kiss Flower?"

"I . . . don't know. How should I know, Susannah?"

"You should know because you told him. You told him, didn't you? Nobody knew except you, me, Simon, and the canoe man. You are the logical one!" Susannah had been sorting this out ever since that night.

"I . . . Why should I do it? Someone must have seen her leave. Maybe he saw her himself."

"You did it to cause trouble between me and Antonio, didn't you. Admit it!"

"Oh, why shouldn't I?" Joaquina decided with a toss of her head. "It worked perfectly. He was mine before he was yours. You stole him, so you're the real culprit. I would have been married to him, instead of doomed to this awful life, except for you! I saw no reason your life should be so sweet. Oh, it was sickening to see the two of you together, while I lived in hell every night. I love him, and now I'll have him at last!"

"How dare you say you love him! You set

him up to be discredited. To jeopardize his appointment and all his dreams. You didn't care a fig, not as long as I got the blame! Well, you won't have him! I'll tell him what you did."

"He won't believe you. Why would he believe you? You, who are always doing things behind his back and causing him trouble?"

"I cannot waste any more time on this foolishness, Joaquina. I have to try to save what I can tonight!"

"Susannah, wait! What should I do if the slaves come here?"

Susannah looked back, seeing instead of a conniving woman only a helpless child, a girl who had never learned that actions have consequences, because she had been too restricted to take any action. For just a moment, looking at Joaquina's frightened face, Susannah felt her anger evaporate in spite of herself.

"Find a place to hide, Joaquina," she told her disgustedly. "The springhouse might be a good place."

Susannah rode again for Twenty Palms, as hard as she could go. But the rebellion preceded her. A heavy vine swung at her out of the trees, a form dangling from it, a terrible face confronting her—staring eyes above a blackly gaping mouth. She was certain it was one of the jungle goblins about which the Indians told grisly tales. She might have thought it a figment of her imagination, except her horse gave a frightened whinny and reared. She clung to its back, too busy maintaining her seat to scream herself. But as she brought her mount under control, she realized there was something familiar about the awful face. It belonged to Rudd

Sloane, swinging there, harmless at last, but looking even more evil in death than in life.

The slaves, she thought, shuddering as she pressed on.

Even before she reached Twenty Palms, she knew she was too late. The smell of smoke was in the air, and a glow lighted the sky. The elaborate log home Cort had built so carefully was a smoldering shell by the time she arrived. Above the house a cotton field, ready for harvest, was burning, illuminating shapes of men running.

"Rachel!" she screamed, urging her reluctant horse toward the house. There was no answer, no sign of life. Not needing the lantern now to see, Susannah threw it aside. Then she galloped among the sheds and barns, calling her sister's name, as tears of dread streamed down her face.

She rode up to the bluff, where the half-harvested cane waited in carts to be pushed down the long chute to the millhouse. The cane had not been fired here, though an odor of sweet scorch drifted over it from other fields. Perhaps Rachel had hidden among the cane stalks, but that concealment would not be safe for long. The fire was coming . . .

"Rachel!" she called.

She heard a footstep and dismounted to investigate. "Rachel! It's Susannah! Where are you?"

A cane cart was perched over the edge of the cane chute, and the sound had come from behind it. But Susannah, in her eagerness to find Rachel, had forgotten how likely it was that the noise had been made by someone else. Rounding the corner of the cart, she came face to face with Conde Marchado. She gasped and stepped backward.

He chuckled. "Why, how delightful, Marqueza," he said, tipping his hat formally, as though they had been passing on a street in Santarém.

"I . . . was looking for my sister," she said, her heart racing. Even in the shadows she saw the lusty look in his eyes.

"So was I. It's a terrible night for a woman to be alone with no husband to protect her." He paused and laughed, pulled on his short thick beard, aware of the double meaning in his words. "You aren't afraid, are you, Marqueza? Not since you're with me."

"Of course not. I was looking for you earlier."

"Why, how flattering, Marqueza." Boldly he slid an arm around her waist. "You've nothing to fear now, my dear. You'll be safe with me."

Susannah shook him off. "I want everyone to be safe, Conde. Sell Maria Rosa to me. You can't sell to Sloane anyway. He's hanging dead back there in the woods. Call back the men who are looking for her and Simon. I will find someone from the Kiss Flower to spread the word they are safe. Perhaps then this destruction can be stopped."

"Stopped? Stopped, Marqueza? A master cannot bargain with slaves. They must be punished, and every white man in the district will take up arms to see to it."

"We must try. We *must* deal with the slaves, Conde. Sell Maria Rosa to me."

"Well," he said with a smirk, "I can't see what I have to lose. Imagine having the good fortune to sell a slave who has escaped."

"Your price, Conde. I will write you a note
and bring you the money tomorrow."

"Marqueza, what must you think of me! To
take a lady's money for a purchase I cannot
even deliver. I will make you a gift of her."

"You are most generous—"

"Surely you will make me a gift too, Susannah. If you would show your gratitude with
only a little kiss . . . We each have our needs,
you know. You need Maria Rosa because that
husband of yours will blame this whole matter
on you. As well he should. It would not have
happened if you had told him long ago about
the escape route from the Kiss Flower. What a
fool Antonio was to marry an American woman.
Ah, but I can see why he did."

Cool air hit her body as he pulled her poncho
over her head. His arm was around her, this
time clutching her so tightly she couldn't pull
loose. She leaned backward, trying to get away,
and felt his hand on her upturned breast. Hurriedly he parted the buttons of her silk blouse.
His lips were on her throat; she emitted a groan
of effort as she fought him. He, in his immense
conceit, mistook it for passion, pressing against
her unthinkably.

"Relax, Susannah. What does it matter if we
enjoy each other? No one will ever know. What's
one more secret to keep from your husband,
eh? You've made it quite apparent that he is not
your master."

"The ground is wet, and I do not make love
with men outdoors like animals," she said
strongly while she trembled in his grasp. "I
require a bed."

Having him ravish her would be no less

digusting in one spot than another, but if she could only get to her horse . . .

But Conde Marchado did not agree to a more suitable place as she had hoped.

"My dear Marqueza, we mustn't let passion cool. It's stopped raining, after all, and the mist is pretty over the palms. I will spread out my cloak . . ."

The moment was all Susannah needed. As he loosened his lecherous hold to place his cloak, she dealt him a hard kick, the heel of her Wellington boot striking his stomach. He gave a grunt, more of surprise than pain, for he was well muscled and she had not struck where she intended. With a curse he caught hold of her again, and giving up all pretense of her compliance, flung her easily to the ground in front of the cane cart.

His weight held her pinned as he fumbled with his trousers, but her hands were free to seize a rock lying near the cart wheel. She intended to pound it against his head, but he saw and gave her wrist a hard twist that made the rock fall free.

What happened after that she experienced in a dizzy horror. She screamed with pain and fear as she lost the stone, and her scream was answered by a distant male shout, "Susannah!"

Then came a strange rumble, a vibration like an earthquake. Over her, darkness suddenly closed out the nightglow and the gleam from the burning fields. Another scream rent the air, so close it seemed to emanate from inside her, but she knew it was the count who had screamed. Even as the world seemed to crash around her, she noticed his mysterious absence. It was as though, after all, there *had* been goblins in the night, protective goblins.

Gradually the tumult subsided. She saw light again beyond the heavy shadow in which she lay. The same male voice called her name again.

"Antonio!" she answered.

She looked up and saw her husband, rain streaming from his hair, glistening on his finely planed face. His cambric shirt clung wetly to his chest and arms, so that he seemed a marble sculpture of magnificent manhood. It was as though he were an apparition, materialized to save her, with an expression in those dear, unexpected eyes that was at once tender and scowling.

She felt his arms around her, pulling her from under the tilted cane cart. She leaned against him weakly, not really surprised that he had been there when she needed him. Hadn't he always, since the night the Yankees had chased her aboard the *River Belle*? And what more in the world could she want than to depend on him?

"Antonio, where is—?"

"Don't think about what happened to Conde Marchado, Susannah," he commanded.

But as usual she disobeyed him. She observed the cane cart, its burden unloaded down the hundred-foot cane chute, stray stalks still clinging all the way.

"Antonio, is he—?"

"He fell into the millhouse. He couldn't still be alive. The weight of cane set the grinder in motion."

The mill had been a new design, the plans

sent to the colony by Dom Pedro himself. It was an American invention he had wanted tested. But Susannah didn't hear Antonio explain it to her. She had fainted.

19

It was the next day before she realized exactly how it had happened. The rock with which she had tried to protect herself had been holding the cart in place, and when Antonio had called her name, the count had raised up to see who was there and had jarred it loose. The cart had rolled forward and tilted, spilling its heavy load and sweeping the count before it.

Susannah herself had been lying beneath the cart, between the wheels, which had passed harmlessly over.

If Antonio had not come back . . . But he had hurried home from Pará, fearful of some sort of trouble. As a master, he was observant enough to sense the shifting moods of his slaves, and he knew that if it had not been Simon, something or someone else would have moved them to rebel. They were the last human beings in the hemisphere held in bondage. The time was simply coming when slavery would end. Antonio had been spending the night in Santarém, intending to return to the Kiss Flower in the morning, when he had heard the news.

Like Susannah, he had thought of Rachel and had ridden to Twenty Palms first, in time to pluck her up onto his horse as she fled from her burning home. It had been appropriate, because Twenty Palms had been in more danger than the Kiss Flower; but even so, as glad as Susannah was to see Rachel, she found herself resenting it. She breakfasted in bed the next morning. She had taken a chill, she told herself, to excuse the indulgence. But that wasn't the reason. Susannah remained upstairs because she didn't want to go down and see the pair of them together.

Antonio had been out all night, after having delivered the two women to the Kiss Flower. It had been past ten in the morning when he had come in at last. Rachel had been waiting shamelessly to serve him coffee and griddle cakes, which she had been keeping hot. Tears of anger sprang to Susannah's eyes as she heard them laughing together below.

Then his footsteps came up the stairs. In amazement, Susannah shifted in her bed, and the dishes on the tray clattered and overturned as his hand twisted the doorknob.

Her heart raced as he stood over her, gazing down impassively at her bare shoulders, exposed in her thin nightdress.

He himself was wearing a breakfast jacket of

velvet with quilted satin lapels and cuffs, the blue color heightening the tone of his skin as though he were fashioned of copper. She let her gaze move up the grateful line of his throat to the firm chin, jutting like one of the little fortified islands at the Amazon's mouth, his eyes fluid and deep, the currents swifts and treacherous as one of the river's black-water streams. What could she see in there? Only displeasure? Or was there longing and vulnerability as well?

"Have you recovered from last night, Susannah?" he asked.

"Oh, yes, Antonio." Susannah forgot all about the imagined chill. In fact she felt very warm all over. She certainly wouldn't say she was ill, not if . . .

But Antonio had other things on his mind. "You shouldn't have gone out last night, Susannah. But of course 'shouldn't' has never stopped you, has it? You were lucky. Conde Marchado wasn't—quite naturally, I suppose. It stands to reason that a man's luck runs out because of you."

"Antonio, surely you don't think that I, that I . . ."

"Invited him? Probably you did; a man of Conde Marchado's character doesn't require much invitation. Undoubtedly you were trying to get something you wanted from him. That's your way with men. You take what you want, without caring about the consequences. But I imagine he deserved his fate. I won't waste sympathy on him, and I'm sure you won't."

Susannah shuddered as she thought of what

had happened to the count, but she answered honestly, "No, I won't."

"What was it you were after, Susannah?" he asked, sitting on the edge of the bed and helping himself to a piece of mango from her tray.

"Maria Rosa. I thought if I could buy her, then I might be able to stop the rioting. Oh, I knew it was dangerous, but what else was I to do?"

The breakfast tray with its dishes betrayed her agitation with its clattering, and he took it and moved it away. It flashed into her head that he might be making room for himself beside her. She stiffened, even as her heart pounded in anticipation.

Why, she would not allow him! Hadn't she any pride? She mustn't let him, after his behavior with Rachel, after what she had seen!

Susannah trembled, but Antonio didn't pull back the covers. "The slaves have gone back to the plantations," he told her. "It took a lot of persuading on both sides, but most of the growers have agreed to a system of shares of next year's crop. The shares are to be credited as payment toward freedom for each man and woman who works. And after a worker earns his freedom, he can contract with whomever he wishes. It would not have been possible without Simon. The slaves wouldn't have been able to understand it at all. It's hard enough now, but they trust their leader. And the growers would never have agreed, if they hadn't had a taste of rebellion, so perhaps its all turned out for the best."

"You've seen Simon?"

"Yes. He's in the slave quarters now, trying

to explain to everyone. I am going into Santarém this afternoon to arrange for a lawyer to draw up the agreement."

"And Maria Rosa?"

"She's with Simon," he told her with a grin.

"Oh, Antonio, to think you've done it! You've accomplished your dream!"

"I've only begun to accomplish it," he told her, smiling. "Susannah, there's something even more important I have to tell you. It's my appointment. I've received it"

"I'm glad, Antonio. But it's no thanks to me, is it?"

"No," he said coolly, "none at all."

They would be moving to Rio, then, leaving the Kiss Flower to survive as best it could under a new overseer. Antonio intended taking Simon and Maria Rosa with him to Rio. It would be too dangerous for Simon now on the Amazon without a powerful protector. He would have too many enemies. Dom Pedro College would be the place for Simon, Antonio thought. The emperor often sponsored scholarships for the gifted; and if he would do so for Simon, he would be the first of his race to attend. Simon would need all the preparation he could acquire to become one of the first important leaders of his race in Brazil.

Susannah got out of bed and looked out her back window, where beyond the well-kept grounds she could see the silver flash of scythes in the sunshine amid the lush cane. She had thought the Kiss Flower beautiful when she first came, but it was more beautiful now. Now she had put her own mark on it. It had been new and unfinished then, but now it had become a home, thriving and vigorous with its children and its crops.

A vision came to her of Robin Hill, its fields empty and brown, its white paint chipped and weathered so gray it seemed the house itself was clad in Confederate uniform. Could that happen to the Kiss Flower while she and Antonio were gone?

A knock came lightly on the door, and her sister entered. "Is he still angry, Susannah?" she asked.

Susannah sighed. "I don't think so, Rachel, It's worse than that. I don't think he cares."

"I know it's my fault what's happened between you and Antonio," Rachel said tearfully.

"Not all of it," Susannah told her.

"Oh, if it hadn't been for me! But Susannah, I couldn't help it! I tried to avoid it. I didn't want to hurt you!"

Susannah stroked Rachel's hair, feeling very much the big sister who had had to take responsibility for them both when Colonel Dunbar had gone off to war. How could she not forgive Rachel? Could Susannah ever forget those days? After the Irving Block, Rachel had lost Robin Hill and then come thousands of miles to fall in love with a man she could never marry. She had hoped to extinguish that love with her marriage to Cort, but now he was gone too. Was it any wonder that Rachel stumbled? Surely Antonio was more to blame. If he had only been a little strong, they would have been spared this grief! Weren't men the cause of most women's grief?

"Love has been unkind to both of us, Rachel," she said. "But we'll always have each other."

"You'll be going to Rio soon."

"You'll come too, of course."

"I can't, Susannah."

"You must! You haven't even seen Rio. You'll love life at court. There'll be music and dancing every day. And excursions, because the princesses aren't cloistered like most Brazilian women. The bay is so beautiful at sunset, and even though you are married, you'll have handsome admirers who'll wish you weren't. Why, the most brilliant and wittiest men from all over the world come to Dom Pedro's court! We'll have the good times the war cheated us of, while Antonio is busy at the Senate. Why, we'll hardly notice he's not around!"

Was that the reason Rachel was refusing to come? Was she afraid of her love for Antonio? We'll both be stronger, little sister, Susannah thought. I'll be strong enough to keep from pining over him, and you'll be strong enough to spurn him.

Could it possibly work?

"I'm not a silly girl anymore, and I don't want parties and admirers. I want to stay on the Amazon and be here for Cort when he comes home."

"Please, Rachel. We can't be separated again! I can't leave you here. And Cort has been gone too long. You must face the likelihood that he won't—"

"He *will* come back, and I am going to be here!" Rachel said, displaying the same kind of hardheadedness that she had about the Confederate uniform. She hadn't really changed so much.

Susannah knew from experience that Rachel could not be dissuaded when her mind was so made up. She considered a moment. "I might as well stay too," she decided.

"You'll lose him, Susannah!" Rachel said.

"I already have. Maybe I'm not sorry. Maybe I was right when I hated him back in Memphis."

But even then, hadn't she hated him because of the devastating power she sensed he might assert over her? Didn't she hate him now more because he didn't assert that power? Wasn't it more that than his infidelity? Would she ever learn to be as indifferent to him as he was to her? How many Rachels and Joaquinas would there be in his life? Staying behind was a beginning to ending his hold on her.

If she secretly hoped that Antonio would refuse to allow her to remain on the Kiss Flower, she was disappointed. When she explained Rachel's need and her own concerns over the establishment, he only nodded agreement. "Why not?" he said. "Running the plantation suits you. And I'll be home when the Senate recesses in July. But whatever trouble you get into, my dear, you'll be on your own."

Oh, if only he would ask her forgiveness for his affair with Rachel, she would be more than willing to beg his for her deceptions about the escape route! But she was sure he could never forgive her. She had come close to spoiling his reputation and his ambitions with her feminine sentimentality. And even if he asked forgiveness, she wasn't sure she could ever truly give it.

So they became the usual Brazilian married couple, wed for convenience. Hadn't that been destined? Wasn't that the way it had begun? Why should she be surprised that was the way it had turned out? Why shouldn't the arrangement suit Antonio?

Susannah almost lost her determination to stay behind when she discovered that Joaquina would be returning to her family in Rio. What had been impossible for a mistreated wife was very different since she had become a wealthy widow. She would spend her days at court again, basking in the admiration of eligible suitors, and no doubt encouraging one gentleman, who by reason of marriage was not eligible at all.

At the dock Antonio hugged and kissed his children. Was it possible that Izabel was almost seven and had changed from a chunky toddler into a graceful stem of a half-grown girl? She clung to her father, weeping, her sleek, looped braids of hair trembling beside her ears.

"Papa, when will you come back?" she pleaded. "Will it be in time for my birthday?"

"Not so soon, sweet one, but I will send you something wonderful from Rio. A dollhouse full of furniture with even its own tiny dishes. Would you like that?"

Izabel nodded, but sobbed harder. Susannah held little Josiah up for his father's kiss; and so when he leaned to embrace the child, his face was close to hers. She could feel the warmth of his cheek, the moist breath of his lips.

Josiah, understanding less than his sister,

wailed even more loudly. Unnerved by his childish racket, Susannah put him down.

Antonio, frowning silently, kissed her chastely on the brow. "Do see if you can't instill some self-control in these children before I come back, Susannah. Especially Josiah, since he's to be a marquess. As for Izabel, what man would want an emotional wife?"

"I'll try, Antonio, but they do need a father."

They were the hold she had on him; they and the Amazon would bring him to her agian. And when he returned after the session of the Senate, was she praying things would be different between them?

The rain set in in earnest after Antonio had gone. The Kiss Flower was isolated, and Susannah's mood was often as dark as the skies. The colony was much smaller now than when they had begun. Some, who had not given up after the early crop failures or the fire-ant invasion, had abandoned the effort after the slave troubles. Remembering the horrors of the American war and not trusting Antonio's solutions, they were making their way back to the States, where at least there was civilization. Scarcely any woman who was left to endure another rainy season on the Amazon did not envy these whose husbands were made of less stern stuff.

With a new Portuguese foreman, Susannah busied herself with detailed plans for the next growing season, deciding which fields to let go fallow and where to plant new stands of cacao for long-term profit, figuring how much cotton should be grown for quick-term profit along with the cane. Rachel concerned herself more with the house and flower gardens, but both of them were lonely.

"It's just us again, the way it was at Robin Hill," Susannah observed bleakly. "We're like a pair of spinsters out in the jungle together. Do you think we'll grow old this way and be known as peculiar and eccentric?"

"How ridiculous, Susannah! Spinsters! When Izabel just ripped my best taffeta skirt playing dress-up in it, and Josiah has been screaming up and down the stairs all day. Antonio will be home in July, and Cort will be coming home too."

It was impossible to display pessimism around Rachel. Rachel was afraid even to entertain the thought that Cort might not return, though Susannah doubted very much that they would ever see him again. He had been gone almost two years.

Next year they must all go to Rio after all. Susannah would give Rachel as the reason, just as she had made her the reason for staying on the Kiss Flower. Rachel must meet new men and begin to forget. Izabel and Josiah missed Antonio, but would Antonio be glad for her to come?

In the evenings after the children were in bed, the sisters often wrote letters. Rachel wrote to Mrs. St. John in Memphis. Susannah corresponded, as she had for years, with Princess Izabel. A reply to one of these missives was the stuff of conversation for a whole day.

"I think we should be glad we are not in Memphis, after all, Susannah," Rachel would say. "Mrs. St. John writes there are four times as many ex-slaves there as when the war ended.

There's not enough work for them, and they are all living in squalor in houses whites have abandoned. Beale Street is becoming a slum, and she has had to move to another part of town because her clients objected to coming to have their clothes fitted there."

"What a shame. I suppose her new place is smaller."

"Yes. Actually, just an apartment behind an elegant little shop. But even there she is afraid of those gangs—the Mackerels, they're called—that run amok and rob and beat merchants. Mrs. St. John says the police are corrupt and the city government is full of graft. The men in Memphis all carry pistols, and women and children keep curfew. There is practically anarchy."

"Poor Memphis. But the town is booming still."

"Yes, but Mrs. St. John says the effects of all the suffering of the war are just beginning to really show. The numbness is wearing off. She says there are dozens of mediums in Memphis, and there are constant reports of ghosts."

"I suppose it's because people are longing so much to see their dead loved ones," Susannah said. She noticed how pale Rachel was looking and changed the subject. "What else does Mrs. St. John have to say?"

"She asks for news of Cort, of course," Rachel replied, and burst into tears.

Izabel's letters were more cheerful, though Susannah wondered if she made them so on purpose. Sometimes she wrote that Antonio had had dinner with them or that she had seen him at some function. Izabel never mentioned Joaquina, who was observing a required year of mourning for her husband. Neither did she ever mention any other woman who was turning Antonio's head. "I almost wish she would say who is chasing after him," Susannah said. "I am sure someone is."

"Maybe he's too busy to pay any attention."

"Maybe." But if Antonio did resist feminine advances in Rio, might it not be for love of Rachel instead of for her? One thing was certain. Antonio was busy. Winning the Paraguayan war at last had meant the dawn of an era of growth and progress for Brazil. Now was the time for social change and the sort of advances Antonio wanted.

But of course, opposition was fierce. Those who had prospered under the established order saw no reason to change it. And Antonio must change their views in time to prevent the kind of upheaval the south had known. The small uprising on the Amazon had been but one spark put out in time. Unless Antonio and Dom Pedro were successful, someday there would be one that would set the entire country aflame.

As the time came closer for Antonio's return, a letter in his hand arrived for Susannah. She was so dizzy with excitement she had to sit down to open it, and then could hardly make her eyes focus on the words. But what she finally read didn't make her happy.

The emperor has decided to make a trip north to Ceará and then another through the coffee country of São Paulo and Santa Catarina. I am going along to view the slave-breeding farms and to talk to people there. It's necessary that an end be put to this sort of thing, and I hope to begin to find a way. Kiss Izabel and Josiah for me and tell them I've sent presents.

*Please have new miniatures of them painted for me. I
must see how they are changing.*

He was not coming home, and he had not
said anything about a kiss for *her* or having *her*
portrait painted for him.

Princess Izabel, who would serve in the emperor's place during the trip, thought Susannah
should plan on coming to Rio for the next session of the Senate.

*Rio is a gay place just now, especially for me with
my husband, Gastão, home from war and a hero, no
less! People are beginning to realize how wonderful
he is and forget that he's a foreigner. Of course, I
hope I'll be able to become a mother at last. That
would please me and Gastão and especially Father,
who is getting a bit uneasy about the line of succes-
sion. Really, Susannah, I'm sure that whatever is
wrong between you and Antonio would resolve itself
if you were here. How I would love to see you—and
those children!*

"Maybe you *should* go," Rachel said, having
been allowed to read the letter. "In fact, I know
you should. He's your husband, and you belong with him."

"Even if he doesn't want me? I've too much
pride for that. Anyway, I'm at least as angry
with him as he is with me."

"Even after all this time?"

"There are some things a woman can never
forgive, Rachel," Susannah said meaningfully,
but Rachel didn't seem to understand her feelings.

"Susannah, maybe the princess is trying to
tell you something. Between the lines, where
she talks about how lively Rio is."

"You think she means it's the women who are lively—with Antonio?"

"Yes."

"You are such a romantic, Rachel! You think if I went there he would sweep me into his arms."

"Well, he cannot, if you *don't* go."

"And you are sure I would like it."

"Oh, yes."

"I suppose you wouldn't go with me."

"You know I can't."

"I know nothing of the sort," Susannah said. "Rachel, dear, this loyalty to Cort is very noble, but it's useless. He isn't coming back."

"Don't talk to me that way, Susannah! When Cort was away in the war, did *you* ever give up on him? Plenty of girls were unfaithful with someone who was more available, even with Yankees. Oh, when I had him, I didn't love him enough! And this is the only thing I can do to make up for it. He'll feel me still waiting for him, loving him, and he'll find his way home. I'll be here, however long it takes!"

So this was the way Rachel was punishing herself for loving Antonio! She would bury herself out here, year after year. But in spite of her concern for her sister, Susannah was almost glad Rachel wouldn't accompany her to Rio. It gave her an excuse not to go either, and meant that Rachel and Antonio would not have the chance to be together again for what had happened once to recur.

So they waited on the Kiss Flower, watching the cane sprout and grow lush far above their heads, while new fields of cotton blossomed with flowers and finally with fluffy bolls. More acres were in production than when Antonio had left, and the few plantations left in the colony were flourishing too. The log homes were giving way to white-columned houses, and carriages pulled by impressive horses traveled with the heavy wagons on roads that had been improved by communal effort. Antonio's plan seemed to be working. The salves labored longer and harder, knowing that the success of the plantations meant freedom.

So much waiting! You could sense it all along the river. The slaves were waiting in hope and fear for the new society, and the whites were waiting too. Everyone was wondering if the entire community would come tumbling down.

But one day, for Rachel at least, the waiting was over. As though he had felt the force of her devotion hundreds of miles into the wilderness, Cort St. John came home.

On a cool sunny morning, Susannah was in the garden trimming the rosebushes, when she turned and saw him coming up the lane, his gait almost a stagger, his fair hair grown shaggy, his face bearded, his clothing ragged. For an instant she caught her breath, believing him a jungle apparition shimmering in the sunlight. Then with a glad cry he saw her and called her name, and she ran into his arms.

"Cort, oh, Cort, is it you?"

"Susannah, dear, that is what you asked the night I came home from the war," he reminded her. "Yes, it is I, though I can hardly believe it myself."

"What has happened to you? You're ill!"

"We were attacked by hostile Indians, Susannah. Jamunda was killed, and I was held prisoner. I couldn't tell you how long. Every day was only more torment; it was worse to keep count. I escaped, but I had no way of knowing where I was. I had only fruits and nuts to eat, no rifle for game or flint for a fire. But I found the river and followed it. Susannah, what a joy it is to see your face!"

All the affection she had ever known for him welled up in her. "Oh, my dear Cort! If only I had had the courage to risk prison, instead of marrying Antonio!"

He bent his lips to hers and kissed her gently. "You were not a coward, Susannah," he told her. "You loved him."

And hearing him say it, all her guilt dissolved at last.

He looked past her toward the house. "Twenty Palms has been burned," he observed. "Rachel?" His voice was a whisper of hope, and Susannah knew it was Rachel he loved, she for whom he had endured so much, for whom he'd come home.

Susannah began to shout, and in a moment Rachel came running from the house, laughing and weeping, her hair flying from its pinnings. Cort started for her, limping as fast as he could go. The impact of their meeting threw them off balance, and they collapsed in a heap in the soft grass.

It was only then that they realized how ill he was, for he lay there unable to rise, gazing up adoringly at his wife, lifting a hand weakly to touch her cheek, which she pressed against it, kissing his palm.

"Oh, Rachel, oh, my love," he murmured.

She shushed him, told him not to try to talk anymore, but Cort had things to say.

"I didn't fail, Rachel," he told her, pulling at a burlap sack beside him. "I've brought diamonds—a fortune!" The gems caught the sun as he spilled them out in a glittering stream. "It's for you to go home to Memphis where you belong. Buy Robin Hill again. I know you always loved it. It's as though a part of you will always be missing without Robin Hill."

"No, dearest," she said fearfully. "We'll rebuild here, where you want to be."

"We cannot," he said.

"We can!" she cried, realizing what he meant. "Cort, you must not! Susannah send for a doctor, now! Right now!"

Susannah ran, racing with all her might for the fastest horse and the best rider on the Kiss Flower. But even as she ran, she knew it was no use. As though only the desire to be in Rachel's arms again had kept Cort alive, he died before the doctor had arrived from Santarém.

20

A month after Cort was buried on the Kiss Flower, Rachel told Susannah she wished to do as her husband had intended and return to Memphis. A letter had arrived that day from Mrs. St. John. So stricken with grief for her son that she couldn't go on with her dressmaking business, she invited her daughter-in-law to take over the thriving establishment while she retired to a less demanding position.

"I really think I'd like to go home, Susannah. There's no future for me here."

"We could go to Rio. There are so many wildly eligible men there, and perhaps next year you'll feel better and want your fun."

Rachel frowned. "I don't like the idea of looking for a new husband. I can't believe I would fall in love with anyone. I wasn't in love even with Cort *that* way, and I think I'd like to be an independent woman and focus my life on something other than matrimony. In Rio there would always be . . ."

Rachel turned away without finishing the thought. There would always be Antonio. Susannah knew that was how the sentence would have ended. Was it really possible for a woman not to center her life on a man, if only in her mind, if only a forbidden lover or a lover who existed only in her heart? She herself had tried to deny her love for Antonio in every way she knew, devoting herself to her children and to the Kiss Flower, which was becoming the showplace of the river. Had Rachel succeeded any better than she?

"You will make such wonderful clothes—ladies will come from New Orleans and St. Louis to buy them, Rachel," she said with a smile.

"I'll have models, too, Susannah, so that gentlemen may come to shop for their wives. Do you remember the first gown we all made together, for you to wear to the dance with Colonel Spangler?

"You were hardly more than a child, and you wished the dress was for you."

"And then the uniform, of course. I was so proud of it."

They were both silent, thinking of the soldier for whom it had been intended.

"Susannah, I am going to buy Robin Hill, just as Cort wanted."

"But it belongs to Colonel Spangler now."

"It doesn't belong to him morally, and he knows it. I have enough money to do exactly as

I wish for once in my life, and I will buy it away, no matter what it takes. And, Susannah, if you ever want to leave Brazil, if you want to come home . . ."

Susannah was unbearably lonely after her sister left, but another session of the Senate would soon be over, and Antonio would surely visit the Kiss Flower then.

Instead, another letter arrived. Antonio told her he was at the forefront of a new bill called the "Law of Free Birth," which provided that the children of slaves would henceforth be born free, to be wards of their mothers' masters until they were of legal age. It was another method of ending slavery gradually, with time for the country to make the transition; but if he left Rio, the opposition would make good use of the opportunity to steal the bill's supporters.

"Please don't bring the children now," he wrote. "There's yellow fever in the city, and although the emperor would be glad to have you at his palace above the city at Petrópolis, you would have to dock in the harbor and pass through Rio."

When the fever had abated, it was Princess Izabel who wrote her that it was safe. "The Condêssa Marchado might be glad to see an old friend, as well as I," the princess said. "She has not remarried, and this steady diet of male admiration must be cloying."

It was very easy for Susannah to read between the lines. She should come to Rio to defend what was hers.

"I will come to Rio when my husband asks me," Susannah wrote back. "It's a matter of pride. I won't force myself upon him. I won't come to Rio to face being ignored by him. If he does not care enough about his family to come home, then he will not be bothered with us."

"I think you're just afraid," Izabel wrote back spiritedly. "It's entirely out of character, Susannah. When did you ever let fear stop you from anything?"

Susannah replied that she had plenty to occupy her on the Kiss Flower, which Antonio had left in her charge, but she knew that Izabel was right. The new overseer had worked out well, and though the innovations and expansions were mostly her doing, the plantation would run well enough without her.

She simply did not have the courage to have him reject her, time having burned away the last trace of his passion for her, like a fireplace left unfueled. A Brazilian man's life did not center around a woman, certainly not his wife. Hadn't she been warned? She had married Antonio for the wrong reason, after all. She had not married him to save herself from hanging or prison. She had married him in the blistering heat of sudden love, and its mark was on her soul. She could not settle for a lesser relationship with him. She would not be merely tolerated. Perhaps he had similar feelings; perhaps the impulsively passionate marriage only embarrassed him now with its lusty memories. Perhaps that was why time after time he failed to return to the Kiss Flower.

In January she received another letter from the princess, with the happy news of the birth of her son, Pedro, and an invitation:

Papa asked me to write to you. He intends to visit America soon. It's a dream of his, and this is the Centennial year, of course. There is going to be a World's Fair in Philadelphia, the first time such a thing has ever been done. If it's a success, it won't be the last, I imagine. The emperor will start thinking of having the next one in Rio, no doubt!

But for now, I'm to invite you to join the entourage, and to tell you the emperor would deem it a special favor. He'd like to have an American beside him who understands the country and can make the trip easier. You are his choice, and he reminded me to tell you that part of the tour will be down the Mississippi on a riverboat, past your old home, Memphis, on the way to New Orleans.

Home! The temptation was too much. She sent off her reply by the next mail and began the task of readying everything. Years in the jungle had depleted her wardrobe, but she left a week for shopping in Pará before the ship arrived that would take her to join the liner *Havelius*.

Once Susannah was aboard with Aunt Caroline and the children, the emperor's trusted old slave Raphael came to meet them and to take Susannah to his master. The emperor greeted her with enthusiasm. "Thank goodness you decided to join me, Marqueza! I'm already in trouble. There are so many Americans aboard, and I cannot understand half of them! Oh, they don't speak like Englishmen at all. You must teach me to speak American. I like the way *you* talk. It's called a Southern accent, isn't it?"

The plump little empress broke in. "He will wear you out before we even reach New York." She chuckled indulgently. "He's already exhausted all the ship's officers with his questions. Come and have some tea, dear. You must be tired, and it won't be long until dinner. They've reserved a private dining room for our party, but Pedro refuses to use it. He wants to sit at table with the other passengers to learn everything he can."

"Of course I do, Mama," the emperor declared. "I came on this trip to learn."

"To think I hoped for a pleasure jaunt," Dona Thereza said with a sigh.

"They are one and the same," Dom Pedro asserted easily. "Susannah, do you know all the verses to 'The Star-Spangled Banner'? I cannot find anyone who does."

" 'The Star-Spangled Banner' is a Yankee song, sir. And like any Confederate, I tried to avoid even hearing it when the army band would play it in Memphis."

"Dear me, how tactless I am! But it's one country again. Won't you learn not to hate the North someday, Susannah?"

"I don't know. I never thought of it as having become one country again. I left so soon after the war. My father was killed and my home left in shambles and with a Yankee owner. It's not easy to forget."

"Pedro, do stop this. It's painful for the marchioness," his wife commanded.

"I apologize," the emperor said, "but, you see, I have learned something. I'll be more careful from now on in matters concerning the North and South. Susannah, will you sing me a Southern song, then? Isn't there one called 'Dixie'?"

"Time enough for that later," the empress said indulgently, and shooed him into another room. "Now we'll have a bit of peace and quiet,"

she said. "That is the only way to deal with
him."

"Is that the secret of your happy marriage,
that you know how to deal with him? Its certainly an unusual method."

"It is merely founded on honesty. Men appreciate knowing what a woman expects. It's
easier than simpering and posturing, especially
for a fat little thing like me. I can't depend on
beauty, certainly."

"I'm sure you are beautiful to the emperor
and to all your subjects, too, Dona Thereza.
They love you so. I did hope to have a happy
marriage once."

"Heavens, dear, it's not too late for you and
Antonio," the empress said, and chuckled, as
though she had a secret. As Susannah was leaving, the empress squeezed her hand again and
told her, "Remember, honesty."

It seemed altogether too simple to work. When
had Susannah ever been honest with a man?
Only when she had confessed to Cort that her
marriage to Antonio had been consummated.
That had nearly cost Antonio his life on the
field of honor.

The empress couldn't be as wise as she
seemed. She'd just been lucky to make a fortunate match.

They anchored in New York harbor on April
15. The emperor, having lost his hat overboard
while exclaiming over the Statue of Liberty, was
sporting a black yachting cap as President Grant's
secretary of state, Hamilton Fish, came onto the
ship to greet him. In a little while the government boat *Alert* returned to shore, supposedly
bearing the royal couple. But Susannah came

upon the pair still standing at the rail of the *Havelius*, contentedly obscure, enjoying their first view of Manhatten island.

"Would you believe it, they completely ignored my request that there be no ceremony," the emperor said. "Besides that, that Fish fellow had no idea where I might be able to meet Longfellow. I translated some of his work into Portuguese, you know, so that Brazilians could read it. Why, in Brazil the poets and artists are at court all the time.

"Here is where you come in, Susannah," he went on. "We are going ashore with the rest of the passengers, and you are to get us a hack to take us to our lodgings at the Buckingham Hotel."

"I am sorry to impose, Susannah," the empress told her. "It's just the way he is."

"I know," Susannah replied with a smile. "I will be honored, Dona Thereza."

Susannah had heard tales of the emperor's European trip. He so hated pomp that he had refused to attend a royal presentation at Buckingham Palace. Queen Victoria herself had had to come to his hotel to pin the Star of the Order of the Garter onto his plain black coat. And in Dresden the king had had to meet his train himself with bands and a military guard to outwit him.

Only a few people recognized the tall Brazilian and his wife, carrying her own satchel, as they drove off incognito beneath flags and bunting. The Buckingham Hotel was an elaborate establishment eight stories high. A skyscraper, the empress thought. It has an ornate elevator and a hundred and fifty rooms. Dona Thereza was glad to rest, since she was bothered by arthritis; but Dom Pedro, having read the president's welcoming telegram, immediately went back to the lobby to inquire the way to Philadelphia.

"Great news," he said when he returned. "The exposition has been postponed for a month."

"What is so wonderful about that?" his wife wanted to know.

"Why, it gives us an entire month to see this country! We'll go to California! I'll arrange for a private Pullman for Monday."

Dona Thereza groaned. "You may go then, but I have been at sea for twenty days, and I am not going to traipse off across a continent."

Dom Pedro frowned, torn between separation from his beloved wife and his thirst for knowledge. "But I must see everything," he said finally.

"Of course you must," she agreed. "I'll join you for the fair. Perhaps Susannah will go on with you. And the children shall stay here with me. We will entertain each other."

"I like traveling, and I cannot refuse my emperor," Susannah replied, laughing, feeling bewildered by it all.

That night they went to the Booth Theater to see *Henry V*. But that didn't prevent the emperor from having her up at six the next morning, impatient to begin his day.

A crowd greeted them at the early Sunday Mass at St. Patrick's Cathedral across the street. Then there was a drive down Broadway, a picture-taking session, and a tour of Central Park, the museum, the zoo, and the reservoir.

On the way the emperor had the chance to see the fire department in action and was impressed with the speed with which the horses ran to their places, harnesses dropping onto their backs automatically as the firemen rushed to their stations.

"That is American efficiency," Dom Pedro cried. "That is what I came to see."

Dom Pedro finished the day by attending a revival meeting, sitting on the platform with his silk hat hung over his umbrella between his knees. Susannah felt herself drooping, her attention wandering. As they drove back to the hotel, she nodded off, aware of it only when her head plunked onto the emperor's shoulder.

"Oh, I beg your pardon!" she said with a gasp.

Dom Pendro chuckled. "It's quite all right, Susannah. You need your rest. Tomorrow will be a big day."

And so it was, beginning with his receiving the governor and the mayor and including his favorite activity of visiting schools. By seven that night they were aboard the Pullman, heading west. In the morning, he was straining for a glimpse of the Erie Canal. In Cleveland he was greeted by an enthusiastic crowd, and in Chicago he was fascinated by the process of rebuilding from the great fire of five years before.

Dom Pedro never let up the pace, sightseeing at every stop, making use of Susannah's being a native American to help him escape formal gatherings. It was she who conversed with hack drivers and even with trolley men. It was she who made purchases, paid, who knew when and how much to leave for a tip.

At Salt Lake City they stopped to test the brine of the lake, and Dom Pedro bought Mormon literature and attended a service at a temple. Beyond there, cattle on the tracks delayed the train, and the emperor seemed to hope to see some of the Indians who still attacked the trains from time to time. By the time they reached California, the emperor had begun to be called "The Artful Dodger" for his habit of slipping away from his Pullman through an empty coach, leaving bands, flags, and girls with flowers behind.

Susannah was indispensable for these escapes, for it was she, carrying her valise and his, who would flag an unsuspecting driver. At the last moment, the emperor would join her, chuckling and ready for more adventure.

Finally they stood at the edge of the Pacific Ocean together, their spirits soaring. They had come all the way across the continent. For Susannah it had been a strange experience, traveling as the companion of an emperor through a land she had fled a decade before. She had been treated royally everywhere, and newspaper reporters had been fascinated by the story of Dom Pedro's American friend. Often she had found herself talking to them about the American colony and praising her husband's efforts to create a haven of freedom and prosperity.

Now, standing on the wet beach, feeling engulfed in vivid blue waves that seemed to tower above them, both the emperor and Susannah felt a lack.

"I wish the empress could see this," Dom Pedro said. "I am not poet enough to describe it."

Susannah, too, felt a desire to be near her spouse. Something in those magnificent waves reminded her of him, made her want him close to her, kissing her in the cool salty air, his powerful arms around her, making her feel as small and helpless as did the colossal ocean swells. Oh, but that could never happen again! The rapture that the shining Pacific recalled was lost forever.

She sighed, and the emperor shot her a glance. Susannah's cheeks pinkened, for it seemed almost as though he knew what she was thinking.

"Come along, Susannah. We mustn't dally," he told her. "I want to see the fishing wharf and the Oriental theater."

Too soon they were headed east again to collect Dona Thereza and travel to Washington to be received by the president. The press remarked that Dom Pedro was the fastest tourist in the country's history. The trip had taken only three weeks.

The royal party had only two days for Washington before the fair opened, and they were off again to the fairgrounds, two hundred and thirty acres in Philadelphia's Fairmount Park.

It seemed strange to be in the heart of Yankee territory. Sometimes Susannah felt almost as much a stranger as the emperor. More, she decided. Dom Pedro made himself at home everywhere. It was so peaceful here; no one seemed to be thinking about the war. Only the sharp Northern accents sometimes revived the old memories. Almost without warning someone would call out in the street, and the images of Colonel Spangler's men pounding at the door of Robin Hill, searching for Cort, would flood her mind. Now and then Susannah's Southern tones turned curious heads, but as often as not, someone remarked with pleasure, asking her where she was from. She always said Brazil, for that was home now.

But when the orchestra and a chorus of nine hundred voices struck up "The Star-Spangled Banner" to open the fair, Susannah felt tears sting her eyes. One country, the emperor had said. Yes, perhaps it was, or one day would be. She glanced around at the emperor, remembering when he had asked her for all the verses. He had them by this time, no doubt. Susannah had never known anyone with such an unquenchable desire for knowledge.

President Grant and Dom Pedro stood side by side and at a signal pulled two levers to start the steam engines which furnished power for the fair. Then the party proceeded to the Women's Building, where the empress, resplendent in a dress of pearl-gray silk with six separate overskirts and a white hat trimmed with white flowers, cut a golden cord to open that pavilion.

The Brazilian Building had facades, doors, and windows of brilliant-colored glass worked out in patterns. The Brazilian arms were in green-and-gold tile. The building had four sections. The first displayed artificial flowers made by Indians from tropical bird feathers. In another was the finest of Brazil's rare hardwoods, and native pottery, glazed with copal. The third contained leatherwork, and the last contained a mineral collection planned by Dom Pedro, with specimens from his own cases.

In the agricultural building Brazil was represented by tobacco, prepared fourteen ways; rubber; cacao; Oriental tea; Brazil nuts; sugar; tapioca; arrowroot; perfumes made of essences of tropical flowers; and objects made from butterfly wings, looking brightly enameled.

A triumphal arch made of fluffy Brazilian cotton had six windows displaying coffees. All around were spread the skins of jungle animals—spotted jaguars, alligators, pumas, and snakes. A painting in the Arts Building depicted a naval battle of the Paraguayan war, and in the Machinery Hall Brazilian silkmaking was demonstrated.

Everything was wonderful, but after a reception on opening night and a banquet the next, Dom Pedro had had all he could take again of formalities.

"The best exhibits aren't even in place yet," he told the empress. "I'd like to take another trip and come back to the fair later."

"Another trip," she said with resignation.

"Yes. To New Orleans. We'll go by train to St. Louis and then down the Mississippi. You know, we did promise Susannah Memphis."

"You won't leave me behind this time," Dona Thereza told him.

"I didn't think so," he said, and the two of them laughed a secret little married laugh that made Susannah envious.

They had to travel more slowly this time. The speeding train made the empress nervous, and since she refused to spend the nights on the Pullman, they had to stop each evening. But Josiah and Izabel loved the train and never wanted to get off.

"The boat will be better," the empress told

the children. "Even I will like that. I have heard so much about Mississippi riverboats."

And she did revel in the leisurely junket downriver on the luxury packet *Republic*, and she wasn't bothered by the fear of a boiler explosion as some of the entourage were. The May air was sweet and warm, and it was lovely to stroll on the decks as they floated past fields where the first green shoots of cotton plants were just showing. In the woods Susannah caught glimpses of early-blooming flowers she had never thought to see again—firepink, wild bleeding heart, and Dutchman's-breeches.

How quiet the South seemed now, and how poor! Here and there the emperor had the boat put in at various landings, and they went ashore to be greeted by clusters of ragged black children, the first generation born into freedom. The entire countryside seemed run-down. Houses were weathered, flower gardens were unkept, overrun with trumpet vine and honeysuckle. The freed slaves lived in shantytowns, homes that were often no more than sheds, with tin roofs rusting brick red.

"Where are all the other children?" the emperor asked as he visited a school. "There are only white ones here."

And having had it explained to him that the races were educated separately, he shook his head. "How can such a great country treat some of its citizens this way? The slaves are better off in Brazil than these people. We must never allow war over slavery in our country. Nothing could be worse!"

Susannah could hardly contain her excitement as they steamed toward Memphis. The first sight of the bluffs made her heart quicken, and she called Izabel and Josiah from their game of hide-and-seek around the hurricane deck to show them the skyline of the city where she had grown up.

They landed beneath flags and bunting, the emperor forgoing his escape this time, so that Susannah could arrive in triumph at the same dock from which she had fled on the *River Belle* so long ago. But Susannah scarcely thought of the Yankees who had pursued her or of clinging to the paddle wheel in the cold, muddy water. Instead, she remembered Antonio ordering her out of her dripping clothes. She remembered the cool silk of his Turkish robe, too intimately his as she had tried to conceal herself in its folds, clutching at its large drooping neckline. In her memory she heard him again command her into his bed as the Yankees approached. And then . . .

She was dizzy with her reverie, all but wishing it were that other time again, for that had been more glorious than this with all its bands and flowers and speeches. But that could never be again. It could never be the same. Perhaps a comfortable devotion like that of Dom Pedro and his Thereza could last, but a fire of passion that had blazed as intensely as hers and Antonio's had been surely doomed to burn itself out. She had not forgiven him, and he did not care.

"Susannah!"

A voice, calling eagerly, brought her back to the present; and there was Rachel, waving. Susannah waved back, glancing at the emperor, who dismissed her with a smile and a nod. In a moment the sisters were laughing and crying in each other's arms.

"Oh, Rachel, how beautiful you look!" Susannah declared, for her sister was blooming. "And your gown! Is it your own design?"

"We call them St. John Originals," Rachel replied, as Susannah inspected the gown of blue spotted foulard, its skirt tied back across the front, with a bustle and train of ruby borché. Rachel wore her hair in a curly fringe over the forehead, pulled into a chignon behind.

The children, having been hugged and kissed and having had their growth remarked upon, were herded into Rachel's carriage; and they were off to view the dressmaking establishment, while the emperor and empress were escorted to the Gayoso Hotel.

After all that had happened, Susannah dreaded her meeting with Mrs. St. John, but Cort's mother only wept tears of joy at seeing her and then took Izabel and Josiah to her quarters behind the showrooms to introduce them to her sour-cream cookies served with lemonade.

"What of Robin Hill?" Susannah asked when they were alone. "You wrote me nothing about it. I suppose you weren't able to buy it."

"Colonel Spangler wouldn't sell, no matter what the price, but it is beautiful again, Susannah. Wait until you see it!"

"See it! That is not likely. Not with a Yankee in residence! Go to Robin Hill with him as its master? Have you gone made, Rachel?"

"Colonel Spangler isn't such a terrible man, Susannah. And he has restored Robin Hill, just as it was. He's even asked me about the details, so that it would be done just right."

"So you've been there? Inside the house?"

"Yes, and so shall you. Tonight. And then I will show you how Robin Hill is to be ours again."

"Rachel, what are you planning? How can Robin Hill belong to us if he won't sell it? Have you thought of some trickery? You know how dangerous that can be! Remember the uniform! Tell me! Confess!"

"No. You will have to wait to see. There's to be a ball at Robin Hall tonight in honor of the emperor. He requested a visit to a Southern plantation, and I persuaded the committee that it be our old home."

"Rachel, I will not go!"

"I'm sure the emperor will be disappointed if you don't. Come and see the gown I've made for you to wear. I have been working day and night on it, and keeping all my customers waiting."

"You've made me a gown?"

"Yes. though if your measurements have changed, we will have to alter it in a hurry."

She led Susannah into a workroom, where a gown hung on a wooden dressmaker's model. The bodice and overskirt were of green satin brocade, the material caught up and draped over an underlayer of pale blue faille. Behind, a train fell in layers, expertly styled, and trimmed in silver rosettes, which were repeated in loops along the edge of the blue.

"It's magnificent!" Susannah declared, pleased as much with Rachel's skill and inventiveness as with the gown itself. "But I still cannot go."

"Try it on at least," Rachel insisted. "I've

selected the colors so carefully to suit your hair and eyes."

When she had it on, they both gasped with pleasure. "You have never looked so beautiful, Susannah. No man could resist you!"

"I am not interested in conquests, Rachel. And certainly I hope you don't mean Colonel Spangler. A Yankee and a married woman!"

Rachel's cheeks turned surprisingly pink. "Oh, don't fly off so, Susannah," she said. "It was just a compliment. Now, please say you'll go to the emperor's ball. We have only this one night to be together, to pretend things are as they used to be at Robin Hill. How can you leave Memphis without seeing it?"

But it was the emperor who persuaded her at last. "I shall take it amiss if you aren't there to show me your old home," he told her. "Remember, it's I, not you, who have been called the Artful Dodger."

In the darkness Robin Hill caught the moonlight and flung it back toward the sky. Carriage lights danced along the shell drive, and waltz music drifted from beyond the lighted windows. Dogwood and azaleas were blooming near the door.

Susannah felt herself in a dream as she passed between the cut-glass sidelights that she had last seen broken and boarded over. Inside, floors glistened, the stairs swept down beside a fine new banister, chandeliers gleamed over immaculate woodwork and fine wallpaper. The furnishings in the foyer were just as they had been when Colonel Josiah Dunbar had marched off to war.

Rachel shot a look at Susannah. "It is perfect," Susannah whispered. "You were right. I wouldn't have missed it."

A hush fell over the gathering as the imperial party entered. Susannah held her head high, for she knew the cream of Memphis society was here, not only to see the emperor and empress, but to see Susannah Dunbar return as the Marqueza da Silva to the home that had once been hers. For a while, it seemed hers again as she greeted old friends, introducing them all to Dom Pedro and Dona Thereza. She had almost forgotten Sam Spangler was in the house, that he, not she, was hosting the ball. Then suddenly he was before her.

She almost didn't recognize this man in his black superfine evening coat with its velvet collar and white waistcoat. She had been looking for a devil in a blue uniform. Here was only a genial man, a little stouter, his mustache replaced by a beard.

Colonel Spangler's eyes paid tribute to her beauty as he took her hand in his. "Marqueza! I was afraid you wouldn't come. I hope you'll take the emperor on a tour of the place yourself. And I hope you approve—of everything."

There seemed to be some double meaning in his words, but Susannah didn't understand it. Sam Spangler bowed to Rachel and asked her to dance. She took his hand, smiling brilliantly as he led her out into a waltz.

Susannah stood for a moment looking after them, somewhat irritated. She had wanted Rachel to be along to share old memories on the tour.

"Susannah?" Dom Pedro at her elbow re-

minded her that he and the empress were eager
to see the rest of the place.

Susannah led the way. In the study the old
desk was still there, refinished and polished.
Susannah's makeshift curtains had been replaced
by brocade draperies.

"This is where . . ." she began, and told the
fascinated emperor how she had shot the present owner here.

In the bustling kitchen she remembered how
Rachel had sat on Cort's hat to hide it; and
upstairs she showed the emperor and empress
the bedroom she and Rachel had shared, the
window where they had watched for Yankee
patrols. But as she talked, Susannah's attention
wandered. How could he have done it all so
perfectly? And why? Even the old mirror that
had come from Virginia when Memphis was
new had been restored, and the portrait of her
mother, which the Yankees had trampled, had
been redone and hung again in the hall.

As she went downstairs again, Colonel Spangler was calling for quiet. Rachel was still beside
him. Susannah expected some toast to the emperor, for their appearance had seemed to trigger his announcement. But nothing could have
prepared Susannah for what Sam Spangler had
to say.

"Ladies and gentlemen, it's my honor and
pleasure to announce that that Rachel St. John
has consented to become my wife!"

Through the cheers and applause, Susannah
felt Dom Pedro steady her as he whispered,
"Remember, Susannah, the war is over now."

Then, before she could gather her wits, a tall,
impressive figure entered the room. Her heart

beat painfully, and her body tingled as though she had been standing close to lightning as it struck.

Antonio!

In an instant she understood it all. The secret that the emperor and empress had shared, why Dona Thereza had been so determined to come on this leg of the trip, why Rachel had worked so hard on the most wonderful gown Susannah had ever owned. It had been planned!

But Antonio had not been in on the plot any more than she. The astonishment in his gaze as their eyes met told her that.

In the tumult of emotion that shook her, Susannah fled, instinctively running back upstairs, shutting herself into her old room and bolting the door as if all Sam Spangler's men were after her.

In a moment there was a rapping. "It's Rachel! Let me in!"

Susannah flung the door wide. "So that was what you meant when you told me Robin Hill would be ours again! He tried to inveigle me into it, and now he's succeeded with you! Oh, Rachel, what a traitor you are! It was bad enough that he had Robin Hill; but I learned to endure it, because at least we had fought and lost honorably. But this! Oh, Rachel, I love you, and I have tried to forgive you for the other. But now there is this! I wish I had never come on this trip. I wish I had never seen Robin Hill again!"

"What 'other' have you tried to forgive me for?" Rachel asked.

"Why, Antonio!"

"Antonio?"

"Oh, don't pretend innocence. I saw you together. I was on the trail the night Maria Rosa tried to escape. And you admitted it. You said you were the cause of our problems."

Rachel gasped. "Do you imagine that Antonio and I . . . ?"

"I saw you with my own eyes!"

"You don't know what you saw, Susannah!" Rachel said spiritedly. "I was riding to the Kiss Flower that night when I met Antonio. Conde Marchado had just been to Twenty Palms. You know how he liked to impress women, and after Cort left, well, sometimes he was an annoyance. He made the mistake of telling me that Joaquina had told him about an escape attempt, and he bragged that he was going to put an end to Antonio's ambitions and then his power would be undisputed in the district. He had been drinking a little, but I suppose he thought I'd approve because Cort had sided with him on the slavery issue. But of course I wanted to warn you. When I told Antonio, he took me in his arms to thank me and comfort me. And that is all you saw. But if I had said nothing to Antonio, Maria Rosa might have escaped, and Antonio would never have known that you or anyone on the Kiss Flower had any part in it."

"Oh Rachel!" An incredible relief washed over her. "What a fool I was! You did what was right. Maria Rosa would not have left without Simon, and she would surely have been caught without Antonio's help."

"Susannah, I love Sam Spangler," Rachel told her. "He isn't a Yankee anymore, only a man who has tried to put a beautiful place back the way it should be. He began to call on me for advice, and we began to work together, and . . . both of us cared so much about what we were doing, it began to be natural to care for each other too. I couldn't help it."

"That is the way love is, as I should know!" Susannah said with a sigh. "I hope you'll be happy at last."

"I will! I will! And you must be happy too! The emperor arranged it, you know. He was tired of seeing Antonio work day and night with no feminine companionship. So he asked Antonio to meet him here, because of his knowledge of the South. Go down to him, Susannah!"

"I . . . Oh, I want *him* to come to *me*. Why won't he? If he hasn't had other women—"

"Then it's likely he's still in love with you. Have you learned nothing about Brazilian men? *You* must go to *him*."

"I'm not sure that he ever loved me!"

"What, didn't he ever tell you so?"

"Yes, once. It was when Izabel was born. I remember it as though it were a dream. I think it probably was."

"Then, didn't he show you with better than words that he loved you?"

"I did think so, for a time. I did think he loved me."

"Don't be a fool again, Susannah! If you are to be a fool, then be a fool in a different way!"

Trembling, Susannah began to straighten her hair and gown before the mirror. "Good luck," Rachel whispered as they embraced. Then, drawing a deep breath, Susannah opened the door.

She saw him from the top of the stairs. Their eyes united again as he looked up at her. Then Rachel was proved wrong in part, for Antonio crossed the room toward her, his pace so urgent that the crowd of partiers divided to make way for him. As they met at the foot of the stairs, he slid his arm around her waist and swung her out into a waltz. The sensation of him so close to her was almost more delight than she could bear as she swirled rapturously to the music of violins.

Her heart pounded against his twilled cashmere dress coat. His breath against her hair was warm and as full of memories as the spring breeze. He gripped her firmly, swinging her about the dance floor with the masterfulness she loved. She closed her eyes, lost in the wonder of his presence, aware that she trusted him to guide her, through the waltz and through all her life.

"Antonio," she said earnestly, "I will not be troublesome anymore. I will not dispute your authority."

"It's too late for that, Susannah," he replied, and sent her crashing into despair. But then he saw her stricken face and laughed. "You were right, my dear, when you said I could not resist you. I have tried to stay away from the Kiss Flower and you. It was too painful there without your love. But how can I stay away from you, when you are everything I want? You are the woman I fell in love with, and I no longer want to change what I love."

"You fell in love?" she whispered in happy wonder.

"Yes, yes, from the very first time I saw you, when your horse ran away on Fulton Street. But how could I admit it, when you married me only from necessity? Do what you will with me,

Susannah. I have always been a victim of loving you."

They were dancing close to a doorway, and suddenly he swept her out through it, into the sweet srping night.

"Antonio," she protested as he took her hand and pulled her down the steps, "you cannot . . . The emperor—"

"Will have to do without you tonight," he told her as he swept her up in his arms and into his carriage.

She clung to him in dazed ecstasy as he raced the horses toward Memphis, down to the dock where the emperor's steamboat, the *Republic*, shone above the dark river.

"Show me your cabin, Susannah," he commanded, and when she had done so, all the world melted into the glory of their embrace.

They twined as one, each quivering with the power of their magnificent love, each yielding totally, one no more than the other, to the dazzling bliss. It seemed that all the world became nothing more than the scene of their union. The river existed only to rock them gently in the arms of love; the moon and stars were only to gild their rapturous bodies, and the sound of violins from the gallery was nothing but the song of their harmony. Finally even these manifestations of earthly existence were left behind in purest transport.

Hours later, the sound of voices in the gangway wakened them as the imperial party returned to the boat. Antonio raised up on an elbow to study her face, leaning to kiss her eyes and nose and lips softly.

"Where now, Antonio?" she asked him. "I shall be anywhere you say."

"We are in need of a real honeymoon, Susannah. We'll follow the emperor on his travels, to New Orleans, and back to the fair. We'll come back to Memphis for Rachel's wedding, and then we'll go home again to the Kiss Flower.

"Oh, yes, Antonio, home together," she whispered, and knew a rush of desire as he pulled her again into his arms.

Epilogue—1888

"She's here!"

The whisper hummed through the crowded throne room of Rio's City Palace. Susannah, wedged next to Antonio, felt the current of excitement, and gazing up into her husband's face, saw his eyes glisten with happy, unshed tears. Next to Antonio was Josiah, as tall as his father now, almost a man. Susannah shushed the younger children: Pedro, Antonio, and the youngest, little Rachel. Izabel was away at college at Vassar, for during his American tour, Dom Pedro had been impressed with the results of American female education and had urged Antonio to send her. And what a woman was about to do today was a tribute to the courage and fiber of their sex.

"The princess is coming," she told the children. "If only the emperor were here!" she whispered to Antonio. But Dom Pedro was lying near death far away in Milan.

For a dozen years since the American exposition, he had worked ceaselessly for Brazil, for better education, cultural growth, economic progress, and government reform. There had been great progress, but there were still problems, still dissent in the country. Some said that by doing what she intended today, Princess Izabel might lose the throne for herself and her son.

Days before, at the palace on the bluff at Petrópolis, Izabel had paced the floor, wondering what she should do. The time was ripe for emancipation, yet she, the regent, was not supposed to make vital decisions.

Antonio had done his best to advise her. In Ceará, he emphasized, the very heart of the slave-breeding country, people had become so disgusted that the provincial legislature had passed its own abolition law. And now the province was a mecca for runaways. The entire nation was honeycombed with an elaborate system of underground railways, and in every province there were societies to provide food and refuge. Thousands of slaves were hidden in the forests behind the city of São Paulo, and no one dared to try to retrieve his property. Lawlessness was rampant, and soon there would be civil war, unless . . .

"We cannot wait," Izabel had decided.

As the spectators parted, the princess, tall and dignified in white satin, walked to the throne and read the two sentences of the decree she had asked Congress to pass. Then she took the golden pen given to her by popular subscription and signed the "Golden Law," the emancipation act.

Suddenly the room was filled with cheers and weeping, and when Izabel appeared at the window of the throne room, the crowds in the street went wild with joy as well.

"If only the emperor lives to learn of it!" Susannah said. A cable was sent at once.

Rio began a festival which lasted nine days, and all the cities and towns across the empire joined in as they heard the news.

In Milan the doctors gave up hope, and a bishop had administered the last rites to the emperor when Dona Thereza came to him with the cable in hand.

"It will excite him too much," the doctors told her.

"But he must not die without knowing that his dream has come true," she insisted.

On hearing the news, the emperor began to rally. "Send cables for me," he commanded. "One is to Izabel. Let it say, 'I hail you, emancipator!' And send another to my people, send my blessings and congratulations. I must go home again, Thereza! I must see my country free!"

He continued to recover.

Bands and crowds greeted him as he came ashore in Rio that August, Susannah and Antonio standing in the sea breeze to receive his embrace. An album bound in solid gold was presented to the emperor, filled with hundreds of tributes, thousands of signatures. For the

empress there was a crown of laurel leaves se
with twenty diamonds.

"How good to have him home again," Susan
nah murmured.

"Yes, but there is still trouble to come," An
tonio warned her. "The proslavery elements ar
joining with republicans, and the army is bore
with peace. I think the empire will fall, Susan
nah."

"There will still be Brazil, and we will d
whatever we must to make our dreams and th
emperor's come true," she replied.

"Susannah, do you never wish you could liv
in Memphis again? Are you ever homesick? Don'
you long for a place that is more civilized tha
the jungles of the Kiss Flower?"

"Why, Antonio, what an idea! The Kiss Flowe
is my home. Wherever you are, I have all
want."

"And so have I, where you are," he told her
taking her hand in his.

She smiled up at him, feeling the familia
current of love between them. "How right th
emperor and empress were about us, after all
Antonio," she said.

Looking at her husband, she felt her hear
beat more rapidly. The years they had spen
together had not dimmed their love. Instead i
shone more brightly than ever, the way fin
silver is polished by use. Their love was familia
now, but still each night together was as infi
nitely new as their very first time. Her tall
vigorous husband, now with a touch of gray a
the temples, excited her as much as though sh
were still a girl; and glancing up at the sky, sh

thought that the hours could not pass quickly enough until darkness. Then, as her eyes met Antonio's, she saw that he, too, could scarcely wait for the moment when he would take her in his arms.

About the Author

GIMONE HALL was raised in Texas but makes her home in Pennsylvania, where she spends her time both writing and raising her two young children. Married to a writer, Ms. Hall is the author of six other Signet historical romances: *Rapture's Mistress, Fury's Sun; Passion's Moon; Ecstasy's Empire; The Jasmine Veil;* a saga, and *Rules of the Heart*.